Sawyer

She li

Sawyer

since she

he woul

gaze dropped to the creamy skin filling out the ruffled neckline of her dress. Jill had grown up, and he'd missed the memo.

"You look beautiful," he said. "Do you have a big date?"

Sawyer wished he hadn't asked. With Jill looking the way she did right now, it was difficult to think of her as his best friend's sister. She was still the lady in red. The woman he wanted to get to know better. He told himself what he'd told anyone who'd been interested in Jill over the years. *Back off, buddy. She's off limits.*

"I loved this book. For me, it was the perfect example of small-town contemporary done right. It's definitely going on my Top Ten Books of 2015 list."

—**SimplyAngelaRenee.blogspot.com**

"I completely enjoyed visiting Christmas again. This novel is full of rich, full-flavored characters with a story line that never lets up and keeps you turning page after page to discover what happens next. I would definitely recommend this story to anyone who wants an intense, involved story that brings in the entire town for the celebration of two people falling in love."

—**KeeperBookshelf.com**

## IT HAPPENED AT CHRISTMAS

"Debbie Mason gives the reader an excellent love story that can be read all year long... You must pick up *It Happened at Christmas*."

—**NightOwlRomance.com**

"A passionate, liberal environmental activist and a straight-arrow conservative lawyer looking to the senate set the sparks flying in this nonstop, beautifully crafted adventure that skillfully unwraps a multilayered plot, adds an abundance of colorful characters and a familiar setting, and proves in no uncertain terms that opposites do attract."

—*Library Journal*

# CHRISTMAS IN JULY

"A heartwarming, feel-good story. I have not read anything written by Debbie Mason before, but now I have to read more of her books because I enjoyed *Christmas in July* so much."

**—HarlequinJunkie.com**

"Debbie Mason's books are the type of books that leave you with a warm and fuzzy feeling... *Christmas in July* is a great read."

**—FreshFiction.com**

"4 Stars! A quintessential romance with everything readers love: familiar and likable characters, clever dialogue, and a juicy plot."

**—RT Book Reviews**

# THE TROUBLE WITH CHRISTMAS

"A fun and festive tale, flush with small-town warmth and tongue-in-cheek charm. The main characters are well worth rooting for, their conflicts solid and riveting."

**—USA Today's Happy Ever After blog**

"4 Stars! This is a wonderful story to read this holiday season, and the romance is timeless... This is one of those novels readers will enjoy each and every page of and tell friends about."

**—RT Book Reviews**

"The lovers are sympathetic and well drawn...Mason will please fans of zippy small-town stories."

"I'm very impressed by [Mason's] character development, sense of humor, and plotting...Ms. Mason wraps this book up as if it were a very prettily wrapped package. Why not open the pages and have a Christmas present early?"

"Debbie Mason has created a humorous, heartwarming tale that tugged at my heartstrings while tickling my funny bone . . . a community that I enjoyed visiting and hope to visit again."

## ALSO BY DEBBIE MASON

# Happy Ever After
# *in* Christmas

# Debbie Mason

FOREVER

NEW YORK  BOSTON

Copyright © 2016 by Debbie Mazzuca
Teaser from *Christmas in July* ©2014 by Debbie Mazzuca

Cover illustration by Tom Hallman
Cover design by Elizabeth Turner
Cover copyright ©2016 by Hachette Book Group, Inc.

Forever
Hachette Book Group
1290 Avenue of the Americas
New York, NY 10104
forever-romance.com
twitter.com/foreverromance

First Mass Market Edition: June 2016

Forever is an imprint of Grand Central Publishing.
The Forever name and logo are trademarks of Hachette Book Group, Inc.

The publisher is not responsible for websites (or their content) that are not owned by the publisher.

The Hachette Speakers Bureau provides a wide range of authors for speaking events. To find out more, go to www.hachettespeakersbureau.com or call (866) 376-6591.

ISBNs: 978-1-4555-3716-7 (mass market), 978-1-4555-6791-1 (mass market—exclusive Walmart edition), 978-1-4555-3714-3 (ebook)

Printed in the United States of America

OPM

10 9 8 7 6 5 4 3 2 1

# Acknowledgments

Heartfelt thanks to my editor Alex Logan, who not only makes each book so much better, but also works tirelessly on behalf of the series. Many thanks to Amy Pierpont, whose insightful suggestions greatly improved Sawyer and Jill's story. To the dedicated sales, marketing, production, and art departments at Grand Central / Forever, thank you so much for all your efforts on behalf of my books. They're greatly appreciated.

Many thanks to my agent Pamela Harty for her support and guidance.

To my wonderful husband, amazing children, and adorable granddaughters, I couldn't do what I do without your love and support. Thank you. I love you all so very much.

Additional thanks and love to my daughter Jess for reading my first drafts and her willingness to answer my endless questions. No matter how many times I've asked them.

And to the readers who take time out of their busy lives to spend a few hours with me in Christmas, Colorado, you have my heartfelt gratitude. Thank you for the lovely e-mails, tweets, and Facebook posts. You guys are the best.

# Happy Ever After
## *in* Christmas

# Chapter One

Deputy Jill Flaherty sat at her desk wrapping her brother's birthday present for his surprise party that night. The yellow helium balloons she'd ordered were currently bouncing in front of her face. She lifted her hand to bat them away, ripping the paper off the present in the process. A present that she'd been painstakingly wrapping for the last ten minutes. Frustrated, she swore under her breath while shaking her fingers to free them of the tape and brightly colored tissue paper.

"You're stuck," Suze announced in an authoritative voice from behind her computer.

"Thank you for your insightful observation," Jill grumbled at the forty-something woman sitting at the dispatcher's desk across the room as she bent her head to pull the tape off her fingers with her teeth.

Suze leaned around her computer and grinned. "I didn't mean literally. I mean you're stuck, stuck. That's why you've been so bitchy lately. You have the pre-thirtieth birthday blues."

"It's my fingers that are stuck, not me. And I'm not..." Jill sighed. "Okay, so maybe I have been a little bitchy. But it's because of all the overtime I've been putting in the past couple of weeks. I'm tired."

She ignored the reference to her thirtieth birthday. She wouldn't admit to Suze that she was partially right. Like an ominous black cloud, the big three-o loomed large in Jill's mind. It always had. Her mother had died two days before her thirtieth. Preparations for Jack's thirty-seventh birthday had served to remind Jill that *her* thirtieth was only five months away.

"Because you don't have a life."

Jill lifted a hand still covered in tape and paper in an are-you-kidding-me gesture. "I do so. I have—"

"Yeah, yeah, I know. You have friends and family and a job you love. Still doesn't mean you have a life. You put yours on hold when Jack was MIA. I had a front row seat so I know what I'm talking about." Suze held up her hand when Jill opened her mouth to defend herself. "I get it. We all knew how hard it was for you dealing with Jack being missing while working two jobs and taking care of Grace and little Jack. It's why I cut you some slack. But here we are two years later, and you still haven't pressed the restart button."

"I have a life," Jill reiterated without elaborating. Suze had stolen her ammunition. If having friends, family, and a job she loved didn't count, Jill didn't know what else to say.

As another balloon danced in front of her face, she thought back to Jack's birthday two years earlier. The Penalty Box, the local sports bar, had been decorated with a hundred yellow balloons that warm night in May. Half the residents of the small town of Christmas, Colorado had shown up to share their memories of Jack and pray for his safe return. By then it had been seventeen months since his Black Hawk had been shot down over the mountains of Afghanistan.

In all that time they hadn't received a single word as to whether he was alive or dead, not even a ransom demand. They'd had nothing to hold on to but hope and faith. At least Jill had been holding on. Right after they'd sung "Happy Birthday" in honor of her brother, she'd found out she was the only one who was.

Still tough to think about, Jill thought as she rubbed the phantom pain in her chest. The memory of the raw, ugly emotions that had cut through her that night. Anger and hurt that his wife Grace planned to move on with her life. The searing burn of jealousy and betrayal that she'd planned to move on with Sawyer Anderson, Jack's best friend and the man Jill'd had a crush on since she was ten, and had fallen in love with when he'd kissed her at her brother's wedding. Not that Grace and Sawyer had ever come out and admitted their intentions or feelings, but Jill had recognized the signs.

And then, within seconds of discovering Grace's betrayal, one of the worst moments in Jill's life had turned into the best. Breaking news had flashed across the television screen behind the bar that Jack and his crew had been found alive.

A chair scraped noisily on the tile floor and drew Jill back from that night. Suze moved the bouquet of balloons and took a seat across from her. "Okay, so tell me, when was the last time you hid the salami?" she asked.

Jill frowned. "What…"

Suze rolled her brown eyes as she peeled the last of the tape and tissue paper from Jill's fingers. "Bumped uglies…Did the horizontal mumbo?"

"I have no idea what you're—"

"Oh for godsakes, when was the last time you got laid?"

Since the answer didn't immediately pop into her head, Jill hedged, "What does that have to do with anything?"

"And there's your problem. You can't remember, can you?" Suze said as she rolled the paper and tape into a ball.

"Yes, I can. Seven months ago," she said, taking a guess. Then realizing the number of months might unwittingly validate Suze's no-life pronouncement, Jill added, "Before you say anything, I've been busy."

Suze pursed her lips and tossed the ball into the garbage can. "Don't buy two-sided tape again. And it was eight months ago with that accountant from Logan County."

"Really? Huh. I could have sworn…" She took in the I-told-you-so look on Suze's lightly freckled face. "Oh, come on, that doesn't mean anything."

"Yeah, it does. It says it all. You have unmemorable sex with unmemorable men. And do you know why you do?"

"No, but I'm sure you're going to enlighten me," Jill said, carefully working the rest of the paper off Jack's present with a pair of scissors.

"Fear," Suze said, taking the scissors from Jill's hand and looking her in the eyes. "You're afraid to get your heart broken. That's why you spend your time fantasizing about the man and life you want and not doing anything about it."

"I do not fantasize about Sawyer," Jill blurted without thinking. She caught the triumphant look in Suze's eyes and quickly added, "Or any other man in town."

"Umhm," Suze said as she opened the gift box, carefully removing the framed photos from inside. It was a collage of Jill's favorite pictures of Grace and Jack with Jill's nephew. "You want this, don't you? The house, the baby, the man of your dreams, the whole enchilada. I want that for you, too, girlfriend."

Jill looked away from the photos and shrugged, turning to pull another roll of gift wrap from the bag at her feet. "I guess. Someday," she said in an offhand manner, unwilling to admit how much she did. But Suze knew her too well to be fooled. She needed a distraction. "What about you? You won't be able to use the boys as an excuse for much longer. They'll be heading to college in a couple years."

Suze arched an eyebrow while sliding the framed photos back into the box. "You wanna play it that way, fine. Here's what we'll do." She taped the box shut, then leaned across the desk to grab two pieces of paper out of the printer. She handed one to Jill.

"What's this for?"

"We're making our life-goal lists. Or in your case, get-a-life list." She took the gift wrap from Jill. "I'll take care of this while you write down yours. I have to think about mine for a bit seeing as how I already have the kids and house."

"Don't be smug," Jill said, looking at the paper like it was bomb about to detonate and she didn't have the code. Maybe because there was a part of her that knew Suze was right. If Jill wrote down what she really wanted, she'd actually have to do something about it. Sometimes living in a fantasy world was easier. You didn't have to deal with rejection, the hurt and disappointment.

By the time Suze had wrapped the present, Jill had one item on her list. It was the only one she felt comfortable enough to write down.

"I knew you wanted to be sheriff," Suze said with a self-satisfied smile, then grimaced. "Make sure you don't show anyone your list. No one's supposed to know Gage isn't running for another term. He'll figure out I accidently overheard his conversation." Suze put her hand over Jill's to stop her from ripping up the sheet of paper. "Don't. You have to write them down. There's a higher percentage that they'll happen if you do."

"Yeah? Where did you read that, Facebook?" Jill asked her friend and coworker who spent more time on social media than anyone she knew.

"Oprah. Now come on. No more stalling. Stop editing yourself and just write them down."

Jill bent over the paper, shielding it with her arm, and wrote down the rest.

"You have to let me see," Suze complained, but before she could take the list from Jill, the phone rang. "Sheriff's department, how can I ...Oh, hi, Boss. What's up? Jill? Yeah, of course she's here. Where else would she be?"

Jill scowled at her and took the phone, rolling her eyes when Suze pressed the speaker button. "Hey, Gage, what's up?"

"I need a favor. The seniors' hockey league are playing

the last game of the season today, and I need you to take my place."

"Ha! Good one. Now, what are you really calling about?"

"I'm serious. We've got two guys down, including me. You know how competitive Ethan is. If we lose the game, he's gonna blame me, and I'll never hear the end of it. Brad already agreed to fill in for one of the other guys."

Brad was a recent hire. Young, smart, and ambitious, Jill had no doubt when word got out Gage wasn't seeking reelection, he'd throw his hat in the ring. Since the guy was also handsome and charming, he could pose a serious threat. Which was probably why Suze was widening her eyes at Jill and nodding like a bobble-head doll. But there was no way Jill was volunteering to play. "I'd like to help you out, but I promised to decorate the Penalty Box for Jack's—"

"Don't worry about it, girlfriend. I'll go over after my shift and decorate," Suze said, stabbing the first line on Jill's list.

"Wow, thanks, Suze," Jill said through clenched teeth. "But I'm sure you have more important things to do. Besides, you'd be better off getting someone who actually knew how to play the game, Gage."

"Come on, you practically lived at the arena and spent more than half your life around Sawyer. You know hockey."

She'd lived at the arena because she had a crush on Sawyer, not because she loved hockey. Though she kinda did now. "Yes, I know how the game is played, but I don't play the game. You need to find someone who does." And they better be good, because former NHL superstar

Sawyer Anderson was on the opposing team. So was Jill's brother.

"He's found someone. You. Don't worry, Gage. She'll be there."

Jill stared at Suze.

"Great. Thanks, Jill. I owe you," Gage said.

"Dammit, Suze, why did you do that?" Jill demanded as soon as her boss hung up.

"Did you not just hear Gage say he owed you? You've had five complaints filed against you this month alone. You need—"

"Four. Mrs. Burnett was exaggerating. The tree branch was a hazard, and I didn't cut her phone line. I tripped over the wire and it came out of the wall." Which was one of the reasons Jill was feeling a little stressed and over-worked these days. Since most of her complaints had come from the seniors in town, Gage had volunteered Jill to work twenty hours a week at the nursing home in hopes she'd learn a kinder and gentler approach.

"Regardless, it's in your file until she withdraws the complaint. But you're missing the point. Brad's a suck-up, and he hasn't been written up. You need to do some sucking up of your own. The only way you'll be elected sheriff is if you have Gage's full support."

"Well, he's not going to feel very supportive if I lose the game for them. Suze, the only hockey I've ever played is street hockey with Sawyer and Jack when I was nine."

"You'll be fine. You're as athletic and as competitive as Brad. You'll get the hang of it in no time." She wiggled Jill's list out from under her arm. "And this is a great op-portunity for you to prove to Sawyer that you're perfect for him."

Jill grabbed the paper from Suze and folded it in half. "I didn't write, *prove to Sawyer I'm perfect for him* on my list. I wrote, *ask him out.*" Saying it out loud caused Jill's stomach to heave. But the more time she'd spent on the list, the more obvious it became that she really had put her life on hold. And clearly, with the approach of the big three-o, she wasn't getting any younger.

"Maybe you should have, because you are. He just doesn't know it yet. And you know why he doesn't, Jill?"

"No, but I'm sure you're going to tell me," she said under her breath.

"He doesn't because you're so busy working, the only time he sees you is in uniform or at Grace and Jack's. You need to show him another side of you. Not the cop or his best friend's baby sister."

# Chapter Two

At that moment, Jill was showing Sawyer her backside. Her heavily padded backside. It was the second half of the third period, and she'd taken a hit from one of the opposing players that sent her flying into the air and onto her knees.

"I give her a four. What about you, buddy?" her brother said from where he leaned over the boards with Sawyer looking down at her.

"She did a perfect one-eighty and got great height, but she blew the landing. So yeah, I'd have to give her a four. You know what, we're winning, and I'm feeling generous. I'll give her a four-point-two," Sawyer said.

"Bite me," Jill said as she pushed off the ice and got to her feet without looking at them.

"What's that, Shortstop?" Sawyer asked, not bothering to hide his amusement.

She turned and lifted her stick at the electronic scoreboard, ignoring his use of her childhood nickname. She was already mad enough. They'd been teasing her relentlessly throughout the entire game. "You might want to take a picture of the score. You won't be winning for much longer," she said, then skated to where the ref waited for her to get into position.

Some people considered the Flaherty temper a character flaw. At times so did Jill, but right now she took advantage of that rush of adrenalin and temper. As soon as the ref dropped the puck, she was on it. What she lacked in finesse, she made up for with grit and determination as she skated up the ice toward the goalie. She faked out the right defenseman—it wasn't that hard. The third line on Sawyer's team wasn't that good, and the reason Jill's team was two goals away from tying the game.

"Jill," Brad called out, tapping his stick on the ice. The auburn-haired and blue-eyed cutie was wide open. But he'd already scored twice. As both defensemen skated toward her, Jill eyed the net the same way she eyed the target at the shooting range. At the top of the hash mark, she wound up and took her shot and...scored.

Her teammates on the bench banged their sticks against the boards while those on the ice rushed her. Brad reached her first. A wide smile split his handsome face as he gave her a hug and lifted her off her feet.

Sawyer's fans booed loudly, and that meant the majority of people crowded in the stands behind the opposition's bench. The competitive midget hockey team he coached was out in full force as were a large contingent of well-endowed blondes. No doubt at one time or another he'd dated each and every one of them.

She glanced at her brother and Sawyer. As if all their

athletic coaching over the years had paid off, the two of them wore proud grins. She wouldn't be surprised if they'd patted each other on the back when she scored. But they weren't looking so proud or happy when she scored three minutes later. Unlike her first goal, her second was a fluke. The picks of her right skate got stuck in the soft ice, sending her into the defenseman who had the puck. Her stick caught the edge of the puck, and it rolled into the net.

But her teammates high-fived her just the same as she took her place on the bench. Ethan, Gage's best friend and district attorney for the county, slapped her on the back. "For five years straight we've lost the end-of-season game to these guys. Now, thanks to you, we have a chance to take the cup. Gage should give you a raise."

A raise would be nice, but she'd rather have her boss's endorsement for sheriff, which would result in more money. But it wasn't fair to take all the credit. "It was a team effort. Brad scored, too."

Ethan didn't respond because he was busy pumping up the team. "Clock's ticking down, boys. Time to bring the cup home," he said as he skated onto the ice with his line.

Sawyer also skated toward center ice. He hadn't played professional hockey in more than seven years. A dirty hit and a severe concussion had ended his career. But he still had the speed and the long, easy strides that had made him a star. The only reason they were able to hold him off was their goalie—a lawyer who worked for Ethan and a former professional hockey player, too. At six four, the guy was built like a tank and filled the net.

"You're something else, you know," Brad said from beside her.

Jill drew her gaze from Sawyer as he faced off against Ethan. "How's that?" she asked, lifting her water bottle to her mouth.

"You're amazing. I've never met another woman like you. There's nothing you can't do."

Jill choked on the water while searching his face for a sign he was teasing. She kind of hoped he was, because if he wasn't, that meant he was interested in her. And she didn't want him to be interested. She didn't want to reject him if he asked her out. Rejection sucked on any level. And he was a nice guy, even if they did end up competing for Gage's job. Plus they worked together. "I can't cook. Well, I guess I could if I had to, but I don't like to. And I can be a bitch, just ask Suze."

He laughed. He had a nice laugh. "You forget I work with you, too. But hey, we all have bad days, and you've been putting in a lot of overtime."

Totally nice guy, dammit. She prayed for a fight to break out on the ice, just not one involving Sawyer. He couldn't risk another concussion. But no, he was tearing up the ice on a breakaway. It was a beautiful sight. She could watch him skate all day. The crowd roared as he showed off his legendary stick-handling abilities. With a flash of a smile and his perfect white teeth, his passion and love of the game lit up his gorgeous face. Then he drew back his stick and took a powerful shot. She held her breath. Disappointment echoed off the building's rafters when the goalie deflected the puck.

She'd been so caught up in the play that she hadn't realized Brad was speaking to her. "Sorry. What did you say?"

"I was wondering if you'd like to get a drink with me sometime?"

She groaned inwardly, wishing she'd either ignored him or said something about the game to distract him. Now she had to figure out a way not to hurt his feelings. "I'd really like to, Brad. But…Gage has a no-fraternization policy." She caught a hint of disappointment in his blue eyes. "I wish he didn't. You're a great guy."

"I feel the same about you. But you're right, I wouldn't want to jeopardize my job."

Before Jill could ask his thoughts about his future with Christmas's sheriff's department, Ethan opened the door to the players' bench. As he and his line filed back in, he said, "Get out there, you two, and do us proud."

"But we're on the third line, not the second," Jill protested even as she stood up. Brad was already over the boards.

"You two are on a winning streak. Now go out there and show them up," he said, pushing her out the door without warning. Her skates went out from under her and she landed on her butt.

Her brother laughed. "You wanna play with the big boys, Shortstop. You gotta get rid of the girlie skates."

"Ouch, looks like that hurt. You might want to sit this one out, Shortstop," Sawyer said, leaning on his stick as he watched her struggling to get up. His mouth twitched with amusement.

"Don't let them intimidate you, Jill. I've got your back," Brad said, slapping at her brother's stick with his.

"Thanks," she murmured and took her place across from Sawyer. Standing six three without skates, he towered over her with them on. He grinned down at her. She scowled up at him. "You won't be smiling once we—"

Five blondes wearing short skirts and white T-shirts

with Sawyer's face covering their boobs drowned Jill out as they shook their pom-poms and yelled, "Go, Sawyer. Go, Sawyer. Go, Sawyer."

Jill rolled her eyes. "They're a little underdressed, don't you think?"

He glanced at them and lifted a padded shoulder. "It's May. Arena's warm."

Seeing him look their way, the women cheered louder and shook their pom-poms harder. Sawyer gave them a sexy smile and waved.

On top of Jack's and Sawyer's teasing, the women and his flirty response set off Jill's temper. She was going to beat them, and she was going to beat them bad. "Ref, you should be calling him for delay of game," she said to the kid with the puck in his hand. It was Trent Dawson. One of Sawyer's star players and his manager's son.

Sawyer laughed. "Good try, Shortstop," he said, slapping at her stick with his.

Jill ignored him and got in position, casting a sidelong glance at Trent. Just as he was about to drop the puck, she said, "I don't flipping believe it. They're flashing their boobs!"

Sawyer lifted his head to look at the same time Trent released the puck. Jill got the drop on Sawyer, shooting the puck to Brad.

"You always did play dirty," Sawyer said, laughing as he whizzed past her.

Within seconds he'd wrested the puck from Brad and was heading back into their end with breathtaking speed.

"The only way to win this game is take Anderson out," Brad said with a determined look on his face as he skated past her.

*Wait? What?* "No, Brad, you…" She started to call after him, but he was already heading for Sawyer. No matter how much she wanted to win—not only to make a point to her brother and Sawyer, but to get in Gage's good graces—she had to stop Brad. Another concussion could cause Sawyer irreparable damage. She skated as if his life depended on it. Sawyer was at the hash mark, Brad a foot behind him. She launched herself at Brad, putting an arm behind him to protect his head as they fell. She let out a whoosh of breath as she landed hard on her teammate, releasing a pained groan when her chin hit the ice.

The crowd roared. Sawyer had scored the winning goal.

\*  \*  \*

Sawyer waited on the sidewalk outside the Penalty Box for Jill. "Why didn't you stick around for the cup presentation?" he teased, holding up the trophy as she approached wearing a white shirt, jeans, and white sneakers.

Her dark, shiny hair swung across her shoulders as she gave her head an annoyed shake. Her full pink lips flattened when she reached his side. "You may not have noticed, but my team wasn't exactly impressed that I lost the game for us."

"Come on, you guys didn't stand a chance. We win every year. But just for curiosity's sake, why did you take out Brad? Did he tick you off?" As Sawyer well knew, it didn't take much to tick her off. She had her brother's temper. Only Jack's twelve-year stint in the military had taught him to control his.

She shoved her sunglasses on top of her head. "No, he

didn't tick me off. He wanted to win, and he was going to take *you* out to do it."

"Wait a sec, are you telling me that you blew the game to protect me?"

Color stained her blade-sharp cheekbones. "What was I supposed to do? Do you want to suffer a permanent brain injury? Because that's what could happen if you take another blow to your fat head." She crossed her arms and looked away.

Sawyer would have laughed if not for the pressure building in his chest. It was rare for Jill to let her guard down. Half the time she was either scowling or growling at him. But every once in a while, like now, she'd show him how much she cared. "I appreciate you trying to protect me, Shortstop. But I can take a hit, you know? It would take someone a lot bigger and badder than Brad to take me down."

She lifted her chin. "All it takes is one time. You shouldn't be playing hockey, even if it is recreational."

"Appreciate the concern, but we have a no-body-contact rule." He frowned, noticing a scrape on her chin and raised it with his knuckle. "You have a bruise. Did you hit the ice when you fell on top of Brad?"

She batted his hand a way. "I'm fine. It's not a big deal."

He slid his hand from her chin to the nape of her neck, then gently massaged the tight muscles. He caught her wince. "You gave yourself whiplash, didn't you?"

She shrugged. "I've had worse."

"Yeah, I know you have." And she never complained. Feeling oddly touched and protective, he lightly squeezed the back of her neck and leaned down to press his lips to her forehead. "Come on, I'll get you some ice and…" He trailed off as he spotted Jack coming down the sidewalk with Grace. His best friend's narrowed gaze moved from Sawyer to Jill.

Sawyer lowered his hand and stepped back from her. "Hey, guys."

Jill turned to greet both her brother and sister-in-law. "Not one word about the game or you don't get your birthday present," she warned Jack.

His serious expression vanished, and he grinned. "You get me another truck?"

Sawyer'd forgotten about that. Jill had bought Jack a truck as a welcome home present. For a woman who was as tightfisted as Jill, it was further evidence of how much she adored her big brother. How much she was willing to sacrifice for him. "Yeah, right, I figure I'm covered for the next five birthdays and Christmases."

"You are," Grace said, moving to Jill's side. "Jack was just telling me how well you played today. I wish I could have been there."

"You probably wouldn't have gotten a seat. Sawyer's fan club was there," Jill said, slanting him a look.

Music filtered out onto the sidewalk as Jack opened the door. "I want to talk to Sawyer for a minute. We'll meet you inside."

Jill frowned, looking from Sawyer to Jack. "What's going on?"

"Nothing, nosy. Now get in there and save me a seat," Jack said, giving his sister a gentle shove. As soon as the door shut behind the two women, he turned on Sawyer. "What the hell were you doing kissing Jill?"

"Oh come on, you can't seriously believe I was making a move on her? Jesus, she's like a little sister to me."

He told Jack about her hit on Brad and her subsequent injury. Even though he was kind of shocked that he had to explain himself.

"Sorry, guess I should have known better. But buddy, you don't have the best reputation in town. You're the last person I'd want dating my sister."

"Ouch. Thanks a lot, pal," he said as he opened the door, following Jack inside. Sawyer stopped short as he looked around the rustic bar with memorabilia from his hockey days hanging on the exposed log walls. A sea of yellow balloons decorated the space, hanging from the rafters and tied to the penalty box and the chairs surrounding the round tables.

Everywhere he looked was a reminder of the night they'd learned Jack had been found alive. The night Sawyer gave up on having the family he wanted. While Jack had been missing, he'd fallen in love with his best friend's wife. He'd stepped aside as soon as Jack came home, giving up on Grace and his dream. But it was a small town, and Jack soon discovered Sawyer's secret. He'd nearly lost his best friend. It had taken weeks to repair their friendship. Sawyer vowed then and there never to put their friendship at risk again. Jack was family. The brother he never had.

"Happy birthday, Jack!" the crowd in the bar yelled.

Jack turned to him. "You did this?"

"Had some help," Sawyer said. "Since the end-of-the-season party fell on your birthday, we decided to kill two birds with one stone." At the time it had seemed like a great idea. Now, not so much because it brought back memories of the last time they'd celebrated Jack's birthday here.

"Talk about feeling like a dickhead," Jack said, grabbing

Sawyer and pulling him in for a hug. "I really am sorry for what I said. I love you, bro."

"Love you, too, you sap. Now get over there and celebrate. I've got some Heroes to make," he said, referring to the drink he'd named in honor of his best friend. "Here, take the trophy with you."

As Jack walked to the table occupied by Jill and Grace, Sawyer took his place behind the bar. He welcomed the distraction of the leggy blonde swiveling on the stool at the far end. She'd organized the cheerleaders for the game. Through the wood rails on the second level, he could see her friends playing a raucous game of air hockey. "What can I get you to drink, Tiffany?"

"One of those looks good," she said, pointing to the Hero he'd made for Jack.

"Sure thing." He set the drink on the tray. "Hang on," he said to the server who was dressed in her uniform of a black-and-white striped shirt and a short black skirt. He went to the bar fridge and took out some ice. Grabbing a baggie, he filled it with ice, then wrapped it in a clean, damp towel. "Give this to Jill," he said, handing the ice pack to the server.

"Sure thing, boss," she said, heading for the man of the hour's table.

Tiffany twirled her blond hair around her finger, batting her fake eyelashes at him. "You were amazing out there today. I just loved watching the way you handled the ball."

He scratched his cheek. "Uh, it's a puck."

She giggled. "Oh right, I knew that," she said and went on to reveal how depressingly little she knew about the game.

Her voice droned on as he mixed drinks. He handed her one, hoping she'd stay quiet for at least a few minutes while she drank it. Instead she took the cherry out of the glass and grinned. "I bet you've never met anyone who can do this," she said, working the stem in her mouth.

Only a couple every weekend. He rubbed his jaw, suddenly tired of the meaningless conversations and hookups. He looked across the bar and caught Jill's eye. She held up the ice pack and mouthed *thanks*. He smiled. Now there's a woman he could have a meaningful conversation with. As soon as the thought entered his mind, he shot a panicked look at his best friend. Afraid Jack had suddenly become a mind reader.

But Jack only had eyes for his wife, who was lighting the candles on a sugar plum cake. She'd made one for Jack's birthday two years earlier. It was her signature cake and had turned the Sugar Plum Bakery's fortunes around. A chocolate sugar plum was hidden in each cake. Sometimes it held a wish or an engagement ring. Two years earlier it held Jack's wedding ring and a good-bye note from Grace to her husband. Jill had been the one who'd gotten the sugar plum that night.

He put the memory of her face—the look of hurt and betrayal—out of his mind and turned off the lights as they once again sang "Happy Birthday" to Jack, only this time he was here. When they finished singing, Sawyer turned the lights back on and lifted a drink. "To our hero," he said, and meant it.

"You're my hero," Tiffany said. At least that's what he thought she said. It was a little tough to make out since she was still trying to tie the stem in a knot.

"Thanks," he said, looking up at the sound of laughter. Jill had gotten the sugar plum again.

She opened it and took out a thin strip of paper, then glanced at him. She chewed on her bottom lip, a nervous habit she'd had since she was a little girl. And there was something about the way she was looking at him that made him nervous. Could she be thinking back to that night, too?

Tiffany pulled his attention from Jill. "I did it," she said, triumphantly holding up the knotted stem. She gave him a suggestive smile. "Any chance you'll be off soon? I'll show you what else I can do with my tongue."

Aw hell, he thought when Jill started to walk toward him with her brother looking on. "Why don't you show me now?" he said, and leaned across the bar to kiss her.

# Chapter Three

After her previous experience with a sugar plum wish, Jill should have known better than to open one last night. She should have lobbed it at Sawyer's head. But instead she'd taken the damn wish as a sign. *Dreams don't come true without action,* it said, so that's what she'd planned to do. She'd headed to the bar to ask Sawyer out and...he kissed the blonde.

"It might be helpful to know more about the victim, dear," Mrs. Lynn, of the tight salt-and-pepper curls and freakishly pale eyes, said.

The residents of Mountainview Nursing Home were searching the grounds for the weapon Jill had hidden as part of a murder mystery game. "She's a twenty-something blue-eyed blonde who was found murdered outside a bar."

"Now, if she was attractive, it was probably a crime of passion. Was she beautiful?" Mrs. Sharp asked.

Jill shrugged. "Some people might think so." Sawyer obviously did.

"Aha, so the motive was jealousy. Which would mean a personal attack. We're looking for a knife, everyone," Mrs. Lynn announced.

She got the murder weapon right, but... "Just because she was beautiful doesn't mean the motive was jealousy. She might—"

"You are beautiful. Marry me. I will make you happy."

Jill turned to the elderly man hunched over his walker, smiling up at her. He'd forgotten his dentures again. But Mr. Gorski was determined, she'd give him that. This was her second marriage proposal in a week. If he was five decades younger, Jill might consider his offer. Her chances of checking a proposal off her life-goal list by the time she hit thirty were bleak. She'd be lucky if she was in a relationship by then.

Mr. Gorski's walker wobbled as he went down on bended knee. Afraid he'd fall and break a hip, Jill reached for him. "Stop. Now," she ordered in her cop's voice. Noting several white heads turn her way, she winced. That probably wouldn't qualify as the kinder, gentler approach Gage was hoping for.

She gave Mr. Gorski a kindly smile and wrapped her hands around his thin arms to keep him upright. He grimaced. *Crap. Brittle bones.* She loosened her grip and said in a sweet voice, one she heard her sister-in-law Grace use, "We don't want to break anything, now do we?"

Her smile faltered. Was that a shimmer of tears behind his dark glasses? *Wonderful, just flipping wonderful.* She didn't have to worry about his bones; she'd broken his heart. "I'm flattered, Mr. Gorski. I really am. You're a great catch. Really, really great."

The words had barely left her mouth when a determined glint replaced the tears. He leaned toward her. "We will marry tomorrow, yes?"

*Relax. Deep breath in and out. You've got this.* She'd distracted him easily enough the last time by pretending she didn't hear him and continuing her self-defense class. But she needed to put a stop to this before he hurt himself. Or scarred her for life, she thought, when he stuck out his tongue and wet his dry lips. Letting go of his arms, she stepped back and blurted, "I have a boyfriend."

One by one the residents of the nursing home stopped searching the manicured grounds for the weapon. They turned their heads, craning their necks in her direction.

Mrs. Sharp looked up from digging in a bed of yellow tulips beneath the gurgling fountain. A cherub, or maybe it was supposed to be an elf, spurted water from his mouth. Whatever it was, it seemed a weird choice for a statue at a nursing home, but what did Jill know? And the elf had provided her with the perfect hiding spot for the knife. "Who is he, dear? Do we know him?"

Jill drew her gaze from the well-endowed statue. Mrs. Sharp was, well, sharp... and relentless. She had to give her something. Since the best way not to get caught in a lie was to stick close to the truth, Jill went with the man who was responsible for her practically nonexistent love life. "No, he, ah, lives in Denver."

He had while he played for the Colorado Flurries. Sometimes she wished he would have stayed there instead of moving back home.

Mrs. Lynn drove her motorized scooter closer. "What does he look like? Is he handsome?"

"Yes, tell us," several of the other women urged, awaiting her answer with breathless anticipation.

Anxious, Jill imagined, to relive their youth through her and her make-believe love affair with a man who saw her as his best friend's kid sister.

It would be easier if she still saw him as the tall, skinny boy he'd once been and not the man he'd become. "He's beautiful. But not pretty boy beautiful, more like Viking warrior or Norse god beautiful. Rugged. He broke his nose, and it's a little crooked, but it suits him. Just like the dimple that shows up in his left cheek when he smiles. He has a great smile," she told her attentive audience. She didn't want to disappoint them. And sadly, for her and her heart, it was true.

"Dark hair or light? What about his eyes?" Mrs. Lynn and Mrs. Sharp uttered their questions in rapid-fire succession.

Jill stuffed her hands in the front pockets of her khaki shorts and rocked on the heels of her hiking boots. "Straight hair, dark blond. But in the summer, it lightens with these amazing wheat-blond streaks that women pay a fortune for. Not that he'd be caught dead in a salon. Half the time it looks like all he does is run his fingers through it. It's always messy and comes to about here." She pointed to the top of her shoulder. "His eyes are dark, same as his eyebrows and scruff."

"I like scruff. Manly. He is manly, isn't he, not metrosexual?" Mrs. Lynn asked.

"Metrosexual is passé, Edith," Mrs. Sharp said to Mrs. Lynn. "It's lumbersexual. I read it in *Cosmo*."

Jill hoped she stopped there. She didn't want to hear what else Mrs. Sharp had read in *Cosmo*. She'd interrupted a heated debate over vibrators the day before last.

"I'm manly, strong," Mr. Gorski said, glaring in the direction of the women while flexing his arms. And that started a who's-got-the-biggest-biceps competition among the men.

"Oh, stop it, you old coots. We want to hear more about Jill's boyfriend. Go on, dear," Mrs. Lynn said.

Mr. Gorski muttered something in Polish and headed for the glass doors.

"Be right back," Jill told the older woman and sprinted ahead of Mr. Gorski. She held the door open. She hoped she wasn't making a mistake, but she felt bad for the old guy. "You've got amazing muscles for a man your age, Mr. Gorski."

"Ninety-five is not old." He grinned, then reached around her for the door.

No, not the door, he was going to..."Ouch." Dammit, he'd pinched her! She rubbed her butt. He had strong fingers, too.

"How tall is he? I hope he's not short," Mrs. Sharp said when Jill returned to her place on the patio. "Short men have a chip on their shoulder." The older woman made a face. "My Barry was five four."

"He's tall. Six three," Jill said, kind of getting into the fantasy now. "In great shape. His arms..." She trailed off when Mrs. Lynn looked past her. The other women seemed to have lost interest, too, fluffing their hair and fanning themselves. Must be the heat. It was warm today. She probably should have kept them indoors. All she'd need was for one of them to drop...

Mrs. Lynn smiled and said, "Sawyer."

Jill stared at her. Mrs. Lynn had told her she saw dead people. Maybe the older woman was indeed psychic after all. It's fine, Jill reassured herself, totally fine. Sawyer wasn't an uncommon name. She'd just…

"How's it going, Mrs. Lynn? Shortstop?" said a deep voice from behind her.

Jill froze, her heart stuttering to a stop in her chest. The muscle slowly came back to life, flooding her face with heat. And other parts; parts that should not be heating. It was that whiskey-smooth voice of his. But this wasn't the time for lust; it was the time for panic. Panic that Sawyer overheard her and knew she was talking about him. Maybe if she ignored him he'd go away. He was used to her ignoring him, sniping at him. Her defense mechanism. The one that saved her from prostrating herself at his feet and declaring her undying love.

Thankfully, she didn't appear to be the only member of the Sawyer fan club. And while she surreptitiously fanned herself with her sweatshirt, he greeted the rest of the home's residents.

"Doing good, Mr. Applebee. You?" He laughed at something the older man said.

Consumed with trying to will the heat from her face and body, Jill didn't make out much of the conversation. Sawyer's close proximity wasn't helping. She could feel him behind her, smell his clean, outdoor scent. And dammit, why did he have to have such a sexy laugh? All deep and rumbly. "You're on. Flurries'll take them four games straight."

*Right. Playoff hockey.* He'd come to watch the game with his old hockey coach, Bill. Sawyer visited him at least twice weekly. And that was it, the thing that made Sawyer Anderson irresistible. Not only was he beautiful on the outside, he was beautiful on the inside, too.

Jill had just about got it together enough to face him when she noticed the speculative gleam in Mrs. Sharp's eyes. Her gaze moving from Sawyer to Jill and back to Sawyer. Old sharp-eyes had figured it out. Jill had to distract her. She clapped her hands. "Okay, people, what is the problem? You've had an hour to find the murder weapon. If you worked for me, I'd fire your ass...butts. Come on, get it together and find the knife."

She heard a choking sound behind her and turned. "What?"

The faint lines at the corners of Sawyer's eyes crinkled with amusement. "Looks like your sensitivity training's going real well, Shortstop."

"Bite me." She wasn't short. She was five eight. Why couldn't he call her Legs? She had great legs. They were her favorite and best body part—long and lean with well-defined calf muscles. Or Hot Cop? Not that she was beautiful; the only way she stopped traffic was by turning on her siren. But since women pretty much thought all male cops were hot, surely men must think female cops were, too.

Sawyer smiled that slow easy smile of his. Even after last night, it still managed to make her toes curl like it always did. "So, how many more weeks do you have to put in before Gage lets you off for good behavior?"

"One." There was a part of her that would miss coming to the nursing home every day, but she could use the extra sleep.

Sawyer glanced at the older men and women as they wandered off to hunt for the knife. He rubbed his hand over his chiseled jaw and manly stubble. "Why exactly do you have them looking for a knife?"

She lifted a shoulder. "Murder mystery game. It keeps

them active. Makes them use their brains." Relaxing now that Mrs. Sharp was focused on the hunt, Jill called out encouragement, "You're getting warmer, Mrs. Sharp. Real warm." Jill noticed Mr. Applebee looking up at the aspen trees that bordered a steep slope on the edge of the property. "Mr. Applebee, buddy, you're not even close. Get back here."

The older man turned and shouted at her, "Maybe if you weren't talking about your boyfriend for the last ten minutes, we would have found the murder weapon by now."

*Danger, danger.* Jill turned to Sawyer and faked a smile. "Better get going or you'll miss the National Anthem. I know how much you like to sing along."

He crossed his arms over his broad chest, the movement putting his biceps on sigh-inducing display. *Show-off.* He raised an eyebrow. "What boyfriend is he talking about?"

"Don't listen to him. He's losing it." She gave him a light shove. "Nice seeing you. Say hi to coach for me."

"Her lumbersexual. He sounds wonderful, doesn't he, Alice?" Mrs. Lynn looked to Mrs. Sharp for confirmation, then turned to Sawyer and said loud enough for the entire town of Christmas to hear, "We're so happy she has a beau. We thought she was a lesbian, you know."

Jill blinked. Seriously? She stared straight ahead, refusing to look at Sawyer. No doubt the interrogation would begin once he stopped silently laughing his ass off.

Movement near the statue drew her attention to Mr. Applebee. The older man stuck his hand in the statue's mouth and triumphantly pulled out the plastic knife. *There is a God.* Jill pumped her fist. "Way to go, Mr. Applebee! Time to celebrate the man of the hour, folks."

Sawyer leaned into her, his warm, spearmint-scented breath caressing her cheek. "You're not getting off the hook that easily, Shortstop," he said, then gently tugged on her ponytail before walking away.

She glanced over her shoulder, following his loose-limbed stride. He pulled his cell phone from the front pocket of his jeans. "Hey, Jack, heard something interesting. Jill has a boyfriend. Yeah, I was thinking the same…"

*Fan-flipping-tastic.* Sawyer and her brother wouldn't let up until they knew every last detail. Every last detail about her fake boyfriend.

She needed a real one. Fast.

\* \* \*

Sawyer caught Jill's reflection in the glass doors as he walked away and pulled out his cell phone. She was getting a little old for him to be ratting her out to her big brother. Maybe if he hadn't seen the flicker of panic in her eyes when he asked about her boyfriend, he wouldn't have made the call, but he had seen it. And all he could think was that she'd picked a real loser this time.

Jill was a good cop with good instincts, but when it came to the men she dated, it was like all her good sense flew out the window. To say she had crappy taste in men was an understatement. Something she'd proven in the past.

"Hey, Jack, heard something interesting. Jill has a boyfriend," he said as soon as his best friend picked up.

"Really? She hasn't said a word to me. Hang on. Grace, did Jill mention that she's dating someone?" Jack called out to his wife. When she answered in the negative, he muttered, "Must be another loser if she hasn't talked about him to Grace."

"I was thinking the same thing," Sawyer said as the doors closed behind him and he walked across the polished tile floor. "I'll ask around at the bar."

"Good idea. I'll talk to Gage and—"

In the background, he heard Grace telling her husband to mind his own business. Sawyer snorted a laugh. "We'll talk later when your wife isn't—"

There was a click, and Grace came on the other line. "I heard that, Sawyer Anderson. Honestly, the way you two act you'd think Jill was fifteen and not twenty-nine. Leave the poor girl alone."

"We would if she didn't pick guys like Peter. Remember the podiatrist, honey?" Jack asked his wife in a teasing tone of voice.

"Well, yes, he wasn't the best—"

Sawyer chuckled at the memory of Peter, and another of Jill's choices came to mind. "What about the accountant? I think his name was Stan."

Jack laughed. "Forgot about him, but he wasn't as bad as Adam the Ornithologist. Remember that guy? He thought he was God's gift. And then there was—"

"All right, you two. You've made your point. If you think you can do a better job, why don't you introduce Jill to someone nice?"

Yeah, like that was going to happen. In Jack's mind, no one would ever be good enough for his little sister. Something he'd made more than clear last night. The redhead behind the reception desk gave Sawyer a flirty wave. "Hey." He smiled. "How's it going?"

"Who are you flirting with now?" Jack asked.

"I'm not flirting with anyone. Just being friendly," he said and headed for the bank of elevators before the red-head waylaid him. He might not be interested, but she was. An older woman moved toward him in her wheel-chair. "Hey there, Mabel," he said, taking a quick step back to avoid being run over. "You're looking beautiful today."

"Seriously, buddy, you have a problem. How many women have you picked up this past month? Besides the blonde you were sucking face with last night," Jack said.

"Jack," Grace said, a warning in her voice.

Sawyer winced at the reminder. By the time he'd ex-tricated himself from Tiffany, Jill had left. "Three." More like none. But he didn't plan on sharing that with Jack and Grace. It was better if they thought he was a player. Otherwise they'd constantly be trying to set him up or worrying that he'd end up alone. More importantly, he didn't want his best friend thinking he was pining after the woman he couldn't have. "Mabel's ninety."

"I forgot you're at the nursing home. How's my new-and-improved sister? Still treating the old-timers with kid gloves?"

Sawyer laughed and told them about Jill's murder mystery game, repeating what she'd said to the seniors.

Jack groaned.

"It wasn't that bad," Grace said, sticking up for her best friend. "And don't either of you dare tease her about this. If you ask me, Gage overreacted. Just because Jill had a run-in with Mrs. Burnett doesn't mean she's not kind to seniors. She's actually very fond of the residents at the nursing home. She talks about them all the time."

"Ah, princess, she cut Mrs. Burnett's phone line," Jack reminded her.

"I don't blame her. Mrs. Burnett isn't very nice, and Jill responded to six emergency calls from her in one night alone. I'd cut her phone line, too."

Grace was being her usually polite self. Mrs. Burnett was a cold-hearted tyrant. She also happened to be a lot like Jill's grandmother. So Sawyer had no doubt the older woman had pushed Jill's buttons. Her relationship with her grandmother hadn't been an easy one. Jill hadn't been guided by a woman's kind and gentle hand. She never knew a mother's love. But, as Sawyer had learned early on, life wasn't always easy…or fair. And if Jill eventually wanted to be sheriff, she had to suck it up and deal. Gage had done her a favor. The job was as much political as law enforcement.

The elevator doors slid open, pulling Sawyer from his thoughts and back to the Flahertys' conversation.

"She cut the branches off Mrs. Burnett's prized cherry tree," Jack said with a hint of laughter in his voice.

"Of course she did. The branches were scratching the windowpane, not an intruder. Really, Jack, I think you're making a big deal over—"

"Maybe you should talk to Fred. Ask him what Jill said when she pulled him over the—"

"Not that this conversation isn't highly entertaining, but I'm going to miss the first period of the game. I'll talk to you guys later." Sawyer said good-bye as he stepped into the elevator and disconnected. A cane appeared between the closing doors. He reached out and held them open, smiling at Mrs. Sharp. "Celebration over so soon?"

She appeared to be too busy studying him to answer.

And the way the older woman was staring up at him as she entered the elevator made him uncomfortable. The words out of her mouth doubled his discomfort. "You have a dimple in your left cheek just like she said." Mrs. Sharp nodded. "It's you. You're Jill's beau. Wait until I tell Edith I figured it out."

Sawyer jerked back, the heels of his tennis shoes hitting the wall. "Uh, no, we're not involved. No, no way. Jill's like a little sister to me."

"The way she talked about you was far from sisterly, young man. And I know it was you." She pointed a finger at his face. "You have a crooked nose and messy blond hair, manly stubble, too. You look like one of those Norse gods just like she said."

Sawyer rubbed his jaw. "She said I looked like a Norse god?" Oh hell, what was he thinking? This was Jill they were talking about. He didn't want her to think he looked like a god. He didn't want her thinking about him in that way period. No, there's no way Jill would say something like that.

"Yes, she said you were beautiful, but not pretty boy beautiful. She's right, you know. You're a very handsome young man. But don't let it go to your head. Nothing's more of a turnoff than a man who's full of himself. Look at Jill, she has no idea how pretty she is and that just makes her more attractive. Now if we could get her to dress a little more…feminine, yes, that would be the ticket."

She studied him. "You better be good to her. Mr. Gorski's asked her to marry him two times this week, you know. She's such a sweet girl. She tried not to embarrass him and let him down gently when she confessed she had a beau."

He held back a laugh. *Jill… sweet?* Then he thought about the next words out of Mrs. Sharp's mouth and his earlier panic vanished. Jill made up a boyfriend to ward off Mr. Gorski's advances. That sounded like something she'd do. But choosing him as her fake boyfriend… Yeah, he wasn't going to think about that. "You have a good night, Mrs. Sharp," he said when the doors opened on the fourth floor.

"You too. Say hello to Bill for me. Tell him I'll check in on him tomorrow. You're a good boy visiting him like you do. Shame that his family never comes to see him."

It was. Bill's kids had come to visit him once since his stroke in December. Sawyer understood that the flight from Florida was expensive and they were busy with their own lives, but Bill had been a good father. He deserved better. "Thanks, Mrs. Sharp. I'll let him know."

Sawyer walked down the sterile white hall toward Bill's room. He stood outside the open door—the National Anthem playing in the background—and took a moment to prepare himself. Even after all these months, he found it difficult to see the once-robust man crippled by his stroke. Could be why Bill's kids didn't come.

Sawyer straightened and entered the room. Bill drew his eyes from the television screen and attempted a smile. The right side of his mouth turned up, his left didn't. He looked frail sitting in the chair wrapped in a blanket. The temperature in the room had to be at least seventy-five degrees.

"All set for the big game tonight?" Sawyer asked, rubbing Bill's shoulder as he moved to take the chair beside him.

Bill nodded. "Should be a good one. McCann's in net."

The words came out slow and slightly slurred, but it was an improvement. At least Sawyer could understand him now.

"Yeah, he's...What the hell happened to you? You didn't fall again, did you?" he asked when the blanket slipped off Bill's shoulder to reveal his right arm in a sling.

"Relax, will you. I didn't fall. Jill did it."

"Wait, what? Are you talking about my Jill?" He cleared his throat. "I mean, Jill Flaherty broke your arm?"

"No, she didn't break my arm. How did you come up with a damn fool notion like that, Ice?" Bill said, using Sawyer's nickname from his hockey days. "She's been coming by to help with my physical therapy. She wants me to stop depending on my good arm."

Strapping Bill's arm had been a good idea. One Sawyer should have thought of. Instead he'd been focusing on stretching the muscles of Bill's weak arm. "All right, you don't have to get all growly, old man. How was I supposed to know?"

Bill snorted and, despite his drooping eyelid, pinned Sawyer with a look he was familiar with. "She still in love with you?"

Sawyer jerked back. "What are you talking about? Jill's not in love with me. She—"

His former coach cut him off with an attempt at an eye roll. "The girl never let you out of her sight. She was on you like a tick on a dog. Don't tell me you didn't see what was right in front of you?"

Sawyer got his nickname for a reason. Nothing on the ice fazed him. He couldn't say the same for now. Especially after what Jack had said to him last night. He shot out of the chair. "I'll be right back."

# Chapter Four

Sawyer's cell rang as he took his morning run along the boardwalk. He pulled out his phone and jogged to the bench under a weeping willow. "Hey, Ma," he answered with a smile as he took a seat. He knew why she was calling.

"Don't you hey Ma me. I just got off the phone from the roofers and was told our bill had been paid in full. Sawyer, you have to stop. Charlie and I can afford—"

He stretched out his legs and cut her off. "I know you guys can take care of your own bills, but I like to help out when I can." His mother had remarried and moved to Arizona eight years ago. Charlie was a great guy, but he was on a fixed income. Sawyer's mother had raised him on her own, working two jobs to ensure he could play hockey. Now it was his turn to make life easier for her, and he'd continue doing so no matter how ticked she might get.

"Honey, you have to save your money. One day you're

going to have a family of your own. At least I hope you will."

So did he. "You don't have to worry about me, Ma."

She sighed. "I complain, but I know how lucky I am to have a son who looks after his mama like you do. You always did. I brag about you all the time to my friends. Oh, that reminds me, next time you come for a visit two of the ladies at my bridge club want you to meet their daughters."

"Thanks, but I think I can find a woman on my own."

"You haven't had much luck so far. I'd like to be a grandma before I'm too old to enjoy them, you know."

He was about to give his usual comeback—you're only fifty-seven—when he saw a woman jogging along the boardwalk. Her dark hair was in a messy topknot, she wore a pair of aviators, a long, black tank top, and Lycra shorts. In Sawyer's mind, there was nothing more attractive than a woman in great shape, and she obviously was. As she drew closer, he admired the definition in her arms and legs, her strong, elegant stride. He wondered why he'd never seen . . . "Jill?" he choked out her name.

"What's that about Jill, honey?"

"Ah, nothing, Ma. I've gotta go. I'll call you in a couple days. Love ya." He disconnected before she had a chance to respond. "Jill," he called out again, wondering why she was ignoring him. Then he spied the buds in her ears.

As he got up from the bench, she glanced his way. "Hey," she said, jogging past him.

Wait . . . what? Why wasn't she stopping? He jogged after her, pulling a bud from her ear. "Hey, yourself. You don't have time for your friends anymore?"

"I wanna get my run in before I head to the nursing home. I've gotta put in a few hours before my shift." She tugged her earbud from his hand.

"Right, it's the last day of your sensitivity training." He nodded at the earbuds. "But you shouldn't be running with those things in."

She gave her head a slight irritated shake. "I'm running on the boardwalk, not on Main Street."

"Still, someone could catch you unawares."

"Seriously? I'm not ten. I think I can handle myself."

Yeah, he could see that she wasn't a kid anymore. Only he was doing his best to ignore the fact. "Nice morning for a run. How come I haven't seen you out here before?" He ran every day at the same time.

"I usually run the trails behind my place, but Parks and Wildlife issued a warning about bears in the area." She picked up speed. "Have a good one."

He matched his stride to hers. "What's up with you? Why are you giving me the brush-off?"

She sighed. "I told you I don't have time to chat. I want to get in five miles before work."

"Fine," he said, breaking into a run. He smiled when he heard her coming up behind him. He knew she couldn't resist the challenge. What he didn't know was why he felt the need to challenge her. Before he had a chance to contemplate that further, and it was probably best that he didn't, she passed him. The race was on. There weren't many women, or men for that matter, who could keep up with him. But she did.

Five minutes later he glanced at her, hoping to see some sign she was ready to give up. She gave him a cocky smile and picked up speed. Then something caught her eye, and she slowed to a jog. She frowned, lifting her chin at a couple of kids making out on a blanket under a stand of trees. "Isn't that Annie and Trent?"

Sawyer stopped and put his hands on his hips. "Hey you two, what do you think you're doing?" They broke apart, jerking upright. Their faces red.

Jill shoved her aviators on top of her head and shot him a ticked-off look. "You couldn't just clear your throat, make some noise? Now you've embarrassed them."

"Are you kidding me? It's broad daylight, and they're making out in public."

She raised an eyebrow at him.

"They're sixteen," he muttered, knowing full well what she was getting at. He followed her across the grass to where Annie and Trent were scrambling to their feet.

"Hey guys, aren't you supposed to be in school?" Jill asked.

"Umm, we have a study period. Exams start next week," Annie said, glancing from Jill to Sawyer.

He crossed his arms. "Yeah, it looked like you were...What was that for?" he said when Jill elbowed him. He rubbed his ribs.

"As long as your parents know where you are, I guess it's okay then." Jill tugged on his arm. "We'll see you later. Good luck with exams," she said, dragging him after her.

"Oh come on, you can't seriously believe they're going to study..." He trailed off as he glanced over his shoulder to see Annie and Trent pulling their books from their backpacks.

"You were saying?"

"They'll be sucking face as soon as we round the corner."

"No they won't, because they've already been caught. Annie's probably worried I'll tell her dad, and no doubt Trent's afraid you'll tell Brandi. You won't though, will you?"

"Damn straight I will." She gave him a look. "Fine, I'll have a talk with him."

She nodded. "Probably a good idea."

"Thanks. I'm glad you...Isn't that Ty?" Sawyer asked, pointing to a guy in a purple Lycra tank top and matching shorts lying spread-eagle on the grass just off the path.

"Ty," Jill called out as she jogged toward him.

The former Hollywood hairstylist, who now owned a salon in town, cracked one eye open behind his red, square-framed glasses as Sawyer and Jill knelt beside him. "If I've gone to Valhalla, don't revive me," he said.

Sawyer frowned. "What's—"

"Viking heaven, right, Jill?" Ty said, moving his eyebrows up and down.

"Oh, okay, then," Sawyer murmured, as his conversation with Mrs. Sharp came to mind. He glanced at Jill, wondering if she'd said the same to Ty. If she had...

"Ouch." Ty rubbed his arm and glared at Jill. "You don't pinch a dying man."

Her face flushed. "You do when someone is faking and scares you half to death."

"Aw, Jilly Bean, you were worried about me." He grinned and pushed himself onto his elbows. "But I wasn't faking. I was dizzy. Maybe I'm dehydrated."

"How long have you been running?" she asked, avoiding Sawyer's stare.

"Oh, about ten minutes, I think."

Jill shook her head, then stood up and offered her hand. "Maybe you should try walking instead."

Ty ignored Jill's outstretched hand and raised his own to Sawyer, who hauled him to his feet. "Thanks," Ty said, patting Sawyer's chest. "Now what have you two been up to?" He waggled his eyebrows. "Anything to share with Uncle Ty?"

"Running, just running," Sawyer said, a nervous hitch in his voice. All he'd need was for Ty to think something was going on between him and Jill. The hairstylist was as big a gossip as Nell McBride. Sawyer cleared his throat. "I better get going. You two have a good day."

\* \* \*

Ty looked at Jill. "Was it something I said?"

"You might as well just have told him that I'm in love with him and think he looks like a Norse god," she muttered as she watched Sawyer jog away, taking in his powerfully muscled legs, tight butt, and broad shoulders. Since she'd been trying to play it cool earlier, she hadn't had much of a chance to ogle him. Her lungs still burned from keeping up with him.

"I did not know this, Jilly Bean. You've been holding out on me."

*Wonderful, just flipping wonderful.* She'd just outed herself to the second-biggest gossip in town. "But I thought..." She crossed her arms. "When we were at the school board meeting a few weeks ago, you told me I was in love with him."

"Because you kept staring at him and Brandi, but I was just teasing you."

"Oh, so what was the crack about Valhalla?"

"Please, the man looks like he walked off the set of a Viking movie." Ty looked at her and grimaced.

"What's with the face?"

He clasped his hands in front of his chest. "I don't know how to tell you this, but Nell was in the salon the other day for her color. She was talking about the couple for the next book in the Christmas, Colorado series. It's Sawyer and Brandi."

Jill did her best not to react. Every couple Nell had used as the romantic leads in her books had ended up getting their happily ever after. Including Jack and Grace. Jill didn't know why the thought bothered her as much as it did. She'd pretty much resigned herself to the fact that she didn't stand a chance with Sawyer. But she supposed she shouldn't be surprised by her reaction. When you've held a dream in your heart for as long as she had, it was tough to let it go.

"Oh, Jilly Bean, I'm sorry. I shouldn't have said anything."

She shrugged. "Don't worry about it. I was going to find out anyway. Besides, Nell's right. Brandi's more his type." His manager was beautiful, blond, and built. They also spent a lot of time together. Both at the bar and outside of it since Sawyer started coaching Trent. And Brandi was raising her son on her own. Everyone knew Sawyer had a soft spot for single mothers because of his own past.

Ty tapped a finger against his lips, looking her up and down. "I disagree. I've seen you together. You have a lot in common. You're both athletic and competitive, and you've known each other for like forever."

"Yeah, that's kind of the problem. He still sees me as a kid and not a woman."

Ty waved her comment off, his eyes roaming her face. "That's an easy fix." He nodded. "You know what, I'm totally up for this. Nell could use some competition. She's not the only one with matchmaking creds. Who do you think got Easton and Chloe together? It sure as heck wasn't Nell. She did her best to keep them apart," he said, referring to the couple in Nell's latest book, *Kiss Me in Christmas*. Ty clapped his hands. "This is going to be so much fun. Are you excited?"

"Uh, excited about what?"

He sighed. "Me taking on your case. I'm going to get you and Sawyer together. You can name your firstborn after me." He grinned. "I can hardly wait to see Nell's face when I tell her."

"No, no telling anyone," Jill said, unable to keep the panic from her voice. "I really appreciate you wanting to do this for... Who are you calling?" she asked when he put his cell phone to his ear.

"Chloe. She and Cat have another week left in their recovery, and Chloe's bored."

Jill imagined she was. The twins had had surgery a few weeks earlier when Chloe had donated her kidney to her sister. And while Chloe had become a friend, the thought of both her and Ty matchmaking on Jill's behalf was enough to send her into a panic attack. It felt like everything was spiraling out of control, and Jill didn't handle losing control well.

"Ty, hang up now," she said in her cop's voice.

He rolled his eyes. "Diva, guess what? We're going to be Jill's fairy godmothers!"

* * *

Jill felt a little emotional walking into Mountainview, and it had nothing to do with seemingly inheriting a couple of fairy godmothers. She'd threatened them with a lifetime of parking and speeding tickets if they breathed a word to anyone about her crush on Sawyer. She also planned to avoid them for the next month. Surely they'd forget about her by then.

No, the tightness in her chest was because this was officially her last day at the nursing home. If anyone had told her a couple of weeks ago that she would be feeling this way, she would have laughed. She hadn't exactly been thrilled about the assignment. But in the end, Gage had done her a favor. After failing to live up to her domineering grandmother's demanding expectations, and being reminded of it every day, Jill hadn't exactly been a fan of the over-seventy crowd.

"Hey, Sandy," she greeted the director as she walked toward her. Sandy wore her uniform of brown slacks and a cream blouse. Her auburn hair was pulled back in a tight bun, her tortoiseshell glasses resting at the end of her straight and narrow nose.

"I have some very sad residents at the home today," she said to Jill.

"Oh no, did someone…die?"

"No silly, they're sad it's your last day with us. They're very fond of you, Jill. I hope you won't be a stranger."

"Of course I won't. I'll stop by lots and play with them."

Sandy choked on a laugh.

"You know what I mean," Jill grumbled.

"Yes, I do. Your murder mystery game was a hit."

Jill grinned. "I thought they'd enjoy it. They're pretty bloodthirsty, you know."

"We do have some characters," she agreed, and then nodded at the dining hall. "They're waiting for you. They've organized a breakfast in your honor. I hope you're hungry."

Her throat tightening with emotion, Jill didn't think she'd be able to eat. "I'm always hungry," she managed to say. But her ability to speak left her completely when she walked into the room and the seniors gave her a standing ovation.

"I have a couple calls to make. Stop by my office before you leave," Sandy said as Mrs. Lynn and Mrs. Sharp came over to get Jill. They led her to a chair at the head of a table. The residents took their seats when she did. Sandy was right. They looked depressed.

Jill cleared her throat and stood. "I'm not really big on speeches, but I want you all to know how touched I am by this. Some of you probably heard that I was sent here at my boss's directive. He thought I needed some help relating to the seniors in town." She looked at their lined faces and smiled. "I wish they were like all of you. This was the best assignment I could have asked for. Thank you for—"

"If you love us so much, then you'd damn well stay and protect us," Mr. Applebee said.

Jill frowned. "Protect you? Protect you from what?"

He lifted his arm. "Someone stole my watch."

Jill moved to his side. "Who did this to you?" she asked, gently touching the bruise on his wrist.

"Must have been the same person who stole my watch," he muttered.

"They stole my necklace and left a bruise right here," an older woman said, pointing to her collarbone.

After a brief interrogation of the residents, Jill discovered two more victims from the weekend before. "Don't worry, I'll get to the bottom of this. I'm going to talk to Sandy."

* * *

"For the third time, no, I'm not getting you a court order to search Mountainview. Jill, Sandy was practically in tears when she called. She said you terrified the staff."

"I did not terrify the staff. All I did was ask a couple questions. But you know what, I don't care if I did. I care about the residents of Mountainview and their well-being. They're vulnerable, Gage. Half of them don't even have family who visit."

"Appears my experiment worked. But Jill, we've never had a complaint against Mountainview before. Sandy cares about the residents just as much as you."

"If she did, she would have let me search the place without a court order. I think she's hiding something."

"Look, Sandy says the residents love you. So my read on the situation is this. They don't want you to leave and have come up with a reason for you to stay. They know you're a cop and you'll do whatever you can to protect them."

She thought about what Mr. Applebee said. It kind of supported Gage's theory. But on the off chance he was wrong, Jill said, "Fine, but I plan on checking in on them every day, and Sandy better not put up a fuss."

"It'll have to be on your own time. I need you here. Paperwork's piled up while you were off."

She stood up. "I wasn't exactly *off*, you know."

"Yeah, I know. But if you want my job, you better get used to the paperwork."

She sat back in the chair across from Gage's desk. "I didn't... Who told you?"

"Suze may have mentioned it," he said with a grin.

That was the last time Jill was letting Suze look at her life-goal list. She was just lucky Jill didn't rat her out to Gage. After all, Suze was the one who'd overheard his conversation and then blabbed the news to Jill. "It was just idle talk, you know. I didn't mean anything by it. I'd never—"

He held up a hand. "Don't worry about it, Jill. Word was bound to get out sooner or later."

"So it's true, you're not running for another term?"

"It's looking that way. My brothers made me an offer that's tough to refuse."

"That's good, I guess. I mean, you're happy about it, right?" She rubbed her hand over her face. She was babbling.

"You don't have to be embarrassed that you want my job. I'd be more surprised if you didn't."

"Really? So, ah, what do you think my chances are? Of getting elected for sheriff, I mean."

He looked at her, seemingly weighing out his words before he said, "There's no doubt you have strong leadership and investigative skills. You're honest. Take pride in your job. And no one in four counties can outrun, outdrive, or outshoot you."

Wow, if that wasn't a ringing endorsement, she didn't know what was. It sounded like she had the job in the bag. She fought back a grin; she didn't want to seem cocky. "Thank—"

"But you have to deal with the town council and the mayor, and you—"

"Your wife's the mayor, and she likes me. She can always smooth things over with the—"

"We're expecting another baby. Madison's decided she won't be running for reelection, either."

"Oh, that's great. Congrats. But I'm sure I can get along with whoever is elected."

Gage rubbed the back of his neck. "That's the problem, Jill. I'm not sure that you can. Diplomacy isn't your strong suit. I had five complaints about you last month alone. Not to mention Sandy's complaint today."

Jill stiffened, heat rising to her cheeks. "I know. I've been working on it. And Sandy—"

"Look, the election isn't until next spring. You have plenty of time to work on your image."

"What's wrong with my image?"

He tapped his pen on a stack of files. "Okay, don't take this the wrong way, but you're kind of a hardass, edgy. You need to...I don't know, get a life maybe. All you do is work."

"You're lucky I do. Who else would you get to put in the overtime I do?"

"You're right, I'm partly to blame. I've asked for an increase in our budget so I can hire another deputy part time, but since we just hired Brad, I doubt it will fly. You know my wife, she can be..." He cocked his head. "If you repeat what I'm about to say to you, I'll deny it. But you remind me of Madison when she first came to Christmas. She gave off that don't-mess-with-me vibe, and half the folks wanted to run her out of town. You felt the same, so don't bother trying to deny it," he said when Jill opened her mouth to refute the statement. Then he continued, "But once we started dating, she let her guard down and showed people her softer and gentler side."

"Really, that's your advice? You're telling me that, if I want to get elected, I have to find a man like you? Someone everyone loves?" It was true. Everyone loved Gage McBride. Tall, dark, and handsome, he was also as nice as he was good-looking.

He looked completely unabashed. "Yeah, I guess I am."

"That's sexist. If Ray wanted to run for sheriff, you wouldn't tell him to—" She began, referring to another of her coworkers.

"Ray's married. And he doesn't have any edges to start with. But don't worry, you have lots of time before election day. Now get out of here, I've got work to do."

If Gage was trying to make her feel better, it didn't work. The conversation had ended up being more depressing than when it started.

# Chapter Five

Jill had succumbed to her fairy godmothers' plans. Her meeting with Gage had tipped the scales in their favor. Obviously, in his opinion, she needed a new image. So she went to the masters. If you needed a makeover, who better to go to than a Hollywood hairstylist and actress. Well, that was what she'd told herself earlier today when she'd arrived at the O'Connor ranch with Ty. She'd soon learned their plans also included...No, she didn't want to think about it. If she did, she might throw up on the thigh-skimming red dress she currently had on.

As she drove past the wrought iron gates of the O'Connor ranch on the way into town, she glanced at the swell of her boobs peeking above the ruffled neckline. Chloe was right, the bra was a flipping miracle worker. But it wasn't as comfortable as her sports bra, Jill thought, rubbing her back against the seat.

"Stop that. You'll put a run in the fabric," Ty said, shoving his hand between her and the seat.

"A little to the left," Jill said and lowered her shoulder.

He rolled his eyes behind his square, red-framed glasses, then gave in and delicately scratched her back with the tips of his fingers. "Remind me to find you a backless dress for the prom."

Her sigh of relief when he hit the right spot morphed into a groan at the mention of the prom. Christmas High's seniors had postponed the event in honor of Chloe. She'd chaired the committee to save the high school from closure. And because they'd announce whether the school remained open or would close that night, all former students were invited to attend.

Jill twisted her sweaty palms on the steering wheel, growing more nervous by the second. "Yeah, about that. I'm pretty sure I have to work on Friday. So there's really no reason for—"

Ty crossed his arms over his black T-shirt. "No way, you're not chickening out. You promised."

She'd promised a lot of things, but as they drew closer to town and the Penalty Box, she was having second thoughts. No, she'd had second thoughts when she arrived at the O'Connor ranch four hours ago. She must be on her twenty-third by now. "I'm not chickening out. But I do have bills to pay, you know. I can't just—"

A grin spread across Ty's handsome face, and he tucked his hands under his armpits, then flapped his arms. "Bawk, bawk, bawk."

"Real mature," she said, trying not to laugh. The itch started back up, and she moved her shoulders as casually as she could so as not to draw Ty's attention. When that didn't work, she pointed out the window. "Look, there's a moose." As soon as he turned his head, she rubbed her back against the seat.

"Where, I don't..." He swiveled his head, trailing off as he stared at her with wide eyes.

She sighed. "I can't help it. This bra is—"

"No, you have a welt on your neck, like a huge one," he said, leaning over to unzip her dress.

"Umm, we're friends, but we're not that—"

"Hives," he said, lightly running the tips of his fingers over her back.

"Oh, yeah, a little harder," she moaned.

"You sound like Meg Ryan in *When Harry Met Sally*. Don't waste it in on me. Save it for Sawyer."

She scratched her neck at the reminder of where she was headed and what she was supposed to do. "I can't go. I'm covered in hives. Maybe I'm allergic to all the crap you put on my face. I hardly ever wear makeup," she said, glancing at herself in the rearview mirror. Startled once again by the stranger staring back at her. She'd never been one of those girls who was overly concerned with her appearance. But she had to admit that it was kind of nice to feel pretty for a change. Not that she'd tell anyone.

"It's not crap, and you're not allergic to it. I didn't put any on your back or neck." He left her dress open and reached for the air conditioner. Icy air blasted out of the vents.

"Okay, so then I'm allergic to the dress. I don't wear—"

"It's not the dress. You're nervous about asking Sawyer to the prom."

She rubbed a sweaty palm on her thigh. Why did he have to remind her? Better yet, why had she agreed? Oh right, she was grabbing on to life and what she wanted before it passed her by. Before she was old and gray and sitting in a rocking chair with no one to talk to and no stories to tell because she'd had no life.

She briefly closed her eyes. Even in her head, she was starting to sound like Chloe. The actress had become a good friend, one Jill cared about, but the woman was a total drama queen. And so was Ty. Jill never should have listened to them. "I'm not nervous. But I'm not in high school. I'm not asking him to the stupid prom."

"Really? You're not nervous?" Ty pointed at her dress.

She grimaced at the palm print. "No, I . . ." She trailed off as a powder blue late-model Chevy pickup came up behind her. There were a couple young guys standing in the back, thumping on the roof of the cab. Her eyes narrowed on the kid behind the wheel. She didn't recognize him, but the truck looked familiar. He sped by, dust and gravel pinging against the side of her Jeep. The two boys laughed as they were tossed around in the open bed.

"Idiots," Jill muttered before connecting to the station. "Hey, Suze," she said when the dispatcher's voice came through the Bluetooth, "run this to see if the truck is stolen." While Jill gave Suze the plate number, she slipped off Chloe's red high heels.

"Sure," Suze said over the tapping of keys, "but aren't you supposed to be having a makeover or something?"

"She did, and she looks amazing," Ty said, holding up his iPhone to snap a picture.

"Ty," Jill grumbled as she stepped on the gas. "This isn't the time—"

He cut her off. "Suze, give me your number, and I'll text you a pic. Ignore the scowl. She looks better without it."

Suze laughed. "It wouldn't look like her without the scowl."

"Geez, would you two stop," Jill said, leaning on the horn to get the kids' attention. When that didn't work, she rolled down her window, gesturing for them to pull over.

"Pickup hasn't been reported stolen. It's registered to old man Adams. I heard his grandson was in town helping him out on the farm," Suze told her, then gave Ty her number.

"Ty, grab my badge out of the bag." Jill pointed to Chloe's tan purse by his feet.

He bent over, entering Suze's number on his phone while reaching for the bag. His head jerked up. "You've got a gun in here."

"Of course I have a gun. Just give me my badge."

He dug around in the purse, then handed it over. Jill held her badge against the windshield in hopes the kids in the back would see it.

"Jill doesn't go anywhere without her gun. Whoa, girlfriend, you look incredible. Ty, schedule me—" Suze began.

"Dammit," Jill said, cutting off Suze when the kids failed to respond as she had hoped. She stuck her head out the window, the wind whipping the long hair extensions across her face. She held them back and yelled, "Pull over."

One of the boys flipped her off while the other one laughed, pounding once again on the roof of the cab. The Chevy picked up speed.

"Do you need backup, Jill?" Suze asked, her voice serious now.

"No, I'm good. Just a bunch of kids out for a joy ride,

but they're heading for Deadman's Curve. I've got to cut them off. Hang on, Ty," she said, shifting gears. Ty stared at her, his mouth falling open when she reversed without slowing down. Yanking on the wheel, she took a sharp turn onto a back road.

"Oh. My. God. I'm on a high-speed chase. This is just like in the movies," he said as he raised his iPhone, dropping it when they hit a pothole.

She glanced at him. "You okay?"

Face pale, he nodded and reached for the strap above the passenger-side window. "No one ever really died at Deadman's Curve, did they?" he asked, his voice going up and down in time with the bumps.

Jill wouldn't be putting her Jeep or Ty through this if they hadn't, but that wasn't something he needed to know. "No."

Given the way he was clinging to the leather strap, she doubted he'd let go. She reached for the bag at his feet. Keeping her eyes on the road, she took out her gun and laid it on her lap with her badge.

He gasped. "You're going to shoot them?"

"No, I'm not going to shoot them." But she had to be prepared in case she'd misjudged the situation and they weren't a bunch of teenagers out for a joyride. Branches from the overgrown brush scraped against the Jeep as they reached the end of the dirt road. "Get out," Jill said, bringing the vehicle to a hard stop.

"Get out? You're leaving me here?" he said, his voice rising an octave.

She leaned across him and opened his door. "Yeah. Go stand behind that tree." She pointed to an oak on the other side of the Jeep. When he opened his mouth, she held up her hand. "Don't argue with me. Get your ass over there. They're close." She could hear Linkin Park blasting from the speakers and the sound of hysterical male laughter.

While Ty got out of the Jeep, Jill slipped the high heels back on. Once he was a safe distance away, she gunned the engine, the tires spinning on loose gravel. She reached the main road and angled her Jeep in the path of oncoming traffic. Twenty feet beyond was Deadman's Curve.

Putting the Jeep in park, she jumped out, cursing the heels as she ran to the other side. She positioned herself in front of the hood. As the pickup sped toward her, Jill realized she was more nervous about asking Sawyer for a date than she was that the truck wouldn't stop. She raised her gun in one hand, her badge in the other.

\*    \*    \*

"Okay, that was seriously hot, but no more cop stuff tonight. This is the new you. The you that will make Sawyer take notice. We're going for feminine and lady-like," Ty informed Jill as she parked on the street between the station and the Penalty Box.

See, even gay guys thought a female cop in action was hot. So why couldn't he leave it at that? Feminine and ladylike...Ty and Chloe were good, but they didn't have magic wands and Jill was no actress. "Yeah, about that. I'll take a rain check. I have paperwork to do."

She didn't. She'd let the kid off with a warning. But it didn't mean she hadn't scared the crap out of him and his friends first. She'd given them a particularly gory image of what would have happened had they taken Deadman's

Curve at sixty miles per hour. Her version of *Scared Straight*. But the kid had family troubles. He'd been sent to live with his grandfather for a few months while his parents worked things out. Her brother had blown off steam exactly the same way when they'd been sent to live with their grandmother.

Ty raised an eyebrow, then pulled out his phone and texted someone. Two seconds later Suze poked her head out of the station's doors. Jill scowled at Ty and got out of the Jeep.

Suze stared at her. "The photo didn't do you justice. Girlfriend, you are going to rock his world."

"Geez, keep it down. Someone will hear you." Mortified, Jill waved a hand in the direction of the Penalty Box.

The dispatcher crossed her arms over her tan uniform shirt. "Oh, I'll keep it down all right. But only if you get your butt in the bar now."

"That's blackmail."

"So charge me," Suze said.

Ty grinned as he closed the passenger's side door. "Thanks, Suzie-Q." He held up his phone. "I'll let you know how she's doing."

"Fine. Let's get this over with," Jill said and stomped down the sidewalk. Though she soon discovered stomping wasn't as effective when wearing high heels. She prayed to God Sawyer was off tonight. Not that she was overly thrilled that anyone would see her looking like this. Earlier she'd allowed herself to get caught up in Ty and Chloe's plan. It had seemed like such a good idea then.

Ty grabbed her by the arm. "Hang on," he said, turning her to face him. While he fixed her hair, Jill scratched her neck, wriggling in an attempt to move the fabric across her back.

He grimaced. "Your hives are back."

"See, I told you this is a bad idea."

"No, it's not. You just have to relax." His eyes lit up. "Okay, so here's what you're going to do. Pretend you're undercover and that Sawyer is a local crime boss you're investigating. And the only way you can get the information you need is to seduce him. Brilliant, right?"

It might just work. But she wouldn't give Ty the satisfaction of telling him so. She didn't like being strong-armed by anyone. Not even a friend. Make that three friends. "I'm not seducing him. I'm asking him...to accompany me to the prom...as a friend. Yeah, that's what I'm doing."

"Whatever you have to tell yourself, Jilly Bean. Just remember, soft and sweet," he said, leading her to the sports bar.

Alicia Key's "Girl on Fire" greeted them as he opened the door. Jill stood stock-still, momentarily frozen with nerves. Ty lightly shoved her inside. She didn't need to look behind the long bar with its high-back black leather bar stools to know the man himself was there. She felt him, sensed his presence like she always did.

The room was crowded. Not surprising since it was a Friday night. There was a hockey game playing on the screen behind the bar. Several couples were on the wood-planked dance floor while two busty blondes sat to the left of the jukebox on a white bench enclosed by white-and-black-painted boards with an electronic clock affixed above. It was the penalty box for which the bar was named. Sawyer routinely put customers in there for causing trouble. Given the time on the clock, the women had obviously been given a major. She wondered if it was for excessive flirting with the owner.

Jill scratched her neck. She shouldn't be here. As though Ty sensed she was about to make a run for it, he grabbed her hand and started singing along with Alicia Keys. Jill couldn't help it; she started to laugh. She sensed someone's eyes upon her and glanced at the bar. Sawyer was watching her while he mixed a drink. He cocked his head, a slow smile spreading across his face, deepening the dimple in his cheek, an appreciative gleam in his eyes. It was the first time he'd ever looked at her that way, and Jill's heart almost jumped out of her chest.

Sawyer Anderson was flirting with her. The long hours she'd spent being made over suddenly felt worth it. But when he looked away to slide the drink to a customer, she gave her head a slight shake. Of course he wasn't flirting with her. She must have misinterpreted the look . . . He glanced at her, nodding to the empty stool at the end of the bar. The heat that seconds ago had touched her cheeks spread.

"Oh. My. God. He's totally hitting on you. Hurry up, go sit at the bar before someone takes your place. I'll be right there. I just want to text Diva and tell her the news. Go make me proud," Ty said, giving her another light shove.

Panicked, Jill grabbed his hand. "Text Chloe later. I need you with me." Now that Sawyer appeared interested, she wasn't sure what to do with him.

# Chapter Six

Sawyer was mixing a martini when the lady in red walked into the bar. Women walked in and out of his bar all the time, but there was something about this one that held his attention. And it wasn't her exceptional long legs in the red stilettos or the way the fabric of the dress she wore clung to her body and emphasized her curves. She seemed familiar.

But there's no way he'd forget that face. She wasn't a typical beauty. She was exotic-looking, stunning. Her cheekbones were high and sharp, a slight bump on the bridge of an aquiline nose, her lips full, her chin strong. He'd always had a thing for blondes, but she had him re-thinking his preference. Her bold features were framed by long, raven-black hair.

Ty stood behind her, saying something that made her laugh. She had a great laugh. And once again Sawyer had a feeling he knew her. Maybe she was one of the hairstylist's Hollywood friends—an actress or model. That would explain why she looked familiar.

As though she sensed him watching her, she lifted her startling blue gaze. It felt like he'd tossed back a shot of absinthe; his world tilted, a fire spreading inside. The reaction wasn't one he'd experienced in a while. Lately he'd been going through the motions. Flirting enough to keep the ladies happy, but not enough to give them hope for more. He was tired of one-night stands and meaningless relationships. He was on the other side of thirty-six and ready to settle down. But he hadn't met a woman who interested him. This one did.

His years behind the bar had made him something of an expert on people. He was good at sizing them up. If he had to take a guess, he'd say by the definition in her arms and legs, the lady in red was in great shape, confident in her ability to take care of herself. But maybe not so confident with the social scene. There was a wary tension in the way she held herself. He'd noticed it when she looked around the bar. He'd also seen the sharp intelligence in her eyes. She was nobody's fool. Intrigued, he cocked his head and smiled at her. He wanted to know more.

She responded to his obvious interest with a startled blink, and her cheeks flushed. His smile widened at the hint of nerves. He was right. At least he hoped he was. He'd be disappointed if she ended up being like the women he met lately. Women like Tiffany who didn't have a clue about the game he loved or were more interested in talking about themselves and their latest shopping expedition.

He slid the martini down the bar to his waiting customer, then glanced back at the lady in red. He raised a

questioning eyebrow, nodding to the empty seat at the end
of the bar. Sheer panic crossed her face, and she looked
ready to bolt. Okay, that wasn't a reaction he was accustomed to. And he was surprised by his own. At the level
of disappointment he felt at the thought she planned to
leave. When she grabbed Ty by the hand, half-dragging
him toward the bar, Sawyer released a relieved breath.
Seconds later he was holding back a laugh. He doubted he
had to worry about her talking about fashion for the next
hour. She walked in her high heels as though they were
her mother's.

The customer across from him held up his glass.
"Another scotch on the rocks."

"Sorry about that," Sawyer said, turning to grab a bottle of Johnny Walker Black Label off the glass shelf
behind him. It wasn't often that he didn't anticipate a
customer's needs before they did. The lady in red was
proving to be a distraction.

He was pouring the scotch when she plunked herself
down on the stool. Sawyer glanced at her, smiled, and
said, "Hi."

She lifted her chin. "Hey, Sawyer."

His jaw dropped. That was Jill's voice coming from
the lady in red's mouth. A woman who intrigued him, a
woman who he'd been fantasizing about sounded like his
best friend's baby sister. He was having an out-of-body
experience.

"What the hell…"

Sawyer's eyes jerked back to his customer. *Jesus*. He
stopped pouring and grabbed the glass overflowing with
scotch. "Sorry, buddy. Next one's on the house." Sawyer
turned away and set the bottle on the counter, and then,

without thinking, tossed the scotch in the sink. Great, his bottom line just took a forty-dollar hit.

He briefly closed his eyes and drew a calming breath through his nose. He'd never needed calming breaths before. He was easygoing, unflappable. At least he had been until the lady...He opened his eyes, looking at her in the mirrored glass. There was no way she was Jill.

"You have got to be kidding me. What a baby. McCann barely touched him," she said, grabbing a handful of peanuts.

Sawyer swore under his breath. It was Jill. And he didn't need Ty hissing her name and elbowing her to know that it was.

"You watching the same game I am, lady? Because McCann slashed him," Black Label said.

"Oh, please. He was in the crease and bumped McCann. Let me guess, you're a Dallas fan," she said, making a face.

Sawyer shot her a shut-it look, wiping down the bar before handing Black Label his scotch. Then he moved to stand in front of Jill, unable to keep from staring.

Ty grinned. "She looks gorgeous, doesn't she?"

Yeah, but that was beside the point. "What's with the dress, wig, and colored contacts? Is there a costume party in town?"

"No, there's not a costume party in town." Ty glared at him, lifting a lock of her hair while Jill stared at the television screen. "These are extensions. Expensive ones, I might add. And why would she wear contacts? She has the most beautiful eyes I've ever seen."

Sawyer had known her since she was five. If she had eyes the color of the ocean, he would know that, wouldn't he? As if in answer, his gaze dropped to the creamy skin filling out the ruffled neckline of her dress, and then he thought of those long, shapely legs in the red stilettos. He'd done his best to ignore the changes the other day on the boardwalk, but now it was next to impossible. Jill had grown up, and he'd missed the memo.

He'd missed something else; her cheeks were red and she wouldn't look at him. He knew women well enough to realize he hadn't just embarrassed her, he'd hurt her feelings. It wasn't her fault that he felt like an ass for flirting with her. "Shortstop"—she drew those startling blue eyes from the screen—"you look beautiful," he said. "Do you have a big date?"

"Oh yes, she does. Or she will once—" Ty broke off, grimacing when she elbowed him in the ribs.

Sawyer wished he hadn't asked. With Jill looking the way she did right now, it was difficult to think of her as his best friend's sister. She was still the lady in red. The woman he'd wanted to get to know. He told himself what he'd told anyone who'd been interested in Jill over the years. *Back off, buddy. She's off limits.* "What can I get you two to drink?"

"Two Divas," Ty said, sliding into Black Label's seat when the other man got up to leave.

Sawyer frowned. "Jill doesn't drink."

"Of course she does. Everyone drinks."

Not Jill, and it wasn't only because her mother had been an alcoholic. Jill didn't like to lose control.

"You know, I am right here. I can speak for myself. I'll take a soda, thanks," she said without looking at him.

Guess he still had some making up to do. "I have something else I want you to try instead. You know the sports drink you sampled last month? I took your advice, and I'm going to take it to market. Tweaked it a bit, too."

She perked up. "Yeah? What did you add, cinnamon or ginger?"

"I'll let you tell me," he said, taking a quick scan of the bar before heading for the refrigerator in the back room. He'd been going to ask her opinion anyway, and it had nothing to do with getting back in her good graces. If it wasn't for Jill, he wouldn't have investigated the idea of developing a sports drink in the first place.

When he returned with the container, she was behind the bar.

"Sorry, no more whiskey for you. You're cut off," Jill said to one of Sawyer's regulars.

"Boyo, she's cut four of us off. And she won't serve Jimmy," added Mr. Murray, another of his regulars and a Flaherty family friend.

"Because he doesn't have any ID, and he looks like he's twelve," she defended herself.

"He's twenty-three," Sawyer said. "Now why don't you sit down and sample the drink before you put me out of business."

"Hey, I was protecting your license." She stepped closer and went up on her toes to whisper in his ear, "Mr. Murray's gout's acting up, and Jerry and whiskey aren't a good combination. I got called to his place twice this week. That's why I cut them off."

With the feel of her chest pressed to his and the smell of her light floral scent, he was having a hard time staying focused. He cleared his throat. "And the other two?"

"The girls you put in the penalty box. They were dancing on a table."

"Okay, good call."

"Yeah, I thought so too," she said, her brow furrowing as she looked toward the end of the bar where Ty sat. The hairstylist mouthed something to her, and her shoulders rose on a sigh. She wound her hair around her finger and gave Sawyer a wide smile.

*Jill. This is Jill,* he reminded himself. "Here." He shoved the sports drink into her hand. "You, uh, should probably go sit down."

"Oh, okay, I'll do that." She glanced once more at Ty and nodded, having a little trouble unwinding her hair from her finger. Once she did, she pushed out her chest and walked away, swinging her hips. She tripped on the rubber runner behind the bar. "Dammit," she muttered. Placing her drink on the bar, she bent over and took off the stilettos.

Sawyer stared at her heart-shaped ass. Jill had been hiding more than her long legs and what appeared to be a nice pair of breasts. Someone cleared their throat. He looked over his shoulder to see Mr. Murray grinning at him. "I'll take that drink now," the older man said.

"You're cut off, remember?"

"Jackson's awfully protective of his baby sister, isn't he? You two still best friends? I wonder how he'd feel—"

Sawyer narrowed his eyes at the old man and got him his drink, his watered-down drink. He set the glass on the bar. "If your gout starts acting up, you've got only yourself to blame." He lowered his voice. "And I'm not interested in Jill. Not like that."

"How come? Something wrong with your eyesight?"

"No, I—" He broke off at the sound of someone

moaning at the other end of the bar. Afraid it was who he thought it was, he prepared himself before slowly turning his head. Brilliant blue eyes locked with his.

"Oh, Sawyer, this is soo good. It's the perfect combo of spicy and sweet," Jill said, her voice huskier than normal. Something had happened to her hair, too. She looked like she'd just been...

"What's..." he cleared his throat "...going on with you?"

She fluttered her lashes and ran her fingernail along the deep V of her dress. "It's the drink. It gave me a rush." Ty said something to her. She pursed her lips, then waved her hand in front of her face. "I'm all tingly and hot. Really, really hot."

"Forget the whiskey. I'll take whatever she's drinking," Mr. Murray said.

Sawyer ignored him and stared at Jill. He didn't know what she was playing at, and she was definitely playing at something. She gave him a flirty finger wave. Jesus, she was flirting with him. No, couldn't be. It wasn't her style. He glanced at Ty because it was his style. "All right, out with it. What are you two up to?"

Ty nudged her.

Jill scowled at Ty while scratching her neck and wriggling her shoulders. Just as Sawyer was about to prompt her again, she looked up at him from under her fake eyelashes. "I was wondering if..." She cleared her throat. "I was..." She trailed off when a fight broke out on the dance floor. She swiveled her bar stool and jumped off, about to head in that direction.

Ty grabbed her by the arm. "No, you promised!"

"I can't just let them..." Jill began, wincing when a

man stepped between the women to break them up and got kneed in the groin. She shook off Ty's hand.

"Jill, I've got it. You—" Sawyer sighed. She was already halfway across the bar. He couldn't help but smile when she barked an order at the two women now rolling around in the middle of the dance floor. She hauled them to their feet, flattening a palm on their foreheads to keep them apart as she read them their rights. Sawyer laughed at the cheerful expression on her face. No doubt about it, she loved her job. And that was the Jill he knew. The one he was comfortable dealing with.

Ty slid off his bar stool with a disappointed look on his face, reaching in his back pocket to pull out his wallet.

"Don't worry about it, Ty. Jill covered both your drinks playing bouncer."

Ty sighed and started to follow her out the door, then backtracked. "You know what? You should name a drink after her." He opened his cell phone and handed it to Sawyer. A picture of Jill filled the screen. She was standing in front of her Jeep, the sun setting behind the Rockies in the distance. She held her gun in one hand, her badge in the other. "Hot Cop works, don't you think?"

Yeah. A little too well.

# Chapter Seven

Jill watched as her fairy godfather stomped out of the station with his wings in a twist. Suze wasn't happy with her, either. Blonde One and Blonde Two were the only ones who hadn't given her grief. They sat in the chairs in front of Jill's desk, quietly sipping extra-strong coffee.

"Okay, your cab should be here any minute. But I'm warning you, if this happens again, I'll charge you with drunk and disorderly," Jill told the women. They didn't have any priors, and once she'd gotten them out of the bar, they'd apologized to her and each other for their behavior.

"We promise, it won't happen again. Now that we know Sawyer's not interested, we'll go to the Garage or some other bar," Blonde One said.

"Uh, my warning goes for any bar, not just the Penalty Box," Jill said. "You shouldn't be drinking to the point you lose control. It's not safe."

"Tonight was a one-off," Blonde Two said, leaning

across the desk. "We kinda had this plan. Sawyer's like real protective of his female customers, you know. So we thought, let's get wasted and he'll have to bring us home."

Jill stared at her.

Blonde One nodded. "And Brandi wasn't there to toss us out on our heinies. But then you showed up."

"Yeah. We were like huh, he's interested in *her*," Blonde Two said, then her eyes went wide. "Not like in a bad way or anything. You're just not his usual type."

When Suze's head popped up from behind her computer screen, no doubt to listen in, Jill said, "Your cab's probably here by now, ladies. Just leave your mugs—"

"Nope, not yet," Suze said. "So Sawyer was interested in our girl here, was he?"

Blonde Two turned in her chair to face Suze. "Like mega. It was kinda depressing, you know? We heard blondes with big boobs did it for him, and then she walks in with dark hair and no boobs, and we're like, what the hey?"

"What the hey, yourself. I have boobs." Dammit, what was she doing? Suze laughed, and Blonde Two apologized. Jill was saved from making a bigger idiot of herself by a horn blasting outside. "There's your ride, ladies. Time to go." She stood up and removed the coffee mugs from their hands. Once she'd seen them safely into the cab, she came back into the station and said to Suze, "That was not helpful and totally inappropriate."

"No, what wasn't helpful was you using them as an excuse not to ask Sawyer out. The man was interested. All you had to do—"

"Sure he was interested, until he found out it was me.

And FYI, I'm sworn to uphold the law. I can't just let two women—"

Suze held her hand to her ear. "Do you hear that? I think it's a chicken. Bawk, bawk, bawk."

"Really, you think I'm a chicken? How about the time I took—"

"On the job, you are not a chicken. But when it comes to Sawyer, you bawk big time, girlfriend."

Jill ignored her and walked back to her desk. Suze was right. Jill had never been so happy for an interruption in her life.

"Brandi's not a chicken. She goes after what she wants. And word around town is she wants Sawyer. Sounds like she's getting help from Christmas's resident matchmaker, too," Suze said.

Jill picked up the mugs and headed for the small kitchen. Suze followed her, leaning against the door frame with her arms crossed while Jill rinsed the mugs. "Where's your competitive spirit gone? I thought that would send you running to the bar. There's still an hour before closing, you know. Seems like a waste of a fabulous dress and makeover."

"You're not going to let up on this, are you?" Jill said as she put the mugs in the dishwasher.

"Nope, not until you've given it your best shot. Come on, how much energy have you wasted thinking about asking him out, wondering what would happen if you did?"

Too much. "Fine, I'll do it. Happy now?" Jill asked, ignoring the nervous jitter in her stomach. A jitter that increased tenfold when she walked into the bar fifteen minutes later. The reason for the tenfold increase gave Jill an up-and-down look as she filled a drink order for one of the servers.

"Hey, Brandi," Jill said, glancing around the bar as she took a seat. "Sawyer around?"

Brandi stared at her open-mouthed, then blinked a couple times. "Jill?"

"Yep, it's me."

"Wow. You look...good. I don't think I've ever seen you in a dress before."

"Thanks. I was in earlier. I didn't see you here." She raised herself up on the stool, once again looking for Sawyer.

"You must have come in when I snuck upstairs to clean Sawyer's apartment and put through a couple loads of wash. Don't tell him I said so, but he's a bit of a slob. Gorgeous, but messy. He needs a wife."

Obviously Brandi was auditioning for the job. Which may have ticked Jill off just a bit because she asked, "So, where is the slob?"

Brandi's red-glossed lips flattened before she said, "He's on an important call. Is there something I can do for you?"

"No, I'll just wait until he's finished." Her back started to itch, and she wriggled her shoulders.

Brandi's brow furrowed and her pert nose wrinkled. "What are you doing?"

"Dancing." She added a few shoulders rolls to make it believable. No way she was telling Brandi she had hives.

"How come I'm not surprised," Brandi said under her breath, as if Jill was proving to be the idiot she'd always thought she was. Then she asked, "You want your regular soda, or are you going to go wild and have a Shirley Temple, better yet, a Virgin Caesar?"

Jill raised an eyebrow. "Do you have a problem with me not drinking alcohol?"

"Well, you are in a bar. Most people who come in here actually drink," she said in a voice laced with sarcasm.

Jill knew she shouldn't let Brandi goad her into having a drink, but she was really starting to get on her nerves. "I'll have..." She looked down the bar and pointed to a man four stools over sucking on a lime. She liked limes. "...whatever he's having." When you've seen as many drunks as Jill had, including her own mother, you tended to avoid alcohol. Well, at least she did. But it didn't mean that she'd never had a drink before. Despite what some people believed.

"Tequila shot coming up," Brandi said with a smirk.

The smirk worried Jill a little, but no way would she back down now. Brandi placed a shot glass of clear liquid in front of her, along with a small bowl of limes and a salt shaker. Jill stared at them. Now what was she supposed to do? She glanced at the man four stools over. He got up and moved beside her. "Looks like you could use some help."

He was very helpful. So helpful that Jill had shot back three rounds of tequila in no time at all. She was sucking on a lime when Sawyer appeared in front of her.

"What the hell do you think you're doing?"

Lips puckered, she held up the lime. "What does it look like I'm doing?" She blinked. Sawyer was no longer there. Her bar stool spun around, and he hauled her off of it. "There you are. I wondered where you went."

"Jesus," he muttered, "you're drunk."

"I'm not drunk. Now Blonde One and Blonde Two, they were drunk. I'm just...a little warm." She wobbled on her heels. "Maybe a little numb, too."

"Come on, let's get some coffee and food into you, and you can tell me what this is all about." He wrapped his arm around her waist and walked her around the bar.

She leaned back and called over her shoulder, "Bye, John. Nice meeting you. Thanks for your help."

"My pleasure, sweetheart. Anytime."

"He's a really nice guy."

"I'm sure he is. Brandi, take care of close for me. I'll be upstairs if you need me."

Jill glanced at the blonde standing behind the bar with her arms crossed over her ample chest. Brandi narrowed her eyes at Jill. "She made me do it," Jill said.

Sawyer looked down at her and raised an eyebrow. "Do what?"

"Drink. She was making fun of me." She mimicked Brandi's voice. "Go wild and have a Shirley Temple, better yet, a Virgin Caesar. As if I'm a virgin. I'm twenty-nine." Jill widened her eyes, raising a hand to her mouth. Why she was blabbing stuff like this to Sawyer? It was like the alcohol had stolen her filter.

"Uh, you know what? I think, for right now, you should keep quiet until we get some food and coffee into you. Sound like a plan?" he asked as he led her up the narrow wooden staircase.

"Yep, good plan. Very good plan. Best plan ever."

Sawyer laughed. "I'll say this for you, Shortstop. You're a cute drunk."

"You think—"

He placed a finger on her lips, and she fought back an

uncontrollable urge to kiss it, maybe lick it. "No talking, remember?" he said.

She nodded, and totally intended to keep that promise, but then he opened the door to his apartment. "So, this is where all the magic happens," she said, looking around the space. Unlike half the single women in town, she'd never been invited up to his apartment.

"Magic?" he choked out, then gave his head a slight shake. "Forget I asked," he said, and steered her toward the kitchen.

With its exposed log walls, the open-plan apartment had a rustic charm, a warm, homey feel. An overstuffed brown leather sectional sat on a cream shag area rug facing a big-screen television above the fireplace. Just beyond the living room, there was a butcher block table with seating for six by a large window. The kitchen was on the small side, but well-equipped, as though someone actually liked to cook.

She leaned to her left to get a look down the hall leading to what appeared to be two bedrooms and pointed. "You're right, that would be where the good stuff happens."

"Maybe I should take you home."

"It's okay. I'll walk. But I'm just going to sit for a minute," she said, pulling out a stool at the breakfast nook. She took a seat and toed off the killer heels. "I don't know how anyone wears these things," she said, bringing her foot to rest on her thigh. She massaged the instep, releasing a relieved moan as she did.

"Uh, Jill honey, you might want to…" he gestured at her leg. "You have a dress on."

She looked down. The hem had ridden up to reveal her

lacy red thong. "Oh, right," she said, adjusting the hem. "At least they match."

"Coffee. I'm going to get you coffee and make you an omelet. Don't move," he said as he walked to the stainless-steel refrigerator. She got a look at the neatly stacked contents of his fridge when he pulled out a container of eggs and a pint of cream.

"I don't know what Brandi's talking about. She said you're a slob, but you look pretty tidy to me. Unless she spent most of her shift up here." She spun on the stool to look around the apartment again... and fell off. "Whoa. That's a slippery little sucker." She laughed from where she'd landed on the hardwood floor.

Sawyer lifted her to her feet, her laughter fading as she looked into his eyes. Until that moment, she thought they were brown. Nice dark eyes, but nothing extraordinary. With his face inches from hers, she saw how wrong she'd been. There was nothing ordinary about his eyes. They were hazel with flecks of yellow. Framed by dark lashes tipped with gold. He smelled amazing, too—a woodsy citrus scent.

His brow furrowed. "Did you hurt yourself?"

"No, I'm...I'm okay." She was better than okay. She was in his arms, and they were alone. It was the opportunity she'd been waiting for. Her heart beat a little faster at the thought of asking him out. But nothing like earlier. Only with her palms pressed to his muscular chest, she was having a difficult time thinking of anything other than how good it felt to be here with him. She let herself lean into him while she worked to get the words out of her mouth. They seemed to be stuck in her throat. Or maybe it was the feel of his hard body pressed against hers messing with her head. Either that or the tequila.

* * *

Sawyer looked down at Jill. He never should have brought her here. Not after how he felt seeing her shooting back tequila at the bar. He'd held her in his arms before, but not like this. Never like this. Chest to chest, thigh to thigh, she was a perfect fit. Soft. Warm. Her light floral scent enveloped him, and he wanted to groan his frustration. Instead it came out as a sigh, as though mourning for what he couldn't have. Because no matter how much he wished it wasn't true, he wanted her. But he wouldn't, couldn't, make that mistake again. He'd nearly lost Jack's friendship once. He wouldn't risk losing it again.

He let go of her and went to take a step back. "Jill..."

Her hands fisted in his shirt, and she tipped her head back, capturing him in her sea-blue eyes. She lifted up on her toes and kissed him. Giving him a taste of what he couldn't have. A forbidden fruit so sweet and tart he wanted to lose himself in the kiss. In her. In Jill. He jerked back. "No. We can't...I can't do this."

She blinked, her hands falling to her sides. "Why not?"

He stepped away, scrubbing a hand over his mouth to erase the taste of her, the feel of her lips on his. "You don't want me, Jill. I'm not the guy for you."

"Yes, you are. I love you."

He heard Bill's voice in his head telling him the same thing. And Mrs. Sharp. How had he not seen what they had? He had to fix this. "No, you don't," he said, his voice coming out forceful and harsh. "You're not thinking straight. You've had too much to drink. That's all it is. You'll find someone who'll love you the way you deserve to be loved."

She wrapped her arms around her waist and shook her head. "I don't want anyone else. I never have," she said, her voice low and soft.

"Believe me, you don't want me, Shortstop. I'm too old for you. I'm not good enough for you. Ask your brother."

She raised her gaze to his. "This is about Jack, isn't it?"

He didn't want to hurt her, but he couldn't let this go any further. "No, it's about me. I'm not attracted to you, Jill. Not like that." She shrank into herself, and his chest tightened and ached. He hated doing this to her, but he didn't have a choice. He put his hands on her shoulders. "The last thing I want to do is hurt you. You're like a—"

"Don't. Don't say it," she said, her voice breaking. "I...I have to go." She turned and bent down to pick up her shoes.

He couldn't let her leave. Not like this. "Jill, come on. Let's talk—"

"No," she said, the word garbled. She ran to the door and flung it open.

He wanted to hit something. He'd handled that all wrong. It didn't matter that he'd been shocked by his reaction to that kiss. Or that thoughts of how Jack would react sent him into a panic. Neither was an excuse for hurting her.

Brandi walked into his apartment. "Why is Jill crying?"

He closed his eyes. He'd made her cry. A girl who rarely did. Over the years he'd seen her hurt—a baseball to the head, a bad fall off her bike, a broken leg when she fell out of a tree, a drunk breaking a chair over her back when she attempted to arrest him—and not one of those times had she cried. He swore under his breath.

"She kissed you, didn't she?" Brandi said, reaching up to rub her thumb over his bottom lip. "And you rejected her."

He stepped back. "I don't want to talk about it."

"It's not your fault she's in love with you, Sawyer. I'm sure you did your best to let her down easy."

Was he the only one who didn't know? He raked his hand through his hair, looking around his apartment. "I didn't. I screwed up. I screwed up bad. I have to go talk to her. Figure out a way to make this right," he said and headed for the door.

Brandi stopped him. "Give her some time. It'll only make it harder for her. Trust me, I've known Jill almost as long as you. She'll be okay." Brandi gave his arm a comforting squeeze. "In the end, you did her a favor. Now that she knows there's no hope for a future with you, she can move on."

# Chapter Eight

Sawyer climbed the outer stairs to Jill's second-floor apartment. He glanced at her small wooden deck as he passed by, smiling at the sight of two hanging baskets swinging in the warm breeze. The purple flowers were dead. He didn't know why she bothered. The woman had a black thumb and was rarely home. It's why he was here early on a Sunday morning.

Because no matter what Brandi said, he had to make this right. Jill was important to him. They'd had their ups and downs over the years, but what family didn't? Jill wasn't always easy. She could be a hardass and a pain in his. It had gotten bad when Jack was MIA. Real bad. Not much got past Jill, and Sawyer was pretty sure she knew he was in love with Grace back then. She hadn't made life easy on either of them. He understood why.

As the months passed without any word of Jack and his crew, Sawyer and Grace had lost faith that he'd ever come home. But not Jill. She'd never given up on the brother she

adored. She was the most loyal person Sawyer had ever
met. But that was all in the past, and they'd gotten back to
normal.

Sure she still busted his balls on occasion, but she no
longer looked like she wanted to cut them off. Well, she
hadn't. Since Friday night, he wasn't so sure that had
changed. But he wasn't about to let a passing attraction—
either his or Jill's—ruin their friendship.

He reached the breezeway. There were two apartment
doors on either side with a view of the pine-covered hills
at the end of the open hall. He knocked on her door.
Watching a hawk gliding over the treetops kept him enter-
tained for a couple minutes while he waited. He heard her
moving around inside; the faint strains of Luke Bryan's
"Do I" playing in the background. He tried again, knocking louder and longer this time. He got the feeling she
was watching him from behind the peephole in the door.

"I know you're there," he said, holding up the carry-
out bag. "I have blueberry scones. They're still warm.
Open up." Since they were her favorite, he was counting
on them to do the trick. Donuts and cupcakes would work
on most women, but not Jill. Maybe because she'd spent
her teenage years working after school and on week-
ends at the bakery. She wasn't a fan of sugary sweet…or
chocolate.

The door opened. His self-congratulatory smile faded
as she came into view. Short denim shorts rode low on her
hips revealing a strip of tanned, taut skin and the bellybutton ring she'd gotten at fifteen. A finger flip to her
controlling grandmother, and to him and Jack, as they'd
forbidden her from getting one. His eyes moved to the
navy tank top that revealed she was braless and…He

quickly brought his gaze to her face. She wasn't wearing any makeup or extensions. Though her hair looked different—softer, sexier—there was no reason for him to be feeling this sudden zing of attraction and heat. She looked like herself. Except she didn't, not anymore.

Once again he reminded himself she was off limits. Maybe that was the problem. Everyone wanted what they couldn't have. He knew all too well what that was like. He'd grown up with a mom who couldn't afford to give him what the other kids had. And as an adult, he'd wanted a woman and a child who belonged to another man. He gave himself a mental kick in the ass. He was here to make things right, not worse.

Jill crossed her arms self-consciously over her chest, a touch of pink coloring her cheeks. "I wasn't expecting company. It's early." She sounded grumpy, more like herself than she had the other night.

The attitude helped. He'd rather deal with this woman than the lady in red. He smiled and held up the bag. "Hockey camp starts in an hour. I wanted to talk to you. Can I come in?"

She sighed and opened the door, stepping aside to let him in. "Fine. But there's nothing to talk about." The color on her cheeks deepened, and she made a face. "Other than for me to apologize, I guess. I, ah, had too much to drink. I can't even remember what I said to you. So if it was…I don't know, inappropriate? I'm sorry." She wouldn't meet his eyes as she reached for the bag and turned away. "Do you want a cup of coffee?"

"Yeah, sure. Thanks." If that's how she wanted to play it, that was fine with him. Well, he thought it was until the next words out of his mouth. "So you don't remember kissing me?" What the hell? He'd gotten a free pass. She'd been willing to act like nothing happened, so why couldn't he?

She was heading into the small kitchen when he'd asked the question. Which might explain why he did. The sight of her ass in the short shorts and her incredibly long legs were messing with his head. He forgot that this was Jill and not his lady in red.

She bent her head and gave it a slight shake before tossing the bag of scones on the white countertop. "Not really. The night's a bit of a blur," she said while opening a cupboard and pulling out two mugs. She glanced to where he stood outside the kitchen by the table. "Can we just forget about it? I apologized. It won't happen again."

He didn't know if he could, but he didn't want her to feel any more uncomfortable than she obviously did. For both their sakes, he had to let it go. No good would come of him continuing down this road. "Didn't think it would, Shortstop. Just wanted to make sure we were okay."

She poured the coffee. "Yep, we're good. Totally—" Her gaze jerked to the table he leaned against, then back to him. "I'll bring you your coffee and scone. Go sit in the living room."

He frowned, not sure where the panicked look on her face was coming from. He glanced at the magazines spread over the table, a glue stick, scissors, and corkboard. "What's this? You working on a project with little Jack?" He smiled.

She scowled. "God, you're nosy. It's nothing. Now, do you want your coffee or not?" She held out a white mug imprinted with the words "Feel safe tonight. Sleep with a cop." and a pair of handcuffs. No way he was letting that image get into his head. It was bad enough he'd spent the past two nights thinking about that kiss. And for the brief amount of time he'd had his mouth on hers, it's not something that should have kept him up at night.

"They were a gift from Suze," Jill said, lifting an identical mug. "She bought me a dozen." She nudged her head at the living room, carrying a plate of scones along with her mug and napkins.

He followed her into a space he was familiar with. The orange-and-brown floral couch and armchair had been her grandmother's. So were the coffee and end tables and the lace doilies decorating both. Jill had inherited the furniture when Grace renovated the apartment above the Sugar Plum Bakery as a surprise for Jack. His best friend didn't have fond memories of living there with his grandmother. Neither did Jill. But as loyal as she was, she wouldn't get rid of the furniture. Plus she was cheap. She didn't like spending money unless she had to.

"Still play?" he asked, nodding at the guitar leaning against the exposed brick wall. He hadn't known she played until she'd performed, with some arm-twisting from her brother, at Jack and Grace's wedding. She'd played "Amazed" by Lonestar, singing along with Jack, who serenaded his beautiful, blushing bride. Jill had been surprisingly good once she got over her nerves. Actually, she'd been pretty amazing.

She shrugged. "When I have time."

"You should play for the seniors. They'd love it."

She snorted. "Yeah, that's not going to happen. I swore I'd never play in public again after Jack and Grace's wedding."

And now, thinking back to that day, he realized the

other night wasn't the first time he'd wished Jill wasn't his best friend's sister. But he'd locked the memory away. He took comfort in the knowledge that he'd been able to. Because as he sat beside her on the couch, taking in those long legs and toned body, he'd begun to wonder if he could.

He drew his attention back to the conversation. "That was what... seven ago? Must be over your stage fright by now."

"Maybe when I'm eighty," she said, lifting a scone to her mouth.

He smiled, remembering how she'd looked the day of the wedding. She'd worn a soft pink dress, her hair a little longer than it was now. She'd been twenty-two; all glowy and innocent. Shy and sweet.

A lot different from the women he'd become accustomed to back then. He'd grown tired of the chase. Not that he had to do any chasing. He was propositioned everywhere he went. He hadn't realized when he'd been signed by the Flurries how much his life would change. And the day of Jack's wedding, he'd gotten the devastating news that put his career in the NHL on the line.

He felt Jill looking at him and glanced at her.

"What's with the face..." she began, then trailed off, putting down her scone and rubbing crumbs from her hands. "Forgot about that. Guess we're even."

"Did I miss something? What are you talking about?"

She shrugged. "You kissed me at Jack and Grace's wedding. I kissed you the other night. So we're even. No biggie. Seriously."

"I didn't..." Relief flooded his body when he realized what she was talking about. "You're right, it's not a big deal. But Shortstop, I gave you a peck on the cheek in the receiving line. It's hardly the same—"

She looked at him like he was an idiot. "I know the difference between a peck and a kiss. And let me tell you, my kiss the other night was a peck compared to the one you gave me when I drove you to your hotel after the wedding."

He stared at her, stunned.

Her eyes widened. "You don't remember."

"Come on, Jill. You know me. If I did, I would have said something." He leaned against the back of the couch. "Jesus."

"I'm not lying. If you don't believe me, ask Barbie... or was it Bambi? I can't remember which puck bunny you were dating at the time, but she opened the hotel room door."

"I believe you, okay. I'm not mad at you. I'm mad at myself." He glanced at her. "I'm sorry, Jill. I never should have kissed you."

"You were drunk. And I..." She lifted a shoulder. "...I was drunk Friday night. Like I said, we're even." She rolled her eyes when he scrubbed his hands over his face. "Would you stop beating yourself up over it? Seriously, it's not a big deal. You were in a bad place that night, Sawyer. I knew that."

"Yeah, it wasn't a good night." And now he realized just how bad it had actually been. What the hell had he been thinking?

"Do you regret retiring?"

There was a part of him that welcomed the change of subject. Knowing Jill, it was probably intentional. "Didn't have much choice."

"If it was up to the owners and coaches, you'd still be playing. Fans and players, too. Including the legions of puck bunnies." She grinned, doing a good job of lightening his mood. "But you made the right choice. All you read about these days is traumatic brain injuries. That was your third concussion, and it was a bad one. You were unconscious for ten minutes." She shuddered. "If you ask me, you should have filed a civil suit against Erik. He punched you in the head from behind, then fell on top of you, shoving your face into the ice. And let's not forget the other dumbasses who piled on."

"Thanks for the play-by-play, Shortstop." But she was right about what had happened that night, and after. They'd all tried to get him to stay on. Even the team's doctor had okayed him to play. Everyone except Bill, his mother, Jack, and Jill. TBI wasn't something people talked about, not like they did today. But Bill had learned everything he could about it and sat Sawyer down two weeks after the hit. He'd laid everything out to him the morning of Jack's wedding. So yeah, he hadn't been in a good place that day. But still...

"Sorry, but hey, you coach a competitive hockey team and play in the seniors' league. Even though I still think you should quit. So it's not like you're out of the game completely. Not like you would have been if you'd taken another hit and ended up a vegetable."

He angled his head. "Really? Are you sure you passed your sensitivity training?" he teased.

"Yes I did. I'm even more sensitive than...Suze."

He laughed. "That's not saying much."

"I'll tell her you said so."

Sawyer glanced at his watch. He didn't have much

time left, but there was something he had to ask her. "Okay, so don't get ticked at me, but I need to know what was going on with you Friday night."

"You're never going to let it go, are you?"

"No, it's not about the kiss. I get that. You had a little too much to drink. It's happened to all of us at one time or another. I meant what was up with the dress, makeup, and hair? You have to admit you weren't acting like yourself even before you shot back the tequila."

She chewed on her bottom lip.

He wished she'd stop. He was doing his best not to think about how soft her lips were. He cleared his throat. "Jill?"

"I had a meeting with Gage on Thursday and it didn't go so well. There's something going on at Mountainview. A few of the residents have suspicious bruising and jewelry has gone missing, some cash, too."

"Really? Did you talk to Sandy about it?"

"Yeah, and that was the reason for my meeting with Gage. She said I scared the staff when I interrogated them, and Gage refused to apply for a search warrant."

"What's with needing a warrant? Sandy should have let you search the place without one."

"I know, right? But Gage thinks they made it all up just so I would stick around."

"There's no doubt they're fond of you, and I can see pretending to lose their jewelry and cash to keep you there, but what about the bruising? Now you've got me worried about Bill."

"Don't be. Until I get to the bottom of it, I'll be dropping by every day."

"I'll keep my eyes open, too. Talk to Bill."

"That'd be great. Thanks."

"So I understand why you'd be upset, but I'm kinda lost as to how the makeover comes into play."

She grimaced. "Gage inferred I needed an image over-haul if I want to be sheriff. It looks like he won't be running for another term."

Relieved there was an explanation, and it didn't have anything to do with him, Sawyer held back a grin. "Just saying, but you may want to go back to the drawing board. You looked more smoking-hot party girl than com-petent cop." *Smoking-hot party girl?* Maybe he should think before he opened his mouth. Now was probably a good time to leave. "I better get going. Thanks for the coffee." He picked up his still-full mug of cold coffee and stood. "And, Jill, I really am sorry."

She leaned back against the couch and groaned. "Can we just stop talking about it?"

"Yeah, of course. And don't worry, I won't say a word to Jack," he said, praying she'd do the same.

"I didn't think you would," she said, getting up off the couch.

He didn't have to ask why. He headed to the kitchen, leaving his mug on the counter. His eyes landed on the board as he walked toward the door. He stopped by the table. "So are you going to tell me what you're doing or is it a secret?"

She nudged the board over a magazine and blushed, not meeting his gaze. "It's a vision board."

He frowned. "Something wrong with your eyesight?"

She looked up at the ceiling for a couple of seconds, then back at him. "No, Sawyer." It sounded more like *dumbass*. "A vision board. You know, like Oprah and those kinds of people tell you to do if you want your dreams to come true."

"Those kinds of people?" he said, struggling to keep the laughter from his voice.

"Yeah, positive people. Chloe had one. It worked, so I..." She trailed off and shrugged.

He took a closer look at her board. There was a white clapboard house with blue shutters and a big front porch facing onto a lake. "Nice house. Place like that would cost a small fortune, though. How long did it take for Chloe's dreams to come true?"

"Twenty years," she said and gave him a light shove toward the door.

He laughed, then saw a woman in a sheriff's uniform. "Wait, is that you?" he said, leaning over the board to get a better look." He glanced at her. "You cut your face out of a photograph and put it on a guy in uniform, didn't you?"

"So what if I did? I couldn't find one female sheriff. Talk about discrimination."

"Keep on Gage's good side, and you'll be able to take that one off your board next spring," he said, then lifted his chin. "Who's the guy with the little boy and girl?"

"My future husband. Chris Pine."

"He's a brunette. I thought you preferred blonds." He knew he'd walked into that one before the words were out of his mouth, but it was too late to take them back.

"Whatever gave you that idea? I've always loved brunettes. The darker the better."

"Oh, okay. I'll let you get back to your board," he said, feeling kinda ticked. Which was ridiculous. He should be happy. He'd come here to make sure they were okay and she wasn't harboring a secret crush on him. They were, and she wasn't. No, she was pining after a guy named Chris Pine. A guy who didn't look like a Norse god or Viking warrior, a guy who didn't look like Sawyer at all. Even though she'd kissed him and told him she loved him. And he`d kissed her back.

# Chapter Nine

It'd been a week since Sawyer had shown up at her apartment, and Jill was just getting around to moving the vision board to her bedroom. As she loaded the last of the magazines into a recycle bin, an actor she'd cut out of one of them fell to the floor. It was Sawyer's doppelganger. Just moments before he'd knocked on the door last Sunday, his doppelganger had stood where Chris Pine did. She'd ripped paper-Sawyer off the board, replacing him with Chris Pine before answering the door. Now she picked Sawyer's doppelganger off the floor and crumpled him in a ball, tossing him in the recycle bin. She tucked the bin awkwardly under one arm as she opened her apartment door and stepped into the breezeway. A rolled-up newspaper flew through the air and hit her on the head.

"Sorry, Jill, didn't see you there," Fred yelled, half hanging out the window of his truck.

"Withdraw your complaint and I won't sue," she

yelled back as she put down the bin and retrieved the newspaper.

"If you're going to sue anyone, you should sue whoever took your picture for the *Chronicle*." Another paper went sailing by her head, but this time she managed to duck. "Have a good day now," he yelled, and burned rubber peeling out of the lot.

She stared at the rolled-up paper, afraid to look. She'd gone to the prom Friday night. Stag, of course. She'd hung around the refreshment table serving punch all night. Spiked punch sounded good about now, or maybe a shot of tequila. Just the thought of the drink made her stomach turn. And not because she'd been hung over the next day. She'd been tipsy, not drunk like she'd told Sawyer. The night wasn't a blur, either. She'd lost both her filter and her dignity. At least the bar had been dark and empty when she left. The streets quiet when she'd made her mile-long walk of shame to her apartment. Her tears and hurt vanquished by anger and pain from walking in the high heels.

She left the bin outside her door and walked back into her apartment, grabbing a cup of coffee before she sat at the table. Slowly she unraveled the paper. Her eyes shot wide when the photo came into focus. She lay her head on the table and groaned at the same time her cell phone rang.

"You don't sound so good," Ty said when she answered. "Let me guess, you got a copy of the *Chronicle*."

"I don't understand why someone would even take that picture of me, let alone why Vivi would publish it," she said, referring to the owner and publisher of the *Christmas Chronicle*.

"Well, maybe they thought it was a catfight. You're

scowling at Chloe and grabbing at her arm. And Nell's acting as editor in chief while Vivi's on maternity leave. But don't worry, no one other than us knows Chloe was asking Nell to make you the heroine for the next book instead of Brandi, and that Nell agreed."

It had been the second most embarrassing moment of Jill's life. "Nell agreed only because she was friends with my grandmother."

"Whatever, at least she's on Team Jill now and not Team Brandi. We'll talk about it later. Right now you have to get your butt in gear and get over here."

"Get over where?"

"Baby shower ring a bell?"

"Ah, yeah, but it's at two." They were having a shower for Vivi. The first one was canceled on account of Cat and Chloe's surgery.

"Nuh-huh, not for you and me. I'm the party planner, remember? It has to be perfect. I need your muscles."

She sighed. "Fine. I have to stop by the nursing home. I'll be there by ten forty-five."

"What are you wearing?"

"Clothes."

"Ha-ha, you have such a droll sense of humor. No jeans or shorts. This is an elegant affair. I don't want you to look out of place. It doesn't have to be fancy; a sundress will do."

"I don't think... Okay, fine, I have one in the back of my closet."

"Rolled up in a ball no doubt."

"How did you know?"

\*    \*    \*

Jill stood beside Ty in Dr. McBride's backyard. "Do you see it?" he asked, pointing to the top of an aspen tree.

She shielded her eyes from the midafternoon sun and followed his finger. "It's a blackbird."

"Shoot it."

"Are you crazy? I'm not going to shoot a bird because you're worried it's going to poop on the table. You should have thought about that before setting up outside under the trees. Besides, you have those little umbrellas hanging over the table. It'll be fine." Seven white umbrellas hung down the middle of a long table draped in white linen. Vases filled with pink water and white peonies sat between each umbrella, while table settings of pink plates with red chargers beneath them finished off the elegant display. Jill didn't say anything to Ty, but the decor seemed more suited to Chloe than Vivi.

"I don't want it to be *fine*. If I want to build my reputation as party planner extraordinaire, it has to be perfect."

"Why? I thought the salon was doing well."

"It is, but it's slow in the summer and Christmas is a small town. I need a cushion. Besides, I love planning parties."

From the expression on his face, she had a feeling business at Diva wasn't quite what he'd hoped for. She glanced at the blackbird. Skirting the table, she bent over and found a small rock nestled in the pine needles beneath the trees and straightened.

"What are you..." Ty trailed off when she drew back her arm and threw the rock at the branch beside the blackbird's perch. It took off with an outraged squawk. Ty hugged her. "You're my hero."

"I don't think I'm his, so let's hope he doesn't—"

She broke off as the twins Holly and Hailey approached wearing formal black-and-white waitstaff attire. Unlike Chloe and Cat, Hailey and Holly, the owners of the Rocky Mountain Diner, were easily distinguishable. Holly wore her dark hair in a beehive, and Hailey had a short, spiky cut that currently sported green tips. The sisters were catering today's event.

Holly gave Jill a smile that oozed sympathy and concern. She looked down at her blue sundress. It wasn't that bad, was it? Though maybe it was since Ty had suggested she should have left it in the back of her closet. She didn't think it was that out of style. She'd bought it eight years ago when Jack brought Grace home to meet them.

When Hailey offered Jill a similar smile, she knew it had nothing to do with her dress. Other than her hair, Hailey was as fashionably unconscious as Jill. Holly rubbed Jill's arm. "How are you doing? We've been worried about you."

Jill briefly closed her eyes. *Brandi*. The three women hung out together all the time. She should have known Sawyer's manager wouldn't keep her mouth shut. Jill had nearly bowled her over when she ran from his apartment. There's no way the other woman wouldn't have noticed that she was upset.

Ty frowned. "Why would you worry about—"

The last thing Jill wanted was for Ty to hear about it. Heart pounding, she cut him off. "We should probably get inside. The guests will be—"

"Because she got her heart broken, that's why," Hailey interrupted Jill while looking her in the eye. "It's not the end of the world, you know. Sawyer's a great guy, but there's someone else for you. You just have to put yourself out there."

"Oh, Jilly Bean, why didn't you tell me? You asked him out, and he said no." Ty pulled her in for a hug. He was the huggiest, touchiest person she knew. Jill wasn't.

"No, no, she didn't ask him for a date. She kissed him. Brandi said he was totally shocked and kind of grossed out." Jill drew back from Ty and stared at Holly, who held out her hands, palms out. "I'm just repeating what Brandi said. But, Jill, what did you expect? The poor guy thinks of you as his little—"

Ty sniffed the air. "Is something burning?"

Hailey's eyes went wide. "Holly! Did you put the canapés in the oven?" Without waiting for her sister's response, Hailey ran for the patio doors with Holly chasing after her.

"I don't smell anything burning," Jill said.

Ty gave a distracted wave of his hand. "I just wanted to get rid of them. Don't worry, I'll keep them busy in the kitchen for the rest of the day." He looked at her, his face scrunched up. "Was it true, what Holly said?"

"Of course not..." She began, then sighed. "Yeah, I went back to the bar last Friday. I kissed him. I can't honestly say how he felt about it, but he dropped by that Sunday and brought me scones. So I guess he wasn't totally grossed out. But, Ty, I'm done. I have to forget about him and move on."

"Maybe. But you know, you should be proud of yourself. It may not have turned out like we'd hoped, but you put yourself out there. I'm proud of you. And hey, it could have been worse. You could have told him you were in love with him."

"Yeah, thank God I didn't tell him that," she said, hoping she managed to keep the truth from her face.

Ty looked at her like maybe she hadn't, but she was saved by voices filtering through the screen door. "They're here. Come on," Ty said.

He dragged her through the kitchen—where Holly and Hailey were taking turns sniffing the oven—to the entrance of the bungalow. Liz was ushering the guest of honor into the house. Since it was Vivi, who in her previous life had been an investigative crime reporter, there'd been no sense trying to keep the shower a surprise.

Chance stood at the door hovering over his very pregnant wife. Vivi wore a white sundress and a scowl, which she directed at her husband. "For the last time, I'm fine," she said, rubbing her back. She caught the direction of her husband's frowning gaze and dropped her hand. "You'd be rubbing your back, too, if you were carrying forty extra pounds in your stomach. So stop worrying about me. I'm fine and our child is fine. So go paint...its room with your dad."

Jill felt a little sorry for Chance. He'd lost his first wife and unborn child six years ago in a car accident, so he was understandably overprotective of Vivi. But as strong and independent as Vivi was, his need to keep her safe drove her kind of nuts. Jill sympathized with her, too, but didn't think Chance was overreacting. At least not today. Normally Vivi had a beautiful, glowing complexion. Today her olive skin held a tinge of gray. Chance caught Jill's eye and lifted his chin at his wife.

Jill nodded, silently promising to watch out for her. Vivi caught the exchange and rolled her eyes, but didn't have an opportunity to call them on it because Chance's dad joined them. "There's my beautiful daughter-in-law," Paul began, then frowned. "Honey, are you feeling all right? You're looking a little—" He broke off when, behind Vivi, Chance gave a warning shake of his head.

"Vivi darling, why don't you come in and sit down," Liz said, intervening before her husband got himself in hot water with the guest of honor.

Vivi nodded and walked toward the great room. She came to a stop and pivoted. "Chance, you told them we're having a girl!"

"It wasn't me," he said, turning as the door opened and Cat and Chloe walked in.

Jill shot Ty a disgruntled look. He'd banned her from wearing pants and a T-shirt, but that's exactly what Cat had on. Of course Chloe wore a hot pink dress and sparkly shoes, but that was Chloe. "Surprise!" the actress said, obviously not getting the memo that it wasn't one.

Vivi ignored her, seemingly determined to find out who gave their secret away. "Paul, did you tell?" she asked her father-in-law.

"Me? No, of course not."

"Told what?" Chloe asked, looking from Dr. McBride to Vivi.

Vivi gestured to the pink tissue paper flowers decorating the fireplace mantel. "That we're having a girl."

Chloe grimaced. "I may have mentioned it. But it was for your own good, Vivi. You would have gotten yellow and green unisex clothes. Now you're going to get adorable pink outfits you'll actually use."

"Okay, time for us to leave, Dad," Chance said, then walked to his wife. He framed her face with his hands. "You need me, you call me, Slick. And don't give me any lip." He whispered something in her ear that made her blush, then kissed her, gently rubbing her baby bump before heading for the door.

Ty sighed. "I love that man."

Chance and Dr. McBride were barely out the door before a steady stream of women started to arrive, including Nell McBride and Jill's sister-in-law.

"Hey." Jill waved at Grace.

Grace smiled and held up a pink gift bag. "Come here. I'll show you what we got."

Jill had contributed to the gift, but let her sister-in-law pick it out. "In a sec. I'm on drinks duty." She hadn't been, but she was now. She was worried that somehow Grace had heard about the episode with Sawyer and would want to chat. Jill didn't want to talk about it with anyone, least of all Grace. And not only because she was married to her brother, but because of the almost-relationship between Sawyer and Grace. It made things even more awkward. Mostly in Jill's mind, she knew.

Grace and Jack were head over heels in love. It was obvious to anyone who saw them together. Sawyer and Jack were good, too. But Jill sometimes wondered if Sawyer still harbored romantic feelings for her sister-in-law. If he did, he did a good job of hiding them. And she knew he would never act on them. He loved Jack like a brother, and he would never do anything to damage their friendship. But still...

Jill was serving a mason jar of pink lemonade to Liz when, out of the corner of her eye, she saw Nell waving her over.

"Time for the games, ladies." Ty clapped his hands to get the women's attention. "We'll go outside now."

Jill sagged in relief. She wasn't a fan of games, but it was the perfect way to avoid Nell and Grace. Two shower games later, Jill decided she'd rather talk about her embarrassing episode than play another one.

"Okay, Jilly Bean, you have to step it up. We lost the last two because of you." Jill was on Ty and Chloe's team. As far as she was concerned, she'd drawn the short straw, not them. "Hey, it wasn't me who put Grace, Madison, and Skye on the same team. They have babies. They know what they're doing." She was reaching. It wasn't like she didn't have experience with babies. Grace and her nephew had lived with her for over a year when Jack was missing.

"What does not knowing which candy bar is which have to do with babies?" Ty asked. Chloe was completely oblivious to their conversation. When she wasn't texting Easton, she was taking photos to put on Instagram.

"If you ask me, that was a stupid game. Not to mention gross." Several diapers with different types of melted chocolate resembling poop had been passed around the room. "Besides, I don't eat chocolate."

"I know, you told us that five times. I think it speaks to a defect in your Y chromosome."

"Oh be quiet and pass the toilet paper roll." This game was as ridiculous as the last. Two team members were supposed to make a diaper on the third teammate out of toilet paper. Jill had insisted that Ty be the diaperee. Since he was wearing pants, she'd thought it would be the least embarrassing. Now she wasn't so sure.

She glanced at the other teams. Liz, Cat, and Skye's stepmother, Betty Jean, stood on one side of them while Nell and her best friends, Stella and Evelyn, stood on the other. But their real competition was the three beautiful blondes standing off to the far right. Skye and Madison were laughing with Grace, who was the diaperee. The two women were pregnant and glowing. Jill couldn't help but wonder if it was hard on her sister-in-law. Jack and Grace had been trying to get pregnant for more than a year. As though Grace sensed her attention, she looked over at Jill and mouthed *You've got this one*. Best sister-in-law ever, she thought. She had to stop avoiding her.

"Ready when you are, Vivi," Ty said.

The guest of honor sat in a comfortable chair with a stopwatch in her hand. "Okay, on your mark..." She winced, then forced a smile. "Get set...Oh," she moaned.

Jill dropped the toilet paper roll and rushed to her side. "Are you..." She glanced at Vivi's stomach. "You should have told us!"

"I didn't want to ruin the party. You all went to so much work and they just started twenty minutes ago. I have lots of time." She groaned and bent over at her waist, as much as she could bend over.

Jill had kept an eye on Vivi's tightening stomach and, if her hunch was right, Vivi didn't have lots of time. "How long have you had the pain in your back?"

"Since around two this morning. But that doesn't have anything to do—"

"Yeah, it does." Ty and the women crowded around them. Jill took the stopwatch from Vivi's hand. "Time the next one," she said, handing the watch to Cat. Jill put an arm around Vivi to help her stand. "Start timing now, Cat," Jill said, holding up Vivi while she breathed through another contraction. "Ty, call the hospital and let them know we're on our way. Liz, call Chance and Paul."

They'd barely made it a couple steps before Vivi's knees buckled as she was once again hit by a wave of pain. Jill wrapped both arms around her, taking all her weight. "Ty, call nine-one-one," she said, keeping her voice calm and even.

Everyone started shouting questions and instructions as Jill headed for the patio door. Cat whistled. "Stop yelling, you're upsetting Vivi. Jill has it under control." Cat darted past her, holding open the patio door.

Jill looked down at Vivi, who was pale and sweating and biting down on her bottom lip. "You're going to be fine. Paramedics will be here in no time at all," she re-assured Vivi as she half carried her through the kitchen and past the entrance to the hall. "Liz, we need a bed with clean sheets." Vivi's panicked gaze shot to Jill. She shrugged. "Better to be prepared, right?"

Liz ran ahead of them with her phone pressed to her ear. She opened a door at the end of the hall. "It's Chance's old room. The sheets are clean."

"You're doing great, sweetie," Madison said, losing most of the color in her face. If Jill remembered correctly, her boss's wife didn't do well with pain. "What can we do?" she asked Jill.

"Do you think a birthing ball would help? I have one at home," Skye said.

Vivi groaned at the offer.

"You know what? Why don't you go...boil some water? That would help." Jill glanced at the other women trailing after her. "Actually, why don't you all go do that," she said as she walked into Chance's bedroom. "Except you, Cat. You come with us." As an ex-cop, she trusted Cat to keep her cool.

"I played a doctor on *Days of Our Lives*; maybe I can be of some help. I did a lot of research for the role," Chloe offered.

Cat pulled back the covers, and Jill helped Vivi onto the mattress. "I wanna push," Vivi said through a strained whisper.

"Um, I'll go boil some water, too," Chloe said, backing out of the room. She grabbed Ty, who'd been wringing his hands in the doorway.

"Cat, can you get behind Vivi on the bed and prop her up a bit, or do you want Liz to do it?"

"I'm good," Cat said. She positioned herself on the bed and guided Vivi into her arms.

Liz leaned over to gently smooth Vivi's hair from her face. "You're doing wonderful, darling. Chance and Paul are on their way."

Nell appeared with a stack of clean towels. "Thought you might need these."

"Thanks, Nell. Vivi, I know it's hard, but don't push yet. I'm just going to wash my hands."

Vivi looked at her as Jill got off the bed. "The paramedics aren't going to get here in time, are they?"

"Doesn't matter. I've delivered a baby before. Nothing to it." Liz, Nell, and Cat glanced at her. It wasn't true. But Vivi didn't need to hear that right now. "Liz, get Chance on the phone. Let him talk to Vivi." And if Jill needed help, Dr. McBride could guide her through the delivery. Because whether they liked it or not, this baby was coming.

Ten minutes later, baby McBride entered the world.

Jill had just cleaned and swaddled the baby when the paramedics and Chance and his father arrived. Cat, Liz, and Nell moved off the bed as Chance pushed through the men and rushed to his wife's side, gently taking her in his arms. He buried his face in her hair. "That was the longest twenty minutes of my life. I'm sorry I wasn't here for you, honey. I tried—"

Vivi pressed two fingers to his lips. "It's my fault. If I wasn't so stubborn, you would have been. I'm so sorry you missed—"

He cut her off with a passionate kiss. "Doesn't matter. Nothing matters but that you're both okay." He stroked her face. "God, I love you."

Jill cleared her throat and carefully offered the baby. "I think someone wants to meet you."

Chance looked from her to the baby, and his eyes filled. He took the baby from Jill, cradling the small bundle to his chest. "She's beautiful. She has your eyes, honey. And your nose." He kissed the baby's forehead. "Daddy's going to have his work cut out for him when you're a teenager." He looked around the room when they started to laugh and frowned. "Well it's true. Look at her."

"You might want to take a closer look, honey. She's a he," Vivi said, her face glowing with laughter and love.

"What? But the ultrasound…" He unwrapped the blanket and blinked, then a huge grin spread across his face. "What do you know? I guess you're going to be as pretty as your daddy."

Once everyone got to meet the baby and congratulate Chance and Vivi, Dr. McBride insisted they go to the hospital and get checked out. He and Liz followed them there while everyone else gathered outside around the table. Jill sat between Nell and Ty. Holly and Hailey were serving the canapés when the patio doors opened. Gage came out first carrying his son, Connor, followed by Annie and Lily. Then there was Ethan with his daughter, Evie, in his arms, and Jack with Jill's nephew in his. Easton and Grayson brought up the rear. Jill sat back and watched as they joined their wives and fiancées. It was like a movie playing out in slow motion. They were all smiling and laughing, the kids cuddling with their mothers, the men sharing loving looks with their women.

Her heart squeezed. She wanted that. She glanced at Nell, wondering if the older woman ever felt like she'd missed out.

Ty sighed. "I guess the three of us will have to be satisfied with being honorary aunties for the rest of our lives."

Nell turned her head to look at Ty. Jill saw the regret before the older woman covered it with a smile. "Not a bad thing to be, son. Not a bad thing at all."

Something wet plopped on Jill's shoulder. Ty's eyes went wide, and he covered his mouth with both hands. Jill looked at the gray blob on her shoulder.

Nell grinned and patted her hand. "A bird pooping on your shoulder brings good luck, you know." She leaned into Jill and whispered, "Probably a good thing because I'm thinking you might need some. Brandi's more determined than I gave her credit for."

# Chapter Ten

Jill was a hero. At least according to this morning's write-up in the online version of the *Chronicle*. Facebook and Twitter, too. Jill didn't have an account on either, but Nell had just texted to inform her that she was trending on local social media. Nell had uploaded a picture of Jill with the over-the-moon parents and too-cute-for-words baby. The photo had broken the record for number of likes and shares on the town's Facebook page. Jill didn't fool herself that the likes had anything to do with her. Chance and Vivi were gorgeous and who can resist a baby?

But the one thing Nell hadn't mentioned, either yesterday or today, was Jill's embarrassing episode with Sawyer. Given that it was Nell, Jill had no doubt the older woman had heard the news. And kept quiet about it. Which Jill told herself was a good thing. A great thing. But, she had to admit, it was also a little depressing. Because it meant that Nell had more than likely realized

what Jill already knew. There was no chance of a romantic relationship between her and Sawyer. And after her
comment about how determined Brandi was, no doubt
Nell had gone back to her first choice for Sawyer's love
interest in book number seven. Since Jill had decided to
move on anyway, she didn't completely understand why
Nell giving up so easily bothered her. Except that Nell
never gave up...on anything.

So maybe that's why it hurt, just a little. Jill had never
felt like she measured up. She was good at sports, but
not good enough for a scholarship. She was attractive, but
not pretty...She just wasn't *enough*. She knew she had
issues. Growing up with a domineering grandmother she
could never please kind of guaranteed she'd have them.
At least Jill knew where hers came from, and she would
deal with them. She figured the best way to do that was
to make a fresh start. Today was the first day of her new
life. She smiled at the thought as she pulled into a parking spot in front of the station. Maybe the positive sayings
she'd pinned to her vision board last night were actually
working. This was the first time in months that she hadn't
had to park a block away.

If things kept going the way they were, the sheriff's
job was as good as hers. Yep, thanks to baby McBride,
her chances of being elected sheriff next spring had gone
up exponentially. And the increase in salary would bring
her one step closer to her dream house on the lake. No
twenty-year wait for her.

Down the street Dan looked up from sweeping the
sidewalk in front of the barbershop. "Great job delivering
the McBride baby. Proud of you, honey. Your next trim's
on the house."

Jill had known Dan since she'd moved to Christmas. His barbershop was only a couple doors down from her grandmother's apartment above the bakery. He used to cut her hair when she was young. "Thanks, Dan."

She smiled, walking a little taller. No better way to start the first day of her new life than as a hero, she thought, opening the door to the station.

Suze looked over from the dispatch desk and grimaced. "Sorry to rain on your parade, but we just got a call from Mrs. Burnett. You'll have to take it."

Jill forced her smile to stay in place. New day, new way was her current motto. "No problem. I should probably apologize to her anyway." Jill held up her hand. Suze tossed her the keys to the cruiser. "Fill me in while I'm driving."

As soon as Jill pulled onto Main Street, she connected with Suze. "Okay, give it to me. Why did Mrs. Burnett call in?"

"This morning or last night?"

It was getting harder to hang on to her good mood. "Are they related?"

"Well, last night she called in a noise complaint, and this morning she says she saw someone skulking about in her backyard. Her words, not mine. And last night's call was actually legit. Brandi Dawson's husband, Steve, got out of jail and came to pay her a visit. It got loud. Brad says Dawson was sober and moved on when he asked him to. He didn't have any reason to charge him," Suze said.

Brad had good instincts so Jill trusted he made the right call. But Brandi's ex was an abusive alcoholic and that concerned her. Gage had worked hard to get the man put away. He'd be about as happy as Brandi was that her ex was in town. Steve had broken parole a couple years ago and ended up back in jail. Jill would like to think that this time he got some help while he was inside. "Why didn't Brandi call it in?" she asked, turning off Main Street.

"Who knows. Maybe Dawson took her by surprise, and she didn't have her phone nearby."

"I suppose. Did you let Gage know?"

"I will as soon as he gets in. He's picking up Chance, Vivi, and the baby at the hospital this morning and taking them home. Bet you earned some serious Brownie points with the boss bringing his nephew safely into the world. That was pretty awesome, girlfriend. I'm impressed."

"Vivi did all the work. I was just there to catch."

"You're a pain in the butt, you know. Take some credit for a change. You did good. Own it."

"Yeah, yeah, I'm owning it. I should be back at the station in an hour. I'm going to stop by and check on Brandi after I finish up with Mrs. Burnett. Knowing Gage, Brad's report won't tell him everything he wants to know. I'll be able to get a better read on her. Do me a favor and check in with Steve's parole officer."

Jill's stomach dipped at the thought of seeing Brandi. She wasn't exactly happy that the woman had witnessed her humiliation and shared it with her friends. But when it came to her job, Jill didn't have a problem putting her personal feelings aside.

"Will do. See you in a bit. Looking forward to hearing all about yesterday's excite..." Suze started to laugh. "Ty just posted a picture of you on Facebook with bird poop on your shoulder. I have to say I liked the one Nell posted better. That Chance McBride is one smoking-hot daddy. Baby's adorable, too."

See, there you go. She knew the likes had nothing to do with her. "So is Chance's wife."

Suze sighed. "I know. Can you imagine looking that good right after having a baby? Too bad she's so nice. I could work up a good hate-on for her."

"You know, you might want to get off Facebook and back to your real job."

"My real job's boring. Besides, you wouldn't believe what people post on Facebook."

Jill turned onto Mrs. Burnett's street. "All right, later. I'm just pulling up to Mrs. Burnett's now," she said as she parked in front of the robin's-egg-blue bungalow.

"Well lookie here, I've solved your case for you. Someone just posted that there was a black bear spotted one street over from Mrs. Burnett's."

"I doubt she'd mistake a person for a bear, Suze. But good to know. I'll check it out. Give Logan at Parks and Wildlife a heads-up."

"Person who posted already did. And you never know, Mrs. Burnett's eyesight isn't what it used to be. It could have been a bear. Better be careful. It may be a mama bear, and the cubs are still around."

Through the passenger's side window, Jill caught a glimpse of the tree she'd cut the branches off of a few weeks ago. "I hope her eyesight is going because it looks like I killed her cherry tree."

"Really? That sucks. Someone posted last week that her husband had given her the tree for their twentieth anniversary. He died a week later."

Jill groaned and rested her forehead against the steering wheel. "I really didn't need to know that," she said, wondering how she'd make it up to the older woman.

It wasn't like Jill had meant to kill the tree. But it's possible she'd overreacted. She sat up and scrubbed her hands over her face. "I guess I can buy her another one. Maybe get a plaque or something to commemorate their anniversary."

"I'll check around for you."

"Okay. Thanks. Later." Jill disconnected and got out of the patrol car. As she walked up the driveway, the floral drapes in the living room window moved. This should be fun, she thought as she scanned the cedars lining the property. She didn't bother knocking on the front door. She'd check the backyard first.

Remembering Suze's warning, Jill jangled the keys in her pocket as she walked along the side of the house, checking for any sign someone had been *skulking* about. None of the furniture on the small patio in the backyard had been moved. No sign the windows had been tampered with. Jill headed for the overgrown garden butting up against the sun-bleached wood fence and Brandi's back-yard. The branches of several scrub trees had been broken. Evidence that someone or something had been back here. She stepped deeper into the brush and crouched down, moving the leaves and branches littering the ground in search of prints. There weren't any that she could see.

"What are you doing in my backyard, Jillian Flaherty?"

Jill pulled a breath through her nose and stood up, turning to the older woman standing at the open patio door. Her white hair was in pink foam curlers that matched her robe and slippers, a cigarette hanging out the side of her mouth. "Morning, Mrs. Burnett. I'm following up on your call." She gestured to the fence. "Is this around where you thought you saw someone?"

"No thinking about it, I saw someone hiding right where you're standing. Lord Almighty, you broke more of my trees, didn't you?"

Jill shoved her hand through her hair. "Look, Mrs. Burnett, I'm sorry about your cherry tree. I'll replace it. But I didn't do this." She held up a broken branch. "There was a bear spotted a street over. Is it possible that's what you saw?"

The older woman took a long drag on her cigarette, then blew out a couple of smoke rings while eyeing Jill. "You mean that? You're going to replace my tree?"

"Yes, and I'll have it planted for you, too. But not where your tree is now. It's dangerous having it that close to the house."

"You think I don't know that? But I don't want a cherry tree. Never did like fruit trees. They attract birds and squirrels, you know. An evergreen would be nice though. A blue spruce I can decorate for the holidays. A big one, mind you."

Jill fisted her hands on her hips. "If you didn't like the damn thing, why did you make such a fuss?"

"It doesn't matter if I liked it or not, it was my tree. You had no business going at it with a hack saw. Besides, you were acting all uppity when I called, like I was putting you out or something. And you cut my phone line."

Jill was mentally telling herself to stay calm and not react when Mrs. Burnett tossed out the last. "I did not cut your phone line. I tripped over the wire, and it came out of the wall."

"Same difference."

"No, there's a very big difference. And if you want your blue spruce, you're going to call the sheriff and tell him what really happened. Deal?"

Mrs. Burnett took another drag on her cigarette and lifted a shoulder. "I suppose. But it better be a big one."

"Five feet," Jill said.

"Eight."

"Six."

"I suppose that'll have to do."

"Good. Now that we've got that settled, tell me exactly what you saw and when," Jill said, taking out a pen and small notepad from her breast pocket.

Ten minutes later Jill made her way to the patrol car. She didn't have much to go on, other than that a man wearing a dark hoodie had been crouched in Mrs. Burnett's garden around seven thirty this morning and was gone when she'd returned from calling it in. And Jill was out at least a couple hundred bucks for a tree. So much for bird poop good luck. Then again, maybe it was all in how you looked at it. Mrs. Burnett's complaint would no longer be on Jill's file. Now she just had to work on the other four... Or was it five?

Jill started up the cruiser, pulled a U-turn, and turned left at the end of the street, then made another left one block over. The first thing she spotted as she drove down the street was a familiar black truck parked in front of Brandi's white bungalow. For a couple of seconds Jill considered calling the woman instead. But she wanted to take a walk around Brandi's property. Jill suspected that Mrs. Burnett's early morning visitor was none other than Steve Dawson.

As she pulled into Brandi's driveway, Jill decided superstitious folklore was for the birds. There was nothing about Sawyer's being at Brandi's that said "This is your lucky day, Jill!"

She turned off the engine and pressed the heel of her palm to her forehead. She was moving on. She shouldn't care that Sawyer was here or why he was or how long he'd been or what they were doing together. It was none of her business. Not anymore, not that it had ever been. Even though she'd wanted it to be. At least a week ago she did. But right now she was here to do her job.

On that thought she got out of the cruiser, wincing when the door slammed behind her. That had nothing to do with Sawyer, she assured herself. Except, indirectly, she supposed that it did. She was afraid Brandi would bring up Sawyer's rejection in front of him. Her neck started to itch, and she stopped on the walkway, about to turn around. But she reminded herself why she was here and headed to the front door and knocked. No turning back now.

Brandi opened the door, her brow furrowed. Like Mrs. Burnett, she wore a pink robe. Unlike Mrs. Burnett's pink robe, Brandi's was silky and sexy and half opened to reveal a matching camisole and sleep pants. And she didn't have curlers in her hair. Her long, blond locks had a bedhead-thing going on. "Jill, is there a problem?"

"Hey, Brandi, I need to talk…" She leaned past the other woman to see if Trent was around. She didn't want to worry the kid for no reason.

Brandi sighed. "Really, Jill, didn't you get the picture last week? I don't know how Sawyer could have made it any clearer that he's not interested. You have to—"

Jill gave her a what-the-hell look. "I'm not here to see Sawyer. Sheesh. I want to talk to you about Steve's visit last night. And I wanted to be sure Trent wasn't around before I did. Okay?"

"Oh, I didn't...Sorry. Trent's in the kitchen." She glanced over her shoulder, a soft smile turning up her lips. "Sawyer's making him pancakes. He's amazing with him."

"Yeah, I'm sure he is. Sawyer's great with kids. So... do you want to talk out here or—" She broke off when Sawyer sauntered to the door wearing a white T-shirt and faded jeans. He had the same sexy bedhead going on as Brandi and his feet were bare. Lucky Brandi.

"If it isn't the girl of the hour," he said with a smile, holding on to the door above Brandi's head, a spatula in his hand. "Come on in and I'll make you a couple flapjacks. You can tell me how it feels to be a hero."

"Jill's here in an official capacity," Brandi said, lowering her voice. "She wants to talk to me about Steve."

Sawyer lost the easy smile. He handed Brandi the spatula and took her by the shoulders, turning her around. "I'll talk to Jill."

"But I—" she began, glancing at Jill before Sawyer interrupted her.

"Trent will wonder what's going on if you're talking to her. Go on," he said, then stepped outside, shutting the door behind him. He rubbed his hand along his jaw. "Gage send you?"

"No, Mrs. Burnett called in a—"

"You didn't cut down another tree, did you?" he asked, amusement lightening the tension she'd seen in his face only seconds ago.

"No, me and Mrs. Burnett are BFFs now."

He laughed. "What did it cost you?"

"A tree," she admitted, then lifted her chin. "She saw someone in her backyard this morning. A guy in a black hoodie."

"You think it might've been Dawson?"

"I wondered. Whoever was back there had been hanging out around the fence. They'd have a clear view into Brandi's place. You happen to see anyone fitting that description?"

"No, but I just got up about thirty minutes ago." He cleared his throat. "Long night."

"Oh, I . . . You stayed here last night?"

He shoved his hands in the front pockets of his jeans, looking beyond her at the neighboring yard. "Yeah, she was upset. She called me after Dawson left. I didn't want to leave her on her own."

"Understandable. I haven't read Brad's report, but Suze said Steve wasn't drunk or combative. Did Brandi feel otherwise?"

"No. But there's a lot of past history there, Jill. You know what the guy put her through. I don't think it's surprising that she'd—"

She held up a hand. "No need to get defensive. I'm not passing judgment. I'm here to make sure Brandi and Trent feel safe, and that Brad didn't miss anything."

"Sorry, like I said, going on a lack of sleep. According to Brandi, Dawson says he's cleaned up his act. He wants to see his son, reestablish a relationship with him. Trent was over at a friend's place. He doesn't know anything about it."

"I take it Brandi's not exactly thrilled with the idea.

I can't say I blame her. But Trent's almost sixteen, old enough to make the call. Either that or they'll have to work it out through their lawyers, I guess. We'll keep an eye on Steve. Suze is getting in touch with his parole officer. We'll make our presence felt on the street." She frowned. "Why are you looking at me like that?"

His mouth twitched. "Citizens of Christmas are safer with you on the job, Shortstop."

Heat rose to her cheeks. "Are you being sarcastic?"

He laughed and hooked an arm around her neck, looking like he was about to kiss the top of her head, but he gave her a noogie instead. Like he used to when she was twelve. "No. I'm proud of you. You did real good yesterday. Saw the pictures on Facebook. Especially liked the one Ty posted."

She lightly punched him in the stomach. "You would," she said, looking up when someone cleared their throat.

"Sorry. I just wanted to make sure everything was okay," Brandi said, standing in the open doorway.

Sawyer removed his arm from Jill's neck and stepped back. "Everything's good. Jill's got it covered."

"If you can keep Trent occupied, I'd like to do a walk-through of the backyard. Ten minutes tops." She caught a flicker of panic cross Brandi's face. "It's nothing to worry about. Sawyer will fill you in."

*   *   *

Jill responded to several calls after checking out Brandi's backyard and made a quick stop at Mountainview. By the time she got back to the station and wrote up her reports, her shift was almost over. She looked up from her computer when Suze let out a gusty sigh. "Let me guess, you're on Facebook again."

"What can I say, it's Man Candy Monday."

"And you don't see anything wrong with objectifying men? Talk about a double standard. If men started up a Woman Candy Wednesday, I can just imagine the uproar."

"Whatever. You should see this guy. I'd sell my first-born, secondborn, too, for ten minutes alone with him."

"You're always trying to sell your kids," Jill said as she got up from her chair. Suze was a single parent of two teenagers, whom she adored. But the boys were a handful. Jill leaned over Suze to look at the screen and blinked. "You wouldn't know what to do with him."

"Says you. I'm going to have Ty do me."

"Ah, Suze, you do know that Ty's gay, don't you?"

"Please. I meant give me a makeover. I just down-loaded the Tinder app on my phone and want to change my profile pic."

"Tinder?"

Suze cocked her head, then straightened and slapped her desk. "I don't know why I didn't think of this before. We'll do it together. You and me. We just need to get you set up on Facebook."

"I have no idea what you're talking about, but I'm not signing up for Facebook. It's stupid and a time suck." And what was she supposed to post? Pictures of her vision board or the hotdogs she was having for dinner tonight?

Suze scrolled down the screen. "You wanna get your-self some of this? He'd make you forget Sawyer in a heartbeat."

Ray, a deputy who'd been around longer than Jill but looked like he was about twelve, was talking to Brad, who'd just arrived for his shift. They glanced over at her and Suze. Jill smiled, muttering out of the side of her mouth, "Would you keep it down?"

Ray patted Brad's shoulder and lifted his chin at Jill and Suze as he headed for the door. "See you in the morning, ladies."

"See you, Ray. Say hi to—"

"Hubba bubba, look at this baby daddy. He'd be perfect for you, Jill."

Ray stopped with his hand on the door and turned. "Something you forgot to tell us?"

"No, it's just—"

Suze wiggled her fingers over the keyboard. "I'm going to set up your profile right this minute. Let the baby daddy hunt begin."

"Ray," Jill called after him, but he was already out the door looking like a man on a mission. She loved Ray, she really did. But the man was as big a gossip as Ty. She ran to the door and opened it, looking up and down the sidewalk. He was nowhere in sight. Okay, that's good. He was probably just anxious to get home to see his wife. They were newlyweds. She'd talk to him in the morning.

* * *

Sawyer looked up from mixing a martini when Ray rushed through the doors, elbowing his way to the bar. It was busy for a Monday. But then again Sawyer had always done a good business with the dinner-hour crowd, and the tourists had started to arrive in town.

"Hey, Ray, don't usually see you—" Sawyer began before the deputy cut him off.

"Jill Flaherty's on the hunt for a baby daddy!" Ray announced loud enough for the entire bar to hear.

"Wait...what did you just say?" Sawyer asked, because there's no way he could have heard him right.

"Sign me up," Jimmy said from the end of the bar.

"Don't know her, but I'm happy to offer my services," one of the tourists said, dirty dancing on the stool.

When two more men began describing in detail how they'd take care of Jill's needs, Sawyer's vision hazed with anger. He slammed the bottle of gin on the bar. "One more word out of any of you, and you can get the hell out of my bar. Jill Flaherty is a friend of mine and no one talks—"

"I've dreamed of tapping her ass. Where do I—"

Sawyer reached over and grabbed Jerry by the front of his plaid shirt, drew back his arm, and punched him in the nose.

"You broke my nose! Ray, arrest him. Arrest him right now!" Jerry yelled through his hands.

"Sorry, big guy. But I don't have much choice. Come out from behind the bar quietly with your hands up."

Ray apologized all the way to the station, opening the door for Sawyer. Jill and Suze looked up from where they were huddled around a computer. Jill's eyes went wide and her mouth dropped open.

Hands cuffed behind his back, Sawyer glared at her. "A baby daddy, really, Jill?"

# Chapter Eleven

Sawyer's arresting officer of a few days earlier sidled up to the bar. "So are we good, big guy? No hard feelings?" Ray glanced at the two men on either side of him and leaned across the bar. "I didn't have much choice when Jerry pressed charges in front of all those witnesses."

"Yeah, we're good." It wasn't Ray's fault. Well, indirectly it was.

If Ray leaned any farther over the bar, he'd be behind it with Sawyer. "Wish I knew what Jill had on Jerry to get him to drop the charges. She didn't happen to share with you, did she?"

"No." She currently wasn't speaking to him. Possibly because, after Suze had explained where the baby-daddy comment had come from, and that Jill was signing up for Tinder, he'd lectured her on the dangers of online dating. As soon as the words were out of his mouth, he knew it was a dumbass thing to say. Jill was a cop. She could take care of herself. But she hadn't been there, hadn't heard what the men said about her.

"Didn't think so. But whooee, whatever it is it must be big. Jerry back downed pretty darn quick."

He did, but whether it was because of what Jill was holding over his head or the way she'd laid into the guy, Sawyer didn't know. As Jill had proved, she didn't need or want a knight in shining armor. Or, as she'd told him, another self-appointed big brother. Sawyer didn't tell her he hadn't been feeling brotherly at the time.

"You want a lemon cola?" Sawyer asked. Ray was in uniform so he figured he'd go with his usual on-duty drink. The deputy liked to stop in on his break to chat and catch up on the latest gossip in town.

"Better give it to me straight. I've got the late shift."

Sawyer held back a laugh as he got Ray his cola. "I thought Jill took the overnight shifts on the weekend," he said, handing him his drink and waving off the proffered bills. "On the house."

"Thanks." Ray took a sip of his cola and looked around the crowded bar. "Not tonight. She's got a hot date. Thought it was about time I took my turn. She's been covering for me since the accident, you know. Least I could do. She works too hard. About time she had some fun."

Ray had nearly died in an accident a year ago May. For a while there, it hadn't looked like he was going to make it. Everyone had been understandably shaken. Sawyer wasn't surprised Jill stepped up. That's who she was; what she did. And while he agreed she worked too hard, an uncomfortable weight settled in his gut at the thought of her on a *hot* date. "She'd be better off finding something else to do for fun. She doesn't have much luck dating," he said, sounding a little testy even to his own ears.

"I bet her date's thinking he's going to have some fun. Her profile pic is hot." Ray's smooth baby face pinked. "Don't tell Lauren I said that." He grimaced. "Jill either. I better get back to work." He left his empty glass on the bar, heading for the door while Sawyer pulled out his phone.

"Be right with you," he told the customer trying to get his attention. Sawyer found Jill's Facebook profile. But it wasn't Jill; it was the lady in red. She'd used the photo Ty had taken of her standing on the road holding up her gun and badge. Ray was right. She looked like she'd be a real fun date.

"Hey, Sawyer." He shoved his phone in the back pocket of his jeans and looked to the spot Ray had just vacated. Jake Callahan leaned against the bar. The man raised an eyebrow. "Having a bad night?"

"No. You come to scope out the competition?" He was yanking Jake's chain. The Callahan brothers owned a club in the next county. The Garage drew a younger, hipper clientele than Sawyer's place.

"Yeah, thought I'd pass out a few flyers." Jake grinned. "I've got a date. Your place is quieter than ours."

Sawyer flipped him off and started filling the order for the customer who'd tried to get his attention earlier. "Sorry for the delay, buddy. You wanna beer?" he asked Jake, as he filled another order.

"Sure. Whatever's on tap."

"So who's your date, anyone I know?" Sawyer asked moments later when he handed Jake the beer.

"Thanks." He passed Sawyer a few bills and change. "Jill Flaherty."

Sawyer nearly dropped the change on the bar. He did his best to hide his reaction from Jake, but it wasn't easy. The anxious knot tightening in Sawyer's chest wasn't the same level of discomfort he'd experienced with any of Jill's other dates. It was over the top and more than a little disconcerting. He decided it was because the dark-haired, good-looking guy standing across from him was a player.

"She's not for you." The words were out of Sawyer's mouth before he could stop them.

Jake slowly lowered his beer from his mouth and frowned. "Huh?"

Sawyer leaned toward him, lowering his voice. "You like fast cars and fast women, and that's not Jill." Then he remembered her Facebook profile and pulled out his phone, turning the screen to Jake. "This"—he tapped his finger on her face with, he belatedly realized, a little more force than was necessary—"is false advertising. It's not who Jill is. She's shy and quiet. Her idea of fun is going for a run or a hike, hanging out with her family. She'd rather sit at home listening to country music and playing her guitar than going to a bar."

"Good to know," Jake said, looking like he held back a laugh. "She sounds perfect." Then he cocked his head to study Sawyer, his expression more serious than amused. "But if you're interested, I'll back off. Jack didn't say anything when he suggested I ask her out. I don't want to—"

Really? He wasn't good enough for Jill but Jake Callahan was? But that wasn't something he could say to either man. "No, are you crazy?" Sawyer cut Jake off. "Jill and

I are just…" He trailed off when the door opened and Jill entered the bar.

She had on a cream-colored blousy top that gathered at the bottom and revealed a tanned strip of skin, her belly button ring visible above her low-riding jeans. Dark jeans that, unlike the ones she usually wore, molded to her narrow hips and long legs. She looked taller, and he craned his neck to get a look at her feet, shocked to see she wore heels. They weren't red; they were black. But just as sexy. And so was her dark hair that framed her lightly made-up face. He'd seen her on a date before and she'd never taken this much care with her appearance. She wasn't playing around anymore. This was serious. What the hell was her brother thinking setting her up with Jake?

The other man followed his gaze and smiled, lifting his hand to get Jill's attention. As she started toward the bar, Jake murmured to Sawyer, "Gotta say, I'm glad to hear I'm not stepping on your toes, buddy."

"What's that supposed to mean…Oh, hey, Jill," Sawyer said at the same time as he shot a menacing stare at the man he was now referring to in his head as Jake the Snake.

Jill gave Sawyer a curt nod, but Jake got an answering smile to his hello and, "Hi, sorry I'm late. Do you want to grab a table?"

"No problem. Sure, sounds good to—"

"Why don't you grab a seat right here?" Sawyer nudged his head at the two men sitting on the stools in front of him. "Scoot down a couple, guys. Thanks."

"No, stay right where you are," Jill snapped at the men, then cast Jake a self-conscious smile before glaring at Sawyer. "Come on, Jake." She walked away. Her dark jeans lovingly cupped her ass while the heels added a sexy sway to her hips that had his customers' eyes going along for the ride.

Sawyer jerked his gaze from her to Jake, who was watching him with a sardonic twist to his lips. "False advertising, my ass," the other man said as he walked away.

\* \* \*

Sawyer had spent the last hour trying to gauge how Jill and Jake's date was going while at the same time pretending not to be.

"Can I get another—"

Sawyer distractedly waved his hand. "I'll be with you in a minute." Why was Jake lifting his hand? He stroked Jill's cheek. You've done it now, buddy, Sawyer thought with a smug smile. Jill won't...Wait, why was she laughing?

He heard a sigh, the sound of a tray landing on the bar, and then, "Coming right up. You too, sir. Sorry for the wait."

Brandi brushed past Sawyer as she retrieved a bottle of rum off the glass shelf and speared him with a ticked-off look. "If you want to know what's going on, why don't you just go and sit with Jake and Jill? Oh, wait, you tried that and she told you to buzz off."

"She didn't tell me to buzz off." Not in those exact words. "You were busy, and they were waiting for their drinks, so I..." He didn't have to explain himself, and since he'd probably dig a deeper hole if he did, he closed his mouth and mixed drinks alongside Brandi. Who was obviously not happy with him. Neither were the customers he'd kept waiting.

She glanced at him as he filled the last of her drinks order. "You're sending Jill mixed signals. It's no wonder she still thinks she has a chance with you."

"She doesn't, and I'm not." He turned to put the bottles of bourbon and rum on the shelf.

Brandi touched his arm. "Sawyer, I saw you with her the other day at my place. You had your arm around her."

"Around her neck. We were playing around like we always do." But it hadn't felt the same.

"Well, maybe you should stop and put some distance between you for a while. For Jill's sake."

Sawyer opened his mouth to argue. But the hollow feeling that expanded in his chest at the thought of keeping his distance from Jill made him think Brandi might have a point. He didn't understand the how or why of it, but somehow his feelings for Jill had changed. It was like he was inches from crossing an invisible line. One that would put him in dangerous and uncharted territory.

"Point taken," he said. "Thanks."

She smiled and picked up her tray. "I'm just thinking of Jill. You're pretty irresistible, Sawyer Anderson," she said, then went to walk away. He'd just released a relieved breath when she backtracked to his side. "Are you busy Sunday night? I was hoping you'd come for dinner."

This is what he'd been worried about. He'd started to see the signs a few weeks ago but had been ignoring them in hopes Brandi would lose interest. He didn't want to hurt her feelings or Trent's. Brandi was his manager and going through a tough time. Besides that, he liked Trent. He saw a little of himself in the boy. Trent looked up to Sawyer the way he'd looked up to Bill. But on the heels of his spending the night, a family dinner would give both Brandi and Trent the wrong idea. "I'd like to, but I promised Bill—"

"I don't want to interfere with your plans. It's just that I have to tell Trent about his father and..." She lifted a shoulder and gave him a half smile. "Don't worry about it."

Sawyer bit back a frustrated sigh. He wanted to be there for the kid when he got the news. "It's okay. I'll be there. Bill will understand."

"Thanks. I really appreciate it. Ethan told me I shouldn't put it off."

Ethan O'Connor was a stand-up guy and the county's district attorney. The morning after Dawson's visit Sawyer had called him to see if he'd be willing to advise Brandi or recommend an attorney. Ethan promised he'd do what he could, refusing Sawyer's offer to pay him for his time. That was the thing Sawyer loved about his hometown—they looked after their own.

Sawyer wiped down the bar as Brandi walked off to serve a table of four. He was thinking about how to ensure that she didn't get the wrong idea about their relationship when Chris DeBurgh's "Lady in Red" came through the speakers. He should have taken the selection out of the jukebox. He glanced to Jill and Jake's table at the far corner of the bar. It was empty. His gaze shot to the dance floor. There they were in each other's arms. Sawyer reached under the bar for the remote. The song stopped, and the jukebox went dark.

There were a couple of groans, which he pretended not to hear, and he went back to wiping down the bar with a satisfied smile on his face. Out of the corner of his eye, he saw Jake give the machine a couple shakes, and the satisfied smile fell from Sawyer's face. Obviously the man liked dancing with Jill and wasn't going to give up. It wouldn't do him much good unless…"What do you think you're doing, Callahan?"

Jake looked up from where he'd moved to the back of the silver-and-blue jukebox. "It shut down. I'm trying to—"

"In the box," Sawyer called out, jerking his thumb at the penalty box.

Jake looked from the black-and-white wooden box to Sawyer. "You shitting me?"

Sawyer ignored Jill, who glared at him with her arms crossed. "Nope, that's what happens when you try to bust my jukebox. Brandi, go set the timer. It's a major." Not long enough. "A double major." At least he'd be sidelined for twenty minutes.

*  *  *

"You sure you don't mind?" Matt Trainer asked Jill as they approached the Penalty Box.

Oh, she minded all right. But that wasn't something she could share with her date. Besides, she, more than anyone, understood that the job came first. Matt was on call and wanted to stick close to Christmas General. She smiled and said, "No, it's fine."

And maybe it was. The whole point of dating was to knock Sawyer off the pedestal she'd put him on in her mind. After what he'd pulled Friday night with Jake, and earlier in the week with Jerry, she was halfway there. Maybe if she'd felt something other than a friendly interest in Jake, she would have been all the way. But she didn't. Despite that he looked like the bad boy version of Chris Pine, there'd been no butterflies, sweaty palms, or secret longings that he'd kiss her. They'd even gone out a second time. Jake had suggested a hike. And although they'd had a good time together, there'd been no sparks.

Jill was hoping this time would be different. The women in town had nicknamed Matt "Dr. McSexy" for a reason. Tonight, wearing a white button-down shirt and faded jeans, he was the poster boy for sexy. And with his dark blond good looks, tall, leanly muscled frame, and easygoing charm, he reminded her a little of Sawyer. Maybe that was why, when he placed his strong, life-saving hand on her lower back as they entered the bar, she felt a warm tingle in her stomach. Then she saw Sawyer.

That warm tingle couldn't hold a candle to the explosion of butterflies taking flight in her stomach when Sawyer raised his eyes and held hers. And neither, she realized, could Matt, at least in the looks department. At least for her. Sawyer's scruff-lined jaw tightened as his eyes narrowed at her and Matt. She wasn't the only one who noticed. Brandi, standing beside him behind the bar in her black-and-white-striped uniform top, looked like she wanted to blow the whistle around her neck and call time out. One by one the butterflies in Jill's stomach climbed back into their cocoons at the reminder of his budding relationship with his manager. Jill knew where he'd spent his Sunday night. While she'd been curled up on her couch, bemoaning her lack of attraction to Jake, Sawyer'd been having Sunday dinner with Brandi and Trent. Jill knew this because nothing was sacred in a small town. But even if Grace and her pals hadn't been buzzing about it, Jill would have found out anyway. Her boss had updated her about Ethan's involvement in the case…and Sawyer's.

Trent was now aware that his father wanted to see him. Like his mother, he didn't want anything to do with the man. Jill had a gut feeling the news wouldn't be well received by Steve. And who knew how that would play out. In her experience domestic disputes were the worst…and the most dangerous for all involved. Jill decided she should probably have a word with Brandi to ensure she didn't let down her guard.

"I'm just going to have a quick word with Brandi," Jill said to Matt, and took a step toward the bar. Brandi held her gaze while putting a proprietary hand on Sawyer's bicep, drawing his attention to her. "On second thought, why don't we just a grab a table?"

"Sure, how about that one beside the dance floor? Or do you want to play a game of air hockey first?" He nodded at the purple table on the second level.

Jill glanced back at him with a smile, the warm tingle reigniting in her stomach. "No contest. Air hockey. But I should warn you, I'm something of a pro."

"I like a confident woman." He laughed, then leaned in and said close to her ear, "But I should warn you, I'm really good with my hands."

Since her confidence in her flirting abilities was next to none, she responded with a grin, silently cheering when a couple of butterflies remerged from their cocoons.

Twenty minutes later they were still there, and she'd even managed to respond to a couple of Matt's flirtatious remarks without blushing. If their date continued the way it…

"Hey, Sawyer," Matt said just as Jill scored another

winning goal. He looked from the black disc to her. "You weren't kidding. You really are good."

She smiled, pretending not to see Sawyer standing beside Matt. Maybe if she ignored him, he'd go away. "Thanks. So are you. Maybe we should—"

"Good going, doc. Not many guys around here can claim to beating Jill."

Matt smiled at her. "Not that good. She beat me two games out of three."

She felt Sawyer watching her, the heat climbing to her cheeks. So what if she'd held back and let Matt win. She tried to let him win the last game, too, but it was too hard to make it look believable. And she'd been worried he'd hurt his hand if he overdid it.

"You're slipping, Shortstop. Come on, let's have a go. You and me."

She clenched her jaw. "No, thanks. Matt and I are going to—"

Sawyer crossed his arms over his tight white T-shirt, giving his head a fake concerned shake. "What did you do to our girl, doc? She's never backed down from a challenge before."

"Jill, go ahead. I don't mind," Matt said.

"Sawyer has to get back to work, and we—"

"I always have time to play with you."

She blinked. Was he flirting with her? She ground her back teeth together. Of course he was. It was just one more trick in his date-breaking arsenal. She picked up her striker. "This won't take long, Matt."

Sawyer grinned and then turned serious as he picked up a striker and got into position. The man was as competitive as she was. He was also as good. Which meant their game went a lot longer than hers and Matt's. Sawyer's shots were like bullets, and it took everything she had to defend her slot. He didn't hold back with her. He never had. And he'd never let her win.

"Good game," she said grudgingly and wiped her forearm across her sweaty brow. He'd beat her by one goal. She looked around and frowned. "Where's Matt?"

Sawyer grinned and lifted his chin at the table beside the dance floor. "He went and sat down about ten minutes ago."

"You are such a..." She made a frustrated noise in her throat and walked off, forgetting she had on heels. She tripped on the stairs. A strong arm wrapped around her waist, holding her against a muscled chest.

"Told you before, Jill. Lose the heels before you hurt yourself."

She shivered at the whisper of his low voice against her ear. Then regained her senses and elbowed him in the gut. "Back off, Anderson."

Matt's gaze moved from her to Sawyer as she walked to the table and sat down. "I'm sorry, Matt. I—"

He smiled. "You let me win, didn't you?"

"No, not all. It's Sawyer. He makes me a little crazy, and I'll do anything to beat him."

"Yeah, you two are pretty competitive. You can tell you've known each other a long time."

"Yeah, since I was five. He's my brother's best friend. But let's not waste the night talking about—" She broke off, staring at Sawyer when he set two glasses of a ginger-colored drink on the table.

He pulled up a chair between her and Matt. "On the house," he said, nodding at the sweating glasses. If Jill wasn't so thirsty, she'd dump it on his head. "Let me know what you think, Matt. It's my new sports drink, Gold Rush."

Jill went to take the other glass, but Sawyer moved it out of her reach. "What the... How come I don't get one?"

"Because they make you..." He looked away and raised a hand. "Brandi, grab a lemon cola for Jill. Thanks." He ignored Jill staring at him and said to Matt, who'd just taken a drink, "What do you think?"

"Good. Really good. Probably the best sports drink I've tasted in a while. Where are you at in the development?"

And that was it. Jill sat back and listened to the two men while sipping on her lemon cola that a ticked-off Brandi had grudgingly delivered a few moments ago. By that time Jill was a little ticked herself. She felt like a third wheel. But after a few minutes, she got caught up in the conversation. You couldn't help but get swept up in Sawyer's passion. Even if he was horning in on her date.

As if he realized he'd been excluding her, Sawyer pulled her into the conversation. It wasn't long before Jill realized they'd done the same to Matt. "Hey, Sawyer, looks like Brandi could use a hand at the bar," she said, hoping he'd take the hint.

"Nah, she's fine," he said, either not getting the hint or refusing to take it. She was betting on the latter and gave him a light kick under the table. He ignored that, too. "So how's it going at Mountainview? Are you any closer to solving the case?"

"It's not really a case. I'm just—"

"You should talk to Matt about it. You do a rotation at Mountainview, don't you?"

And that was it. Jill sat back while Sawyer laid out *her* concerns to Matt. Only this time she wasn't going to let him monopolize Matt's attention or the conversation. She mentioned two of the workers who'd been on vacation for the past two weeks. She hadn't noticed any suspicious bruising on the residents since they'd been off.

"Not much I can tell you given doctor-patient confidentiality, but it may be nothing more than that their skin is thinner and tends to bruise more easily as a result. And the majority of the residents are on some form of blood thinners. If it makes you feel better, I've never seen any signs of abuse. I'd report it if I did."

She hadn't realized that, indirectly, it may have sounded like she thought Matt wasn't doing his job. "I know you would. And I'm sure you're right. There probably isn't—"

"Doc's probably right, Shortstop. I talked to Bill about it after you mentioned it. He hasn't seen anything that gave him cause for concern. As far as any abuse going on, that is. But he's a little worried that Mrs. Sharp has the hots for him." He started to laugh and told her about Mrs. Sharp's latest conversation with Bill.

"If you think that's bad, Mr. Applebee woke up to find Mrs. Sharp in bed with him last week," Jill said, and that led to one story after another.

It wasn't until Matt pushed back his chair from the table that she realized they had once again excluded him from the conversation. "I'm going to take off. Leave you two alone," Matt said as he stood up. "Jill, if it doesn't work out between you and Sawyer, give me a call."

# *Chapter Twelve*

It was the afternoon of little Jack's birthday party, and Sawyer watched as his best friend climbed the oak tree in his backyard. "You look like a big egg that sprouted wings," he informed Jack.

"I'm a pterodactyl, dickhead. My son's favorite dinosaur." Jack reached back to detangle the pink wing on his costume.

"A lot you know. A pterodactyl isn't a dinosaur." Sawyer shook his head with a laugh as his best friend got comfy on a branch with a crested hat on his head, swinging his claw-slippered feet.

"I don't know what you think is so funny. You look like a green glowworm with sparkly red triangles down your back."

"Hey, I'm a tyrannosaurus Rex. The biggest and baddest of them all. And I'm your son's favorite. He told me so himself."

"Yeah, yeah, that was just to get you to stop whining

and wear the costume. Grace told him to tell you that."
From inside the house came the squeals and shouts of
what sounded like twenty kids. "Okay, Rex, you better
find a place to hide. You don't want my sister to find you.
She's got a gun."

"Are you kidding me? Why would you let Jill carry a
gun at a four-year-old's birthday party?" His voice went
up an octave. He hoped Jack, Gage, and Ethan didn't pick
up on it. He could admit to himself that he was a little
nervous, but he didn't need to announce it to them. Jill
was ticked at him, and rightly so. He'd been an ass. He
still couldn't figure out what had come over him. Something else he planned to keep telling himself. But he
was hoping for a chance to at least apologize to her today. Preferably when she didn't have a gun in her hands.
Maybe he'd get lucky and one of the other women and
their team of dinosaur hunters would find him before she
did. The team who was first to take down a dinosaur won
the game.

He heard District Attorney Ethan O'Connor laughing
from behind a bush on the other side of the backyard.
"Do you hear the fear in his voice, guys? He's worried
Jill's going to hunt him down after he ruined her date with
Matt."

"I didn't ruin her date, O'Connor," Sawyer said,
stomping toward the shed in his huge clawed feet. Just
for that, he wasn't telling Mr. DA his pointy purple head
was sticking up from behind the bush. He could get shot
first.

"That's not what she told Grace, buddy boy. And you
ruined her date with Jake, too. I had high hopes for them.
You're just lucky she's carrying a water gun and not a

paint gun. Those suckers hurt," Jack said from his perch in the tree.

"Maybe you should test your wings, flyboy, and take a flying leap," Sawyer grumbled as he ducked behind the shed. Slightly ticked and, if he was honest, still a little hurt to learn that Jack had set up Jill with Jake. What was so special about Callahan anyway?

"That's rich coming from you, Jack. You've been scaring off her dates since she was old enough to start dating. How was Sawyer supposed to know the game plan had changed?" Gage asked.

Sawyer stuck his head around the corner of the shed and looked up in the tree. "Yeah, how was I supposed to know? Thanks, Gage," he said, glancing to the rosebushes where Jill's boss was hidden. "Buddy, your tail is sticking out."

"He knows because he's the one who told me we should start setting her up," Jack informed Gage. "So I did, and he blew it. Twice."

Sawyer grimaced. He'd forgotten about his panicked phone call from outside Bill's room. Then he realized what else Jack had said. "You set her up with Trainer, too?"

"No, Grace did. Now, can we stop acting like girls? They're getting the kids into their squadrons. Stay strong and stay safe, my dinosaur friends." Leaves fluttered down from the tree. "Rex, get your ass in the shed. They're going to see you straightaway."

"Thanks," Sawyer said, running around the side of the green-and-white shed that he'd thought would serve as camouflage. Apparently he was more neon than army green. He opened the shed door.

"Anytime, buddy. I've always got your six," Jack called down from his perch in the tree.

He did. Unless it came to his sister. Sawyer got inside, pulled his eight-foot tail in behind him, and closed the door.

From inside the tight space, he heard the back door open and bang against the house a couple of times. He winced at how they were wrecking his paint job. He and Jack had renovated the purple Victorian a couple years back as part of their community service. Sawyer had a soft spot for the old house. It had gone a long way to helping him and Jack repair their friendship after Sawyer nearly destroyed it.

Hooting and hollering broke out as the kids swarmed the yard. Jack wouldn't be impressed with their squadron leaders lack of control.

"Dino team three, with me now," Jill barked out.

Sawyer started to laugh.

"We're hunting T. Rex," she said.

Sawyer stopped laughing and edged to the corner of the shed where there was a sliver of light. He pressed his eye to the hole, scoping out the yard. All he had to do was make it to the back door without them taking him down, and he'd be King Dino for the day. More importantly he'd be dry. He had no doubt the water gun Jill was packing was of the Super Soaker variety.

He caught sight of Nell McBride leading her merry band of hunters down the driveway. Madison, with her son, Connor, in her arms, followed Nell to the front yard. Sawyer moved a little to the right. Skye, carrying her daughter, Evie, with her troop following close behind, was headed toward the bushes where her husband was hiding. There was no way she'd miss...

"Oh, look at the pretty butterfly," Skye said, turning her back on the bush and waving her hand behind her. When Ethan jumped up and sprinted for the back door, Sawyer opened his mouth to call her out for cheating. He quickly closed it when a leggy brunette in faded jean shorts, a blue T-shirt, and flip-flops came into view. He'd been right. Jill was carrying the mother of all water guns.

As she started for the shed, Sawyer came up with a plan. He had the element of surprise on his side. Shuffling toward the door, he flung it open and roared. Jill shot him in the face.

\* \* \*

"You weren't choking for that long. All you had to do was stop roaring. Now quit whining and keep moving," Jill said, her chest pressed to his, her hands tied behind her back.

If he was whining about choking on the gallon of water she'd shot down his throat, it was because he was trying to distract himself. They were roped into being partners—both literally and figuratively—by Nell and Ty. The chocolate dinosaur egg they were transporting to the nest was cradled in Jill's cleavage. "Our egg is melting," he said, unable to take his eyes off the smear of chocolate on her chest. He had an uncontrollable urge to lick it.

Her gaze jerked to his. "Don't even think about it, Anderson. Your tongue comes within an inch—"

How the hell did she read him like that? "You have a dirty mind, Jill. I wasn't thinking about licking your...I was thinking about my T-shirt. I don't want to get it covered in chocolate."

She rolled her eyes. "You've had that T-shirt for at least ten years. It's about time you tossed it."

His response was on the tip of his tongue, but it stalled there when her hipbones rubbed against him. There was barely room for a whisper of air to move between them. He felt every inch of her pressed up close and personal against him. Too close, too warm, too soft. If they didn't deliver the egg soon, he was going to find himself in an embarrassing situation. Possibly dangerous if his best friend caught on. Forget his best friend—Jill would probably take care of the problem with a knee to Sawyer's groin.

He bit back a groan as they moved a few more feet. More rubbing, more friction, more heat. Jesus, he knew this was a mistake as soon as Nell and Ty paired them off. Maybe if Jack hadn't challenged him, Sawyer would have backed down, but he and his best friend had been in competition since grade school.

"Come on, princess, we're almost there," Jack encouraged Grace, their team of munchkins cheering them on.

Right, there were kids watching. Not that Skye, Ethan, Gage, and Madison seemed to care. They were all having one hell of a good time keeping their eggs between them. Sawyer would be surprised if their baby dinosaurs came out of it alive. He'd be having some fun, too, if he wasn't partnered with Jill. Wasn't having these inappropriate thoughts of melting chocolate and licking it off every inch of her glowing skin…*Aw hell. So much for PG.* He glanced at Jill.

Her breath hitched, and her face flushed.

Yeah, obviously she could feel every inch of him, too. "Stop rubbing against me," he said from between clenched teeth.

"I'm not doing it on purpose," she said, pulling back. The egg dropped to their waists. Instinctively they both pushed their lower halves together at the same time. She sucked in a sharp breath.

Sawyer bit back a groan. Jack looked at him as he and Grace inched past them. For a couple seconds, Sawyer considered letting the egg fall. But it'd be a little hard to hide his physical reaction to Jill if he did that now. "So you and the doc, any chance of a second date?"

She glowered at him.

"Okay, I'll take that as a no. Probably for the best anyway. Anyone who'd give up on you just because they think they've got a little competition isn't really worth—"

"He didn't have any competition," she snapped at him.

"Yeah…yeah, right." He lifted his chin. "We're gaining on them. Just a couple more steps to go and we've got this in the bag, Shortstop." And that was the key, he thought when the blood returned to his head. He had to keep calling her Shortstop.

They passed Grace and Jack. "Thank God," Jill murmured when they drew apart and dropped the egg into the nest that sat on a sawed-off log. At least what was left of the egg.

"Yay, Mama Jill and Daddy Sawyer delivered their baby safely to the nest." Ty, who'd planned the dinosaur-themed birthday party, came over to untie their hands. But Jill had already undone hers. "Looked to be some friction there, you two. Anything you want to share with Uncle Ty?" He moved his eyebrows up and down behind his red-framed glasses.

Jill shoved the rope into Ty's hands and stomped off.

"Hey, I was just teasing," Ty called after her. "I thought it was a great game, didn't you?"

"For an adults-only party," Sawyer said.

"Oh really, do tell."

* * *

Somehow Ty and Nell had missed the memo that Jill was over Sawyer. So had her body if her reaction to him while playing the dinosaur egg game was anything to go by. Though she could just as easily blame it on no under-the-covers action for a while. A really long while. She came out of the guest bathroom after washing the chocolate from her chest and nearly walked into Nell.

Jill glanced toward the formal living room and the kitchen at the back of the house. Since no one was around, she took advantage of the opportunity. "Ah, Nell, you know how Chloe suggested Sawyer and me for your next book?"

"Yep, didn't see that coming. I was all set to work my matchmaking magic on Sawyer and Brandi. She could use a good man, you know. But Chloe's probably right. Readers like the brother's-best-friend-with-the-little-sister romance. I was still on the fence until after I saw what I did today. Wasn't sure Sawyer could get past the—"

"He can't. We can't. I'm not interested, and neither is he. I'm serious, Nell. We're just friends so you should probably find another couple for your book." She couldn't bring herself to say Sawyer and Brandi.

Nell winked. "You leave that up to me. I'll go wherever my muse takes me, and right now, she seems to be stuck on you and Sawyer."

Wonderful, just flipping wonderful. And to think she'd been hurt when it looked like Nell had dumped her. She needed a distraction. Something to keep Nell occupied. "I don't want to take time away from your writing, but I have a case I could really use your help with." She lowered her voice. "But you can't tell anyone about it," she said, then shared what was going on at Mountainview.

"Evelyn, Stella, and I will get on it right away. We'll go in undercover."

This was working out better than Jill expected. Not only would Nell be focused on something other than matchmaking, she might actually help Jill solve the case. "They're always looking for someone to do arts and crafts with the residents. Think you can handle something like that?"

Nell rolled her eyes. "You've known me for how long? Not much of a detective if you have to ask me that." She patted Jill's arm. "Don't worry, the girls and I've got it covered. We're the Crime Stoppers, remember?"

Jill had a sudden flashback to Nell, Evelyn, and Stella's attempt to solve another case. She'd had a serious lapse of judgment. "Um, Nell, you know what, maybe I—"

Grace appeared in the hall. "I wondered where you two were. Come on, it's time for little Jack to open his presents."

Jill followed Nell and her sister-in-law into the yard. Her nephew sat between Sawyer and Jill's brother on a blanket surrounded by his friends. Little Jack was adorable in a pair of camouflage shorts and a T-shirt, a plastic safari hat on his head. Looking at her nephew with his curly dark hair and his big blue eyes, she forgot all about Sawyer and Nell's matchmaking. She'd fallen in love with little Jack from the first moment she'd held him in her arms.

"Mama, Auntie J, sit with me." He waved them over.

Sawyer smiled and made room for her between him and little Jack. Seeing his love for her nephew shining from his eyes, it was hard to stay mad at him for ruining her dates with Jake and Matt. Like her, Sawyer would do anything for their godson, and that pretty much made him a star in her eyes. Which was probably another reason why she had such a difficult time letting go of her feelings for him.

"Did you remember batteries?" he murmured when little Jack began tearing off the paper from their present. Since they were his godparents, they'd always given him a joint birthday gift.

"Of course I did," she said, her eyes on little Jack, waiting for his reaction to the Mighty Megasaur Remote Control Dinosaur they'd bought him. He didn't disappoint, squealing with delight and demanding that they open the box right away.

Sawyer chuckled. "It's a hit."

"Thank your Auntie Jill and Uncle Sawyer," Grace said.

Little Jack launched himself at them, wrapping his small arms around their necks. He gave them each a smacking kiss. "Now you kiss," he said, pulling their heads together. Jill glanced at Sawyer. He looked about as uncomfortable as she felt. It was like the memory of the dinosaur egg race shimmered and danced between them. It could shimmer and dance all it wanted; she wasn't going to think about it. Another memory for the vault. She pushed it in and slammed the door, then leaned in and kissed Sawyer's cheek. His return kiss was as perfunctory as hers.

"Okay, are you ready for Mommy and Daddy's present now?" Jack asked his son.

Little Jack frowned. "I got it. I'm getting a baby."

"Wait…what? Are you guys pregnant?" Jill said, looking from Grace to her brother.

Jack put his arm around Grace, and they smiled at each other. "Yeah, we were going to wait another couple of weeks to tell you but—"

"Oh, my God." Jill leaned over and pulled them both in for a hug. "I'm so happy for you guys."

"Hey, are you crying?" her brother asked.

She slugged him. "No, I got something in my eye." She let go of her brother and hugged Grace tighter. "You should have told me."

"I was going to at Vivi's shower, and then with all the excitement…"

"Hey, let me in there, Shortstop," Sawyer said, nudging her out of the way. Jill moved aside to let him and everyone else congratulate the mommy- and daddy-to-be.

Jill stood and picked up little Jack, swinging him in a circle. "You're going to be the best big brother ever. Just like your daddy."

He giggled, then ran off with his friends when she put him down.

Sawyer came over and slung a companionable arm around her shoulder. "Congratulations, Auntie."

She smiled. "Same to you, Uncle Sawyer." They both stood and watched Jack and Grace with their friends. "I was getting worried they weren't going to be able to have another baby."

"Yeah, so was Jack. I couldn't figure out why they asked Ty to plan little Jack's party." He nodded at the decorated yard. Ty had once again gone all out. Shiny green-and-blue fabric covered the table with a runner of brown felt down the center. On top of the runner, Ty had placed rocks and small logs with stuffed dinosaurs in between. "Looks like we better prepare for Jack going into overprotective-daddy mode."

"Probably, but Grace won't mind. He missed out on so much with little Jack. And now..." She trailed off, afraid she was going to cry.

Sawyer's arm tightened around her shoulders, and he rocked her gently against him. "Look around you, Jill. He's got everything he wanted and more."

"You're right, he does. And no one deserves a happy ever after more than my brother and Grace." She sniffed, wiping a furtive finger under her eye.

He smiled down at her. "You'll get your happy ever after, too, Shortstop."

She'd like to think that she would. But she wasn't sure it was possible. The only man she'd ever wanted happy ever after with was Sawyer.

# Chapter Thirteen

Jill had been feeling pretty proud of how she'd dealt with her matchmakers. Nell and her best friends were volunteering Tuesdays and Thursdays at Mountainview, running a workshop on creating life-story books, a combination of scrapbooking and narrative. Sandy had agreed it was a great activity and a good way to stimulate the residents' minds. It was also a great way for Jill to preserve her sanity. She'd even been able to arrange for Ty to do hair at the home on the same days. He earned a little extra cash, and it kept him out of *her* hair. So yes, with her matchmakers occupied for the last couple days, she'd been breathing easier.

Until now.

Standing in Jack and Grace's kitchen, she discovered she had another matchmaker to contend with. One who was more devious and dangerous than Nell and Ty combined.

Jill crossed her arms and leaned against the counter. "What do you mean Sawyer's staying here, too?" Two months earlier she'd agreed to stay with her nephew while her brother and Grace attended a wedding in Virginia. They were leaving in an hour, and Grace had conveniently forgotten to tell Jill that she was sharing babysitting duty with Sawyer.

Grace avoided meeting Jill's eyes, focusing instead on an imaginary spot on the island. "I just thought it would be easier if you both were here. That way it won't interfere with your work schedules. Sawyer can take the days, and you can take the nights." She continued rubbing the black granite countertop with the white cloth. "And, um, Sawyer knows how to cook. You don't."

"Please, I know you. You probably have the meals all made up with the instructions taped to their lids."

"I do, but I've never been away from little Jack this long. I thought it would be more fun for him to have you both here. If he gets lonely, it'll be easier for the two of you to distract him."

Jill pushed off the counter and covered Grace's hand with her own. Knowing her sister-in-law as she did, Jill should have realized what was going on. Grace wasn't playing matchmaker after all. "He'll be fine, Grace. We'll keep him so busy he won't even know you're gone, I promise."

Grace turned her hand beneath Jill's and squeezed. "Thanks. I've tried to cancel twice, but Jack really wants me to go."

"Of course he does. You guys haven't been away together since your honeymoon. Now you can have a babymoon. You two deserve some alone time."

"That's what your brother said." Grace's cheeks pinked while a small smile played on her lips.

"And from that smile on your face, I can guess what else he said. And I'm just going to bleach those thoughts from my mind because that's not something I want to think about. Ever."

Grace laughed. "Best friends share that kind of thing all the time."

"You don't have to tell me that. I've heard you, Madison, Skye, and Vivi when you get together. I just don't want to hear that kind of stuff about my brother."

"What don't you want to hear about me?" Jack said, coming in from the backyard with her nephew in his arms.

"Details about the babymoon," Jill said, holding out her arms for little Jack. "Hey buddy, are we going to have fun when Mommy and Daddy are away?"

"I know we are," Jack said, moving to stand behind Grace. He wrapped his arms around her and nuzzled her neck.

"Ah, baby and baby sister here," Jill reminded him, though she secretly loved seeing how much her brother adored his wife.

"I'm no baby. I'm a big boy," little Jack said, struggling to get out of her arms. She put him down and gave him a light pat on his butt. Her nephew didn't like to stay still for long. "Where's Uncle Sawyer? I wanna play."

"Hey, what am I, chopped liver? I can play, too, you know," Jill said.

"You're a girl."

She crossed her arms and looked down at him. "So what does that have to do with anything?" She glanced at her brother and Grace, who were trying not to laugh. "What are you teaching my nephew?"

Before they had a chance to answer, the front door opened. "Hey, little Jack, come see what Uncle Sawyer brought you?"

"What a suck-up," Jill said as she reluctantly followed the family to the front hall. Sawyer leaned against the doorjamb wearing a black golf shirt, khaki shorts, and a smug smile. He gestured to the bright green John Deere truck complete with dump bed sitting on the wraparound porch.

"No freaking way," Jack said, looking as delighted with the truck as his son, who raced out the door on his chubby little legs. Sawyer scooped him up, and the three of them admired the John Deere with manly grunts of approval.

She and Grace crossed their arms at practically the same time, but it was Jill who spoke first. "Do not tell me you bought a four-year-old a motorized vehicle."

Sawyer glanced at her with a raised eyebrow. "Okay."

"Buddy, this is too much. You guys just bought him the dinosaur for his birthday," her brother said.

"One of my customers sold it to me cheap. He's moving. His kid barely rode the thing. It's in mint condition."

"Jill's right, Sawyer. Isn't he a little young for a motorized car?" Grace asked.

"Nope, I checked it out. And see here." He pointed inside the truck. "There's a second gear lockout to prevent him from going too fast."

Little Jack was already climbing in the truck. "Go now."

"Okay, buddy. Auntie Jill and I will take you for a walk. Mommy and Daddy will probably be gone by the time we get back so you better say good-bye now."

She caught her nephew's hesitation, the slight quiver of his chin before he climbed out of his truck to give his mommy and daddy a good-bye hug and kiss. Sawyer may be a suck-up, but he was a smart suck-up, a thoughtful one, too. It'd be easier on both Grace and little Jack if he was tooling around in his impressive new toy when his parents left.

Jill's good-bye took longer than her nephew's. Grace had at least forty notes with instructions that she wanted to go over with Jill before they left. At note number twenty, she finally said, "Grace, you do remember that the three of us lived together for over a year, right? You can text me, call me on the hour if you need to, but get your butt in gear before you miss your flight."

Grace's eyes went all shimmery and wet. "It's not you I'm worried about, it's me. I'm really going to miss him."

Jill pulled her in for a hug. "I know you are. And he'll miss you, too. But he'll be fine and so will you. You're only gone for four nights. It'll fly by."

Her brother, who'd been talking outside with Sawyer, walked into the house. Grace moved out of Jill's embrace and furtively wiped at her eyes before turning to her husband with a shaky smile. "All ready to go."

His expression softened. "Princess, if you don't want to go, say the word and we'll stay home."

"No, you can't disappoint Holden. You're his best man." She touched her stomach. "Don't mind me. I'm more emotional these days."

Holden was one of the men who'd been held captive with Jack in Afghanistan. Their shared experiences had created an unbreakable bond between the two men, between the rest of the crew as well. They'd all be at the wedding. Jill thought it was important that her brother was, too. It would be good for them to celebrate something happy and life-affirming.

Jack covered Grace's hand with his and smiled down at her. "We'll take care of your stress when we get to the hotel room. I ordered chocolate strawberries to be delivered as soon as we arrive. And there's—"

"Eww, baby sister here," Jill said and reached up to kiss her brother's cheek. "I'm going now. And you two better be gone when we get back."

"Count on it. Thanks again, Jill," he said as she headed for the door. "Oh, and I read Sawyer the riot act. But just in case he forgets, no sleepovers with his legion of lady friends. I don't want him scarring my son or baby sister."

"Jack, don't be ridiculous. Sawyer would never do something like that. Besides, he's not dating anyone right now," Grace said, nibbling on her bottom lip as she cast a concerned glance Jill's way. So she'd been right after all. Grace was trying her hand at matchmaking.

Her brother laughed. "I think I know my best friend better than you do, princess. He doesn't *date*."

No doubt Jack did know Sawyer better than they did. So Grace could put her matchmaking schemes to rest. Jill didn't know why she found the thought a little depressing. She should be happy her three matchmakers were now out of the game.

* * *

She hadn't counted on a fourth matchmaker. Little Jack wrapped his arms around their necks as she and Sawyer tucked him into bed that night. "Kiss," he said for the third time. They did the cheek thing again. "No, on the yips."

Sawyer looked down at him. "I'm going to have a talk with your mommy and daddy."

Jill made a panicked sound in her throat, shooting daggers at Sawyer when little Jack whimpered, "I want my mommy and daddy."

Sawyer grimaced. "I know you do, buddy." He rubbed little Jack's shoulder, looking at a loss as how to comfort the now-crying child. "How about you and Auntie Jill call them on FaceTime?"

She angled her head and gave him a what-the-hell look. The last thing her overanxious sister-in-law needed to see was an upset little Jack.

"I want them come home now," her nephew said on a hiccoughed sob. His little hands clutched his dinosaur sheets and balled into fists, his face turning red, his expression mutinous. Jill recognized the signs. The Flahertys were known for their tempers, and little Jack was no exception. She sensed a tantrum in the offing.

Jill leaned over and reached for her guitar. When little Jack and Grace were living with her, she used to calm her crying nephew by playing. She'd brought the guitar with her today, thinking she'd start teaching him to play while his parents were away. She didn't realize she'd be competing with a motorized truck.

Sawyer, who'd changed tactics and was currently trying to distract little Jack with bribes of a visit to the Penalty Box the next day, glanced at her when she started to play. As a slow smile curved his lips, she nudged her head at the door. His smile widened, and he shook his head.

She briefly closed her eyes, then pushed her self-consciousness aside when little Jack sniffed, "Sunshine."

Her nephew liked him some John Denver. She obliged, strumming her guitar, holding back a sigh when he ordered her to sing. She hesitated and glanced at Sawyer, wondering what to say to get him to leave. But in the end she didn't have to ask because his cell phone rang. He mouthed "Jack," tousled their godson's dark curly hair, and left the room, closing the door behind him.

The tension left Jill's shoulders and she sang while she played "Sunshine on My Shoulders." Then "Rocky Mountain High" and "Annie's Song." As her nephew's eyes began to close, she finished off with one of her favorites by Fleetwood Mac, "Landslide." She had a faint memory of her mom singing the song while playing the guitar in Jill's childhood bedroom.

She'd been young when her mother died and thought maybe she'd imagined it. But when Jack first heard Jill play the song, he'd told her she sounded like their mom. So it hadn't been a dream after all. She supposed that's why she'd kept playing even when her grandmother told her to stop. It was as though it kept some part of her mother alive, a good part, a good memory. The thought caused her voice to get a little husky as she sang the chorus one last time.

Jill smiled as her nephew released a shuddered sigh. She eased off the bed and rested her guitar against the dinosaur-decorated wall. Tucking his covers around him, she bent down and kissed his forehead, then tiptoed across the room. She turned on the monitor and opened the door. Sawyer sat on the hardwood floor, his back against the wall, his arms crossed over his chest, his head lolling on his shoulder. She supposed she couldn't blame him for falling asleep. She'd been surprised little Jack wasn't comatose before his head hit the pillow. The kid never stopped.

She was considering whether or not to wake up Sawyer when he opened one eye, stretched, and smiled. "You don't need your badge or gun for crowd control, Shortstop. Just whip out your guitar and sing. Guaranteed to put anyone to sleep."

"Was that supposed to be a compliment?"

"Of course it was," he said, rising to his feet. "You should play at the bar. I'll pay you. You can put it toward your dream-house fund."

She shuddered at the thought of playing for an audience. Been there, done that, got the T-shirt. "No time, but thanks." She glanced at him as they headed for the stairs. "Everything okay with Jack and Grace?"

"Yeah, he just wanted to check to see how bedtime went before they headed out."

"Did you tell him it was going well until you mentioned his mommy and daddy?"

"Are you kidding? He pretends he's calling because Grace is missing little Jack, but he's just as bad."

"Yeah, he's a marshmallow." Just like the man following her into the kitchen. Sawyer would make a great father one day. She stopped short and stared at the island. "Tell me again why we didn't just heat up one of Grace's casseroles for dinner?"

"Because it wouldn't have been as much fun for little Jack. He loved making his own pizza. So did you."

"Yeah, but I forgot we'd eventually have to clean up the mess." They'd gone out for ice cream right after dinner and for a walk along the boardwalk to feed the ducks.

She ran a fingernail under the pizza dough stuck to the countertop. "Does granite scratch?" she asked, thinking they might have to use a chisel.

"I'll clean up later." He opened the fridge, taking out a beer and a can of cola. He tossed her the soda. "Let's go sit on the front porch and watch the sun set."

"Don't you have to go to work?" Now that they were without their pint-size chaperone, she wasn't sure being alone with Sawyer was a good idea. Not that she had to worry about him making a move on her, and of course, she wasn't about to make one on him. She had that T-shirt, too. But they'd had fun today. He was easy to be with and great with little Jack, so it was possible her mind might start playing the what-if game. A game she'd told herself she wasn't allowed to play anymore.

"Nope, took the night off. Brandi can handle it." Twisting the cap off his beer, he headed for the front hall. "Are you coming or not?"

She hesitated, then looked around the kitchen again and decided sitting watching the sun set sounded better than cleaning. "Coming." She grabbed the monitor off the top of the refrigerator, then checked the locks on the back door before making her way to the front porch.

Sawyer glanced at her when she closed the screen door. He was sitting on the swing at the end of the porch, taking up most of it with his big, athletic body. He patted the seat cushion covered in sunflowers. The warm summer night air was filled with the scent of the wildflowers filling the front yard.

Jill pretended she didn't notice his invitation, leaning instead against the white porch rail. She set the monitor down and took a sip of her cola.

"I don't bite, you know," he said, once again patting the cushion.

Afraid he'd read more into her refusal, and he'd be right, she picked up the monitor and sat down. He leaned into her. "You have little Jack under surveillance?"

"Houdini, remember?"

The amusement in his eyes faded. "Yeah, I wish I didn't."

"Me too," she murmured, though she hadn't actually been referring to the day that little Jack nearly drowned. Another memory she'd locked in the vault. But there it was again, as clear as though it was yesterday and not two years earlier. She could hear the fear and devastation in her brother's voice telling her they didn't know if little Jack would make it. Jack's and Grace's shell-shocked faces at the thought they might lose their two-year-old son. She'd experienced the same terror, but stayed strong for them. He was their child, not hers. But Sawyer saw through her act. He was the only one who did. He'd held her until she couldn't cry anymore.

With his arm resting across the back of the swing, Sawyer stroked her hair. "I'm good," she said.

"You said the same thing at the hospital that day."

He had a good memory. There were things she wished he'd forget, like the night at his apartment. She wished she could forget, too. His fingers in her hair and his big body crowding hers were making that difficult to do. She needed to change the subject. "So where were Jack and Grace off to?" she asked, shifting as though to look at him when what she was really trying to do was put some distance between them.

He moved his hand from her hair to rest it on the back

of the swing. It didn't help. Now she felt the heat and weight of it against her back.

"Out for dinner at some fancy Italian place with the wedding party. Maria's going, too."

"I didn't know she was invited to the wedding," Jill said, unable to keep the nervous hitch from her voice. Maria was the journalist Jack and his crew had been sent in to rescue when the RPG brought down their Black Hawk. The woman had tried to break up Grace and Jack when she'd come to Christmas. Jill was partially to blame.

"Yeah, Jack and Grace were a little surprised, too." He gently tugged on her hair. "Don't worry, she's not there to cause problems for them. She's engaged and doing well from what Jack said. She and Grace are going shopping tomorrow."

"Wow, that's great...I guess."

He smiled. "Feel better?"

"Why would you ask that?"

"Don't try and pretend you didn't feel bad for encouraging her, Jill. Everyone knew who gave her—"

"Whoa, really? You've got a lot of nerve bringing that up when you were the one in love with your best friend's wife." She bit out the words, anger reverberating through her as the feelings from two years ago swamped her. The betrayal she'd felt when she saw Sawyer and Grace together and sensed their growing attraction.

"You've been keeping that bottled up for a long time, haven't you?" He rested his elbows on his knees, then glanced at her. "We didn't think he was coming back, Jill. And never, not once, did I act on those feelings."

"So you did love her." She hated how saying those

words made her feel. It felt like he'd betrayed her as much as he'd betrayed his best friend. Even if he hadn't acted on those feelings. Even though she had no right to hers.

"I thought I did. But I'm not sure anymore. I wasn't jealous that Grace was with Jack and not me. If I had loved her, like a man loves a woman, I don't think I could have been around them like I was without feeling something. And the only thing I felt was happy for them." He lifted a shoulder, then took a swallow of his beer. "Maybe what it came down to was I felt closer to Jack when I was with Grace and little Jack." He glanced at her again, the pain of his memories etched on his handsome face. "He may be your brother, but I've always thought of him as one, too. I was hurting as much as you were, Jill. I needed to do something for him. So right or wrong, I stood in for him with his family."

And he'd stepped aside as soon as Jack came home. Not once had she seen any sign that Sawyer's feelings for Grace were anything more than platonic since then. As much as she'd needed to be there for Grace and little Jack, so had he. And he had been. "I'm sorry."

He sat back. Stretching out his long sun-bronzed legs, he rested his head on the back of the swing and looked at her. "It's probably something we should have talked about back then, but I was afraid you'd shoot me. You still believed with all your heart Jack was coming home. I couldn't be the one to tell you he wasn't." He smiled. "I've never been so damn glad to be proven wrong. And once he was home, I figured, if Jack could forgive me, so could you. I actually thought you had. Guess I was wrong."

"I did. I have." And it was true. At least now it was.

# Chapter Fourteen

Sawyer woke up the next morning feeling oddly un-
settled. He stretched and looked around the sunlit guest
bedroom, wondering if something about the room had
caused the sensation. The Victorian was old, but it
didn't appear as though its long-dead original owners
had come to pay him a visit. A crib box leaned against
the opposite wall while a couple of paint cans sat on the
hardwood floor alongside a tray of brushes and rollers.
The room was obviously intended for baby Flaherty
number two.

And maybe that's what was behind the small hollow
ache under his ribs. The thought that he'd better get his
act together before he missed out. Playing house with Jill
wasn't helping. There'd been a couple of times yesterday
when he'd caught himself watching her with little Jack
and thinking maybe he'd missed out with her. She and little Jack had been feeding the ducks, their dark heads bent
together as she held his small hand toward the gosling

paddling their way. She'd been laughing at her nephew's nervous squeal when she looked up at Sawyer.

With the sun shining on her face, her skin glowed, her love for little Jack lighting up her beautiful eyes. His world tilted, and he'd had to work to return her smile. In that moment she wasn't his best friend's baby sister; she was just an incredibly attractive woman. One who intrigued him. One, if he was honest, who he wanted to kiss.

Again.

He'd had a similar reaction when he'd sat outside little Jack's bedroom listening to her sing in that low, raspy voice as she expertly played her guitar, lulling him into yet another what-if fantasy. When she came out of the bedroom to find him there, he pretended he was sleeping. He'd needed a minute to hide how much she affected him. He hadn't quite shaken off the image of those long, talented fingers on him or that husky voice whispering that she loved him.

It's why he'd suggested they sit outside and watch the sun go down. If the conversation hadn't ended up taking an unexpected direction, he might have told her that he'd been wrong that night at his apartment and admitted he was attracted to her. But the conversation had blown way off course and back to the past. Maybe he should be grateful that she had unwittingly reminded him why she was off-limits before he did something stupid like ask her out.

He rubbed his chest and got out of bed, thinking that at least something good had come out of last night. Jill had forgiven him. It'd been a bit of shock to discover she hadn't. He supposed he shouldn't have been surprised.

Jill played her cards close to the vest. Always had. Until that night at his apartment.

He scrubbed his hands over his face to rid himself of the memory. Thoughts like that wouldn't do him any good. They had a couple more days of living under the same roof. He glanced at his watch. The hum of the ceiling fan and the birds outside were the only sounds in the house. Maybe Jill had already left. If she hadn't, she was going to be late for her day in court.

At the thought he grabbed a pair of jeans and a T-shirt from his duffel bag on the floor and quickly pulled them on. He checked on little Jack first, inching open the bedroom door. His comforter was a tangled mess, one of his pillows on the floor. Sawyer smiled. Apparently the kid didn't stop moving even in his sleep.

The refurbished wood floors creaked as he walked toward Jill's room at the end of the hall. He glanced in the small bathroom; no sign she'd showered in there. Then he remembered there was one off her bedroom. He stood outside her room and pressed his ear to the door. Nothing. No sound of the shower. He rapped his knuckles on the door. "Hey, Ji . . . Shortstop, you up? It's seven."

He waited a second and tried again, knocking a little louder this time. He knew from her brother that she slept the sleep of the dead. Or she had when they'd lived in the apartment above the Sugar Plum Bakery. He opened the door. "Hey Shortstop, rise and—" He broke off, unable to make his tongue work. Possibly because it was hanging out of his mouth. She reached for a pair of black pants on the bed wearing nothing but a lacy black thong. Jill Flaherty wore a thong. That's the only thought that was

going through his head as his eyes followed her long legs
to the curve of her tight ass to her waist and...

She turned around. Oh Jesus, he'd been right. She had
very nice breasts. No, they were actually pretty spectacular. Round and firm with...

"What the hell? Get out of my room," she yelled at
him, whipping out her ear buds. Then, as though just realizing her naked breasts were on display, she made an
embarrassed sound in her throat and crossed her arms
over her chest. She seriously had nothing to be embarrassed about. She...Jesus, what was he thinking? Right,
he wasn't thinking because he couldn't. He jerked his
eyes to her face. "Sorry, Shortstop." Who was he trying to
kid? He'd never be able to think of her as Shortstop again.
Hot Cop? Oh yeah, definitely Hot Cop.

"Get out!" she yelled again.

"Sorry, I didn't mean to, ah..." He slapped his hand
over his eyes and backed out of the room, pulling the door
shut. Dizzy and slightly off-balance—and really, really
hot—he leaned against the wall. *Holy hell.* Jill Flaherty
wore a thong and had incredible breasts. And a gun.

He knocked on her door. "Jill honey, I'm sorry. I didn't
mean to..." What? Stare at you like a kid who'd gotten
his first look at a *Playboy* centerfold? Yeah, that would go
over real well. "I didn't see anything, honest." The image
would be burned in his brain forever. He thought he heard
a choking sound. "Are you okay?"

"Shut up and go away."

"Oh, okay. Do you want coffee? I could make you
some pancakes, how about that?" He waited. "I'll just go
and make that coffee for you."

What he needed to do was grab a cold shower. But

she'd probably take off while he was in there and he had to see her before she left. He had to know she accepted his apology. He checked on little Jack before heading downstairs. Surprisingly the kid had slept through it all. Guess he was like his aunt.

Dark roasted coffee dripped into the pot as Jill came down the stairs. She walked into the kitchen. He didn't know if she had an I'm-going-to-cut-your-balls-off look on her face because he hadn't made it there yet. He was staring again, and not because she'd forgotten to put her clothes on. She wore black pants and a feminine-cut black blazer with a white blouse underneath. She looked sophisticated and sexy. Coolly professional and all grown-up. He lifted his eyes to her face. "I'm sorry, Jill. I didn't mean to—"

She arched an eyebrow. "Stare?"

He felt his face flush and rubbed the back of his head. "Yeah. I think I was in shock."

"That I have boobs?"

"If you don't mind, I'd rather not think about your... boobs."

"Good. I don't want you thinking about them, either," she said and walked by him to grab a thermos out of the cupboard. She didn't punch him or threaten him with bodily harm so he figured he was forgiven.

She walked to the refrigerator and took out the cream.

He looked down at her feet. She had on high heels and her toenails were painted fire-engine red. He cleared his throat. "You look nice."

She glanced at him, her dark hair falling over her face. "Thanks."

He grabbed the pot of coffee, gesturing for the thermos.

She handed it to him. She smelled good, too. "So you never said what case you have to appear in court for."

"Assault and battery. The wife's finally agreed to testify against her husband."

"Hope he gets what he deserves," Sawyer said, handing her back the thermos.

"Yeah, me too. Thanks. I'll be a few hours. There's a schedule and a list of dos and don'ts for little Jack on the fridge. Grace pretty much covered everything, but if you need me, call. My phone will be off when I'm in court though."

"We'll be fine. I've got it covered, Jill. Don't worry."

"You're sure? Because I can see if the sitter can take him."

"No, I'm good until you get back. I've got a couple guys handling hockey camp, and I don't have to go into work until eight tonight."

"Okay, see you later," she said and turned to walk away. He couldn't help but notice she had no panty lines. "Oh, there's a box of . . . Are you staring at my butt?"

\* \* \*

"Hey, Brandi, sorry I didn't return your call sooner. Little Jack got hold of my phone. Hang on a minute," Sawyer said. "Buddy, don't dig up those flowers, Mom . . . Auntie Jill won't be happy if you do."

"Why?" he asked.

"Ah, because she loves roses. And you won't find any dinosaur bones there. Go back to where you were digging near the tree. That's a perfect spot." Sawyer knew this because he'd buried some plastic bones there.

Little Jack got in his John Deere and motored over to the tree, turning his head when the back gate opened. "Annie," he yelled, jumping out of his truck to run to the dark-haired teenager.

"Cool truck," she said, picking up little Jack. She waved at Sawyer.

He cocked his head. "So let me guess. Your mom doesn't think I can handle little Jack on my own for the day?"

"No, she…" She shrugged and grinned. "Kinda. She thought you might need a break."

Did he. The kid hadn't stopped since he got up three hours ago. "Appreciate it, Annie. Thanks." He put the phone back to his ear. "Sorry about that. What's up? Everything okay?"

"All right, I guess. Trent's just a little bummed that you won't be at the arena today."

"He won't even notice I'm not there once Tony and Adam start putting them through the drills."

"That's not true. You know how much he loves spending time with you."

The muscles in Sawyer's neck tensed. He knew Trent enjoyed spending time with him, but he was beginning to think Brandi was using her son as an excuse to get closer to him. He glanced to where Annie and little Jack were digging under the tree and walked to the picnic table at the far corner of the yard. "Look, Brandi, I enjoy spending time with him, but—"

He heard a door shut, then she lowered her voice and said, "Steve called this morning. He wants to see Trent."

"What does Trent want?"

"I didn't tell him. I don't want to upset him. But I don't

want him to see Steve. I don't trust him, Sawyer. I don't trust that he's changed."

"I get it, but if Trent wants to see him, you can demand that the visits are supervised. Did you let Ethan know that he called?"

"I wanted to talk to you first. I'll call him as soon as I get off the phone with you. You'll be at the bar tonight, won't you?"

"As far as I know, unless Jill has something she needs to do."

There was a long pause before she said, "It's none of my business, but do you really think it's a good idea that you're staying with Jill? It must be uncomfortable for you knowing how she feels."

After this morning he was pretty sure Jill was the one feeling uncomfortable. "Don't worry about Jill. She's a big girl." He rubbed his jaw when an image of her in nothing but her thong flashed before his eyes. "She'd been having a bad day and had too much to drink that night at my apartment. She didn't mean anything by it."

"That's not how it looked to me. But like I said, it's none of my business. I just hope—"

At the beep of an incoming call, he checked the screen and cut Brandi off. "I've gotta go. There's a call coming in from Mountainview. I'll see you tonight." He disconnected and answered. "Sandy, everything okay?"

"No. Where have you been? I've been trying to reach you for the last hour. Bill had a bad fall. He's at the hospital. They think he may have had another stroke."

Panic tightened his throat. "I'm on my way," he managed to say before disconnecting. He jumped off the picnic table and realized where he was. He had no choice.

He had to take little Jack with him. Maybe Annie'd come, too. "Hey buddy, we have to go to the hospital."

"No. I no like hospitals."

He hadn't considered that possibility. It'd been two years since the accident, but the kid was smart. He probably remembered the time he'd spent there.

"Is something wrong?" Annie asked.

"You know Bill?" She nodded. "He had a fall, and they think he might have had another stroke. I have to go see him." Not only did he want to be there for Bill, he had to be. Sawyer had power of attorney, including the authority to make health care decisions for Bill.

"I can look after little Jack."

"I don't know, Annie. He's a handful."

"I'm almost sixteen. I babysit Connor and Lily all the time."

It took Sawyer a good fifteen minutes to go over Grace's lists with Annie. He left her some money to order a pizza so she wouldn't be preoccupied making little Jack lunch.

"Call me if you need anything, anything at all. I'll try to be back within the hour." He'd go back to the hospital as soon as Jill came home. He crouched in front of little Jack. "You be a good boy for Annie, okay?"

"Yeah, me a good boy."

"I know you are, buddy. You're just a little busy. Kinda like the Energizer bunny."

Annie laughed when little Jack started hopping around the kitchen. He followed Sawyer to the door. "There's a dead bolt," he said, pointing it out. "Use it. Thanks, Annie."

It took Sawyer another fifteen minutes to get to the

hospital and find a parking spot. He called Jill on his way to the emergency room. His call went straight to voice mail. He left her a message, telling her what happened to Bill and that he'd left Annie with little Jack. He asked her to call him as soon as she could. Times like this, he'd call Jack, but he wasn't about to bother him while he was away. Sawyer felt antsy, tension stringing his muscles tight. He wished Jill wasn't in court and that she'd call him back. He needed someone to tell him Bill would be all right.

As soon as Sawyer walked through the emergency room doors, he spotted Matt Trainer at the nurses' station. The doc looked up as Sawyer approached and met him halfway. He put a hand on Sawyer's shoulder. "Relax, he had a fall, but as far as I can tell, he didn't have a stroke. He's having a CT scan now, and I'll run some more tests on him just to be sure."

Sawyer took a deep breath and blew it out his mouth. "Okay. Thanks. That's good news at least."

"You can fill out the paperwork while you wait. I'm going to keep him overnight as a precaution."

Sawyer nodded, starting to feel more like himself as the tension inside him released. "I'll give his kids a call. Any other injuries I should know about? Bill tell you how it happened?"

Matt's eyes narrowed, and he crossed his arms. "Are you asking because of our conversation at the bar?"

"No, I'm asking because Bill fell. He's in Mountainview to make sure accidents like this don't happen."

"Look, I know you're upset. But no matter the facility or the level of care provided, falls do occur, Sawyer. It's not a reflection on Mountainview. They got to him seconds after he fell. If he'd had a stroke, that would have meant the difference between minimal and extensive damage. As to your question how he fell, that's something we have to look into. He said he got dizzy, disoriented. It could be as simple as an infection or dehydration, but don't worry, we'll get to the bottom of it."

"Sorry if I'm coming across as an ass. I trust you, doc, and this hospital. I know he's in good hands."

"You're worried about Bill, I get it. He's lucky he has you." Matt's brow furrowed as he studied Sawyer more closely. "Uh, is everything okay with you?"

"Other than Bill ending up in hospital, yeah, I'm good. Why?"

"For one, you forgot your shoes. For another, you have paint all over your T-shirt, and . . ." he pointed to Sawyer's head. "What is that?"

Sawyer followed Matt's finger and pulled a hunk of goop from his hair. "Pancake batter. Little Jack wanted to help. And we were finger painting." He looked at the handprints on his T-shirt and shrugged. "What can I say? He's a creative kid. 'Fraid I don't have an explanation for the lack of footwear, other than I might have been a bit panicked. You have any of those bootie things I can borrow?"

Matt grinned. "Sure thing. So you're looking after little Jack while his mom and dad are away?"

"Yeah." He eyed the man. Even though he was a guy, Sawyer could see why the ladies thought Matt was hot. As he'd just proven, he was also a good doctor and a good guy. Something a woman like Jill would appreciate. And after seeing a mostly naked Jill, he didn't want to think of her playing doctor with Matt. Which may be the reason why he added, "Jill and I are staying with him at the house."

"Is that so?" Matt's lips twitched.

Sawyer sighed. "Just get me the booties, will ya? People are starting to look at me funny."

"That could be for any number of reasons, my friend." Matt nodded to the nurses' station. "Come on, I'll get you suited up."

An hour later Sawyer had yet to see Bill and his frustration was starting to grow. Though it was possible that had more to do with talking to Bill's kids. They'd had a hundred and one excuses why they couldn't come see their father. Sawyer wondered if it was because they knew he was there to take care of Bill. Even though that was true, it didn't cut it for him. If his mother was in the hospital, he'd drop everything to be by her side. He was about to give her a call when his cell rang.

"I can't find him, Sawyer! I can't find little Jack!" a hysterical Annie yelled over the line.

# Chapter Fifteen

Hey, are you okay? How's Bill? I was going to—" Jill began before Sawyer cut her off.

"Where are you?"

Her hands tightened on the wheel at the rough rasp of his voice, praying he wasn't going to tell her that Bill died. "Couple minutes from the station. I have to—"

"No, don't. Just come home, okay?"

"Sure, of course," she said, almost certain now that Bill had died. But she couldn't bring herself to ask. Sawyer sounded like he was barely holding it together. "Is there anything you need? Can I—"

"Jill, I need you…" He trailed off, and she heard him speaking to someone. The words were muffled as though he'd covered the phone. But it sounded as if someone was crying in the background. He came back on the line. "Just hurry up and get here." He swore under his breath. "Just get here as fast as you can."

"Less than ten minutes away now. Hang in." She

disconnected, wondering if she should call her brother or
Sawyer's mother. Bill's death would affect him deeply.
Whether Sawyer would admit it or not, the older man was
like a father to him. She decided to hold off to see how
he was doing first. Knowing her brother and Sawyer's
mother, they'd jump on the next flight out if they thought
he needed them.

She wished she would have been there for him when
he got the news. Or at the very least called as soon as she
got his message. But she hadn't had a chance to respond
when court recessed for lunch because the prosecution
wanted to review her testimony.

As Jill turned onto Sugar Plum Lane, she saw Gage's
white Suburban parked in front of the house along with
another patrol car. Several people were running into
the backyards of the houses on either side, including
Skye. Gage came out of the house followed by a pale
and obviously distraught Sawyer, who was raking his
hand through his hair. Annie was there, too, her arms
wrapped around her waist, shaking her head when Gage
spoke to her. Jill's heart started to race, as though her
body already knew what her mind refused to believe.

As she pulled behind the Suburban, Gage and Sawyer
turned. She saw the look on Sawyer's face and her body
went hot, then cold, then weak with fear.

*He was missing. Little Jack was missing.*

A wave of nausea rolled over her. She pressed her lips
together, breathing slowly through her nose, ordering the
confusion from her brain. *Get out of the damn car. Move.*
The door opened. She looked at her hand, surprised to
find it had obeyed her command.

"It's going to be okay, Jill. We'll find him."

She lifted her eyes to Sawyer, her heart twisting at the grim expression on his face, the fear in his eyes. "How..." Her throat was too tight and too dry to say more. She swallowed. "How long has he been gone?" She finally managed.

Sawyer reached in and helped her from the Jeep. "At least an hour. Annie searched the house and yard before calling me," he said, closing the door.

It was worse than she thought. He could be anywhere. The woods, someone's backyard pool. She pressed her fingers to her temple, willing the worst-case scenarios away. She had to get it together. She was wasting precious time. Every minute, every second counted in a missing child case. She knew that, goddammit, so why wouldn't her brain work?

Sawyer cupped her face with his hands and ducked his head to look her in the eyes. "We're going to find him," he repeated as he gently brushed his thumbs across her damp cheeks.

She was crying. She was standing on the street crying. She swore under her breath and pulled away from him, wiping angrily at her face. "The neighbors two doors down have a tree house—"

"I already checked," he said, taking her hand as they walked toward the house. He told her everywhere they'd looked for little Jack so far. The exact same places she would have looked had she been here. But of course Sawyer would; he knew her nephew as well as she did.

Annie and Gage met them on the sidewalk. The young girl looked at her through tear-swollen eyes. "I only left him for a few minutes. H-he was coloring at the table when the pizza guy came, and then..." She glanced at her father and mumbled, "Trent stopped by to say hi. But I didn't let him in, and we only talked at the door for a minute or two—" She broke off with a sob.

Jill lay a hand on the teenager's shoulder, clenching her jaw as she fought back the ugly, unfair urge to shake the young girl. "It's okay, Annie. No one's blaming you." She looked at Gage, seeing her own fears reflected back at her in his eyes, and it was all she could do to hold it together. "Did you talk to the pizza delivery guy?"

Gage nodded, and then he and Sawyer shared a silent exchange to which Sawyer gave an almost imperceptible shake of his head. "What...what aren't you telling me?"

Gage rubbed the back of his neck. "Mr. Potter noticed a late-model white pickup parked down from the house. The guy sat there a good ten minutes and seemed to be watching Grace and Jack's place. Potter was going to call it in, but by then the pickup had moved on."

"Timeline?"

"Coincides with when little Jack went missing," Gage admitted.

Jill swayed on her heels. Sawyer grabbed her. "Don't go there. It's probably just a coincidence. As far as Mr. Potter could tell, the guy never got out of his truck. He didn't see any sign of little Jack, either. Come on, you need to sit down."

She pulled away from him. "No, I have to help. I have to look for little Jack." She had to do something or she'd go crazy with worry. She felt desperate and out of control.

"Jill, look at me," Gage said. "Let us handle it. I have everyone on it. We're doing a house-by-house search in a two-mile radius. He can't have gotten that far."

"Little Jack's truck. Did he—"

Sawyer briefly closed his eyes. "We found it in the lane at the end of the street."

Her stomach heaved. She pictured her nephew driving down the street with a smile on his adorable face. Grace's and Jack's faces when she told them their precious son was missing. *Pull it together,* she inwardly snapped at herself. She had to start thinking like a cop and not an aunt. "What about the woods, the park? Maybe he's going to the bakery looking for Grace, or...or the boardwalk. We were there yesterday."

Gage and Sawyer turned as several cars and trucks pulled up. Jill blinked back tears, her throat tightening at the sight of Nell McBride, Ted and Fred, Ty, Easton, and Chance, Suze's teenage sons, piling out of their vehicles.

"You stay here in case he comes home, in case someone calls," Gage said, giving her shoulder a gentle squeeze.

When Gage moved away to organize the volunteers, Sawyer placed a hand at the small of her back and nudged her toward the house. Her legs felt heavy as she walked to the front porch. Unable to move another inch, she collapsed on the steps.

"Annie, do me a favor and stay in the house and take any calls that come in," Sawyer said.

She nodded, stopping in front of Jill. "I'm really sorry. I didn't—"

"I know you are. We call him Houdini for a reason. He—" Unable to continue, Jill closed her eyes. When she opened them, Sawyer was crouched in front of her.

He took her hand. "We will find him, Jill. I promise."

"You can't make that promise."

"I just did." He pressed his lips to her palm. "I'm going to look for him. You call everyone you know. Anyone you can think of. Get them out looking."

Gage and Sawyer might believe the guy in the truck had nothing to do with little Jack being missing, but Jill couldn't let it go. "What if the guy in the pickup..." She shuddered, unable to finish, but then a thought came to her and she twisted at the waist. "Annie, come here."

The young girl opened the screen door. "Yes?"

"How long was Trent here?"

Annie bit her lip and looked down at her black high-tops. "Just before the pizza guy. But I didn't let him in. And I kept checking on little Jack. I swear, he was only out of my sight for two minutes."

"Did Trent mention his dad? Has he seen him around town, like he was following him?"

She nodded. "He didn't want to tell his mom."

"Thanks, Annie. You can go back inside."

She hesitated, then met Jill's eyes. "Are you going to tell my dad and Trent's mom?"

"Yeah, I am. If... Yeah, I have to tell your dad. But you can call Trent and give him a heads-up. Gage." She waved him over.

"So you think it was Dawson in the white pickup?" Sawyer asked as Gage jogged up the walkway.

"I do."

Once she filled Gage in, the two men left on foot to search for little Jack. Gage went one way and Sawyer the other. Jill called Suze to get her to do a search on Steve's truck for the make, model, and plate. Within five minutes Suze had the information she needed. Jill went over Gage's head and ordered an APB on Steve. She didn't believe he was involved but he may have seen something that would aid in the search.

She looked up to see Skye coming up the walkway. She joined Jill on the steps and gave her a hug. "They'll find him, you know. Ethan said to tell you he can't get away from court, but his lead investigator and several of his office staff are on their way to join in the search."

"Thanks, I...we appreciate it. Where's Evie?"

"Betty Jean has her. Daddy's out looking for little Jack. Now tell me what you need me to do."

"I have to make some calls."

"Okay, I can do that." She pulled out her phone.

Ten minutes later they both looked up as a black Mustang roared down the street, double parking in front of the house. Chloe and Madison got out of the car.

"Honestly, someone should take Chloe's license away from her. Look at poor Maddie. She's as white as a sheet."

She did look pale, but Jill had a feeling it wasn't from the ride. Madison held Jill's eyes as she came up the walkway. "I'm so, so sorry. I never would have suggested Annie—"

Jill raised her hand. "No, it could have happened to any of us. You know that. But you should probably go talk to her. She's pretty upset."

Madison gave Jill a quick hug. "Can I get you anything, something to drink or... You probably can't think of food right now, can you?"

"No, but thanks."

As Madison disappeared into the house, Chloe ended a phone call and hurried up the walkway. "That was Cat and Grayson. They're out looking, too. Grayson called in some of his buddies from the FBI, and Paul rounded up a bunch of the staff from the hospital. Now, what do you need me to do?"

Skye held up her phone. "We're making calls."

Chloe chewed her thumbnail. "I don't really know many people in town. But honestly, I think they're all out looking for little Jack. Maybe that's what I should do. I can drive around—"

"No," Jill and Skye said at almost the same time.

"My goodness, you'd almost think..." Her eyes narrowed. "I'm a good driver, you know."

Jill patted the step. "Just come and sit with us."

Chloe joined them on the front porch and slid an arm around Jill's waist. "He'll be okay. They'll find him."

"He has to be. I don't know what I'd do if..." She closed her eyes as she thought about breaking the news to Grace and Jack. She scrubbed her hands over her face. "I better make those calls." Just as she was about to start, her cell phone rang. She checked the screen, praying it wasn't her brother or Grace. It was Sawyer. "Did you—"

"Auntie J, I got losted. Uncle Sawyer found me at the doggie's house. No, I wanna talk to Auntie J. Can I have pizza? I'm hungry. Uncle Sawyer said no treats for me. No, it's my turn. There's Auntie Nell—" She could hear cheers and laughter in the background.

Half laughing, half crying, Jill sagged against Chloe. "Sawyer found him."

"They found him," Chloe and Skye yelled. Madison and Annie came running from the house. Several neighbors appeared on the street, cheering when Chloe once again shared the news.

Sawyer's voice came over the line. "We'll be home in a few minutes. No, you can't have cupcakes, either."

"He's okay?"

"Yeah, I found him a couple blocks over. A bunch of kids' toys in the backyard and a dog. No one was home. He was asleep in the playhouse."

"How did you know he was there?"

"The dog. No, you're not getting a dog, either. You made your Auntie J cry. Annie, too." She heard sniffling, then Sawyer sighed. "All right, you can have a cupcake and pizza, but only if you promise not to leave the house again. Ever."

"You're a marshmallow," Jill said. And her hero. Today he was her hero.

\*   \*   \*

Sawyer crept up the stairs, wincing when they creaked. He didn't want to wake up Jill or little Jack. It was late. Once everyone cleared out after celebrating little Jack's return, Sawyer had gone to the hospital and spent some time with Bill before heading to the bar. He smiled as he reached the landing. Jill wasn't taking any chances tonight. She'd put a baby gate in little Jack's doorway and attached a couple of bells. His smile faded as he heard what sounded like someone sniffling. He walked down the hall. Her door was ajar.

He tapped. "Jill, you decent?"

"Yeah, but..." She hurriedly wiped her face as he walked into the room. "I didn't tell you to come in."

He ignored her. "Why are you crying?" he asked, sitting on the edge of the bed. She lay on top of the floral comforter wearing blue-and-white-striped sleep shorts and a lace-trimmed white tank top with the baby monitor resting on her flat stomach.

"I called Jack," she said.

He drew his eyes from her bellybutton ring and winced.

"I know we agreed to wait until they came home, but I was afraid he'd find out," she said. "I told him not to tell Grace."

"I called her," Sawyer admitted.

Jill sighed.

"For the same reason *you* called Jack," he said, pulling out his phone. She leaned over and grabbed hers off the nightstand. He frowned. "What are you doing?"

She arched an eyebrow. "Texting Jack to tell him Grace knows. What are you doing?"

"Texting Grace to tell her Jack knows."

Their cell phones pinged with incoming messages. "He'd already told her," Jill said at the same time Sawyer said, "She'd already told him." They smiled at each other.

"Jack said he's taking back your best friend card."

"Grace said the same about yours." He leaned over and wiped the moisture from her cheek. "You going to tell me what the tears are about? Jack knows better than anyone how easy it is for little Jack to pull a disappearing act, so no way he would have laid into you."

"Of course he didn't, but I..." She ran a finger over the monitor, a tender smile curving her lips. "He looks like a little angel when he sleeps."

"Yeah, too bad he has a little devil on his shoulder." He took the monitor from her. He never would have forgiven himself if something had happened to little Jack. He loved him like he was his own. He cleared his throat. "Look at him twitching in his sleep. He's probably dreaming about his next big adventure. Let's hope baby number two is more like Grace than Jack." He set the monitor on the nightstand.

"I don't know how they do it. Today decided it for me. I'm not having kids."

"Is that why you were crying?"

"What is it with you? I wasn't crying. I got something in my eye."

"Uh-huh, seems to be happening to you a lot lately." He didn't plan on letting her off the hook that easily, but it was a little hard having a conversation with her when he couldn't keep his eyes off that long, toned body. He blamed it on this morning's peep show. He stood up and lifted his chin. "Get under the covers. You're—" He broke off. Telling her she was cold would give him away.

She glanced at her chest and pursed her lips, then rolled over and got on her hands and knees to crawl beneath the sheets. Sawyer held up the covers and looked away.

She stared at him as he tucked the comforter around her, ensuring that not a hint of her tanned skin showed. Satisfied there was nothing left to tempt him, other than her face, he once again sat on the side of the bed.

"You know, it's getting late. I should probably..." She trailed off as she looked at him more closely, then grimaced and touched his hand. "I'm sorry. You've had a shittier day than me. How's Bill?"

He smiled and took her hand in his. "He's good. He didn't have a stroke. He has a bladder infection."

"Well that's a relief. It's late. I thought maybe..."

"No, I stayed at the hospital until he fell asleep, then dropped in to check on things at the bar."

"Ah...How's Brandi?"

"Not in a happy place. She's mad at Trent for dropping by when Annie was babysitting. She apologized, by the way. And she's angry he didn't let her know Dawson's been following him around."

"I can't say I blame her. But Trent's just a kid. None of this can be easy for him. I hope you told her we don't blame him or Annie for what happened with little Jack."

"I did. And I…" He hesitated, knowing she wouldn't be happy with him.

"You what…" She searched his face and groaned. "You confronted Steve, didn't you?"

"What did you expect me to do? I can't sit around and do nothing while the guy stalks Trent. They don't have anyone else to look out for them. I wanted Dawson to know that they did, so I called him and laid it out for him."

"What I expect you to do is let Ethan and the sheriff's department do their job. You have no idea how volatile these situations can be, Sawyer. Stay out of it."

"Their hands are tied, mine aren't." They'd pulled Dawson over to question him and let him off with a warning. Sawyer gave him one, too. Only he'd backed his up with a promise. "Now, no more sidetracking me. I want to know what upset you."

She sighed, tipped her head back, and closed her eyes. "Nothing. It was nothing. Go away and let me sleep."

"No."

"Ugh. You're so annoying." She rolled over and gave him her back.

He had an idea what was going on with her. When they'd nearly lost little Jack two years earlier, she didn't let anyone see her pain or fear. She put everyone before her, trying to take care of them, making sure they were all right. She'd done the same thing when her brother was missing. Today she'd let her guard slip. But with everything going on before and after, he hadn't had a chance to make sure she was really okay. He moved in behind her and put his arms around her, trying to ignore the feel of her lean, supple body tucked against him, the sweet smell of her hair, the feel of its soft, silky strands against the side of his face.

"Nothing's going to happen to him, Jill. Tomorrow we'll handcuff him to one of us for the day." She sniffed and nodded. He leaned over her. Her eyes were closed. "Are you crying again?"

"No," she muttered.

He was surprised she didn't elbow him or push him away. If anything, she seemed to snuggle deeper into his arms. And that show of vulnerability bothered him more than the tears. Maybe that's why he brushed his lips over her cheek and whispered in her ear, "You don't have to pretend you're tough with me. I know you are. But it's okay to be emotional after what happened today."

"After? Maybe. Not during. I couldn't even do my job."

He drew back. "What are you talking about?"

She rolled onto her back. "You saw me. I froze. If I was Gage, I'd fire my ass. I sure as hell wouldn't recommend me for sheriff." She bit down on her bottom lip, looking up at the ceiling.

He cupped her face, drawing her eyes to his. "No one, least of all Gage, expected you to react any differently. Jesus, Jill, you were the one who figured out it was Dawson in the white pickup. Do you know what a relief that was? It was bad enough having little Jack missing, but to think he could have been..."

"I didn't do enough. If I can't keep it together, I don't deserve to be sheriff." She looked away. "Doesn't matter, I wouldn't have been elected anyway."

"You're too hard on yourself. You always were. You don't see it, do you? You don't see how amazing you are."

"Right, if I'm so amazing, why did you turn me down the..." She shook her head and held up her hand. "Ignore me. I'm being an idiot."

"Stop it. You know why I turned you down."

"Yeah, I do. You're not attracted to me. So if I'm so amazing explain—"

"So what part of me standing here this morning staring at your incredible breasts and your ass in that thong with my tongue hanging out makes you think I'm not attracted to... Well, hell," he muttered.

She stared at him. "You think I have incredible boobs?"

"I'm lying in bed with you wearing nothing but a skimpy T-shirt and itsy bitsy shorts, so now is not the time to remind me about your incredible boobs."

She lifted up the covers and looked down at herself. "I guess they're okay, but incredible..."

"Trust me, they are. But the point I was trying to make was that I turned you down because of Jack."

She snorted. "You did not."

"I did too. And you know—"

"You're a good guy, Sawyer Anderson. I appreciate you trying to make me feel better. Thank you."

"Oh for chrissakes, shut up," he said and kissed her to prove to her that she was amazing and intriguing and had the most incredible breasts he'd ever seen. Only it didn't stop with one kiss. It might have, if she hadn't kissed him back and kicked off the covers and pressed that long toned body against him. Or made those sexy sounds in her throat that had him putting his hands on her ass and drawing her closer. Or that when he did, she rubbed against him and lifted her mouth from his to whisper, "I guess I was wrong. You really are attracted to me. Really attracted."

And he was, even more attracted than he'd realized.

# Chapter Sixteen

Jill'd had sex before: good sex, decent sex, taking-you-to-a-happy-place sex. But never anything close to what she'd experienced with Sawyer last night. She thought that mind-blowing, seeing stars kind of sex happened only between the pages of a romance novel. The descriptions in those books were so over the top that she'd find herself laughing out loud, skipping them, or wondering if maybe she wasn't doing it right.

After being with Sawyer, she decided it wasn't so much her but the guys she'd been with. Sawyer—with a face that could launch a thousand women's fantasies—had used his powerful warrior's body to make hers come true. He'd rocked her world. He'd known exactly what to do to make her body hum with pleasure and make her beg for more. And Jill wasn't someone who begged. She also wasn't the type of woman who gave up control. But with Sawyer, she'd lost it as soon as he'd put those experienced hands on her.

She probably should be thanking the legions of women who came before her. But thinking of those women made her wonder if there would be more coming after her. Her chest tightened at the thought. And that reaction said it all, she supposed. Until Sawyer, she'd never made love with a man she was actually in love with.

His morning-after routine could use some work, she thought, as she glanced at the indent of his head on the pillow beside her. No kisses, no cuddles, no declarations of undying love. She grimaced and threw back the covers. She was getting a little ahead of herself. Just because they'd had sex and it had been seeing-stars amazing didn't mean Sawyer was ready for a relationship. The man showed all the signs of being a confirmed bachelor, which she found kind of sad. And not only for her.

On that somewhat depressing thought, she stood up and glanced at the baby monitor on the nightstand. The memory of yesterday crowded in on her at the sight of her nephew still asleep in his bed. She pushed back thoughts of the debilitating fear that had overtaken her, her failure to act. No matter what Sawyer said, her inability to respond professionally had put her nephew at risk. The sheriff on her vision board was coming down as soon as she went home.

And when Jack and Grace got back, she was going to suggest they have a GPS tracker surgically implanted on her nephew. Though Nell, Mr. Murray, and several of the other old-timers who'd come back to the house to celebrate after little Jack had been found did a pretty good job of putting the fear of God into her nephew. They'd all agreed that some good old-fashioned discipline—a swat on the behind—would solve the problem. They were outvoted and had settled for giving her nephew a "good talking to." Jill didn't have a problem letting them step in. Sawyer was another story. He'd gotten an earful when Nell and Mr. Murray overheard him telling a teary-eyed little Jack that he'd think about getting him a puppy.

Once she'd grabbed a quick shower and blew her hair dry, Jill dumped the clothes she'd brought with her onto the bed and contemplated what to wear. Something she'd never given much thought to before. Maybe it was because, with her nephew still asleep, she was hoping to entice Sawyer back to bed. Or maybe she was just stalling because she wasn't sure what to say to the man who'd rocked her world last night.

Twenty minutes later she walked into the kitchen wearing the white shirt Sawyer had taken off last night and left on the end of her bed. She thought it looked sexy without trying too hard. And just the thing to lure him back to the bedroom. The shirt also smelled amazing.

Her heart did a little flip when she saw Sawyer standing with his back to her looking out the window over the sink. All the sexy morning-after lines left her head at the sight of his damp hair, sweat from his run molding the black sleeveless T-shirt to his broad back, his black sweat shorts riding low on his narrow hips.

For maybe a second, she contemplated throwing herself into his arms and kissing him. Something Chloe would do, but she was no Chloe. Jill didn't have a tenth of her confidence. Confidence that the man currently guzzling a glass of water with the phone pressed between his shoulder and ear felt anywhere near what she felt for him. Despite evidence to the contrary last night.

He put the glass on the counter, then massaged the

back of his neck. "You know we're good here, Jack. Se-riously, there's no reason to cut your holiday short." He paused and listened to her brother. "Okay, I get it. I prob-ably won't be here when you get in. Jill's off, and shit's piling up on my plate. Yeah, she's fine. Her usual, you know. Giving me grief." He turned as though sensing her standing there, and his eyes swept over her before return-ing to her face. He grimaced. "Right, we'll talk when you get home."

She crossed her arms. "Is grief what they're calling or-gasms these days? You seemed to have enjoyed the two you had." She did her best to keep the hurt from her voice. She should have known better than to expect that things had changed.

He looked surprised, then quickly recovered, his voice laced with frustration and maybe a hint of nerves. "So what? You would have preferred me to say 'Yeah, me and your baby sister got it on last night, and she blew my mind?'"

"I blew more than your mind," she muttered, despite the small flicker of hope that maybe she had. But she was too angry at the way he'd casually dismissed their night together to let it sink in.

He stared at her, the muscles in his corded neck mov-ing as he swallowed hard. "Yeah, you did. But if you think I'm going to share any of this with your brother, you're crazy. I don't have a death wish. You have to give me a little time to—"

"To what, blow me off? You know what, let's forget last night ever happened. It was a mistake."

He came to her and placed his hands on her shoul-ders, dipping his head to look her in the eyes. "I couldn't forget last night even if I wanted to. But babe, you gotta cut me some slack. For more than fifteen years I've been warning every guy I've ever met not to do what I did last night. Give me some time to get my head around it, okay?"

She lifted her shoulder and looked away. "Whatever. I'm a big girl. It was just sex. I'm not expecting you to put a ring on my finger if that's what you're worried about," she lied, maybe not about the ring so much as what last night meant to her.

"It wasn't just sex, and you know it." He dropped a kiss on the top of her head. "I wish I could stick around today, but I've got a lot to do. You going to be okay on your own?"

She pressed her lips together and nodded. His kiss said it all.

His smile looked strained as he walked away. He stopped on the bottom step and turned. "Until we figure this out, it's probably best if you don't share it with Grace and your girls."

"Don't worry, Sawyer. I'm not planning on taking out an ad in the *Chronicle*."

He bent his head and gave it a slight, frustrated shake before looking at her. "You have no idea what's going to go down when Jack finds out about us."

And there it was—his friendship with her brother meant more to him than she did. "I'll make it easy on you. Don't say anything. There's nothing to tell." She held up her hand when he opened his mouth. "No, we had sex. And no matter how great it was, that's all it was."

She didn't add *all you want it to be*. One of them had to be the realist in this non-relationship. It might as well be her. Along with the sheriff, she'd also remove Sawyer from her vision board when she got home. And then she remembered she'd already done that. Too bad she hadn't thought about that last night. In her defense, once he'd had his mouth on her, he'd made it pretty hard to think.

Bells clanged upstairs and little Jack yelled at the top of his lungs. "Auntie J, Uncle Sawyer, I want out."

Jill wasn't sure if it was frustration or relief she saw in Sawyer's hazel eyes.

* * *

Sawyer stared at the computer screen in his office at the Penalty Box. He wasn't any further ahead on his paperwork than when he started it an hour ago. He kept seeing Jill standing there in his shirt looking like she'd taken a hit. That was tough, but what was worse was remembering the way she felt over him, under him, and beside him. Her low, sexy moans, her long, talented fingers, and that mouth, that amazing mouth. She was passionate and giving and she'd done what no other woman had done before her, she'd made him laugh and she'd made him smile and she'd made him... Jesus. He didn't want it to end this way, no matter what she seemed to think.

He pulled out his phone and texted her: *Why don't you bring little Jack by for a root beer float? I'll be here for another hour*. They didn't open until noon, and Jack and Grace wouldn't be back until late tonight. Sawyer still had a crapload to do, including stopping by the hospital for a couple of hours before working at the bar until close. But he'd gotten at least one good piece of news today: the NHL was considering endorsing Gold Rush. Something he wanted to share with Jill. Who was he trying to kid? He wanted to see her. Wanted to convince her to give them a chance.

He checked his phone at the sound of an incoming text. He smiled at the emoticons filling up his screen, and then a blurry picture of little Jack with what looked to be Jill's hand reaching out. The kid must have gotten hold of her phone.

Another text came through: *Nix the float. He doesn't need any more sugar. But if you're up for a game of air hockey with him, we're there.*

Relieved that she wasn't avoiding him, he responded with a smile: *Always.*

*See you in fifteen.*

Sawyer shut down the computer and pushed back his chair from the desk. He'd pick up a couple of blueberry scones at the bakery and put on a pot of coffee for Jill. It sounded like she might need one.

As he headed for the front of the bar, Brandi flung open the door. "Hey, what are you doing here this early...What's wrong?" he asked, taking in the panic on her face.

She glanced behind her, clutching her purse to her chest. "Steve. I haven't seen much of you the past couple of days so I thought we could catch up before it got busy. He followed me here."

Now wasn't the time to think about what her need to catch up meant. There was a more urgent matter to deal with. He couldn't believe his warning hadn't registered with the asshole. "He still out there?"

She gave him a quick nod. Her eyes were bloodshot. She looked tired and a little frantic. "He says we have to talk. I don't want to talk to him, Sawyer. I can't deal with him anymore."

She had to deal with the situation, but she didn't have to deal with her ex. "You don't have to. I will. Stay here," he said, helping her onto a stool before heading for the door.

Sure enough, Dawson was approaching the bar. He jerked to a stop when he saw Sawyer. "I wanna talk to Brandi," he said with a belligerent thrust of his bearded chin. He looked like he'd walked off the set of *Duck Dynasty* wearing camo pants and an army-green T-shirt. He was an inch or two shorter than Sawyer, but he had him by a good fifty pounds.

Sawyer moved to stand in front of him and crossed his arms. "What part of *she doesn't want to talk to you* did you not understand yesterday? You got questions, go through Brandi's lawyer."

"You got no business sticking your nose in this. They're my wife and kid."

"You got a problem with your hearing, Dawson? 'Cause I'm sure I told you this yesterday, but in case you didn't quite get it the first time, I'll repeat myself. Brandi and Trent are my business. I see or hear that you were within ten feet of them, I'll have you charged with harassment."

"Who the hell do you think you are? You don't get between a man and his family."

"A man, Dawson? I don't think so. A man doesn't whale on his wife with his fists. And a man holds down a job, supports his family. He doesn't drain their bank account and steal his wife's tips to go get shit-faced with his pals."

Dawson's face flushed, his meaty fists curling at his sides. *Do it. Give it your best shot,* Sawyer thought, so he could give him one back. He needed to release the anger building inside him at the reminder of what this no-good asshole had put Brandi through.

"I did my time. Now I wanna do right by my—"

Several people on the sidewalk across the street glanced their way. Sawyer lowered his voice. "Twice, Dawson. You didn't learn your lesson the first time. Why should Brandi believe you now? You stalking them sure as hell isn't giving her reason to. Keep it up and you'll end up back in jail. Now be smart and get in your truck and leave."

He stabbed Sawyer's chest with his finger. "This ain't over, pretty boy. I'm getting my family back one way or another."

Sawyer put his own threat in his smile as he wrapped his hand around Dawson's and squeezed. "You'll have to go through me to get to them."

"Jesus, let me go." The other man's face contorted, his knees buckling. "I'll have your ass for assault."

Sawyer squeezed harder, lifting his chin at the security camera above the Penalty Box. "Won't fly, I've got it on tape. Just protecting myself." He released his grip on Dawson's hand, shoving him back as he let go. The other man stumbled into the hood of his pickup. "Instead of stalking Trent and Brandi, why don't you get a job? Start making up for all the child support you never paid."

Holding his injured hand to his chest, Dawson fumbled with the door to his truck with his other hand. He stared at Sawyer as he got in the pickup. Sawyer couldn't get a good read on the emotion swirling in the man's dark eyes, but he got the feeling he hadn't seen the last of him.

Sawyer pulled out his cell phone and left a detailed

message on Ethan's voicemail. He'd fill Jill in when she got here. No doubt she'd be ticked he'd confronted Dawson, but Sawyer wanted to ask her about filing a restraining order. And he wanted her to give the man's probation officer a call.

When he walked into the bar, Brandi was still sitting where he left her. He didn't like what he'd seen in her eyes. The same beaten-down look he'd once seen in his mother's. It wasn't easy being a single parent, especially on what a waitress brought in. It's why he'd made Brandi his manager and put her on salary. He needed to do something more. If Gold Rush went as well as he suspected it would, he'd have plenty of coin. Not that he was hurting. He'd been paid extremely well by the Flurries and he didn't play loose with his cash. He was saving for a house. But he'd bought his mother a nice place in Arizona that set him back some. And it wasn't like he was raking it in at the bar.

He leaned on the back of the stool beside hers. "You need a holiday. Why don't you take a couple of weeks off? You and Trent could—"

She shook her head. "No, I like working, and I need the money."

"Paid holiday, Brandi. And I've got a friend who has a great resort outside of Aspen. Trent would have a blast..." He held up his hand when she went to protest. "My treat. You've earned it."

"I can't leave. Not until this thing with Steve is settled. I feel safer in town. We have you and our friends looking out for us. Besides, Trent has hockey camp."

"Just think about it, okay? Hockey camp's over at the end of July."

She searched his face. "Is this because of something Steve said?"

"No, it's because you deserve a break."

"So you got through to him? He's going to leave us alone?"

He put his hand on her shoulder and gave it a comforting squeeze. "He'll back off for now, but only until he regroups. The best thing for you to do is get your case in front of a judge as soon as possible. He doesn't have a hope in hell of getting visitation until he gets his act together. And I don't see that happening anytime soon."

"I can't afford a lawyer, and I won't be Ethan's charity case."

"No problem, I'll take care of it. I'll take it out of your check. Spread it over the next two or three years, whatever works. I was planning on giving you a raise anyway. Gold Rush is taking up more of my time, and I'll need you to take over some of the paperwork."

She bowed her head, and her shoulders began to shake.

"Hey now, come on. Don't cry. It's going to be all right. I promise," he said, folding her into his arms.

"I don't know what I'd do without you. You're always there for me and Trent." She sniffed into his neck, then pulled back, looking at him through tear-filled eyes.

Sawyer hadn't been able to get a read on the emotion in Dawson's eyes, but he knew exactly what he was seeing in Brandi's. He was screwed. And he didn't know how badly until she curved her hand around his neck and kissed him. It was not a grateful kiss or a kiss shared by friends. This was a wet kiss, filled with longing and heat.

"See, Uncle Sawyer's kissing her yips."

# Chapter Seventeen

It'd been more than a month since Jill and little Jack had walked in on Brandi kissing him. They'd gone from considering a relationship to definitely not having one. At least in Sawyer's mind they'd been thinking of taking their friendship to the next level. Jill had made it clear the morning after the best night of his life that it had been sex and only sex. A one-time aberration.

She didn't seem to care that Sawyer wanted more. But after the "kissing on the yips" incident, he'd reluctantly come around to her way of thinking. Probably because, after he'd chased Jill down to try and explain, he'd returned to the bar to face Brandi, who, unlike Jill, was definitely on board with taking their friendship to the next level. No matter how carefully Sawyer had broken the news that he wasn't interested in pursuing a relationship with her, but was extremely interested in one with Jill, Brandi hadn't exactly been jumping for joy.

She'd made a couple cracks about what a relationship

with Jill would cost him, reminding him how close he'd come to losing Jack's friendship in the past. And even though Sawyer understood where the comments were coming from, they'd reinforced his own concerns and guilt. Which was how he'd ended up on the same page as Jill.

But seeing her now in the hall outside Bill's room at Mountainview, Sawyer felt a moment's regret that they hadn't given their relationship at least a shot. She wore her faded jean shorts, a long-sleeve gray T-shirt, and sandals. With one long, shapely leg bent at the knee and her foot pressed to the wall, she thumbed through her phone. Her hair was held back by her sunglasses. Longer now than the night those dark, silky locks had brushed across his bare chest. His regret intensified at the memory, as did his desire when she turned her head and those stunning blue eyes locked on him.

A flicker of emotion flashed across her face before she contained it, and he wondered if she shared his regret, his desire. But he pushed aside any more thoughts of what they were missing out on when he realized she must have a reason to be standing outside Bill's room. He jogged down the hall. "What's going on? Has something happened to Bill?"

She put out a hand, stopping him from entering the room. "Calm down. He's fine," she whispered. "His physiotherapist is with him."

"Oh, okay." He leaned against the wall beside her. "Why are you whispering?"

"Because he's not improving like he should. So I'm listening in on their session. She's not providing the full forty-five minutes. You're getting ripped off."

Like Jill, he hadn't thought Bill's recovery was progressing as it should, so he'd hired a physiotherapist a couple weeks ago. He supposed he should be happy Jill was keeping an eye on Bill, and he was. But there was a part of him that resented her for giving him further proof that she was a woman worth fighting for. "Thanks, Shortstop. Appreciate you looking out for him, and me."

She slanted him a look, and it wasn't a happy one. He figured she didn't appreciate him reverting back to her childhood nickname. And since he was slightly ticked at her, he said, "Sorry, I know you prefer 'babe,' but I reserve that for women I'm dating."

"Probably smart since, according to my brother, you change them out on a weekly basis. At least you don't have to worry about remembering their names," she said, looking at her screen.

He would have laughed, enjoyed sparring with her, if she hadn't mentioned that the information came from her brother. Then he reminded himself it was his own fault Jack thought he was a player. He'd been the one fueling the misconception for a couple years now. But she knew better. "And you know that's bullshit because you wouldn't have let me near you without a condom if you thought it was true," he whispered in her ear.

Their heavy make-out session had nearly ended when he'd discovered there were no condoms in the house. It wasn't as if he'd expected to get lucky and had come prepared. And since it was late and the stores were closed, it had looked like they'd end the night with a cold shower instead. Until Jill volunteered that she was on the Pill. And he'd admitted he was seven months and counting into a dry spell, which was the reason he didn't have a supply at his place. Until Jill he'd never had sex without a condom before.

She responded with a noncommittal sound, a dark flush coloring her high cheekbones. Then she cleared her throat and without looking at him said, "If she holds true to form, she should be leaving anytime now."

"Huh, I'm disappointed. I was expecting another smart-ass comeback."

She opened her mouth to no doubt give him one when, just as she'd predicted, the physiotherapist walked out of the room. She stopped when she spotted them, looking from Jill to him. "Hi, session's over for the day. You can go on in," she said with a cheery smile.

Jill lowered her foot from the wall and straightened. Turning her cell phone to the forty-something woman, she swiped the screen. "If you look close enough, you'll see the timestamp on the photo. You arrived fifteen minutes ago."

The physiotherapist's cheery smile fell from her face to be replaced with an outraged gasp. "Are you checking up on me?"

Sawyer crossed his arms and let Jill have at it. He always enjoyed watching her go into cop mode.

"Yeah, you got a problem with that? Because I've got a problem with you ripping people off."

"I am not. I—"

"Your agreement with Sawyer states that you'll provide forty-five minutes of physiotherapy to Bill. You provided fifteen. At your last three visits. In my eyes, that constitutes fraud."

"I don't have to listen to this. You have no right to accuse—"

Jill raised her eyebrows and lifted her T-shirt to reveal her badge hooked onto her belt loop.

Now that...was hot. And for a man who'd been effectively returned to friendship status, not something he needed to see.

The woman sent Sawyer a panicked look. "He won't let me work with him. He refuses to cooperate. What am I supposed—"

"Inform Sawyer."

"I am!"

Jill rolled her eyes. "I'll let you handle this," she said and walked past the woman and into Bill's room.

Five minutes later, after agreeing to give the woman a second chance, Sawyer walked into the room to find his Hot Cop handling Bill. "I don't care. If you want to get out of here, you have to do your exercises."

"Yeah, yeah, turn my TV back on."

"Not until you squeeze the ball five more times." She tossed a yellow tennis ball at Bill. He caught it in his good hand...and drilled it back at Jill, who caught it easily. She smirked. "Good try."

"You're a pain in my butt. Now go catch some criminals and leave Sawyer and me alone. We have business to discuss."

"A pain in the butt who's trying to help you out, old man. Show some respect," Sawyer said as he moved toward the chair by the bed. He pulled the strap of his messenger bag over his head. The cans and bottles inside clanged as he placed it on the table.

Jill looked from the bag to him. "Don't tell me you've smuggled in beer. He's not allowed to drink."

This time it was Bill's turn to smirk. "That was last

week. This week he's brought me some samples of Gold Rush."

Sawyer thought of Jill's reaction to the sports drink and said, "You can't have any." He didn't think he could deal with it after the brief flash of her badge and flat, tanned stomach. She'd obviously spent some time in the sun over the past few weeks.

She made herself comfortable on the edge of the bed, ignoring Bill's *watch my feet* and Sawyer's raised eyebrow. "What? I'm the one who gave you the idea so I should get to see, too."

She had him there. No sense arguing with her anyway. She was stubborn. "All right, but the labels aren't quite where I want them yet," he said as he removed the three cans and three bottles from the bag, lining them in a row on the table.

Both Jill and Bill pointed at the bottle at the end and said, at almost the same time, "That one."

He wasn't really surprised. It was his favorite, too. Jill leaned over to pick the bottle up and examine the label. "Have you thought about asking Grace to help you with this? She's artistic and has a great eye for design."

"I hadn't, but I will now. Appreciate the suggestion." He smiled.

She returned it with a "You're welcome."

Bill dragged his paralyzed arm over his chest, then folded the other one across it. "So what's her share?"

Sawyer had been looking for a way to take care of Bill financially without wounding his pride. He'd come up with the idea of giving him a share in Gold Rush. Telling Bill that he'd been instrumental in coming up with the idea. It wasn't true. But Jill had been. "We haven't talked about that yet."

She frowned. "A share in what?"

He needed to change the subject before Bill started putting it together. He twisted off the caps, handing one to Bill, the other to Jill. Her frown deepened. "You said I couldn't have one."

"Changed my mind. Thought we'd drink a toast to Gold Rush's success," he said, twisting the cap off the third. They clinked bottles. His eyes followed Jill's to her mouth as he prepared for her reaction.

She took a long swallow, then said, "Oh my God, this is soo good. I'm getting all hot and tingly." She glanced at him. He touched his mouth, checking for drool. She grinned. "It's good, but it's not that good. If you haven't guessed by now, Ty was egging me on that night at the bar."

"Wouldn't have guessed. You're a good actress."

"She's not that good. She doesn't sound anything like that Meg Ryan gal," Bill said with a challenge in his eyes.

Never one to refuse a challenge, Jill took another long swallow then gave it all that she had. The performance that followed was even hotter than the one at the bar. Only he wasn't thinking of that night; he was thinking of the one he'd spent in her bed. He reached over and took the bottle from her. "Show's over, Meg. You have people to serve and protect. Off you go now."

Bill chuckled into his bottle.

"Why? I thought we were going to talk—"

Okay, something was not right. It was a small town, and they'd seen each other around over the last few weeks. Jill hadn't been cool with him or tried to avoid him, but he also didn't get the impression she'd wanted to stay too long in his company. Until now.

"Who or what are you avoiding?"

Bill laughed and pointed his bottle at her. "Nell roped you into helping with her life book thing, didn't she?"

"Careful or I'll volunteer you for next Thursday." She angled her head as though thinking it over. "Actually, that's not a bad idea. I'll talk to your physiotherapist about it. She can make up for all the time she's lost."

"And to think I used to think you were a sweet kid. You're an evil woman, Jillian Flaherty."

"You sweet talker, you." She put down her bottle, then lifted it back up. "Have you looked into bottling companies yet?"

"A couple. Why?"

"Do you remember when that brewery tried to make a go of it about eight years ago?"

"Can't say that I do." He'd still been playing with the Flurries at the time and living in Denver.

"You might be evil but you've got brains, I'll give you that. Jill's right. You should talk to Calder Dane. Wouldn't be surprised if the brewery left their equipment in his warehouse when they folded."

He hadn't thought about cutting out the middle man, but it wasn't a bad idea. "Great. I'll give him a call."

"And Jill, you wanna get out of Nell's life story thingy, just ask her about her and Calder. I'm sure you'll get a free pass once you do."

"If I do, so do you. Thanks." She put the bottle back on the table, running her fingernail under the label before looking at him. "Jack mentioned that it looks like the NHL is going to endorse Gold Rush. It's going to be big, Sawyer. I can feel it." She gave him an almost-shy smile. "I'm...We're proud of you." She hesitated for a second, then placed a hand on his chest and reached up to kiss his cheek. "You deserve all the success that comes your way."

He wrapped his arms around her and hung on a little too long. "Thanks."

And that's when Sawyer realized he and Jill weren't on the same page at all. He wanted her as much as or maybe more than he did that night six weeks ago.

*  *  *

*You idiot.* Jill berated herself as she headed for the bank of elevators. For more than a month she'd kept her distance, and then she had to go and throw herself in his arms. Yeah, like she needed a reminder of what it felt like to be held by Sawyer Anderson. She dreamed of him every night. Of *that* night. Okay, so she'd dreamed about him before. But it wasn't the same now that they'd made love. If the men she'd dated before couldn't measure up to him, the ones who followed didn't stand a chance. She might as well save herself the frustration and stop dating.

Or maybe she should apply for a transfer. Because no way would Sawyer take a vow of celibacy. Her cheeks flushed as she remembered their panted conversation of that night, the night to end all nights. He may have been going through a dry spell, but she had no doubt it wouldn't last for long. And when it ended, which she supposed it kind of had with her, which made it worse, she'd have to stand on the sidelines and watch as he dated

one voluptuous blonde after another. Not that that was
anything new; she'd been doing it for years. But it was
different now.

She had a flashback to the day she and little Jack
walked in on him and Brandi and shuddered. It didn't
matter that he hadn't initiated the kiss. She believed him
when he told her he hadn't. Still, it was tough to see him
in another woman's arms.

As the elevator dinged and the door slid open, Jill
stepped inside knowing she had to come up with a strat-
egy to move on from Sawyer. It would be too difficult to
relocate and leave her brother and his family, especially
with a new nephew or niece on the way. Throwing herself
into her job had worked in the past. No reason it shouldn't
work again. Maybe she'd get a second job in security.
Since she'd decided not to run for sheriff, she'd need the
extra cash for her dream-house fund. And, dammit, that
was one dream she wasn't giving up on.

She felt a little better as she stepped off the elevator.
Until she remembered where she was supposed to be.
She'd thought she would have caught the person responsible for the thefts and bruising by now, and that Nell
and her posse would have moved on to bigger and better
things. She hadn't, and neither had they.

But as the thefts and bruising continued Sandy had become as concerned as Jill. She'd allowed Jill complete
access to the employees and their files, and Gage had
agreed to Jill working a few days a week at Mountainview. Yesterday she'd ruled out the staff's involvement.
If her suspicions were right, her thief was one of the residents. Several of whom were currently waving her into
the craft room.

Nell looked up when Jill pulled out a chair at a table littered with sparkles, stickers, and some other crafty crap. "Where the Sam Hill have you been?"

She opened her mouth to say with Sawyer and Bill, but didn't want to put the matchmaking glint back in Nell's eyes. "I stopped by to check on Grace. Morning sickness, you know."

Nell's eyes narrowed. "It's the afternoon."

Jill didn't have to think up a comeback as the older women at her table let loose with hair-raising stories about the horrors of their own pregnancies. Jill cringed at Mrs. Sharp's detailed description of giving birth at home...by herself. All Jill could think was thank God there were no pregnant women around. If she hadn't already decided not to have babies the day little Jack went missing, that story would have done it for her.

Nell, who seemed to be enjoying the conversation about as much as Jill, clapped her hands. "Okay, time to get down to business. We have the room for only two more hours. Get your memory keepers out."

"Jill doesn't have one," Mrs. Lynn informed Nell.

Before Nell could offer her one, Jill said, "I'm here to help you guys, not do one of my own."

"Oh no, dear, we're going to share them once we're done, and we want to see yours, too."

"I've got an extra one," Nell said and walked over to the table, plunking a book in front of Jill. The thing had to have at least fifty pages in it. What was she supposed to fill it with? "You'll have to bring pictures with you next time." Nell grinned. "I probably have some of Sawyer."

Every white head at every table looked her way. Jill

bowed her head, then lifted her eyes to Nell. "So what's this I hear about you and Calder Dane? You've been holding out on us, Nell."

It was the first time Jill had ever seen the older woman at a loss for words.

"Oh, they were quite the item back in the day," Mrs. Sharp said. "A regular Romeo and Juliet, only they didn't kill themselves. The Danes and McBrides have been in a feud since their great-granddaddies founded Christmas." The older woman looked up at Nell, whose face now matched her red hair. "I always thought you'd get back together when his wife died. She was such a lovely woman. What was her name again?"

"Meredith," Mrs. Lynn said. "I taught her in grade school. Sweet little thing. Not as smart as Nell, mind you." She twisted to look at Nell. "I never had a student as bright as you, dear. I was so proud when you became an electrical engineer. Bragged about you to everyone I knew. That girl's going places, I'd say."

"I suppose that was a problem for you and Calder. Men of that generation were intimidated by an ambitious woman. Is that why you broke up, Nell?" Mrs. Sharp asked.

"No," Nell said gruffly and pulled her cell phone from the back pocket of her jeans. "Jill, you'll have to take over the class. Fred's back is out and he needs me to drive him to the doctor."

"But I..." Jill trailed off as Nell rushed from the room. Well that's not how it was supposed to go. She never should have mentioned Calder. Not only because she was now stuck running the show, but it was obvious Nell was upset.

A few hours later Jill sat with Grace on the porch swing discussing the day's events. Well, the events that didn't involve Sawyer. "Did you know about Nell and Calder?" Jill asked.

"I'd heard rumors that they'd dated, but nothing specific. We should call Madison and let her know Nell was upset." Grace got up from the swing, causing it to rock. Jill put a hand on her stomach when it rolled with the motion.

Grace frowned. "Are you still feeling nauseous?"

"I don't have the flu if that's what you're worried about. More like motion sickness. Maybe I've got an inner ear thing." She shrugged. "Or it's because I'm so tired. I've been putting in a lot of overtime again."

Grace lowered herself carefully onto the swing. "How tired?"

"Tired tired, but that's not unusual when you work as much as I do. Wait a minute, is there some weird bug going around that I don't know about?"

Before she answered, Grace leaned forward and looked in the living room window, then whispered, "Is there any chance you're pregnant?"

Jill laughed. "Of course not. Why would you even think that?"

"I don't know, probably because half the women we know are." Grace smiled and patted her hand. "Sorry, I shouldn't have asked. It's just that you haven't been your energetic self and you've seemed kind of off."

"Just work." It wasn't like she could tell Grace that she and Sawyer had... *Oh, crap.* No, no way. She was on the Pill. But sometimes she forgot to take one and doubled up. She had to get home and count them. "Umm, speaking of work, I should probably get home and get some sleep." She pushed off the swing.

"It's only six o'clock, and Jack's barbecuing his famous chicken for..." Grace took one look at her and said, "There is a chance, isn't there?"

"I didn't think so until you mentioned it," Jill grumbled.

"I knew it! I knew something happened between you and Sawyer."

"Oh my God, would you keep your voice down? The whole neighborhood will hear you."

"Sorry, you're right. The last thing we need is for Jack..." She got up from the swing and took Jill by the hand. "Come on."

"Where are we going?"

"To get a pregnancy test." She glanced through the window again. "In the next county."

An hour later Jill tossed the used pregnancy test in the wastebasket beside the toilet. "Give me another one."

"That was the last one."

"So we'll get more."

"Sweetie," Grace said, peeking her head around the bathroom door, "one positive test might be false, two, maybe, but not three."

# Chapter Eighteen

Up until his best friend stormed into the bar, Sawyer had been having a good day. He caught a glimpse of Jack's face through the mirrored glass and turned, frowning when Jack shoved the stool back viciously from the bar and took a seat.

"Who pissed in your cornflakes?" Sawyer asked. It had been a long time since he'd caught a glimpse of the renowned Flaherty temper, but it was obvious that it was in full force now.

Jack put his elbows on the bar, scrubbed his hands over his face, and looked at Sawyer through his splayed fingers. "Some asshole got my baby sister pregnant," he gritted out between clenched teeth, then cursed and raked his hand through his hair. "I need a drink. Give me a shot of tequila."

Sawyer felt like he'd taken a puck to the head and grabbed the black leather bumper on the bar. *Jill? Jill was pregnant?*

Jack looked at him, nodding. "I know just how you feel, buddy. You and I looking out for her all these years and some no-good bastard knocks her up."

Sawyer didn't know how to break it to his best friend that there was a possibility he was the no-good bastard. He grabbed two shot glasses and a bottle of tequila, forgoing the lime and salt. This was not a social drink. Quite possibly, it was Sawyer's last. "So...how, ah, when..." Jesus, it felt like he had a mouthful of marbles. His hand shook, splashing tequila over the edge of the shot glass.

Jack lifted his eyes from the overflowing shot glasses. "Ah, I think we both know how..." He trailed off with a groan. "Thanks a lot for putting that visual in my head. I do not want to think of Jill..." He tossed back the tequila.

Oh, yeah, he knew all right. And like Jack, he felt like groaning, too, only for an entirely different reason. Then he reminded himself Jill was on the Pill. "How far, ah, along is she?" he asked, his tongue not working any better than it had moments ago. He tossed back the shot in hopes it would help.

"Around six or seven weeks, I think."

Sawyer choked and pounded his chest with a fist. At Jack's raised eyebrow, he rasped, "Went down the wrong hole. Go on."

"You sure you're okay? You look kinda pale."

Sawyer fake coughed. "Think I'm coming down with something."

Jack moved back a bit. "No offense, but if it's contagious, I don't want to pass it on to my wife. Anyway, I overheard Grace on the phone with Jill, and now she's giving me the *it's not my story to tell* crap. And Jill's not answering her... Wait a minute. We were at the wedding six weeks ago. Jill dated Jake... and Matt about a week before we left for Virginia. I'd put my money on Jake. The doc would at least know to suit up." He made a face, no doubt at the thought of his sister having sex, then tossed back another shot.

Sawyer grimaced. Though not for the same reason as Jack. Sawyer didn't want to think of Jill having sex with anyone but him. But he knew her well enough to know she wouldn't have sex with any random guy. She sure as hell wouldn't jump in the sack with Jake after two dates. And her date with Matt was a non-starter. So that meant... *he* was Jill's baby daddy.

Sawyer was in the process of tossing back another shot when Jack muttered, "This is all on you, dickhead."

Sawyer choked, spewing tequila across the bar.

While he attempted to get his coughing under control, because this time the alcohol really had gone down the wrong hole, Jack leaned across the bar to grab a towel. Eyeing Sawyer as he wiped it down, he said, "You know what? We're taking you to the doc to see about your cough. Once we get Matt in the examination room, we'll find out if it was him. If it was, we'll beat the crap out of him. If it wasn't, we'll head to Jake's garage. And if it's not him, we'll—"

Sawyer wasn't letting his best friend run around Christmas half-cocked, interrogating every man in town. Jill didn't deserve to become fodder for the town's gossip mill. At least not until she was prepared for it. It was time for Sawyer to man up. "It was me," he rasped, not totally recovered from his coughing fit.

"No kidding. If you hadn't come up with the brilliant

idea of us matchmaking for Jill, I never would have set her up with—"

Sawyer glanced around at tables that were steadily filling up with the after-work crowd. He leaned across the bar and lowered his voice, "No, I'm pretty sure it's me who got Jill pregnant."

"My baby sister Jill? You're telling me you slept with my sister?" he roared.

"Would you lower your damn voice? I didn't mean for it to happen, Jack. We got carried away when you were at the wedding. But I'll make it right. I'll—"

Jack stared at him. His nostrils flared, his blue eyes shooting fire, but he wasn't yelling, and Sawyer made the mistake of thinking they could talk reasonably, like adults, like the longtime friends they were.

"She was upset, Jack. I was comforting her and then..."

"You had sex, in my house, with my *baby sister*." He dragged out each word, his voice rising on each one until he shouted the last two.

The customers were staring now and so were his servers. "Look, let's go to my office and we'll—"

"And what? Talk about how you, a man who I trusted to take care of my baby sister, got her pregnant?" he yelled, then launched himself across the bar.

\* \* \*

How could something the size of a pea turn your life upside down so completely? And it would only get worse once everyone found out she was pregnant. *Pregnant. Her. She was pregnant. There was a baby growing inside her.* It still hadn't sunk in. She'd been walking around in a fog since finding out last night. She'd sworn Grace to secrecy. She trusted her best friend to keep her secret for as long as Jill needed her to. She looked down at her stomach. If she was lucky, she had a couple of months to figure everything out. Her heart pounded a nervous beat, and she turned onto the back road. When she reached Lookout Point, she shut off the engine and slumped in the seat.

Her brother would lose it. Her brother? What about the baby's daddy? Sawyer was the one who had every right to go batshit crazy when he found out the consequences of their one-night stand. But he wouldn't. He was too nice of a guy to make her feel bad for messing up her damn pills. She'd missed two, and she didn't even know when she had, that's how irresponsible she'd been. Swept away on a storm of lust, she'd been unable to think clearly. Of course the fact she was in love with the man didn't help.

A man who thought it was his duty to save and protect single mothers everywhere. She rested her forehead on the steering wheel. And she was carrying his baby. It was going to get bad. She could feel it. With Sawyer's single-mommy issues, she wouldn't put it past him to tell her he loved her. She could even see him go so far as convincing himself that he did to ensure his child had the kind of family he'd always wanted. At least she knew him as well as she did and wouldn't make the situation worse by buying it. Because, feeling about him like she did, it would be easy to do.

Panic closed her airways, and her stomach heaved. She threw off her seat belt and shoved open the door, jumping from the car. Afraid she was going to be sick, she bent over and placed her palms on her knees. She breathed deeply through her nose as she waited for the feeling to pass. It wasn't morning or afternoon sickness; it was sheer, unadulterated panic.

She'd experienced the same symptoms when she got out of bed in the middle of the night to make a list of all that she had to do to prepare for the baby. She straightened and started to pace as she thought about each item on the two-page list. A little more than seven months, she reminded herself—lots of time.

She stopped pacing and breathed in the early September air. The sweet, spicy scent of decaying leaves and a hint of wood smoke filled her nose. She loved this time of year. From where she stood, she could see over the tops of the evergreens and yellow-leafed aspen trees to the small town below. The purplish haze of the Rockies surrounded the pastel-colored homes and shops.

She thought of how many of the inhabitants from those homes and shops had come out the day little Jack went missing. It was a good town with good people. A good place to raise her child. An extended family. And her own would be there for her, too. She knew that. They'd help out as much as she'd let them. So would Sawyer. He'd be an amazing father. Her child couldn't ask for better. They'd figure out the co-parenting thing. Make it work.

She placed a hand over her stomach and made her child a promise. She promised to be a better mother than hers had been. She'd protect her child like a parent was supposed to. They'd never feel invisible or worry whether they'd have something to eat or whether their mother would get out of bed that day, that week. And then one day she didn't get up. She'd abandoned them to her sixty-eight-year old mother who didn't want to deal with a little boy and girl.

Jill shook off the maudlin thoughts and got back in the cruiser, wrapping herself in the calm that had come over her before she took the trip down memory lane. A call came through the Bluetooth as soon as she turned on the patrol car. It was Suze. Someone else who would be there for Jill over the next few months...and years.

Before Jill had a chance to say *hey*, Suze started in on her. "Why are you not answering your cell phone? Never mind, I have a pretty good idea why since everyone's trying to get hold of you. But what I don't understand is why you didn't share the biggest news to hit Christmas, in like forever, with your best friend."

The only news Jill could think of was her own. And it sounded like everyone knew. Where was her phone? She searched the passenger seat, the floor, and the backseat. It wasn't there. She already had pregnancy brain and had forgotten it at home. She probably shouldn't be driving or carrying a gun.

"Hello. Are you there, baby mama? And even though I'm mad at you, I commend your taste in baby daddies, but boy oh boy, girlfriend, do you have a lot to make up to me. You didn't even tell me you were sleeping with Sawyer. The man of your dreams. The—"

"Oh my God, Suze, stop. This is serious. I just found out last night. How in the hell is this already all over town? Grace was the only one who knew, and she wouldn't tell. Did someone see me buying the—"

"I like Grace. I really do. But face it, that woman would not keep a secret from her husband."

Jill rubbed her back against the seat. "My brother knows?"

"Yep, he stormed in here looking for you. Said he'd left you ten messages and you weren't responding."

"Call him and say I'm undercover on a case...for the next month," Jill said, scratching her neck.

"Now that might work on your brother, but the man you were playing with under the covers came looking for you, too. He says he left you twenty messages. And so you don't get upset when you see him, 'cause that's not good for the baby, he's sporting a fat lip and bruised cheek courtesy of your brother. It's all over Facebook."

While Jill headed for home and her phone, she gave Suze the details because she threatened to keep calling her until she did. After answering her embarrassing questions and getting lectured on safe sex, Jill got the condensed version of *What to Expect When You're Expecting*. She made a mental note not to buy the book.

"Thanks, Suze. Sorry I didn't let you know, well, about everything. You're my go-to girl from now on. I'm at my place. I'll have my radio on, but I'm going to swing by my brother's."

"Take your time. It's quiet out there tonight. I expect a full report, though. Next day off, we'll head into Denver for some baby shopping." She heard the tapping of keys. "Oh my God, you should see...Never mind, I'm going to make a baby Flaherty board on my Pinterest page. You can check it out later."

It was, she knew, useless to argue with Suze. Jill also ignored the small pang of irrational disappointment that Suze didn't plan on calling it the baby Anderson board. That was useless, too.

Jill ran up the stairs to her apartment and grabbed her phone from where she'd left it beside her list. While heading back to the cruiser, she thumbed through her messages. Suze wasn't exaggerating. Jill had at least fifty messages waiting for her. Grace had sent her ten apologies with an explanation of how Jack found out.

Her brother's Flaherty temper was alive and well in his texts: *What the hell were you thinking? Who is the father? Where the hell are you? Pick up your damn phone!* The rest were more of the same, except for the last one: *Stay away from Anderson. I don't want you anywhere near the asshole. I mean it. Call me.*

She briefly closed her eyes. Sawyer had been right. Because of her, his and Jack's twenty-two-year friendship was over.

But Sawyer didn't mention anything about her brother in his texts. He didn't rant or yell at her like Jack. All he wanted was to give her a heads-up that the baby news had gone viral, make sure she was okay, and apologize for not taking better care of her. The last five texts from him got a little more frantic. No doubt afraid she'd had a breakdown at the news.

She slid behind the wheel, taking a moment before responding to him. Tonight was his hockey team's first exhibition game of the season, so she sent him a text instead of calling. He'd be behind the bench by now. Her one lucky break of the day. She'd put off talking to him for as long as she could. *Sorry. Left my phone at home. Really sorry Jack acted like a jerk. I'm working. Talk tomorrow.*

She shut off her phone. Now to deal with the jerk.

Jill walked into the purple Victorian without knocking

and strode to the kitchen. Grace was setting the table with little Jack's help. Her nephew spotted her first. "Auntie J, you come to play?"

"Sorry, buddy. Auntie's working. I need a word with your daddy." *Dickhead daddy* is what she really wanted to say.

"Here honey, you put the napkins out for Mommy, okay?" Grace handed them to little Jack then came to Jill. She gave her a hug. "I am so sorry. Please don't be mad at me. I didn't realize he was going to be home early from work," she said for Jill's ears alone.

"I'm not mad. At least not at you. Where is he?"

"Out back barbecuing. Probably taking his anger out on the poor chicken."

"Little late for you guys to be eating, isn't it?"

"He ran downtown, then ran back home."

"That didn't work very well, did it?" Her brother ran to stay in shape, but he also ran when he was angry or upset. "He gave Sawyer a fat lip and a bruised cheek."

Before Grace could respond, though her wince said it all, a little voice asked, "What's wrong with Uncle Sawyer's yip?"

She looked down at her nephew. "You have big ears. And you're sneaky, too."

"Jill, don't be too hard on your brother. He—"

She raised her hand. "Don't defend him. And do me a favor, both of you stay inside. Close the windows, too."

Jack looked over his shoulder when the screen door banged closed behind Jill. He slammed the barbeque lid shut. "I've been trying to reach you for the past four hours. Where the hell have you been?"

"Was that before or after you beat up Sawyer?" She

crossed her arms and shook her head. "I'm twenty-nine, and this is not the dark ages. I do not need you to defend my honor. I'm perfectly capable of doing that myself. And in case you forgot, it takes two to make a baby. Sawyer—"

"Do not defend him. He took advantage of you and my friendship."

"He didn't take advantage of me, Jack. I wanted—"

"Really, Jill? You think I want to hear about you and... What the hell were you thinking? The guy's a total player. A man ho. For chrissakes, he was in love with my wife. He—"

"You don't believe that. If you did, you would have cut him loose long before this. He took care of them while you were missing. Took care of all of us. He's a good man. He'd do anything for you."

"Sure he would. I told him to stay away from you, and what does he do... You know what, I don't want to talk about him anymore. I want to talk about you." He walked over and put his hands on her shoulders. "Are you okay?"

And there he was, her big brother who'd been protecting her for as long as she could remember. He was the one who'd bandaged her scraped knees, helped her with her homework, made sure she got to school on time. She couldn't stay mad at him. She knew where his anger was coming from. It had been the two of them against the world. Until they'd moved to Christmas, and then it was three. Her, Jack, and Sawyer.

"A little panicked and overwhelmed, I guess." She met his eyes. "I want to be a good mom. I'm just not sure I know how."

He took her in his arms. "You've got no worries there, honey. You'll be a great mom. You've already had lots of practice with little Jack." He leaned back. "And you have us. Grace and I've already talked about it. You can move in here until you get on your feet."

"Jack, you have another baby on the way. I'm not going to—"

"We have the room. You gave up almost two years of your life to be there for my wife and son. Let us do this for you." He shook his head when she opened her mouth. "Don't say anything right now. Just think about it. You don't have to do this alone. We're here for you."

"I know you are. And that helps a lot. But no matter how angry at him you are now, Jack, you know Sawyer. He'll be there for this baby. And me, if I need him."

He stepped back from her and shoved his hands in the front pockets of his jeans, looking out over the yard. "Doesn't matter. I can't forgive him for what he's done."

"It was a mistake, an accident. It's nobody's fault. It just happened. Don't ruin your friendship over this."

He looked at her, his eyes shadowed and a little sad. "I wanted you to have the perfect life. A beautiful one. Like me and Grace. And he stole that from you."

She pressed her lips together, fighting back a smile. "Did you steal Skye's rose-colored glasses?"

"What are you talking about?"

"Uh, the time your wife was going to ask you for a divorce?"

"Extenuating circumstances."

"What about the time she kicked you out of the apartment and you moved in with me?"

He sighed. "Fine. We've had our ups and downs. But

even then, I knew she was the only woman for me. And I was the only man for her. I want that for you, Jill."

So did she. But she didn't think she'd ever be the only woman for the man who was her only guy. "Sheesh, you're such a romantic. But just because I'm having a baby doesn't mean I won't find someone to love."

"It won't be as easy. The baby will be your priority. And it's not as if you've had much luck—"

"Stop while you're ahead. I'm still thinking I have a pretty awesome big brother."

He grinned and kissed her forehead. "We'll get through this together, Shortstop. We always do."

"No more Shortstop, please. I'm going to be a mother." And for the first time since the stick turned blue, Jill smiled at the thought. "I gotta get back to work." She reached around him and lifted the barbeque lid. "Looks like you better order in."

# Chapter Nineteen

Jill left her brother's feeling happier than when she arrived. But as she reached the cruiser, a call came over the radio that there was an altercation at the arena. Suze, unprofessional as always, told the other cars that Jill would take the call. So it looked like she'd be talking to Sawyer tonight after all.

She pulled into the Anderson Arena parking lot. *Yep, that's your daddy, baby. He's a big shot in town. Though you wouldn't know it by the way he acts.* She laughed at herself as she got out of the cruiser. Her conversation with her child was unexpected. She never thought she'd be the type. But she doubted she'd get as crazy as Skye and rename her baby every month before he or she was born.

As Jill approached the building with its sky-blue siding, she remembered the day the town had renamed the arena in Sawyer's honor. It was seven years earlier. His mom and Bill had been there busting with pride. Jill had been proud of him, too. He'd donated money to renovate the old arena and add a second ice surface. It was pretty state-of-the-art for a town the size of Christmas.

No doubt Sawyer'd have their child on skates as soon as he or she could walk. He'd taught Jill to skate when she was ten. Even as a teenage boy he'd shown signs of the man he'd become. He never got frustrated with her no matter how many times she fell or how many times her Flaherty temper erupted because she couldn't get it right the first time. He'd just laugh and tease her out of her mood. She smiled at the image of the three of them skating together. It was a nice thought, a happy thought. Much better than the ones she'd had in the middle of the night and this morning.

She pulled open the door and walked through the lobby, getting a whiff of popcorn and cotton candy from the concession stand to her left. Her stomach rumbled. She'd forgotten to eat. Something that would have to change now that she was eating for two. She was tempted to grab some popcorn, but decided against it. It wouldn't look very professional if she arrested someone with a bag of popcorn in her hand.

A cheer went up from behind the half-glass doors leading into the rink. She pushed them open and glanced at the electronic scoreboard. The game was tied with fifteen minutes left to go. She approached the security guard, standing, watching the game at the glass. "I got a call there's a problem."

"Hey, Jill. Sorry to call. But I can't get Brandi Dawson to leave. Ref's going to run the clock if she doesn't get out of here."

Jill grimaced. This wouldn't be fun. She and Brandi had always gotten along okay. But since the night at the bar, and the day she'd walked in on the woman kissing Sawyer, there'd been an obvious chill in the air whenever Jill ran into her. If Brandi heard the news about the baby, she imagined her reception would be frosty at best. The woman wanted Sawyer, and she wanted him bad.

"What did she do?"

"Trent took a dirty hit from the captain of the opposing team. Ref missed it, and Brandi hasn't stopped giving him and the player grief. And before you ask, language was foul, and she caused a scene. Referee kicked her out of the game."

"So why didn't you—"

"I tried. She refused to go. Said she'd sue me if I laid a hand on her."

Jill sighed. *Wonderful.* "Okay, I'll handle it."

"Great. Appreciate it. Home side." He lifted his chin to the top of the stands, then his eyes went saucer-wide. "Kid's father from the other team is heading toward her. I better come with you."

Jill had already clocked the father and was on her way to the stairs. She caught sight of Sawyer behind the bench wearing a black suit. His handsome profile marred by a fat lip. He had a foot on the bench and a hand on one of the player's shoulders, talking to them. Jill was pretty sure it was Trent. Sawyer turned his head and straightened, then looked up at the stands before his eyes came back to her. She gave him a wry smile, which he didn't return. His face was hard, a muscle pulsating in his clenched, bruised jaw. The man was clearly not happy. And some of that unhappiness appeared to be directed at her and not just Brandi.

Maybe Jill had been looking at the situation through

rose-colored glasses. Her chest tightened as family out-
ings were replaced with him not wanting to have anything
to do with the baby, or with her. She pushed the thought
away. This wasn't the time. Brandi and the father from
the other team were in a screaming match.

"Your son's a goon. He's not good enough to play in
this league. All he knows how to do is hit. You teach him
that, asshole?"

"Problem is your son's a mama's boy, lady. You teach
him to dive so he doesn't hurt his delicate self?"

Idiot hockey parents, Jill thought as she jogged up the
cement stairs.

"Careful," she heard a deep male voice call after her.
It was Sawyer. But she didn't have a chance to reassure
him, or flip him off, because Brandi chose that moment to
put her hands on the barrel chest of the six-foot man and
shove him back. This did not surprise Jill. When a woman
had been abused like Brandi had been, it was common
for her to strike first. No one was going to get the best of
her again. Be that as it may, the man could legitimately
charge her with assault.

"Brandi, back off," Jill ordered as she jumped over the
bleachers to reach her.

But the man had already grabbed Brandi. "Keep your
hands off me, bitch."

Seeing the look that came over Brandi's face, Jill
lunged, shoving herself between them. She knocked the
man's hand aside, grabbed it, and twisted it behind his
back. Not hard enough for him to feel pain, but hard
enough that he knew she meant business. "Calm down.
The both of you."

Before either of them had a chance to say anything, the

referee blew his whistle, gesturing that they were out of there, raising two fingers. "He can't do that. He can't kick me out for two games. Ref, you—"

"Brandi," Jill snapped. The woman looked at her as if seeing her for the first time. And if the lip-curling expression that came over face was anything to go by, she didn't like what she saw. "I won't tell you twice. Get going."

"Who do you think you are, Jill? Give you a badge and a gun and you think—"

Jill rolled her eyes and turned her back on Brandi, releasing the man's arm. "Sir, the ref has asked you to leave. Frank"—she nodded at the security guard—"will escort you outside to wait for your son."

"Me? What about this wack—"

"Look, if you want go to your son's next game, I suggest you leave quietly. And I'll be taking care of the wack…Ms. Dawson."

He nodded, then leaned around Jill to look at Brandi. "Get some help, lady. You're lucky I don't charge you."

Jill looked at Frank and nudged her head at the father, silently urging the security guard to get him out of there now. "Don't say another word," she said to Brandi when she glared at Jill and opened her mouth, "or I'll arrest you for disorderly conduct. Now move."

"Don't think I won't be talking to Gage and lodging a formal—"

She took Brandi by the arm and ushered her down the steps. "Knock yourself out."

Two women whispered behind their hands when they hit the last step. Brandi whirled on them. "Are you talking about me, Leeann and Pam? Because if that was your kid—"

Jill tugged on her arm. "Stop it. Think about your son," she said, lifting her chin at the bench several feet away from them. "Don't you think you've embarrassed the poor kid enough?"

"How dare you!" Brandi said and shoved her.

"Do that again, and I'll arrest you right here," Jill said as she reached out to steady herself on the board. "In front of your son and his coach. Now move it before I change my mind."

Brandi started walking, but kept talking. "You don't have a clue what it's like to have a child. Come and talk to me when you do." She shot a nasty look at Jill over her shoulder. "Wonder how your kid's going to feel when they find out you tried to trap its father by getting pregnant. Never works, you know. Not even with a man as honorable as Sawyer. That was really low, Jill. And I'm not the only one who thinks so," she said with a pointed look at Sawyer as they passed behind the bench. "Trent honey, I'll meet you at the car."

Jill really, really wanted to arrest her. Even more so when Sawyer glanced at them and said, "I'll bring Trent home, Brandi. Jill, call me after your shift." The way he looked at her seemed to imply Brandi wasn't the only one who had an ax to grind.

"I won't be home until after midnight. I'll call you tomorrow," Jill said, and without giving him a chance to respond, moved past Brandi. She held the door to the lobby open. Brandi sashayed past Jill in a pair of painted-on black jeans, spike heels, cream sweater, and a self-satisfied smile on her lips.

She lost the smile as soon as she stepped out of the arena and came to an abrupt stop.

"What…" Jill trailed off when she spotted the reason for Brandi's reaction. A white pickup, its lights on, was parked directly across from the arena doors. "Brandi, go to your car and go home. I'll take care of Steve."

\* \* \*

A large man sat in the shadows at the top of the outer stairs leading to Jill's apartment when she arrived home in the early hours of the morning. Her hand went to her gun.

"Don't shoot. It's just me." Sawyer's deep voice traveled on the crisp night air.

"I don't want to do this right now. It's been a long night," she said as she approached the stairs, feeling both cranky and tired.

He lifted a takeaway bag from the Rocky Mountain Diner. "I brought you soup and a club sandwich. You have to eat," he said as he stood up, the outdoor light above her apartment door illuminating his wind-blown blond hair and battered face.

She nodded. Her legs felt both heavy and a little weak as she climbed the stairs to reach his side. She took out her keys, glancing at his mouth as she unlocked the door and pushed it open, gesturing him inside. "Looks like that hurts. You should probably charge my brother with assault."

He shrugged. "I've had worse. In his place I would have done the same." He walked past her and put the bag on the table, seemingly unwilling to look at her. She felt the tension coming off him in waves. He wasn't going to make this easy. She'd half expected him to take her in his arms and tell her everything would be okay. His texts gave every indication that that's how he felt, but maybe she'd misread them. She thought back to the look in his eyes at the arena.

She went to lock the door. Maybe it would be easier to say what she had to without seeing the anger and accusation in his eyes. "I didn't get pregnant on purpose, Sawyer. I would never do that to you or any other man. But it's my fault we're in... I mean, that I'm in this situation. I forgot to take my birth control pills a couple times. I'm not even sure when. I guess because I haven't been seeing anyone for a while..." She trailed off as he moved in behind her.

He put his hands on her shoulders and turned her to face him. "I heard what Brandi said to you. I'm sorry that she did. The thought you might've gotten pregnant on purpose never crossed my mind, Jill. Not once. I should have said something then, but it wasn't exactly the time or the place. I set her straight when I brought Trent home. If it's anyone's fault, it's mine. Can you forgive me for not taking better care of you?"

She angled her head and raised her eyebrows. "Okay, first of all, I'm pretty sure I'm the one who said not to worry about the condom because I was on the Pill. I may have even threatened you with bodily harm if you stopped." His mouth lifted at the corner and he winced. "Secondly, I'm almost thirty. And I don't know why I have to keep reminding you and my brother that I am old enough to protect myself. Plus that's pretty much part of what I do for a living. So can we stop with the guilt thing, please?"

"I'm guessing the 'I'm a man and you're a woman and it's my job to protect you' wouldn't go over well, would it?" he said, a touch of amusement glinting in his hazel eyes.

She snorted. "Good call."

He smiled, then his expression grew serious again. "And let's get one thing clear right now. This 'situation'"—he made air quotes—"is not yours, it's ours. We're in this together, Jill. I'll be with you every step of the way. Don't even think about fighting me on this," he said when she opened her mouth to argue. "And not because it's the right thing to do. I want to be." He took her by the hand, tugging her after him. "Come on, let's get you fed. Your stomach's growling."

She swallowed past the tightness in her throat. He'd said exactly what she needed to hear. Though maybe not what she'd *wanted* to hear, she thought when her vision misted. In her fantasies, he would tell her he loved her, that he was over-the-moon about the baby. And they wouldn't be celebrating with soup and a sandwich. He would have swept her off her feet and carried her to bed.

"I'm just gonna grab a shower," she said, forcing a smile before hurrying off to her bedroom as every one of the feelings she'd experienced since learning she was pregnant hit her. The last thing she wanted was for Sawyer to see her cry. Again. And she couldn't use pregnancy hormones as an excuse. Even though she thought they might be to blame. She kind of hoped they were because this was becoming an annoying habit.

\* \* \*

Sawyer watched Jill practically run from the room and forced himself not to go after her. The last thing she'd want was for him to see her cry. So far he was doing a lousy job handling the situation. First with Jack, and then with Jill. He should have told her he was happy about the baby. That he wanted to be a father. Because it was true. After the shock of hearing the news from Jack and getting a fist in the face—not that Jack's reaction was a surprise—a small swell of excitement had filled him when it started to sink in.

If he'd been smart, he would have gone with her when she arrived to escort Brandi from the building. But he'd been furious with his manager and didn't trust himself not to lay into her, and he wouldn't do that in front of Trent and the other kids on the team. Half the time his players acted more mature than their parents. If Sawyer had his way, he'd ban them all.

But once Trent went off to play video games in his room, Sawyer told Brandi in no uncertain terms that unless she could keep it together, he didn't want her at Trent's games. It wasn't the first time she'd pulled a stunt like tonight. Trent was a talented player, but there had been coaches who didn't want him on their team because of Brandi. Until tonight Sawyer had kept that information to himself. But he'd laid it out to her. In part because of what she'd said to Jill. He'd nearly jumped over the boards when he heard the bullshit she was spewing. And he was going to make damn sure everyone in town knew that's all it was. Even if he had to take out an ad in the *Chronicle*.

He glanced at his watch. It was two forty-five. Jill was probably beat. He should let her get her rest. They could talk tomorrow. As he grabbed the takeaway bag to put it in the fridge, a piece of paper fluttered to the floor at his feet. He bent down to pick it up, unconsciously scanning the contents of the page before he realized what it was. She'd covered both sides of the paper with things she had to do to get ready for the baby. Her fear and panic evident in every line.

Looked like he was sticking around after all. She wouldn't sleep if she was worrying about this, and he could alleviate the majority of her fears. While he heated up the soup, he found a tray and loaded it up with crackers, the sandwich, and a glass of milk. She might as well eat in bed. When they were finished talking, she could roll over and go to sleep. He put the cream of cauliflower soup in a cup and placed it on the tray, stuck the list in the pocket of his jacket, then made his way to her bedroom. The shower had turned off ten minutes ago so he figured he was safe. He knocked on her door, then pushed it open. He nearly dropped the tray.

She scowled at him as she pulled the black sleep shirt the rest of the way over her head.

"Sorry," he grimaced, then tried to make light of it, "but hey, it's not like I haven't seen you naked before."

"What are you doing in my bedroom?"

He held up the tray. "You're tired, thought it would be more relaxing for you to eat in bed while we talk."

"You don't have to take care of me. I'm not dying, I'm having a baby. Women do it all the time. They even deliver them by themselves, you know. Which, for the record, I have no interest in doing. And after hearing Mrs. Sharp's story, the natural thing is out, too. So make a note to keep Skye away from me, in case I forget."

He held back a laugh. He had the impression it wouldn't be appreciated. It wasn't often he saw Jill nervous, and right now she was babbling. It was kind of cute. "No Skye, and lots of drugs. I've got your back, babe," he said as he put the tray on the nightstand, then held up the covers. "In you get."

"Thanks," she sighed, then wrinkled her nose as she got into bed. "What is that smell?"

"Cauliflower soup," he said, placing another pillow behind her back and one on her lap before setting down the tray. "You need to start eating vegetables."

"I knew you were going to be annoying."

"Better a guy who cares than a jerk who doesn't, don't you think?" he said as he toed off his shoes. His chest tightened a bit at the thought of anyone other than him being her baby's daddy. He wasn't exactly sure why and knew it wasn't fair. She deserved to be having a baby with a man who loved her; a man she loved. But life rarely went the way you planned. Besides, she was lucky it was him and not one of the losers she'd dated in the past. At least he'd make sure both Jill and the baby were well cared for.

"That depends on how annoying you become." She took a tentative taste of the soup, then raised her eyebrows. "Not bad."

He stretched out beside her. "Glad you approve. Now keep eating while I explain how we're going to handle this. And before you accuse me of snooping," he said, pulling her list from his pocket, "the paper fell off the table, and I picked it up."

"Sawyer"—she went to grab the list from his hand—"that's private."

He held it out of reach. "Careful, you're going to spill your milk," he said, nodding at the tray. "Look, I know it's private. But it has to do with the baby, and since the baby's mine, too, it should be private to everyone but me." She gave him a look. "Okay, I admit that's a stretch. And I'm sorry for invading your privacy. That's not really true. I'm glad I saw the list. You're worrying about a lot of stuff that you don't have to worry about. Like this one: *If something happens to me, who's going to look after my baby?* First off, nothing is going to happen to you. But God forbid it did, I would take care of the baby." He read the second one and looked at her. "Okay, this one kinda scares me, too. What do you think the chances are that our kid will be as wild as little Jack?"

She slowly lowered the sandwich she'd just raised to her lips. "I've lost my appetite." She put the sandwich on the plate and returned the tray to the nightstand. She lay back down, turning on her side to face him.

He smiled and stroked her cheek. "We pretty much helped raise little Jack, so we're ahead of the game. We know what to expect. We can figure out the rest as we go along."

She tentatively touched the side of his mouth. "I'm sorry this has come between you and Jack. He had no right to hit you."

He turned his face and kissed her fingers. "Right now all I care about is you and the baby and making sure you're both healthy and happy."

"I guess we're lucky to have you then, even if I have no doubt you're going to become stupidly overprotective." She looked at him, absently rubbing her stomach. "You'll be an amazing father, Sawyer. Little Jack adores you and so does Trent and the kids on your team. You're great with them."

"I'm sensing a *but* in there."

"No *but*. I'm just a little concerned about how Steve perceives your relationship with Trent. And Brandi. I'm assuming she told you about my conversation with him tonight."

"Yeah, she did. But she didn't mention anything about me."

"Because I didn't tell her. She has enough to worry about. And Steve was smart enough not to make an outright threat against you, but I need you to be careful. No more confronting him. Leave that to us."

"Come on, he's just shooting off his mouth. He doesn't have the balls to—"

"You don't know that. In Steve's eyes, you are the reason Brandi won't take him back. And the reason his son doesn't want to see him. It sounded like Brandi may have implied that your relationship is more than it..." She glanced at him from under her lashes. "I guess I shouldn't assume—"

"Brandi and I are just friends. I explained that kiss to you, Jill. I thought you believed me."

"I do. But you didn't owe me an explanation then, and you don't owe me one now. I'm just telling you why I'm concerned about Steve. More so now that he's lost his job."

"I didn't know he had one."

She nodded. "In construction for a few weeks. That's why Brandi hasn't heard from him. He was hoping to prove to her that he's changed, but the company lost out on a job they were counting on. Steve was the last man hired so he was the first to be let go."

"I'm sure it's not easy for an ex-con to find a job, but

I'm having a hard time sympathizing with the guy. And we both know Brandi's not taking him back."

"You're right, and I don't blame her. But I wonder if maybe she shouldn't let Trent see him. Steve believes that he wants to, but that Brandi, and *you*, won't let him. Do you think it's possible Trent used Brandi as an excuse so he didn't have to tell his father he didn't want to see him?"

"I didn't know he'd even spoken to Trent. I thought he'd just been following him around this summer."

"Steve says he did, and he was pretty convincing. Maybe you should talk to Trent. If he does want to see his father, it might go a ways in diffusing the situation."

"Court date's set for late October. Might be best to wait until then."

"Your call, but I'm serious about you confronting him. You see him around, you call it in."

"Yeah, like I'd rather see you confronting him. It was bad enough watching you run into the stands and put yourself between that guy and Brandi."

"That's my job. I'm trained to do it. You're not."

"I'm not the one carrying our baby."

"I'm not even going to acknowledge that you said that."

"Ignore me all you want, but you won't be able to ignore the fact you're pregnant for long." He put his hand over hers on her stomach, and she scowled at him. "Don't get testy. I'm just stating a fact. When will Gage put you on desk duty... next month?"

"No, not until I request it or it starts getting in the way of me doing my job."

He slid his hand under hers. "Won't be long. You're already starting to show."

She rolled her eyes and tugged up her sleep shirt. "Really, it looks like I'm pregnant? My stomach's flat."

"Nope, there's a definite baby bump," he said, stroking his fingers over her warm, soft skin. He only meant to tease her, but instead he was torturing himself. The memory of the night they made the baby still burned in his brain. The muscles in her stomach contracted under his hand, and he wondered if she was remembering, too. Wondered if, like him, she wanted another chance to explore that explosive chemistry they'd had. He lowered his head and kissed her stomach, felt the quiver beneath his lips, heard the sexy, low moan. He turned his head while trailing his lips over her dips and curves and met her heavy-lidded eyes.

"What…what are you doing?" she said, then gasped and arched her back, her fingers tangling in his hair. "Never mind. Just keep doing it."

# Chapter Twenty

Jill sat curled up in a chair in the corner of Bill's room at Mountainview. She was there to catch a thief, but the man who'd stolen her heart was going to blow it if he didn't quit calling her. "What now?"

"It's a good thing I have healthy sense of self-esteem or that greeting would have done a number on my confidence, babe," Sawyer said.

"You called me three times in the last hour and a half."

"What can I say? It's a quiet night at the bar, and I like to hear your voice."

She liked to hear his voice, too, except when he was being annoyingly overprotective. "Like I told you when you called twenty minutes ago, I'm not leaving until I solve this case."

"It's two in the morning. You need your rest."

"Were you planning on coming over to check up on me when I get home?"

"Good possibility of that happening. You have a problem with that?"

"No, other than to point out for someone who is so concerned about me getting my rest, you have no qualms about keeping me up half the night."

He laughed. "Yeah, but I don't have to worry about you getting hurt when you're in my arms."

She didn't know about that. Even though they'd been spending a lot of time together these past three weeks, she still had no idea where their relationship was headed. For all she knew, he was just hanging out with her to look out for his baby mama and enjoying the fringe benefit of some pretty amazing sex. "Gotta go. I hear someone in the hall. I'll text you when I'm on my way home." She disconnected before he had a chance to respond.

"If you'd just marry the boy, he wouldn't be calling you at all hours of the night," said a gravelly voice from the bed.

Bill had been pushing for them to get married ever since he'd heard the news. He wasn't the only one. Half the residents in town and at Mountainview had given their opinion on the matter. To the point where Jill had been worried Sawyer would cave to the pressure, then she'd worried when he hadn't. Which was silly because she wouldn't marry him even if he asked. Maybe it was selfish, but when she got married, she wanted it to be because the man loved her, not just her baby. "I thought you were asleep."

"Hard to do when he calls you every blasted minute. And when he's not calling you, you're nodding off. You snore, by the way."

"I don't know how you'd hear me. You sound like a

freight...Shh, I hear something in the hall." This time she wasn't making it up. The familiar *tap tap tap* of a cane drew closer. Mrs. Sharp appeared in the doorway in her white nightgown and housecoat, backlit by the light in the hall. Jill pulled her feet tight to her chest as the older woman moved her cane from right to left and walked alongside the bed. Mrs. Sharp sat on the edge of the mattress, giving no reaction to Bill's muttered, "She's sitting on my hand."

The older woman bent over and picked up Bill's gold watch from the nightstand, staring at it for a moment before getting up and walking out of the room.

"Go after her. That's my retirement watch."

It was just as she'd suspected. Mrs. Sharp was her thief. At today's life book session, the older woman had revealed that she'd walked in her sleep as a young girl. Her mother had done the same. Only her mother had eaten when sleepwalking while Mrs. Sharp collected bright, shiny objects. The older woman said she'd outgrown the condition, but Jill remembered hearing about Mr. Applebee's nocturnal visitor and put two and two together.

"Don't worry. I'll be back as soon as I find her stash and get it sorted out with the staff."

Which took a lot longer than Jill anticipated. Mrs. Sharp had several more rooms to visit before heading back to her own. Jill found her stash at the back of her closet. And from the looks of it, she'd been collecting bright and shiny objects for a very long time. The only thing Jill had wondered about was why money had gone missing. Her answer was in the box—money clips. Because of the amount of cash and number of items, the staff called Sandy in. No charges would be brought against

Mrs. Sharp, but they came up with a plan to keep the older woman safe. Jill would sit in on the meeting with her later that day.

Bill was having breakfast by the time Jill returned his watch. She barely had enough time to shower and change into her uniform before heading back out for the business owners' meeting at the town hall. She was the liaison for the sheriff's department.

Madison was calling the meeting to order when Jill arrived. "Sorry," she murmured and went to take a seat. One that was pulled out for her by a disgruntled-looking Sawyer. She was surprised to see him. It was unusual for him to attend the meetings. Typically, Brandi attended on his behalf. She was there, too, looking about as unhappy with Jill as Sawyer was.

"Sorry I forgot to text. Busy night, morning, I guess."

His eyes roamed her face. "You look like hell."

"Thanks. You don't look so hot yourself," she lied. Between the inch or more of scruff on his handsome face, his messy hair, and the worn, brown leather jacket that emphasized his broad shoulders, he looked sexy and disreputable.

Brandi sat on his other side, doodling on her notepad with a smirk on her face. Naturally the other woman didn't look like hell. She had on her signature tight jeans, a form-fitting blue sweater, and her blond hair looked like she'd recently been at Ty's salon.

Grace rushed into the room. "Sorry I'm late," she said, taking the seat beside Jill. Grace glanced at her and grimaced. "Do you have morning sickness now, too?"

"No, she doesn't. She's making herself sick working overtime," Sawyer said, of course loud enough for everyone to hear.

Madison gave her a concerned look. "Jill, if Gage is overworking you, you have to tell him."

"Happy now?" Jill whispered out of the side of her mouth to Sawyer, lightly kicking him under the table. "I'm fine, Madison. Gage had nothing to do with me working late. Just wanted to wrap something up at Mountainview."

"Give me the scoop. Did you catch the thief?" Nell asked. The older woman had forgiven Jill for bringing up Calder and was now back running the life story group.

"I'll tell you about it later. I'm sure Madison wants—" Jill broke off as the man himself walked into the room. Calder Dane was a handsome man with a thick head of lustrous white hair and a beard. Tall and barrel-chested, his cheeks were rosy, and his blue eyes twinkled with good humor. He looked like how you imagined Santa would. Which was probably the reason he played the jolly old elf in the town's annual Christmas parade and at Santa's Village.

"Apologies for being late, folks. Truck wouldn't cooperate this morning." His gaze moved from the empty chair beside Nell to Sawyer.

"You can have my seat, Calder," Jill said, finally cluing into why Sawyer was here. He and Calder required the town's permission to reopen the old plant. She stood and walked around the table to pull out the chair beside Nell. Sawyer crossed his arms, raising an eyebrow at her.

She pretended she didn't notice and turned her attention to Madison.

"Thanks, girlie," Nell murmured.

Jill slouched down in her chair and whispered, "Just sayin', but that is one handsome man. Maybe you should, you know, let him know you're interested."

Nell whispered back, "Maybe you should take care of your own love life instead of worrying about mine. Brandi's been looking for a man like Sawyer since she cut Steve loose."

Jill glanced across the table. Brandi was leaning into Sawyer, whispering something in his ear. He nodded, then, as though he sensed Jill watching, looked up and held her gaze. He tilted his head, a slow smile curving his lips. The ass knew she was jealous. She rubbed her middle finger along her cheek. She heard his low laugh, and a second later, he teasingly rubbed his foot against her leg. She caught Grace looking at them with a smile on her face. Brandi wasn't smiling, which made Jill smile. Yes, she was petty like that.

Jill's smile morphed into a yawn. She smothered it, relaxing in her chair to listen to Madison read the minutes from the last meeting. Her voice faded into a low drone. Jill woke up with her head on Nell's shoulder. Oh, crap, she thought, straightening to glance across the table. Sawyer wasn't in his chair. And that was because he was beside hers. Gone was the sexy, flirty man of earlier. He was in overprotective baby daddy mode. "Thanks, Madison. I'll send you the prospectus tomorrow. Calder can fill you in on the rest," he said, then scooped Jill into his arms to everyone's delight but hers, and obviously Brandi's.

"Sawyer, if you don't put me down, I swear I'll—"

"Quiet, or I'll kiss you in front of everyone to shut you up."

"You wouldn't da—"

\* \* \*

Sawyer glanced at Jill as he turned onto her street. The kiss had shut her up, and now she wasn't talking to him. She was talking to the passenger's side window in his truck. She was too exhausted to drive, but obviously not too exhausted to curse him out.

"...Looked like an unprofessional idiot. Big jerk. I've never been so embarrassed in my life. It'll be all over Christmas—"

"Babe, you got something to get off your chest. Probably better to say it to me than my window."

"I'm not speaking to you."

He pulled into the parking lot of her apartment complex and turned off the engine. "You fell asleep in the middle of a meeting because you were up for twenty-four hours so don't get mad at me when I worry about you."

"You can worry about me, but you cannot go all caveman on me and carry me out of a meeting. It was embarrassing. And then you kissed me in front of everyone!"

"I gave you fair warning."

She made a frustrated sound in her throat and unsnapped her seat belt, holding up her hand when he undid his. "I'm mad at you. And I don't want to talk to you right now. I'm going to bed."

"I'm sorry. Maybe I overreacted—"

"Ya think?" she asked as she opened her door.

"Okay, I was an idiot. But just let me walk you to your—"

She slammed the door.

He dug out his cell as he watched her walk to the stairs of her apartment. His fingers tightened on his phone when she stumbled. She was the most stubborn, hard-headed woman he'd ever met, and she was making him act like an idiot. He began punching in a number when he realized it was Jack's. He disconnected. He hadn't spoken to his best friend since that day at the bar. Sawyer's texts and calls had gone unanswered. Both Grace and Jill had tried, he knew, to intervene on his behalf. But the man was as stubborn and hard-headed as his sister.

He called the one person he knew would never let him down. "Hey, Ma," he said when she answered.

"Honey, what's wrong? You sound down."

"I'm good. How about you and Charlie?"

"We're both doing well, honey. Now are you going to tell me what's wrong or do I have to call Nell?"

He'd been holding off telling her until Jill was at the three-month mark. He figured it was close enough to share the news. Plus he had to tell her if he wanted her perspective on the situation. "I've got some news that I think will make you happy, Grandma."

"Did you…did you just call me grandma? Oh my God. Charlie. Charlie, we're going to be grandparents! Sawyer's having a baby," she yelled, then got back on the line. "Who's the baby's mama; do I know her? When's the baby due? I'll have to call Nell, and she can help me coordinate the shower from there. I could—"

He laughed, which he considered somewhat of a miracle given how he was feeling. "Ma, slow down. One question at a time."

"Sorry, I'm just so excited, I'd about given up on you. So who's the girl? Is she wonderful? Are you engaged?"

He sighed. "It's Jill, Ma."

"Jill, our Jill?" she said, sounding confused.

He leaned back against the headrest. "Yeah, Jill Flaherty." There was a long pause. "You still there?"

"Yes, I'm just a little surprised, honey. Don't get me wrong, you know I've always loved Jill. She'll make a wonderful mother. But I never thought she was your type. I didn't realize you were even dating. She's a lot younger than you, isn't she?"

He was beginning to think there was another reason he'd put off telling his mother. This wasn't exactly the supportive conversation he'd been hoping for. "No, only seven years. And you know we've always been close. One thing led to another."

"Oh, I see." And it sounded like she did. He'd never been able to put one over on her. He didn't know why he'd expected to now. "You know, honey, friendship is a great foundation for a marriage. You are planning on marrying Jill, aren't you? Giving my grandchild a name and taking responsibility for both Jill and the baby?" Her soft voice held a hint of steel.

He hadn't given much thought to marriage. Probably because he'd always assumed he'd be in love with the woman he proposed to. But his mother was right. It was the next obvious step. And as he'd realized over the last few weeks, he enjoyed spending time with Jill. And not just in bed, though there was definitely not a problem in that end of their relationship. He'd begun to resent their schedules, especially hers, and how much time they spent apart. At least if they were living under the same roof, they'd have more time together. It'd make it easier when the baby came along. "Come on, Ma. You know me better than that. It's all pretty new. We've only known about the baby for a few weeks."

Her voice softened. "I'm sorry. I shouldn't have said anything. I know exactly what kind of man you are. Jill is a very lucky girl. She'll never have to worry about a thing. Neither will that child. Look at how you took care of me."

"Taking care of Jill is causing a bit of a problem. She thinks I'm overprotective," he said, then told his mother how he'd been handling things so far. More like how he'd been screwing them up.

"Well, it sounds like you're still finding your way. Probably a good thing you started out as friends," she said, a hint of laughter in her voice. "Why don't you relax a little? Stop worrying about her so much. I can see how the daily e-mails about what she should and shouldn't be eating and other health risks might get on her nerves. Sure as heck would get on mine," she said under her breath.

"I heard that, Ma." He thought of the one he'd sent Jill earlier today. "So do you think I should warn her about the risks involving firearms? They say it's bad for the baby's hearing, and Jill's exposing herself to toxic chemicals when she's cleaning her weapon. And God knows the woman loves her weapons."

"Well, honey, I might be careful about sending her any more e-mails. Any more e-mails at all."

"Okay. Thanks. Love you, Ma. Talk soon." He hung up and immediately texted Jill: *Babe, I e-mailed you earlier today by mistake. Do me a favor and delete it. Sorry again for being an ass.*

# Chapter Twenty-One

"You look fantastic. Pregnancy suits you." Vivi smiled at Jill as she rocked her son's carriage with her foot. They were sitting outside on Vivi and Chance's patio with a gorgeous view of the lake, enjoying the unseasonably warm fall weather. Sawyer and Chance had left about an hour ago to do something manly. At least that's what they'd told her and Vivi. Jill figured it was good for him to hang out with Chance. She knew he was missing her brother.

She ran a thumb under the waistband of her navy yoga pants. "I'm not even three months, and I've graduated to stretchy pants. My jeans don't fit anymore, and I had to order a new uniform." She glanced at her boobs, noting how they stretched her navy hoodie. "It's Sawyer's fault. Every time I turn around, he's shoving food at me."

Vivi laughed. "Get used to it. Chance still does it, and Sam's four months old."

"That's not what I wanted to hear. You're supposed to tell me it's a passing phase."

"I've come to the conclusion it's just who they are, Jill. Guys like Sawyer and Chance—the majority of men in Christmas, really—have a protective streak a mile wide. They can't help themselves. They'll do everything they can to take care of their families. You'll get used to it. Sort of. When you think about it, we're lucky. Most women would kill to have a stand-up guy whose sole focus is to take care of them and make them happy. And you have to admit, they look real good doing it."

Jill stared at her, wondering what had happened to Kick-Ass Vivi Westfield. "When did you start drinking the Kool-Aid?"

She grinned and lifted a shoulder. "I don't know. Motherhood has a way of making you reevaluate life. Changes your priorities, I guess. And watching Chance with Sam..." Her face went soft, her violet eyes misty. "Sorry, hormones are still off the charts." She dabbed at the corner of her eye with her finger. "Trust me, I understand better than anyone how you're feeling. But believe me when I say that it'll be worth it in the end."

"So when he picks me up in a meeting and carries me out of the room, kisses me to shut me up, and sends me e-mails about the dangers of firearms, I'm just supposed to suck it up?"

Vivi laughed, then said, "Sorry, I heard about the meeting. And just so you know, all the women in town thought it was a swoon-worthy moment."

Jill crossed her arms. "So I heard." Someone, her bet was on Nell, had snapped a picture of Sawyer kissing her as he carried her out of the room and posted on the town's Facebook page. It got more likes than her bird poop photo. She'd caught Sawyer looking at it the other day with a grin on his face. "Thanks for not putting it in the *Chronicle*."

"Hey, us kick-ass girls have to stick together. And to answer your question about sucking it up, that would be a *hell no*. They wouldn't want us to. They like the challenge even when they complain that we're being hard-headed and stubborn."

Jill glanced over her shoulder at the sound of a truck coming down the gravel drive. "Our manly men are returning. Any idea what they've been up to?"

"I've been sworn to secrecy. But I will say your baby daddy is going to earn some serious Brownie points. I'm beginning to think these guys put their heads together to help the next one in line. Because as far as romantic gestures go, Sawyer's outdone them all."

"Umm, you're probably trying to make me feel better, but it's actually not working. Why does he need a romantic gesture?"

"Maybe to make up for embarrassing you at the meeting?"

She nodded. He had been trying to rein himself in the past week. She still received a couple texts a day, but they were more of the *how's it going* kind or to share something funny that had happened at the bar than the annoying ones that made her want to thump her phone on her head, or his. "Right. That must be it." She narrowed her eyes at Vivi, who appeared to be silently laughing. But then the baby started to fuss, distracting them both.

"I swear he has Chance-radar," Vivi said, standing to bend over the carriage. She moved the mosquito netting and lifted the baby into her arms. "You hear your daddy, don't you, sweetie?" Sure enough, the men's conversation filtered to the front of the log home, and the baby wriggled in Vivi's arms.

"He's getting so big," Jill said, joining Vivi to stroke Sam's soft, chubby cheek. He had the same beautiful olive complexion as his mother, but with the blond tufts of hair and bright blue eyes, he was the spitting image of his father.

Vivi looked at her. "Don't say it."

Jill laughed. "Okay, I won't. But you have to admit the resemblance is uncanny."

"Which his father tells me at least three times a day."

"What do I tell you?" Chance asked as he and Sawyer came down the grassy incline carrying a green canoe between them. Sawyer winked at Jill as they headed for the dock.

She raised an eyebrow at Vivi and nodded at the canoe. "That's your idea of an amazing romantic gesture?" She lowered her voice so Sawyer wouldn't hear her. In part because she didn't want to hurt his feelings, but also because she didn't want him to think she thought of their relationship as a romantic one. *Friends with benefits* was a more apt description.

Vivi grinned, responding to her husband instead. "That your son is the spitting image of his mother."

Chance snorted as he lowered his end of the canoe. "He's his daddy's mini-me. The next one will look like you, Slick."

Sawyer said something to him as they walked toward the flagstone patio. They laughed, the sun's rays shining down on their outrageously handsome faces and turning their blond hair to gold. They could pass for brothers. Both were tall with muscular builds, though Sawyer was leaner than Chance. And while Sawyer reminded Jill of a warrior with his rugged good looks, Chance had actually been one. Every once in a while that cold fierceness showed on his face, until he looked at his wife and baby boy like he was now.

"He's lucky he's hot," Vivi murmured.

Jill felt the same about Sawyer. She'd be ticked as hell at him one minute, and then he'd give her one of his slow smiles and her anger dissolved, leaving her all melty. She was feeling a little melty right now as he walked to her side. He had on khaki shorts that showed off his long muscular legs and a black Flurries hoodie with the sleeves pushed up to his elbows to reveal his powerful forearms.

"Miss me?" Chance said, giving his wife a kiss and taking the baby from her.

"You were gone less than an hour," Vivi said, tickling her son's tummy when Chance turned the baby to face them.

"Hey, big guy," Sawyer said, leaning in to stroke the baby's face. "Mind if I hold him?" he asked Chance.

"Sure," he said, handing him over.

Sawyer cradled the baby in his arms and nuzzled Sam's cheek. "He smells good."

Chance laughed. "Not always."

Vivi caught Jill's eyes. She knew what the other woman was thinking without her saying a word. Totally worth putting up with his annoyingness for a moment like this.

\* \* \*

Twenty minutes later Jill was no longer feeling the warm fuzzies. She was fighting the urge to throw Sawyer overboard.

"Babe, you gotta pull the blade through the water like this." For what felt like the third time in so many minutes, he demonstrated the action with his paddle.

"That's what I'm doing," she muttered, sitting at the front of the canoe wearing a life jacket. "Where are we going?"

"In circles if you keep paddling like that." She shot him a look over her shoulder, and his lips twitched. "Should have remembered you always have to have everything planned out. Can't we just enjoy the day together?"

"I guess." It would be easier to if she knew what he had planned. She kept thinking about what Vivi said and it was making her nervous. She didn't like surprises.

"Okay, if it'll make you happy..." He lifted his paddle and pointed across the lake from Vivi and Chance's "...That's where we're headed."

She followed his paddle, squinting behind her sunglasses. She glanced at him. "I don't see anything but a bunch of trees."

He lowered his sunglasses on his nose, looking over them at her. "Trees? You don't see the gorgeous fall foliage? Look at those reds and oranges. At the way the aspen leaves shimmer in the breeze."

She pressed her lips together, then cleared the laughter from her throat. "You're right, it's really beautiful. And the mountains are looking pretty spectacular today, too, with their snow-covered peaks." She skimmed her paddle over the water. "The lake's so still it looks like glass."

"It's the same color as your eyes. I hope the baby has your eyes. They're beautiful."

"Oh, I…" He'd foiled her teasing with a compliment. "Thank you. Yours are, too."

"Thanks," he said, a hint of amusement in his voice.

They paddled without speaking for a few minutes. The sound of the wooden blades slicing through the water and the small waves gently lapping against the boat were peaceful and calming. She felt the release of tension from her body and admitted, "This was a good idea. I'm glad you thought of it."

"Jack and I used to come here every summer. We fished in the marshes over there." He pointed at the bulrushes to the left of them. There was a man in a white rowboat, partially hidden by the weeds. "Caught some good-sized trout."

"You miss him, don't you?" Her brother was being a stubborn jackass. Grace couldn't get through to him and neither could Jill.

"Of course I do. But what I miss the most are the times we all spent together. The five of us hanging out, having barbeques and family dinners."

"Me too. It's not the same without you."

"I thought he'd come around by now. When I pictured me having a kid, getting married, he was always there. It's not the same without him. It would have been nice to share today with him."

She froze, praying he didn't mean what she thought he did. She felt movement behind her, the gentle rocking of the canoe. "Jill, I want to ask you something." Eyes wide, she stared at the shoreline. "Turn around real slow and face me, babe. I want to do this right."

She whipped around. "Sawyer, I..." In her panic, she forgot to put down her paddle. He was on one knee, holding a small blue box in his hand, when the blade hit him on the shoulder, knocking him off balance. "Oh, crap."

"Jesus, don't—"

She stood up to reach for him...and overturned the canoe.

\* \* \*

"I didn't say no. I said I'd think about it," Jill tried to explain to Sawyer as they pulled the canoe onto the rocky shore. They hadn't bothered trying to get back into it. They'd stripped off their clothes, hanging on to the canoe as they kicked their way to shore. The man in the rowboat had offered to help, but by the time he would have reached them, they'd probably have made it to shore, so they'd politely declined. Chance, who'd been standing at the end of his dock, offered his help, too. Since he'd been laughing his ass off at the time, their response wasn't as polite. They'd flipped him off.

"You were so panicked you nearly took my head off with the paddle, then you overturned the canoe. That doesn't sound like *I'll think about it* to me," he muttered, shoving his wet hair from his face. Droplets of water glistened on his chiseled pecs and his washboard abs, his black boxers molded to his...

"Jill?"

Her eyes jerked to his face, and she winced at the hurt and confusion in his eyes. "I'm sorry. I didn't mean to ruin your proposal."

"Even if you hadn't overturned the canoe, it was going to be ruined when you rejected me."

"I didn't reject you. I just don't think this is something we have to rush into. We can revisit it in a couple months, okay?" And maybe by then he'd fall in love with her. If he'd said those three words, she would have said yes in a heartbeat. Even if she'd had the smallest hint that he might be falling in love with her, she would have said yes. But she didn't because he wasn't.

"I don't understand why you want to wait. We're friends. We spend practically all our free time together anyway." He moved her hand from the snaps of her life jacket and undid them for her. She raised her eyes to meet his and shivered at the heat she saw there. "We're compatible out of bed and in. The sex is amazing and gets better every time. We're great together, Jill. We get along better than half the married couples I know. Or am I missing something? Have you not been as happy as me these past few weeks?"

Everything he said was true, and maybe if she was willing to settle for a man who loved her, but wasn't *in love* with her, she'd say yes. But eventually it wouldn't be enough for either of them. She'd always want more, and then one day he might meet the woman of his dreams, and where would she be then? She'd witnessed the devastation a broken heart could cause firsthand. She wouldn't intentionally do that to herself or her child.

"Guess not," he said and moved away to retrieve his sweatshirt, shorts, and her yoga pants from the top of the canoe.

She slid off the life jacket, letting it drop onto the rocks, then wrapped her arms around his waist and rested her cheek against his cool, damp back. It was easier to say what she had to without looking at him. "We've known each other since we were kids, Sawyer. Sometimes I think you know me better than I know myself. So you know that I've been as happy as you." And she had been, even when he was driving her crazy. Suze had been right. Up until a few weeks ago, Jill had been coasting through life. Sawyer and their baby had changed that. "I'm just asking for a little time. It's all happened so fast. Marriage is a big step. I don't want to ruin what we have. I'm not just thinking about us, I'm thinking about the baby, too."

He turned in her arms and looked into her eyes, then gently pushed her hair from her face. "Okay. We'll do it your way. But..." he said, pulling back to dig the ring box from the pocket of his shorts. He took her hand and placed it on her palm, folding her fingers around the box. "I want you to hold on to this."

She looked down at his big hand covering hers. "Maybe you should keep it. What if you change your mind?"

"That won't happen."

"You don't know—"

"Yeah, I do, and I'll show you why. Come on." He placed his hand on the small of her back, nudging her forward.

Through the grove of aspen trees she made out a clapboard house. It was a little run-down, but it was a good size with a welcoming front porch. And it was obvious someone lived there. She smelled the woodsy fragrance of a fire, a tendril of gray smoke coming from the river rock chimney. She held back. "Maybe we should call out. The owners might not take kindly to trespassers and shoot us."

# Chapter Twenty-Two

Sawyer sat in his office playing a game of desktop hockey. His right hand was beating his left. Instead of celebrating the official endorsement from the NHL that hit his inbox ten minutes ago, he was shooting a pea-size puck at a card-size net trying to figure out the woman who said he knew her better than she knew herself. If that was true, she would have said yes to his proposal. At least one of them.

For a minute there, when he told her the house on the lake was theirs, he thought she might give in and put him out of his misery. He'd taken advantage of her stunned silence, the tears turning her eyes ocean blue, and picked her up, carrying her across the threshold in a move he thought might tip the scale in his favor. It didn't. And neither did the rose petals he and Chance had scattered over the sleeping bags laid out on the battered floorboards in the living room.

He'd even done as Ethan suggested and filled the place with vases of long-stem pink roses. They hadn't helped his cause, either. Neither had Ty's suggestion that he fill the house with candles or Chance's that he make her s'mores. Against his better judgment, he'd roasted hot-dogs for her in the fireplace as Gage recommended. And Sawyer hadn't said one negative word about the crap in her favorite meal.

He frowned as he thought back to the events of yes-terday and put down his miniature hockey stick, leaning his head against the back of the chair. She'd told him how much she loved and appreciated the efforts he'd gone to. And then she'd rocked his world in front of the crackling fire, leaving little doubt that he'd scored an A-plus in the romantic gestures department.

So maybe it was his proposal that needed work. Not only his first, but his second one, too. If anything, it might have been worse than the first. And since they'd been ly-ing in front of the fire in a blissed-out state instead of half drowned, he was trying to remember what he'd said that put the chill in the air.

It was possible she was just ticked he hadn't let it go as she had asked him to. Because really, what woman wouldn't be thrilled when a man told her how much their unborn child already meant to him? Everything he planned to do to ensure their baby always knew how much it was wanted and loved. He picked up the hockey stick and tapped it on his desk. He needed a woman's opinion. But after his last conversation with his mother, he didn't really feel like telling her he'd screwed up again.

There was a tap on his office door, and Brandi stuck

her head inside. She looked at him and winced. "Guess I don't have to ask if everything's okay."

"That obvious, huh?" He straightened in his chair. "What's up?"

"I just wanted to check on you." She shut the door, then crossed his office to take the seat in front of his desk. "I'm sorry Jill didn't accept your proposal. I'm kind of shocked she didn't, actually. Maybe—"

He stared at her. "How did you know?"

"It's all over Facebook. Someone posted a picture of the two of you on Christmas's home page." She pressed her lips together, obviously fighting back a laugh, then said, "Of you guys falling into the lake yesterday afternoon. It was captioned 'Sawyer's epic proposal goes epically wrong.'" Brandi continued over his groan, "So people were commenting on it and congratulating you both. Then someone posted this morning that congratulations were premature."

He gave his head a frustrated shake. Bad enough to live in a small town; add social media into the mix and you couldn't make a move without it going viral within hours. He probably should give Jill a heads-up. She was hanging out with Grace and little Jack today.

"So is it true? Did she actually reject your proposal?" she asked carefully.

"Not really. She just wants some time to think about it." Brandi was a woman, a single mother, maybe she could tell him what he'd done wrong. "I need your opinion on something. Let's say a guy goes all out. He buys you the house—"

"You bought her a house?"

"Yeah, on Mirror Lake. Across from Chance and

Vivi's place. It needs some work, but...Anyway, obviously the first proposal didn't go according to plan, so I asked again." He told her everything he said. Even got a little emotional himself because that's how heartfelt the proposal had been. He glanced at Brandi to see if she was tearing up. "Great proposal, right? She totally should have said yes right there and then."

Brandi raised her eyebrows at him. "Were you proposing to the baby or Jill?"

"It's the same thing, isn't it? They're a package deal."

"Sometimes I think there's a reason I stay single," she said as if speaking to herself, then she placed her hands on her thighs and leaned forward. "Sawyer, you're a great guy. Jill knows that. She doesn't need to marry you to know you will be there for her and the baby."

"But it'd be better for all of us if we—"

"Men," she sighed. "Sawyer, take me for an example. I'm not in love with you." He raised an eyebrow at her. "Okay, so I totally think you're hot, and I'd do you in a heartbeat. And if you asked me to marry you, I'd be dragging you to the altar. You know why?"

"Ah, no." He probably should have called his mother instead of asking Brandi for advice.

"Because my son needs a father. An amazing man like you who he can look up to and learn to become the stand-up guy I want him to grow up to be. And I'm tired of doing it all on my own. But Jill, she's not like me. She's in love with you, Sawyer." She rolled her eyes when he opened his mouth to argue. "Trust me, a woman knows these things. Jill doesn't need to marry you to give her baby a daddy, she's got that already. She wants to marry a man who loves her as much as she loves him. And you know what, I think you already do."

"Love Jill? Well, yeah, she's always been like—"

She bowed her head and gave it a slight, frustrated shake. "Take my advice, do not tell her you love her like a sister."

"Yeah, right, that'd be kind of... That's not what I meant, anyway. We're friends. I love her like a friend."

She scooted forward on her chair. "Okay, tell me about Jill. Don't think about it. Just say whatever comes to mind when you think of her."

"She's stubborn as hell, that's for sure. Strong. Independent. Loyal to a fault. Funny. A little shy. Doesn't have a clue how amazing she is. She loves her job and this town. Adores her family. Would do anything for anyone. She's selfless. Works harder than anyone I know. She's talented. You wouldn't believe how well she plays the guitar. And her voice when she sings, gets you right here." He patted his chest. "Same as when she smiles. And her eyes, I've never seen eyes that color before. Or the way they..." He sat back in the chair. "Jesus, I'm in love with Jill Flaherty."

"My guess is that you have been for a very long time. You just didn't want to admit it to yourself." She smiled and stood up. "You might want to try proposing to her a third time. Only this time, tell her what you just told me."

"Brandi," he said as she opened the door to leave, "thank you. One day soon, you'll find that guy you're looking for. But until you do, I'm here for you and Trent. That's not going to change."

"I know—" She jerked back as Jack pushed through the door.

"Sorry," he apologized to Brandi, then strode across

the room, slapping his hands on Sawyer's desk. "This has gone on long enough. It's time for you to step up to the plate and take responsibility, Anderson."

Brandi gave him a good-luck look and shut the door. Sawyer wasn't feeling too friendly toward his ex–best friend and future brother-in-law, so he said, "Guess you haven't been on Facebook, dickhead."

Sawyer straightened in his chair, pulled his keyboard toward him, and logged onto the town's Facebook page. There were three photos: one of Jill nearly taking his head off with the paddle, a second one of them falling into the water, the third of them paddling toward shore. He looked closer at that one, smiling when he recalled part of their conversation. And as he studied the angle of the shot, he knew without a doubt who'd taken the photos. Chance had some explaining to do. Then again, now that Sawyer had *hopefully* discovered the way to Jill's heart, the photos would be a nice memento.

Jack released an impatient sigh and came around the desk, leaning over him. "Why the hell did she attack you with the paddle?" He shot him a glare. "What did you do to her now, dickhead?"

"Look closer, dumbass. I asked her to marry me."

Jack leaned toward the screen and grinned, then he frowned. "She said no? Why the hell would she say no?" He sighed and parked his ass on the desk to look at Sawyer. "You screwed up the proposal, didn't you? If you would have asked for my advice, the first thing I would have told you is to rent a rowboat instead of a canoe."

Sawyer leaned back in his chair and crossed his arms.

"You weren't speaking to me or taking my calls, remember? Now I'm not talking to you. So buzz off. I have things to do."

Jack shoved his hand through his hair. "Okay, I deserve that. But you gotta know how I was feeling. It was a shock. She's my sister—"

"And I was your best friend."

"You're not going to make this easy on me, are you?"

"I'm not going to punch you in the face if that's what you're asking."

He winced. "Sorry about that. I didn't break anything, did I?"

He snorted. "Please, you punch like a girl. Always did."

"Really? I'm trying to apologize."

"Make it quick. I have things to do."

"I'm sorry for being an ass"—Jack narrowed his eyes at him when Sawyer gestured for more—"of epic proportions and messing up your pretty face. I love you like a brother, and I've missed you. A lot." He held out his hand. "Can we be friends again, dickhead?"

"Yeah, flyboy," he said, shaking his hand. "We can be friends. And if you get out of my office and I can convince your sister I'm in love with her, we can be brothers-in-law, too."

"Wait... come again? You're in love with *Jill*."

"Yeah, and you wanna tell me why you said it like that? Your sister is an incredible woman. She's sweet and—"

Jack started laughing. "You sure you're talking about my sister? Because Jill isn't exactly—"

"Don't piss me off."

He stared at him. "You're not joking. You are in love with her. I've gotta—" He broke off when his cell phone rang. "Hey, princess. What?" He nodded, glancing at Sawyer. "I'm with him now. We're on our way. Tell her... tell her everything will be all right."

Sawyer saw the concern in Jack's eyes and stood up. "Is it Jill? Did something happen—"

"She's cramping, and she's bleeding."

"How... I don't understand. She's been feeling great. A little tired, but... They can stop it, can't they?"

"They're on their way to the hospital. Let's go, buddy. Come on, I'll drive you."

\* \* \*

Dr. Evans, Christmas General's resident ob-gyn, touched Jill's arm. "I'm very sorry for your loss. If you have any questions or you just want to talk to someone, please call me." She gave Sawyer's shoulder a gentle squeeze as she walked out of the hospital room.

He dragged the chair closer to the bed and stroked Jill's cheek. Her face was pale and pinched, her eyes bloodshot and swollen. His throat ached, his eyes burning from holding back his own emotions. He wanted to say something that would take the devastated look from her face. If only for a few minutes. He wanted her to know they were in this together. But he could feel her slipping away from him, building up her walls. "Jill, honey, please look at me."

She slowly turned her head. "It's over. You don't have to stick around anymore."

"Don't shut me out." He brushed her damp hair from

her face. "We'll deal with this together. I love you. Just tell me what I can do—"

She curled her fingers around the sheets. "Don't say that. You don't have to tell me you love me."

"I know I don't, but I do. I do love you, Jill. I want to marry you."

A tear rolled down her cheek. "Please go. Please just leave me alone," she whispered.

"I know you were the one carrying the baby, but I'm hurting, too. I want to be with you."

"Don't you think I can't see it in your eyes? You blame me," she half cried, half yelled. "It's my fault I lost the baby. I didn't eat like you told me to or slow down at work or get—"

He took her by the shoulders and gently shook her. "Stop it. Stop it right now. I don't blame you. You heard the doctor. There was nothing you could do. Nothing you did wrong. It just happens sometimes." He went to pull her into his arms.

"Get out. Just get out. I don't want to talk to you. I don't want to do this." She pushed him away.

He bowed his head, scrubbing his hands over his face, then slowly came to his feet. "If you need me, just call." She rolled on her side, facing away from him. He wanted to crawl in beside her and take her in his arms, but she didn't want him. He felt like he'd not only lost the baby, but he'd lost Jill, too.

Grace, Jack, and Matt were standing in the hall. They turned when he walked out of the room. Grace crossed to him and wrapped her arms around him. "Oh, Sawyer, I'm so very sorry."

He held her for a minute and then pulled back and

rubbed his eyes. "She won't...She doesn't want me, but she needs somebody. Go to her, Grace. Make her understand this wasn't her fault. I don't blame her."

Her eyes filled, and she gave him another hug. "She knows that. She's just hurting. We're here for both of you. Whatever you need—"

"I need you to go to her, Grace," he said.

"I'll do that right now. It's going to be okay, Sawyer. I promise it will," she said before heading to Jill's room.

Sawyer heard Grace trying to comfort Jill as the door closed behind her. His hands balled into fists at the sound of Jill crying. He squeezed his eyes shut and strong arms closed around him. "I'm here for you, buddy. We'll get through this together. Whatever you need, you've got."

He nodded as he pulled back from Jack's embrace. "Thanks," he said, his voice gruff. "I'll be fine. It's Jill I'm worried about."

"So am I. But you're hurting, too."

"She doesn't want to see me. I think I've lost her, Jack."

Matt came to stand beside them and handed Sawyer a cup of coffee. "Give her time. It's not uncommon for women who've miscarried to push the people they love away. On top of the grief, even to carry on a conversation can feel overwhelming. The next few days will be tough. Hormones will make it worse."

"What can I say to stop her from blaming herself?" Sawyer asked Matt.

"It won't matter what you say. It's a natural reaction. And that's about all you can keep telling her. Everything she's feeling is natural and normal. But Jack's right, you have a right to grieve, too." He gave Sawyer's shoulder a comforting squeeze. "Call me anytime if you need to talk. Jill can go home whenever she's ready."

"Okay. Thanks, doc," Sawyer said, looking up when Grace came out of the room. She wouldn't meet his eyes. "She doesn't want to see me, does she?"

"She wants to be alone right now. I'm going to take her home and stay with her as long as she'll let me. Why don't you go home with Jack? Call her tomorrow."

He called her every day, e-mailed and texted, too. When he couldn't keep away any longer, he went to her apartment. She wouldn't answer the door. He dropped off things he thought she needed, leaving them outside her door. They were always gone the next day. He tried to reach out to her through Grace, and Jack, but she'd cut them off, too.

Two weeks later, he couldn't do it anymore and gave up.

# Chapter Twenty-Three

Jill sat on the couch eating one of the blueberry scones Sawyer had left outside her door yesterday. It had been her birthday. She didn't feel like celebrating then or now. Didn't feel much like doing anything. Other than eating the scone. Surprising since she hadn't felt like eating anything since she'd lost the baby. She waited for the tears and anger to come at the memory of that day. All she felt was...numb.

She supposed that was an improvement. Feeling nothing was better than dealing with the crippling emotions—the guilt and heartbreak—of the past two weeks. But somehow she had to find a way to move on. Or at the very least to pretend she was. She hadn't been out of her apartment since the night Grace had brought her home. Hadn't talked to anyone or responded to their texts or calls. She'd crawled inside herself and stayed there. But Gage would be understanding for only so long. She couldn't afford to lose her job on top of everything else.

At the sound of someone knocking on her apartment door, she closed her eyes. She didn't want to face Sawyer. Didn't want to see the pain and confusion in his eyes. The accusation he'd tried to hide. Didn't want to remember the days and nights they'd spent together. How close she'd come to having her dreams come true. The only thing that had been missing was his love.

Real love. True love.

He may have said the words, but he didn't mean them. If he did, he would have told her the night he proposed. He'd had two chances. His second proposal had been more telling than the first. It had been all about the baby. And the baby was gone.

The pain hit her like a shot in the dark, leaving her gasping for air and her chest aching. And for the first time she acknowledged that her heartbreak was not only about losing the baby but for the loss of Sawyer as well. But she didn't have a chance to fall apart because someone was knocking on her living room window. Her eyes shot open to see Ty standing on her deck with his hands cupped to the glass, peering in at her. His eyes bugged out behind his glasses before he covered his reaction to what she imagined was her sorry-ass self.

"Jilly Bean, I need your help. Nell's going to ruin Cat and Grayson's wedding," he yelled through the window.

They weren't getting married until the twenty-fourth, she thought with a frown. It couldn't be...It *was* the twenty-fourth. She placed the scone on the coffee table and pushed to her feet, mentally preparing herself for Ty's sympathy and condolences. It's what she'd been avoiding. In the beginning, she'd tried to pretend the doctors were wrong. That her child was still safe and growing inside her. She'd held onto the fantasy as long as she could.

She opened the sliding door. "Are you crazy? You could have fallen and broken a leg."

"I know." He checked behind him. "Or ripped my pants." Then he gave her a quick up-and-down look—not doing a very good job hiding his shudder—and put his hands on his narrow hips. "And it would have been your fault. Next time, answer your door. Go hop in the shower; we're losing precious time. Wedding's in five hours."

She sighed as he walked past her. "Stop sniffing me. I don't smell. And I'm not going anywhere," she said, closing the door behind him.

"Ah, yes you are. You promised last month, and I need you to deal with Nell. She replaced the beautiful crystal glasses I ordered from the supplier with...mason jars." He scrunched up his face and raised his hands. "Who does that? We better hurry before she wrecks my vision for the big day. And I still have four heads of hair to do."

"Ty, I'm not—"

He put his hands on her shoulders, the sympathy she'd been grateful he hadn't offered shining in his eyes. "Your little girl would have been as beautiful and as strong as her mama. You are strong, Jilly Bean. You'll get there, but not by hiding away in your apartment."

She bowed her head, a tear rolling down her cheek before she could stop it. Her throat tightened painfully. She'd needed to know if she'd been carrying a boy or a girl. Though over the past week, she'd sometimes regretted that she'd asked Dr. Evans to do the test. And even as a spurt of anger flared inside her at Ty's accusation that she was hiding in her apartment, she knew he was right.

"I'd give you a hug, but I think I'll wait until you've had a shower," he teased, ignoring her show of emotion as he turned her toward the bedroom.

"I'll go, but I'm not staying for the wedding," she said as she reached the doorway.

"Oh, dear God," he said, surveying her room. "You get in the shower, and I'll take care of"—he waved his hand—"this."

"You don't have to clean my—"

"Go," he ordered, pointing to the bathroom door.

As she stood in the shower, some of the tension and pain she'd kept bottled up inside swirled down the drain. Ten minutes later, when she turned off the water, she could hear Ty talking to himself in her bedroom in his typical dramatic fashion—several *oh, my Gods* followed by clapping. A rusty laugh escaped from her mouth, startling her. She'd thought it would take months before she felt like laughing again. Ty flung open the door before the small pang of guilt took hold.

"Ty, I could have been naked!" She scowled at him as she tightened the towel around her chest, steam billowing around them. Her bedroom was freezing. She glanced beyond him. Her window was wide open, the wooden blinds billowing and clacking.

"We have to hurry." He dragged her out of the bathroom. "Chloe decided she wants an updo instead of wearing her hair down. She's such a drama queen. Now I have both her and Nell to deal with. Thank God, I have you. Get dressed and don't forget your gun. Two hawks were circling the tent this morning."

"I'm not shooting a hawk, so you can forget about me bringing my gun. Besides, the wedding's at five; they won't be around by then." She looked around her room, which was spotless. There was fresh bedding on her bed and a vase of orange chrysanthemums on her nightstand. "Thank you, you didn't have to do…" She tilted her head. "My neighbor had a pot of those on her deck. Did you steal them?"

"Maybe." He grinned and shoved a dress in her hands.

It was the red dress she'd worn to the bar. She cleared her throat. "I told you. I'm not staying for the wedding." She turned, grabbing a pair of jeans and a hoodie from her closet.

\* \* \*

She shouldn't have let Ty talk her into coming, Jill thought as they drove through the decorated wrought-iron gates of the O'Connor ranch. Of the eight vehicles parked in the circular drive, she recognized seven of them. But Ty had taken a cab to her place so she'd had to drive him here. Didn't mean she had to stay though.

"I don't believe her," Ty muttered, ordering Jill to stop the Jeep. She'd barely pulled to the side of the drive-way when he jumped out to rip orange bows from the gates. He tossed them in the backseat. "Might as well park here," he said.

That suited Jill. Less likely that someone would block her escape. She locked the Jeep and joined him on the walk up the circular drive to the elegant stone bungalow. "Oh good God, I'm afraid to see what else she's gotten up to," he said when they reached the dark Spanish-style double doors, ripping off heart-shaped yellow wreaths fastened with orange ribbon to the doors. "I swear the woman is color blind."

"They're not bad, Ty."

"The color scheme is aubergine and cream, Jilly Bean. Not yellow and orange." He looked around the front porch, made a face, then removed two tasteful wreaths from behind the large planters that held branches decorated in white lights. The wreaths, obviously Ty's handiwork, were made up of cream tulle and elegant deep purple flowers. He looked at her as he stuck them on the door. "I'm counting on you to keep her busy while I'm finishing up the bridal party's hair and makeup. Check the barn to make sure she hasn't been adding more of her *special* touches in there," he said as he opened the door.

Jill didn't understand what Nell would be doing in the barn until she remembered Chloe telling her—with a sniff of her small upturned nose—that both the dinner and reception were being held there. Not the barn that housed the horses of course. When they walked into the foyer to discover more of Nell's *special* touches, Jill figured she should have brought a pair of handcuffs with her. Ty looked ready to commit murder.

Feminine laughter greeted them as they walked toward the kitchen. Jill rubbed her sweaty palms on her jeans when she recognized Grace's, Madison's, and Skye's voices. She was just about to tell Ty she'd head to the barn when she made out their conversation.

"Poor Gage, he was running all over town last night trying to find me dill pickles. It must be a girl. I never had cravings with Connor," Madison said.

"I'm pretty sure I'm having a boy. I was never this sick with Evie," Skye said. "Delivery day can't come soon enough. Are you feeling better, Grace?"

"Much better, thanks. I could do without the heartburn

though. But if I end up with a little girl with her daddy's gorgeous head of... Why are you both—" She broke off and turned around. Her face fell. "Oh, Jill sweetie, I'm so sorry. I didn't... We didn't know you were there. We never—"

Jill curled her fingers at her sides, her nails stabbing her palms as a wave of anger and hurt rushed through her. It was so unfair. They already had beautiful babies. Why couldn't she have just one? All she wanted was one. A happy baby girl with her daddy's gorgeous hair and eyes. What did she do wrong? Didn't she deserve to be happy, too? Hadn't her life been crappy enough growing up with a mother who didn't love her enough to stick around, a grandmother who didn't want her, and then a man who only wanted her because of the baby she carried.

She dug her nails so hard into her palms she was sure she drew blood. "Don't worry about it," she said in a voice devoid of emotion, even though she was practically seething with it. "I'll head to the barn, Ty." She turned and walked away without looking at the women.

"Jill, wait." Grace came after her. "Please, wait."

She stopped at the mudroom door, staring out at a stand of aspen trees. Their ghostly branches were almost barren of leaves. She'd always loved this time of year; now it just reminded her of death. She'd felt the same as a little girl, but she'd grown past it as a teenager. Now here she was full circle.

"I'm so sorry, Jill. The last thing I want to do is remind—"

"Yeah, well, that'll be a little tough seeing as you're pregnant and I'm not. Maybe you guys should think about how lucky you are instead of complaining about a little heartburn and morning sickness," she said, shoving the door open and letting it slam behind her. She regretted the words as soon as they were out of her mouth. But it didn't make them any less true. And she didn't know if she could face Grace and apologize. She would, just not now. She had to get out of there. She heard the mudroom door open behind her as she headed for the front of the house.

"Jill, wait."

She bowed her head at the sound of the familiar voice, then glanced over her shoulder. "Nell, I can't stay. I—" She broke off at the look of sympathy and understanding on the older woman's face.

"Come with me, girlie. We need to talk. Just you and me."

Maybe because what Jill needed most these past couple of weeks wasn't a friend, or a brother, or a lover, but a mother, she nodded. They walked in silence across the yard. Nell stopped at the small bridge that separated the O'Connors' home from the barns and outbuildings. She leaned on the railing, patting the spot beside her. They stood there for a few moments listening to the gurgle of the stream beneath them before Nell broke the silence. "You see those rocks?"

Jill nodded, and Nell continued, "They're like us, girlie. The water's our troubles. Over time, if it finds its way into the cracks, freezes, and expands, the rocks weaken and break apart. But you heal those cracks and it smooths over the hard edges and ridges, and makes you stronger."

"I feel like God's punishing me, Nell. That I did something so horrible I'm not meant to be happy."

"Your grandmother was a friend, but that doesn't mean I always agreed with her or how she raised you kids. Told Jack the same thing. She'd get some damn fool notions in her head, and I can see she put them in yours." She shifted and looked at Jill. "You were a parent, not for long, but you were. You may not have held your baby girl in your arms, but you held her in your heart. If you could, would you have done everything in your power to protect her?"

"Of course. Of course I would."

"So why wouldn't God do the same for you? He doesn't make bad things happen, Jill. They just do. That's life. But he's there to lift you up, to show you a way through the difficult times. He puts people in your life who will do the same. If you let Him, and them. Last thing those women in there meant to do was hurt you. Gracie would cut off her arm for you. But you know that, don't you? We've all seen our share of troubles, Gracie, Skye, Maddie, Liz, Chloe, and Cat. Not anyone in this town who hasn't. Look at your brother."

Jill closed her eyes. Nell was right. No one knew that better than her. Compared to what some of them had suffered, her loss must seem insignificant in comparison. They hadn't hidden away like she had. They'd dealt with their pain head-on. They were stronger for it, too. The thought wasn't helpful. It brought back the old feelings that she was not enough. Not strong enough. Not good enough.

"No, don't go comparing what you've suffered to anyone else. You're entitled to your grief. Everyone deals with their sorrow differently. One way's no better than the other. I'm just saying that everyone in there, everyone in town, can empathize with your pain. They're here for you. Just tell us what you need. You have a lot of folks who love you, girlie. You just have to let us in. Sawyer, too. Men don't show it like we do, but he's hurting, too."

"I can't, Nell. You don't know him like I do. It's better this way."

"Take it from me, I learned the hard way, Jill. Don't shut him out. You don't let him back in, he'll move on."

"Are you talking about Calder?"

Nell nodded. "I got pregnant when I was seventeen. Last year of high school, it was early June. I'd never been as scared and angry as I was the day I found out. Couldn't tell anyone, not in those days. It was worse because of our parents. They didn't want us to see each other, but we were in love. We'd talked about Calder coming with me when I left for school. We'd get married, start a life away from Christmas. And then I found out I was pregnant."

She looked down at the water splashing against the rocks. "I was furious at him, blamed him for the baby as if I hadn't played any part in it. And then in late August I woke up in the middle of the night to god-awful cramps and my sheets soaked with blood. I'd lost the baby. Just as I had become accustomed to the idea of having one, I lost it. I thought God was punishing me, too."

Jill stared at Nell as though seeing her for the first time. "What did you do? Did your parents find out?"

"No. I got myself cleaned up as best as I could. Changed the bed, then rolled up the sheets and went out in the backyard and buried them. The baby, too, I guess. Two days later, I went off to college. Didn't say good-bye to Calder, just left. Felt a lot like I imagine you did these past couple weeks. But I didn't have anyone. Not many women went to college in my day, so I had lots of time to think, and I came to realize how unfair I'd been to Calder. How much I missed him." She lifted a shoulder. "How much I loved him. Planned to tell him when I came home on the Christmas break. First thing my mother says to me when I walk in the door is that no-good Dane boy is getting married."

"I'm so sorry, Nell. I don't know how you dealt with it all by yourself."

She arched an eyebrow. "Isn't that what you've been doing the past two weeks?"

"It's not the same. You didn't have anyone to turn to. My God, Nell, you took care of everything by yourself. And you were so young." Jill squeezed her hand. She couldn't imagine what that would have been like.

"If I'd let him, Calder would have been there for me. So would Stella and Evelyn and Ted and Fred. Though they probably would have killed Calder."

"Why didn't you go to him that Christmas? Tell him that you loved him."

She gave her a sad smile. "I did, but it was too late. Calder's a lot like Sawyer. He's a good man, an honorable one. He didn't want to hurt Meredith. And in his own way he loved her. They had a happy marriage. Raised two fine sons and a daughter and had a passel of grandchildren."

And Nell ended up alone.

"I know what you're thinking, Jill. But I've had a good life. You don't have to grow a child in your belly to love it or to be loved in return. I've had that with Paul and the boys. Maddie and the girls. You should know that. You've had the same with little Jack."

Jill's eyes filled. She couldn't speak so she nodded. It took a moment for the muscles in her throat to relax. She swiped at her eyes and looked at Nell. "You could still have your happy ever after, Nell. I've seen the way Calder looks at you."

"And I've seen the way Sawyer looks at you."

"He doesn't love me. He's doing what Calder did with Meredith. He's doing the honorable thing."

"So the man buys you a house, asks you to marry him, shows up at your apartment every day for two weeks to bring you food and flowers because he's being honorable?" She laughed and shook her head. "And here I thought your generation was supposed to be smarter than ours."

"Nell, I said white votive bags along the aisle, not pumpkins," Ty yelled, gesticulating wildly from where he stood in front of the tree where Cat and Grayson would be married.

"Halloween's a week away. You have to have pumpkins," Nell yelled back at him. "Now come on, I want to show you what I've done to the barn."

"Thank you, Nell. Your talk, saying what you did, it meant a lot to me," she said, hugging the older woman. "It helped."

Nell patted her back. "Anytime. You always had your brother, then Sawyer, and Grace, so I didn't think you needed me. I would have stuck my nose in long before this if I thought you did. You're my people, too, Jill. Remember that."

She smiled, her stupid throat closing up on her again. "I'll just go help Ty, and I probably should go talk to Grace and the girls. I'll see you in the barn in a few minutes."

It took her several moments to calm Ty down about

the pumpkins. She helped him replace them with the paper votive bags, then she went inside and apologized to Grace. Jill allowed the women to pull her into the wedding chatter and fun. She talked to Chloe for a bit and Cat, who looked stunning in a floor-length cream sheath wedding dress. Thanks to Nell's talk, Jill was able to act like her normal self, even if she hadn't quite gotten there yet. Her smiles were more fake than genuine. But she felt like she was taking a step in the right direction. Until she went to the barn to check on Nell.

Sawyer was setting up a bar in the far corner with Brandi. He had on a black suit, and Brandi had on a tight black lace dress that hit her mid-thigh. They were laughing. Jill didn't know what hurt more, that they looked beautiful and happy together or that Sawyer was able to laugh. A natural, normal laugh. While all she could do was fake it. It didn't seem fair, and worse, it seemed like he'd already gotten over the baby. And her.

As though he sensed her watching them, he glanced up. Jill left the barn. She heard him call her name and kept walking, stopping when he grabbed her arm.

"So that's how it's going to be? Every time you see me, you're going to walk away?"

She slowly turned, keeping her eyes on his white shirt, the open button at the collar. "I didn't want to interrupt you. I'm not good company right now. And you looked like you were having a good time."

"Just because I was laughing doesn't mean I don't hurt, too, Jill. You don't hold the monopoly on grief." He blew out a breath and looked away. "I've been trying to reach you for two weeks. Two weeks...and nothing, not one word. I thought we had something. I thought you—"

"We had a baby together, and now we don't."

He searched her face, then gave her a curt nod. "I won't bother you anymore," he said and turned to walk away.

"Sawyer," she practically yelled his name, the fear that she'd lost him for good coming out in her voice. She cringed at the needy, pleading tone. "Thank you for everything you did for me these last few weeks. I know it's been hard for you, too. I'm sorry I couldn't be there for you. I-I hope someone was."

The light she saw in his eyes when she called him back faded. His face went hard. "Lots of people. Only not the one I wanted. But we don't always get what we want, do we, Jill?"

\* \* \*

The gorgeous blonde wrote her number on a napkin, then leaned over the makeshift bar and slid it into the pocket of Sawyer's jacket. She took her time doing so and smiled up at him. "Call me anytime or drop by the set." She was an actress who had a part in the movie with Chloe. They were filming in Aspen.

He nodded and gave her a smile. He'd already told her he wasn't interested. But she was the type of woman who wouldn't take no for answer. There'd been a couple of them tonight.

Jack approached the bar, turning to watch the woman walk away. He raised an eyebrow at Sawyer. "You wanna tell me why you're letting women give you their numbers when you're in love with my sister?"

His chest tightened at Jack's mention of Jill. When

he'd looked up to see her in the barn, all the anger and frustration he'd been feeling for the past two weeks vanished. He'd wanted to go to her, take her in his arms, and just hold on to her like he'd wanted to since the day they'd lost the baby. Thinking she'd come to apologize for shutting him out. To tell him they were going to be fine, that she loved him. He couldn't have been more wrong.

"Don't know why you care. Your sister sure as hell doesn't."

Jack winced. "You know Jill. She just needs some more time. Grace said she was here earlier. She overheard the girls talking about their pregnancies. It was hard on her. She was upset."

His jaw clenched. "I know how she feels. What can I get you to drink?"

"Hey"—he touched Sawyer's arm—"you think I don't know it's been hard on you, too? Who have you been hanging out with these past couple weeks? I get it, buddy. I do. But she was the one carrying the baby. It makes it more—"

He didn't need Jack to remind him it was more difficult for Jill. He knew that. Knew what she was going through both mentally and physically. Matt had been by the bar a couple times to check up on him and explain things. "I didn't just lose the baby, I lost Jill, too."

"Come on, you haven't lost her. Don't give up on her. She loves you, and you love her."

"You weren't there. You didn't see her. If she was ever in love with me, she isn't now." Since the night at his apartment, she hadn't once told him she loved him. And he was beginning to doubt she ever did. "Think about it, Jack. If something like this happened to you and Grace, you'd pull together. It wouldn't rip you apart."

"I hear you, but it's not the same. You guys got together because of the baby. And now—"

"There's no reason to be. Jill said pretty much the same thing. She looks like hell, Jack. Her clothes are hanging off her. She's looks like she's lost twenty pounds. Her eyes are swallowing her face, and she's pale. You and Grace have to make her let you in." He'd been shocked when she turned to face him. He'd wanted to scoop her up in his arms and take her home and feed her. Kiss away the pain in her eyes.

"Or maybe you have to, Sawyer. You love her. If I didn't think you did before, I know you do now."

In every e-mail, in every text, he'd told Jill how much he loved her. He'd even bought her the damn house she wanted. He'd been working out there every chance he got in hopes they'd get back together. He'd run around buying stuff that he thought might make her smile, help her deal with the pain, and left them at her door like a lovesick schoolboy. "I gave it my best shot. It wasn't good enough. I'm done."

# Chapter Twenty-Four

Jack sat wedged between a branch and the trunk, hammering a nail to secure the witch to the tree. Harder than Jill thought was necessary, but then again, he was ticked at her. He lifted the witch riding a broomstick and stared down at her. "This is how you're acting, only substitute the W with a B."

"You did not just call me a…" She looked around for her nephew, then remembered Grace had taken him inside to help dip the candy apples in sprinkles "…B. I. T. C. H." She spelled it out to be on the safe side.

"That's exactly what I'm calling you. You broke my best friend's heart."

Her brother had been on her case about Sawyer since Cat and Grayson's wedding last week. Until today she let him talk. She hadn't been in the mood to argue or fight back. But she was starting to feel more like herself again. "Give it a flipping rest. He is not *in love* with me. He loves me like he loves you and Grace and little Jack."

"Really? I didn't talk to him for over a month. He left four messages for me. How many did he leave for you? Don't remember him showing up at my place for two weeks straight, either."

Everything that she loved, that had some special meaning for her, he'd dropped at her door. Like the iPod loaded with all her favorites songs. Gibson guitar picks and strings for her guitar. A framed photo of them falling out of the canoe. One of her feeding the ducks down by the boardwalk with little Jack. Bottles of Gold Rush and her favorite scones.

"And you know what, Jill? Sawyer Anderson does not lie. Never has and never will. He told me he was *in love* with you, and I believe him. Maybe it's time you start believing him, too. Because honey, there's a lot of women out there who would be more than happy to take your place."

She stared up at him. "He told you he loved me?" Jack gave her a clipped nod. "Before or after I lost the baby?"

"Before and after, and what does that have to do with anything?" He pointed his hammer at her. "Don't answer. Don't overthink it and make excuses. Just put the man out of his misery and tell him you love him. Unless you don't."

"I do...I do love him. I just thought..."

"Stop thinking and go to him before it's too late."

She didn't like what he seemed to be implying. "Has he been seeing someone else?"

"Not that I know of. But he's been hanging out at Brandi's quite a bit this past week. The three of them went out for dinner last night to celebrate the win in court. Heard from a reliable source they were looking pretty cozy." He grinned. "Nice to see your scowl back. Get going and make my best friend a happy man."

"I'll drop by and see him after work. I'm off at four."

"Okay, the guy bought you a house and showered you with presents, did everything he could think of to win you back, and you're going to…drop by after work? Seriously, you don't have a romantic bone in your body."

\* \* \*

"Your brother's right. You have no game," Suze said.

Jill should have kept her mouth shut instead of sharing her plan to apologize to Sawyer—and Jack's opinion of it—with her friend. "What's wrong with my plan? He loves the pizza from the diner, and he loves Grace's pumpkin spice cupcakes, too." After Jack's reaction Jill had added an impromptu dinner before asking Suze what she thought. For the most part Sawyer's attempts to feed her had annoyed her, but looking back now, Jill found them sweetly romantic. So she'd taken a page from his playbook.

"As apologies go, it's not horrible. But Jill, you rejected the guy's proposal, and he went all out. Like the most epically romantic proposal of all time."

"It wasn't that great. We fell in the lake," she muttered. Suze's comparison of Sawyer's romantic gesture to Jill's made her realize just how pathetic hers was.

"He bought you your dream house, girlfriend. And let's not forget the trouble he went to the past couple of weeks trying to get you to let him back in."

Jill rested her elbows on Suze's desk and buried her face in her hands. A romantic dinner wouldn't come close to making up for what she'd put him through. Sawyer was one of the kindest men she knew. He was also laid-back and easygoing. But he wasn't a pushover. He could be as tough and as unbending as the next man. She thought back to the day at the barn. Both the expression on his face and the look in his eyes didn't bode well for a reconciliation. She was worried she'd pushed him away one too many times.

Suze pulled Jill's hands from her face and dipped her head to look into her eyes. "He knows what you were dealing with. We all did."

Suze had forgiven Jill for not letting her in. Everyone had. But Jill hadn't been the only one who'd been hurting. She should have been there for Sawyer. "I think I hurt him pretty bad, Suze. I'm not sure he's willing to give me a second chance. In his place, I don't know if I would."

"And that's why you've gotta pull out all the stops. Leave no doubt in that man's mind that you love him."

She didn't fail to notice that Suze didn't argue with her. As hooked into Christmas's gossip as Suze was, Jill wondered if she knew more about where Sawyer's head was at than she did. "Jack mentioned that Sawyer, Brandi, and Trent were out for dinner last night. He said...He heard they were looking pretty cozy."

Suze avoided looking at her. "I'm sure they were just relieved the judge ruled in Brandi's favor and wanted to celebrate."

"Show me the picture, Suze."

"I can't sign into Facebook when we're at work. Now let's get back to the plan."

Jill would have laughed if not for her growing worry that the picture revealed that Sawyer and Brandi were looking more than cozy. "Be serious, you spend half your shift on social media. Just show—"

"What are you girls up to?" Ray asked as he and Brad walked into the station. Gage had finally given in to Ray's demands that he be allowed out on patrol. But only if another deputy was with him.

Jill didn't miss that Suze looked more than a little relieved by the interruption. "Get over here. We need a guy's opinion." They came over to Suze's desk, and she proceeded to tell them about Jill's plan to win back Sawyer.

Jill wondered how her plan to apologize—now she was thinking more on the lines of groveling—had become a plan to win him back. Obviously Jill knew it was a win-him-back plan, but when had it become one in Suze's mind? Jill already knew the answer—right after she brought up Sawyer and Brandi's night out.

"That's easy. Show up in a trench coat with nothing underneath and wear a pair of hooker heels. Works every time," Brad said.

Ray, who was blushing to the roots of his hair, nodded. "Maybe a fur coat and boots. It's getting a little chilly out."

Jill bowed her head and groaned.

They all looked over when Gage came out of his office and straightened, pretending they were working. But their boss didn't pay any attention to them. He was on the phone. "Okay, take it easy, honey. I'm sure Annie is fine."

The four of them looked at each other. That didn't sound good. As soon as Gage disconnected, Jill asked, "Everything okay?"

Her boss rubbed the back of his neck and glanced at

them. "It's parent-teacher interviews at the school today. Annie was supposed to be helping Aunt Nell decorate at Mountainview for the Halloween party. Trent was going with her. They headed out on their bikes about an hour ago. Aunt Nell said they haven't shown up, and Madison can't reach Annie on her cell phone."

Jill did her best to hide her reaction to the news. She wouldn't be surprised if the teens had stopped along the way for a little make-out session. Not something she'd share with Annie's father. "I'm sure they're fine. They probably just got sidetracked. I'll head over to Mountainview," Jill offered, happy for the opportunity to get out of the station. At least she wouldn't have to listen to any more win-back-Sawyer plans. "Why don't you give Brandi a call and see if the kids stopped by her place?"

Gage nodded. "I will. Let me know as soon as you find them."

"For sure," she said and headed out of the station.

As she walked to her patrol car, Brandi was opening the door to the Penalty Box. The curvy blonde had on leopard print leggings, an over-the-butt black sweater, and a pair of short black boots with killer heels. Her long hair was as wild as the leggings she had on. She had the look of a woman on the prowl.

And Jill had a fairly good idea who she was hunting down. It appeared she'd also brought food to entice her prey. Jill had no doubt the bakery box in Brandi's hands contained Sawyer's favorite cupcakes. So much for her win-back-Sawyer plan, and looking at Brandi, Jill wondered if she should even bother coming up with a new one.

But she wouldn't let her jealousy stop her from doing

her job. "Brandi, did Trent and Annie stop by your place?"

"No, they're helping out at Mountainview." Her brow furrowed. "Why, is something wrong?"

"Nell says they haven't arrived yet. I'm sure everything's fine. You know what kids are like, they're probably goofing around. I'm heading over there now. I'll have Trent call you when I catch up with them."

"Hang on, I'll call him. Save you a trip." Brandi fumbled the bakery box as she went to retrieve her phone from her bag.

"Careful, you don't want to drop your pumpkin spice cupcakes," Jill said, regretting the words as soon as Brandi confirmed that they were.

"How did you know that's what's in the box?" she asked as she put her phone to her ear.

"I could smell them," Jill lied. It was better than telling the woman she'd guessed it was part of her plan to seduce her boss. Jill couldn't help but wonder if it would work. It's not like she'd given Sawyer any reason to hold out hope for them. She'd made a lot of mistakes in her life, but Jill was beginning to think this was the worst. She thought about calling him while she waited for Brandi to reach Trent. She'd already checked out his usual parking spot and knew his truck wasn't there. She decided against it. Making up over the phone or via texts was as bad as breaking up that way.

"Trent, call me when you get this. I better hear from you within the next fifteen minutes, buddy, or you're in big trouble." She looked at Jill, a hint of worry shadowing her eyes. "I tried a couple of times, and it went straight to voice mail."

"Cell service can be spotty on the road up to Mountainview. Don't waste your energy worrying. I'll find them, and I'll call you as soon as I do."

"Okay, I'm sure you're right. Thanks, Jill," Brandi called out as Jill reached the cruiser. "I'm sorry about the baby. I know how excited you both were. Sawyer…" She trailed off and forced a smile. "I'm glad you're back to work. Let me know as soon as you find the kids."

"Yep, will do," Jill said, forcing a lightness to her voice that she didn't feel. Over the last couple of days, she'd gotten better at accepting the offers of sympathy and condolences. It wasn't as painful as it had been. Every day got a little easier. But she felt a sharp stab in the vicinity of her heart at the realization that, while she hadn't been there to comfort Sawyer, Brandi had. And that was on Jill.

She got in the cruiser and radioed into the station instead of wasting time running back in. "Let Gage know that the kids aren't at Brandi's place. She tried to call Trent, and he's not answering his cell, either," Jill informed Suze.

"Umhm, I bet he's not. You might want to check out the abandoned farm on Ridge Road. Lots of kids go there to make out and party." As the mother of two teenage boys, Suze would know.

"Thanks. I'll keep that in mind. Gage and Madison might want to start giving Annie's friends a call, though."

"I think they've already started. He's getting a bit antsy."

Jill could sympathize. "Won't take me more than ten minutes to reach Mountainview. Hopefully we can put his worries to rest by then."

Five minutes later Jill knew that wouldn't be the case. In the field bordering the road to the nursing home, sunlight glinted off chrome. Jill pulled onto the loose gravel and got out of the cruiser to cross the field. There was a black bike and a purple one lying half on, half off each other. They looked like they'd been tossed there.

"Annie, Trent," she called out. There was a stand of trees about three hundred yards in front of her that would have afforded the teens some measure of privacy. But her cop's instincts were telling her there was more going on than a couple of kids making out in the woods. She jogged back through the field and then walked along the side of the road searching for clues. Twenty yards in front of her cruiser, she spotted what she was looking for. Tire tracks and signs of a struggle. She ran back to the patrol car and jumped inside. As she gunned the engine and pulled a U-turn, she radioed it in.

For a brief moment, she second-guessed what she was about to say. Her confidence in her abilities had taken a hard hit when little Jack went missing. But if she was right they didn't have any time to waste. And if she was wrong, she'd look like a complete fool, but she was willing to take that risk. "Suze, put an APB out on Steve Dawson's pickup." She quickly explained what she'd discovered and what she thought had happened.

"Oh God, no, Jill. How am I going to tell Gage? He's going to freaking lose it. I'm losing it, and they're not even my kids. Crap, Brandi just walked in."

"Keep the line open and tell Ray and Brad what's going on. Get Ray to question Brandi about Steve. She may have an idea where he is. Then get Brad on the phone to Steve's probation officer."

"And Gage?"

"Give me two minutes to check on something and then patch me through to him," she said, then tried to call Sawyer. Her call went straight to voice mail, and her heart started to race. She ordered herself to keep it together and called her brother. "Jack," she said as soon as he answered. "Where's Sawyer?"

"About time you got your—"

"Jack, I don't have time for this. Do you know where Sawyer is?"

"He and Calder were going to take inventory at the plant." She turned on the siren, pulled another U-turn, and floored it. "Jill, what's going on?"

"If I'm right, Steve abducted Annie and Trent, and he's going after Sawyer next. He blamed Sawyer for keeping him away from his wife and son, and now with the judge ruling against him, my bet is he's out for revenge." She didn't know how she could so calmly recite her theory, and what that meant for the man she loved, when her insides were frozen with fear. And then, because she knew her brother so well, she added, "Do not go anywhere near the plant, Jack. I mean it. I'll update you when I have a chance."

"I can't just sit here and do nothing. He's my best friend, and he's in trouble."

"I've got him, Jack. I'm not going to let anything happen to him. I've gotta go." Just as she disconnected, Gage's voice came over the radio. She could hear a hysterical Brandi in the background. Jill told him the same thing she'd told Jack, then added, "He has no reason to harm Trent and Annie, Gage. Just remember that, okay?"

He needed something to hang on to. So did she. The knowledge that Sawyer was smart, in great shape, and strong helped. Both physically and mentally, Steve Dawson was no match for Sawyer. He could take the man easily. Unless Steve was armed. Jill would like to believe that as an ex-con it would be impossible for him to get a gun, but she knew that wasn't necessarily true. Where there was a will, there was a way. And he didn't need a permit for a knife.

"Where are you?" Gage asked, his voice low and gruff.

She turned off the siren. "Five minutes from the plant."

"How the hell did you get there so fast...Never mind, just hang back until you have backup. We should be there within twenty minutes."

"Too long," she said as the cruiser jolted over the bumps and dips on the dirt road. She slowed down. She didn't want to announce her arrival. When she rounded a bend in the road, she made out the plant through the trees. Sawyer's truck was there along with a white commercial van. The logo of the construction company Steve had worked for was on the side panel. Her fingers grew sweaty on the wheel, her heart racing. "He's here. I'm going to park on the road and walk in. There's good coverage. I'll be fine."

"All right, dammit, but you keep yourself safe. I mean it, Jill. Keep your radio—"

"No, I'm going silent, Gage. I can't risk him getting spooked. See you in twenty," she said, then turned off her radio and pulled off the gravel road. She got out of the cruiser, carefully closed the door, and locked it. Then she headed down a small incline toward the plant. She stayed low, using the trees and scrub brush for cover.

She did a quick scan of the area before sprinting across the clearing to the parked vehicles. She crouched behind Sawyer's truck, relieved to see no signs of violence or blood. Then she heard a dull thumping coming from the back of Steve's van. As she moved to approach, a shot rang out.

# Chapter Twenty-Five

The first shot was followed quickly by a second and then a third. They were fired from within the warehouse. She heard the ping of one hitting metal, the sound of a man crying out in pain. She couldn't make out who it was, but she was betting it wasn't Steve. Somehow the bastard had gotten hold of a gun. The thumping in the van grew louder.

Jill crouched down and duck-walked the few feet. When she reached the cover of the van, she straightened and opened the door. Trent and Annie sat with their backs together, their wrists and ankles bound with ropes, their mouths gagged. Relief surged through her that they appeared to be unharmed, traumatized from the looks in their eyes, but physically okay. Someone inside the warehouse wasn't.

She jumped inside the van, removing the gags from their mouths first. "As soon as I untie you, you're going to run through the bush and up to my patrol car. I'll cover you until you're out of sight. How many guns does Steve have? Does he have any other weapons that you could see?" she asked as she removed the knife from her utility belt and cut the rope binding their ankles.

Trent followed her lead and whispered back, "One, I think. Maybe a hunting knife, too."

"The gun looked like yours, Jill," Annie said.

*Good girl*. That's exactly the information Jill needed. A Glock was accurate at close range, not so much at a distance. She couldn't be sure of the size of the magnum, but on the high side, he'd have fifteen rounds. He'd used three unless... "Did you hear any gunshots before the last ones? Did he have any more clips?"

Annie shook her head and rubbed her wrists. "No. I didn't see any."

"Great. You guys are doing awesome. Now let's get you out of here. Just let me check first." She jumped from the van and scanned the area. She heard a crash from within the warehouse, then a shouted curse. Now that sounded like Steve. She helped the kids out of the van and gave them a reassuring smile. "It's going to be fine." She pointed to where her patrol car was and handed Annie the keys. "Your dad's on his way. I want you to run that way, and not in a straight line, okay? Don't worry, I'll keep you safe."

Annie's eyes filled with tears. "Sawyer and Mr. Dane—"

"Don't let him get away, Jill. Don't let my... Steve get away."

She pulled them both to her and gave them a quick hug. "Sawyer and Calder will be all right. And trust me, Trent. Steve isn't going anywhere but jail. Now go, run."

As she watched the kids race across the clearing, Jill turned on her radio and gave Gage an update, ordering an ambulance for whoever had been hit. Once Annie and Trent disappeared from view, she ran toward the warehouse with her gun drawn. Right now she had the element of surprise. She prayed that would work to her advantage.

With her back to the building, she turned her head to see if she could hear anything. As she listened, she worked on relaxing her muscles and slowing her racing heart. She had to believe Sawyer and Calder were all right. If she planned on keeping them that way, she didn't need her reaction time impaired by fear.

Another crash and the sound of breaking glass came from within the warehouse. Jill judged it to have come from somewhere around the middle of the plant and on the opposite side to her. She didn't have time to waste. She ran for the entrance doors. She carefully inched one open and shouldered her way inside, allowing in as little light as possible. She crouched down, scanning the space.

The plant was the size of a football field. The only light came from the windows, but she could make out the basic layout. Three rows of conveyor belts, boilers at one end, various types of bulky machinery in the center aisles, and other equipment like rolling ladders and metal shelving throughout. Lots of places for Sawyer and Calder to hide. But if she had to guess, she figured they were hiding out in the offices at the far end of the second level. They were accessible by a set of metal stairs. The window in what appeared to be the main office had a clear view of the floor.

Jill slipped off her boots, then made a run for the boiler across from her.

"I'm getting tired of playing hide-and-seek, Anderson. The old man must be bleeding out by now. You want him to live, come on out and face me like a man."

Steve was one aisle over from her, closer than Jill had thought. She knew Sawyer, and if there was any truth to what Steve said, she had only moments to act before... She heard the door of the office open and cursed under her breath before yelling, "Steve, you're surrounded. Drop your weapon."

He turned in the direction of her voice and fired. She ducked behind the boiler, the bullet pinging off the conveyor belt. She heard him running in the opposite direction, toward Sawyer and the office. "Sawyer, shut the door and get down," she shouted. Not waiting to see if he listened to her, Jill edged around the boiler in case she'd misjudged the direction Steve had taken. She hadn't; he had a foot on the first step leading to the upper level. She had no choice. She ran several feet, closing the distance between them, and got in position. "This is your last warning, drop your weapon or I will shoot."

He spun around with his gun raised. She fired. He jerked back, clutching his shoulder. He started to raise his gun again. "Drop it. It's over." She recognized the hopeless look that came over his face and, before he got off another shot, she fired again. Shooting the gun out of his hand. She kicked it out of the way, holstered her own, then flipped him onto his stomach, Mirandizing him as she cuffed him. She turned on her radio. "Suspect is contained. Repeat, suspect is contained." She looked up to see Sawyer carrying Calder from the office. The older man's pant leg was cut off at the knee, the fabric tied above the bleeding wound. "We have one male victim with a gunshot wound in a lower extremity. Suspect has a gunshot wound to the upper right shoulder and hand. Ambulance ETA?" Jill asked as she hauled Dawson to his feet.

He struggled, cursing her out and threatening to charge her with excessive force.

"Two minutes," Suze said at the same time Brad ran up the aisle. Jill handed off Dawson to the deputy. Brad gave her a fist bump. "Good job, Jill."

"Thanks," she said with a smile, turning as Sawyer came down the stairs. Her gaze moved over him, searching for injury. Tension and adrenalin were replaced with relief that he was unhurt. Their eyes met and held. "You okay?" she asked.

"I'm good. You?" he asked, even though he'd visually checked her over the same way she had him.

"Better now that I know you're both okay. You had us worried." She wanted to touch him and kiss him and hold him. Tell him that she was sorry and that she loved him. But she felt awkward, unable to read the emotion in his eyes.

"I know how that feels," he said quietly as they walked down the aisle to the front of the warehouse. "You should have waited for backup."

She glanced at him. "It may have been too late if I did. You shouldn't have opened the office door. You could have been shot."

He lifted a shoulder, then nodded at Calder, who appeared to be barely conscious. "Didn't see that I had much choice."

Jill touched the older man's arm. "Calder, you're going

to be fine. The ambulance is here to take you to the hospital. They'll take good care of you."

"Thank you. You too, Sawyer." His voice was whisper thin, his eyes half open, but at least he was talking.

The paramedics met them when they reached the front doors. As Sawyer helped the men settle Calder on the stretcher, Jill gathered up her boots and put them on. Once Calder was belted in, they followed the paramedics as they wheeled him out the doors. Patrol cars, two ambulances, and several vehicles crowded the warehouse parking lot. People were piling out of cars and SUVs, including her brother, Brandi, Nell, and Madison. Gage was standing beside his patrol car with Annie in his arms and a hand on Trent's shoulder.

If Jill wanted a few moments alone with Sawyer, she had to act fast. "Sawyer, I wanted to talk to you for a minute. Do you think—"

He looked down at her, then glanced in Brandi and Trent's direction. "I better check on them first. They'll both be shaken up. I'll—"

"I won't keep you," she said, struggling to keep the hurt from her voice. She started to walk away.

She heard him curse softly, then his hand closed around her arm. He turned her to face him. "Why do you keep walking away from me? You didn't give—" He broke off as Brandi and Trent ran to him. He gathered the sobbing mother and son in his arms, looking at Jill over their heads.

He'd made his choice. She clenched her jaw to stop her chin from quivering and walked toward her brother, who was talking to Gage and Madison. Annie broke away from her father and mother and ran into Jill's arms. It felt good to hang on to someone. "You should be proud of your daughter," she said to Gage and Madison when they joined them. "She's brave, observant, too."

"She thinks you're the bomb," Gage informed her with a smile, rubbing his daughter's head. "So do I. What you did…" His chest expanded on a deep, inward breath. "That was probably some of the finest investigative work I've ever seen. You followed your gut, and your instincts were right on. I'm not only recommending to the town council that you take over for me as sheriff, I'll be your campaign manager."

"Sorry honey, that job's mine. You can be my assistant though," Madison said, pulling Jill in for a hug. "I can't ever thank you enough."

"Just doing my job," Jill said, a little overwhelmed by the attention and support.

"Yeah, I heard all about what you did," her brother said, curving his hand around her neck to give it a gentle squeeze. He kissed the top of her head. "Don't sell yourself short."

"Your brother's right, Jill," said a familiar deep voice from behind her. She glanced over her shoulder. She might have appreciated Sawyer's comment more if he didn't have his arm around Brandi's shoulders. Even as Jill processed the thought, she knew it was unfair. Brandi had every right to lean on him after what she'd been through.

Both Madison and Annie released her. The young girl went to stand with her boyfriend, glancing at her father before shyly taking Trent's hand. Gage blew out a breath while Madison placed a hand on her husband's arm.

Brandi offered Jill a watery smile. "Thank you. Gage

told us that, if it wasn't for how quickly you put everything together, things might have—" She lifted her hand, placing it over her mouth.

"You should be proud of Trent. Both he and Annie were great," Jill said, once again feeling guilty for begrudging Brandi Sawyer's support.

Jack went to his best friend and hugged him. "You had all of us worried, buddy. I don't know how my sister kept it together. She—"

"I'll see you all later. I, ah, have to get back to the station." Jill cut her brother off before he embarrassed her by telling Sawyer she loved him in front of the woman he'd moved on with. "Come on, Jack. Walk me to my car."

"But—"

"Jack." She widened her eyes at him and nudged her head in the direction of her car then, having made her point, started walking. Did he follow her? No, of course he didn't. She bowed her head when she heard him talking to Sawyer.

"Any reason in particular why you wanted to shut your brother up?" Sawyer asked when he caught up to her a few moments later.

She ground her teeth and stared straight ahead. "You should get back to Brandi and Trent."

"Jack's taking them home. I'll go over later. I thought you wanted to talk to me."

"Nope, I got my answer."

"Interesting, I don't remember you asking me a question or answering one."

"You made your choice. It wasn't me."

"Is that right? So now you're not only Christmas's top cop, you're psychic, too?"

Sawyer nudged her to side of the road as the ambulances drove by with their sirens on.

"I don't need to be psychic to know that you've moved
on with Brandi. Everyone in town saw the picture of the
two of you at the restaurant. And—"

His mouth lifted at the corner. "Three. The three of us
at the restaurant."

"Whatever. You were looking pretty cozy. Well, that's
what everyone keeps telling me. And I saw Brandi today
in her man-hunting outfit, and she bought you your favorite pumpkin spice cupcakes."

"Man-hunting outfit?" He shook his head with a laugh.
"Babe, that would be her win-the-new-principal-over outfit. The cupcakes were for him. It was parent-teacher
interviews today. The principal isn't happy with Trent's
grades and threatened to suspend him from extracurricu-
lar activities until they improved."

"Oh, I . . ." She trailed off, glancing up at him as he
started backing her off the side of the road and into a
tree. She closed her fingers around his forearm. "What are
you—"

"It's not me who moved on, Jill. That was you.
You shut me out of your life. Are you trying to tell
me you want to let me back in?"

"Yeah, that's what I wanted to tell you. But you
were"—she gestured at the warehouse—"busy with
Brandi and Trent."

"That's what friends do. They comfort one another."

"Brandi's not just a friend. She's in love with you."

"Nope, she was looking for a father for Trent. But she
does think I'm hot and would totally jump my bones if I
wanted her to."

She crossed her arms. "I don't think you're funny."

The amusement left his face. "I love you. I haven't stopped. It's you, Jill. You're the one who keeps walking away from me, from us. I asked you to marry me. Maybe you don't remember, but you said no."

She touched his face and held his gaze. "I'm sorry. I'm sorry for everything. For shutting you out and not being there for you like you tried to be there for me. I thought you'd convinced yourself you loved me because of the baby. But after talking to Jack, I realized that you really did love me."

He angled his head. "Really? After everything I've said and done, you didn't believe me. Yet one word from your brother and—"

She lifted up on her toes and touched her mouth to his. "I'm sorry. I love you." She drew back at the look in his eyes. "You don't believe me, do you?"

"Jill, I've told you I loved you about a hundred times. You've only told me once before now. The night at my apartment, and you said you were drunk."

This was not the reaction she was hoping for. She wanted him to take her in his arms and kiss her until she melted into a puddle of lust. Swear his undying love. "I wasn't drunk. I've loved you since I was ten and you let me tag along with you and Jack. I've loved you since you taught me to skate. Since the day you caught me skipping school and didn't tell on me. I've loved you forever, Sawyer Anderson."

He smiled. "Those are the memories of a little girl. But the woman I know, she keeps walking away from me. So—"

"I saved you!"

He started to laugh. "Yeah, you did. But that's who you are. It's your job. Sometimes, babe, actions speak louder than words."

"Okay, how about this?" She fisted her hands in his plaid shirt and dragged his mouth to hers. She put every one of her feelings for him into the kiss: love, lust, admiration, hope, friendship, even the pain of their loss. For several beats of her heart, she wasn't sure he would respond. But then his hands cupped the back of her head, protecting her from the rough bark of the tree as he responded with a long, slow kiss that left little doubt he wanted her. If it had, his body pressed against hers would have wiped them away. She felt his heat, his desire, as much as she felt her own.

She couldn't get close enough to him and moved against him. He groaned into her mouth. She moaned into his.

A horn blasted. "Deputy Flaherty, that's hardly the behavior I expect from one of my officers," Gage shouted out his window. He laughed when Sawyer flipped him off and didn't stop kissing her.

"Hey, dickhead. That's my baby sister you're making out with. Get a room," Jack yelled out his truck window.

Sawyer gave her one last toe-curling kiss while flipping her brother off, then pulled back, staring down at her.

"Do you believe that I love you now?" she asked.

He took her chin between his fingers. "I know that you want me," he said and gave her a quick hard kiss before stepping away and taking her hand. He walked her to her cruiser, opening the door for her. "I'll see you tonight."

"So does that mean we're okay? We're together again?" She was having a hard time getting a read on him.

"I told you, Jill. I love you. I didn't stop."

What was she supposed to make of that? As he walked back down the road, she reached over the seat and grabbed the bullhorn. She yelled into it, "I love you, Sawyer Anderson." She was pretty sure all of Christmas heard her.

He laughed and smiled back at her. But she still wasn't sure if he truly believed her or not.

# Chapter Twenty-Six

The same gut instinct Jill had gone with earlier today was telling her that a romantic dinner of pizza and cupcakes wasn't going to cut it. She had to do something more than shout out her love through a bullhorn and feed the man. The longer she thought about Sawyer's reaction, the more she began to think that it wasn't so much that he doubted she loved him. It was that he doubted she had it in her to stick around. So somehow she had to prove to him that she was as invested in their relationship as he was. She was in it for the long haul, through the good times and the bad. No more running for her. Now if she could just figure out how to do that.

When she'd arrived back at the station, Ray, Brad, and Suze slapped a list of suggestions on her desk. Along with a *Jill Flaherty for Sheriff* sign. The sign had been appreciated. Their suggestions...not so much. She'd thought they, out of anyone, would believe—like she had at first— that saving the man would be enough to win him back.

Instead they'd presented her with a list that ran from hysterical, to absurd, to possibly illegal in some states. She was going to keep a close eye on Brad from now on.

No further ahead than she was several hours ago, Jill was feeling a little desperate as she headed for home after work. The clock was ticking down. Sawyer had texted that he'd see her in a couple hours. He was going to stop by and visit with Bill after he left Brandi's. And Jill still had no clue how to convince the man she loved to trust her not to hurt him again. She supposed she could put it off for another day, but her trusty gut instinct was screaming that would be a bad move.

She called Grace. "So I need to come up with an idea to...um, convince Sawyer he's my forever love." The phrase sounded so weird coming out of her mouth that she felt the heat rise to her cheeks. Her brother was right, she didn't have a romantic bone in her body, but Grace did.

"Aw, that's so sweet. Jack—"

"What are you doing? If you share that with my brother, I'm taking away your best friend card."

"Sorry," Grace apologized, not doing a very good job hiding the amusement in her voice. "Okay, how about this? You know how much he loves my pumpkin spice cupcakes, so why don't you come over and I'll help you make him a batch?"

Jill sighed. "I thought you'd be better at this."

"I'm very good at this; just ask your brother. Oh, wait, there was this one time—"

"Okay, your voice just got all breathy and excited so I know where this is going. I'm hanging up now."

Grace laughed. "Call us if you need help."

"I did, and you weren't any. Good-bye." Jill heard Grace calling to Jack as she disconnected.

She called Chloe. The woman was an actress, and she'd won over Easton McBride; surely she'd have some great advice. "I already saved him, and it didn't work," she said when Chloe finished outlining what Jill was pretty sure was a scene from the movie she was filming in Aspen. One in which Jill would be the hero of the day instead of Chloe.

"Really? I guess I can understand why it didn't. That's kind of what you do for a living. Oh, wait, I've got it. Easton told me he fell in love with me when I renovated his house. Ta-da, problem solved."

"You're rich, and I'm not. Besides, I have to do it tonight. Like in two hours."

"Hhmm, that's fast. Don't worry though, I have a very creative mind. I should be able to come up with something cheap and quick. They're calling me for my scene. I'll get back to you as soon as I'm finished."

"Thanks," Jill said, but she didn't hold out much hope Chloe would come up with something in time. Not when she was filming a scene.

Jill thought about calling Ty, but his solution would no doubt be elaborate and time-consuming and involve a makeover of some kind. But just as she was about to give up, she thought of the one person who wouldn't let her down. Nell McBride. She was perfect for the job. She wrote about romance and romantic gestures all the time.

Her call to Nell went straight to voice mail. Undeterred, Jill headed for the hospital. She'd seen Nell climb into the ambulance with Calder, despite the paramedics telling her not to. The woman at the information desk told Jill that Calder was out of surgery and gave her his room number. When she reached the third floor, Jill spotted Nell's friends in the waiting room. Ted and Fred looked upset. So did Evelyn and Stella.

Surely the woman at the desk would have told her if Calder hadn't made it. Jill's chest constricted at the thought that something had happened to the older man after surgery. "Is Calder okay?" she asked.

"He didn't die if that's what you're asking," Fred grumbled, crossing his arms over his chest.

"If he's okay, why do you guys look like you've lost your best friend?"

"Because Nell's going to get her heart broken again," Stella said.

"Now, Stella, Calder's a nice man. He loved Nell once; maybe it will work out this time," Evelyn said without much conviction, wringing her hands.

Jill hid her smile at the thought the shooting had brought Nell and Calder back together. Obviously Nell's friends wouldn't be happy to hear that Jill was thrilled for the older couple. Then again, they didn't know the whole story. She did.

"I'm just going to check on Calder and Nell. I'll talk to you guys later," Jill said. If Nell didn't have any suggestions, maybe one of her friends would.

"Tell Nellie not to be a damn fool," Ted called after her.

She found Calder's room easily enough and was just about to step inside when Nell came out with an aggrieved expression on her face. "Is everything okay?" Jill asked.

"I called a nurse two minutes ago to bring him more blankets and pillows, and they haven't shown up."

"They're pretty busy this time of day. I'm sure they'll get to you as soon as they can. How's Calder doing?"

"Paul says the surgery went well. He expects him to make a full recovery," she said, referring to her nephew who was chief of staff at Christmas General. Nell slapped her forehead. "What the Sam Hill am I thinking? I haven't thanked you for saving him." She gave Jill a fierce hug, then leaned back. "Grateful, girlie. And proud of you, too. Maddie's already put out the word for volunteers for your campaign. We couldn't ask for a better sheriff."

"Thanks, Nell. I appreciate all the support. But I want to talk to Sawyer before I commit myself to running." Now that was something else she never expected to hear herself say.

"No doubt you'll be running then. Sawyer's not the type of man who'd hold his woman back from pursuing her dreams."

No he wasn't. He was the type to make their dreams come true. And that's when Jill realized the house, all the gifts he'd left outside her door, weren't romantic gestures. It was Sawyer being Sawyer. His way of taking care of and loving her. Her anxiety and panic left her. She knew exactly what she had to do to prove to Sawyer that she would love him forever.

"I don't want to keep you. I'm sure you want to get back to Calder. But if you have a second, I'd like to run something by you," Jill said.

"Always have time for you. Give it to me."

Once Jill was finished, Nell grinned. "I have to say, I

didn't think you had it in you, girlie. But that just might be the best romantic ending the Christmas series has ever had."

Jill scratched her neck. "You're putting it in our book?"

"Of course I am. I mean, if it works."

Jill groaned.

"Now stop that. I'm sure it will. And stop scratching your neck. You have a huge red mark." She frowned and pointed to Jill's collarbone. "You have one there, too."

Jill pressed her back against the wall and rubbed. "Hives. I get them when I'm nervous."

Nell patted Jill's cheek. "You'll be fine. I don't want to leave Calder, so make sure you film it." Jill stared at her. Nell chuckled. "The before and during, not the after. I can use my imagination."

"I guess I better get going." With one last rub, Jill pushed off the wall and gave Nell a hug. "I'm happy for you. For you and Calder. I hope it works out this time."

Nell glanced at the door to his room. "I was stubborn for too long. Holding on to my foolish pride. Protecting myself, I guess. But when I thought I was going to lose him... Well, it makes you think. I wasted a lot of time. Calder's determined we don't waste any more."

"Sounds like you're going to get your happy ever after, Nell." It couldn't happen to a more deserving woman. Nell had spent so much time making sure they all got theirs that she'd nearly missed out on her own.

Nell lifted a shoulder in a we'll-see gesture, then smiled. "That's the title for your book. *Happy Ever After in Christmas.* So you better get going and make it come true."

Jill scratched her neck again. "I'll do that. Give Calder

my best," she said as she started to walk away. She pivoted. "Nell, do you have a couple in mind for book number eight?" Jill wasn't asking because she was curious. Okay, she was a little curious. But the real reason she wanted to know was because she wanted to be prepared. There seemed to be a correlation between Nell's books and an uptick in Jill's workload at the station.

"I might take a break. Work on my own love life for a change," Nell said with a wink.

\* \* \*

If Bill kept dawdling, Sawyer would be lucky to get to Jill's place before midnight. He didn't know what was up with the old man. Every time Sawyer went to leave, he came up with another excuse to make him stay. Maybe Bill had been more shaken about what happened at the warehouse than he let on. Sawyer had been pretty shaken himself. Especially when he heard Jill's voice and saw her through the office window coming after Dawson with her gun drawn. He'd wanted to be the one to protect her. A natural response, he supposed. But one he'd have to learn to curb since it looked like she was going to be sheriff in the near future.

Maybe he was getting ahead of himself. He wasn't exactly sure he had a place in Jill's future. He wanted to. But the memory of the last few weeks made him cautious. He didn't doubt that she loved him. He smiled, thinking of her yelling it through the bullhorn. She'd surprised him. And after that and her kiss, the last thing he'd wanted to do was give her more time to think. But she needed time. He had to be sure she wasn't acting out of fear and the adrenalin from the shooting. That's why he'd gone to spend some time with Brandi and Trent. Why he'd come to Mountainview to hang out with Bill. He wanted to give her space before he saw her tonight.

He rubbed his jaw. "Old man, what are you doing in there?"

"I'm coming, I'm coming. You never used to be so impatient." The bathroom door opened.

He blinked. Bill had on a suit. When he'd sent Sawyer to hunt down a bag of peanuts for him thirty minutes ago, he'd been in sweatpants and a shirt. "You wanna tell me what's going on? Are you making a break for it or we going out trick-or-treating?"

"We're going to the Halloween party downstairs. Hurry up or we'll be late."

Sawyer wasn't going to argue. He'd been trying to get Bill out of his room for months. "You got a hot date?" he asked.

"Might be someone special I'd like to see," Bill said, making his way slowly down the hall.

"Let me guess. Mrs. Sharp?"

Bill snorted a laugh. "She's ninety-three if she's a day. Nope, Jean, my physiotherapist, said she might pop by."

"She's thirty-three if she's a day."

"Forty-seven, smartass. And before you say it, I'm young at heart. These days a thirty-year age difference isn't that big a deal."

Guess he'd been angsting about his and Jill's age difference for nothing. Though admittedly he'd stopped thinking about it the first night they'd been together. Now he kind of wished that was all he had to worry about.

He slanted Bill a look as he hit the down button. The

old man was looking good. Now might be the time to share his idea with him. It'd give Bill something to shoot for. If he agreed to it, that is. "So I've been thinking about what you're going to do once you get out of here. I'm planning to move into the house on the lake, and I want someone to live in my place above the bar. Would you be interested?" he asked as he held open the door. It'd be a good setup for both of them. He could keep an eye on Bill, and the old man would have a nice place to live rent-free.

"Could work. But you're charging me rent. I don't take handouts."

He leaned against the elevator wall. "How about we compromise? You help me out at the bar in exchange for rent. I'm going to be busy in the next couple months with Gold Rush."

"Gonna be lonely out at the lake rambling around in that big house all by yourself, isn't it?" Bill didn't look at him, but he saw his lips twitch.

"I wasn't planning on being alone. I was hoping…" He shrugged as the doors opened. "I'll have a better idea what's happening with me and Jill after I see her tonight."

"I'm sure you will," Bill said with a full-on grin.

"You know something I don't, old man?"

Bill didn't respond as he made his way toward the party room. "Well, would you look at that? We missed it," he said.

It looked like they had. All the lights were off. But Sawyer could have sworn he saw movement a second ago. "Maybe it's in another room," he suggested, feeling bad for Bill after he'd gone to all that trouble to get ready.

"Well, would you look at that? We missed the party," Bill yelled, moving toward the room.

"I heard you the first..." Sawyer trailed off as the soft, flickering glow from dozens of lighters lit the room.

"Ow, I burned my thumb."

"Careful, Edith, you'll catch my hair on fire."

Several voices shushed them, but at that point, Sawyer was oblivious to anyone but Jill sitting on a chair in the middle of the room. She had on the red dress she'd worn to the bar, and she was strumming her guitar.

She looked up at him as she sang "Marry Me" by Train.

The woman who vowed never to play in public again was playing for him. She was putting her heart on the line. Asking him to marry her in front of their family and friends. He saw Jack and Grace with little Jack in the audience, Skye and Ethan, Chance and Vivi, Gage and Madison, Annie and Trent, Brandi, Suze, and Ty. They were all there waiting for him to give her an answer. He didn't think he could. His throat was tight with emotion, with love for Jill.

As he started to move toward her, a voice in the crowd yelled, "Yes, yes, I will marry you. You are beautiful. I will make you happy."

Sawyer held her gaze and smiled. "She is beautiful. But, Mr. Gorski, I think she's proposing to me."

"Sing 'Sunshine,' Auntie J," little Jack called from the audience as she strummed the last note.

"Sorry, buddy," Sawyer said, taking the guitar from her hands and placing it on the floor. "She's coming home with me." He scooped her into his arms, looking into her true-blue eyes. "The answer is yes, in case you were wondering."

She wrapped her arms around his neck. "Thank God, because I had nothing for the second act."

"Uncle Sawyer kissed Auntie J on the yips."

\* \* \*

*Jill Flaherty and Sawyer Anderson finally get their happy ever after.* Jill smiled at the Facebook link Suze had just sent to her phone.

Sawyer had a hand on the wheel while his other one stroked her hair. She was snuggled against him on the drive to the house on the lake. He was bringing her home. "What are you smiling at?"

She turned the screen.

He grinned. "You outdid me, babe. Best proposal ever. Ty and Chloe help you come up with it?"

"No, I came up with it all by myself." She told him what everyone else had suggested.

"Okay, I take back my yes. You have to propose to me again. Any one of Brad's ideas would work for me."

"I'm sure they—" She broke off as he turned onto the road to the lake. The high beams shone through the trees, illuminating the clapboard house. Someone had obviously spent time working on it. Now more than ever the house resembled the one that had been on her vision board. It had been painted white, its shutters blue.

"What do you think? I didn't change anything inside. I was hoping we'd do that together."

She moved out from under his arm. "You did this?"

"Yeah. I needed to keep busy."

And she knew why. "I wish I could turn back time. Be

there for you like you tried to be there for me. I don't know how to make it up to you, Sawyer. I—"

He placed two fingers on her lips. "Stop. I don't want you to apologize anymore. You needed time. Besides, you more than made it up to me tonight." He kissed her. "Stay here for a minute. I have something else I want to show you."

"Seriously Sawyer, you can't keep spoiling me like this. I'm not as good at this romantic stuff as you are."

"This is for both of us. I thought…" He lifted a shoulder. "Well, you'll see."

She frowned as she watched him jog to the house, not sure how to read his mood. Her phone pinged with a message from Nell. Jill had sent her a text, attaching a video of the proposal. Nell had responded with a selfie of her and Calder giving a thumbs-up. Jill didn't know when she'd ever seen Nell looking as happy as she did now.

She showed Sawyer as soon he opened her door. "Way to go, Calder. I wondered if he'd finally work up the nerve to ask her out. She's all the guy talks about. I've been giving him advice. Glad to see it finally sank in."

"Maybe you should be writing an advice column for the *Chronicle*, Mr. Romance. And no offense, but I think it was my advice to Nell that did the trick. Well, that and Calder getting shot."

He grinned. "If we decide we want a change in careers, we'll go into the matchmaking business together," he said as he wrapped a heavy wool blanket around her shoulders. "I hate to cover up that dress, but it's chilly out. And I really hate to change these heels out for rubber boots, but knowing you, you'd kill yourself walking on the path."

His hand curved around her calf while he drew the fingers of his other hand slowly down her leg to remove her shoe. By the time he got to her other foot, she was practically moaning. She fisted her hands in his jacket and pulled him down for a hot, wet kiss, then drew back and said, "Maybe we should save our walk for tomorrow."

He kissed her back. "It won't take long." He nodded at the chimney. "Gotta give the fire time to heat up the place."

"Um, we're not going canoeing tonight, are we?"

He laughed. "Babe, I'm not getting in a canoe with you ever again."

She crossed her arms. "I wasn't that bad."

"Thanks to Chance, I have evidence to the contrary. Come on." He closed the passenger's side door, then took her hand and turned on a flashlight.

The air was cold, her breath crystallizing in small puffs. She clumped alongside Sawyer in the oversize rubber boots. Leaves crunched beneath their feet, the smell of wood smoke on the air, the full moon cutting a golden path across the black water. "It's so peaceful here. I can't wait until we live here full-time."

"Say the word. We can move in next week."

"Really?"

"Yeah, really." He brought her hand to his mouth and kissed it, then he stopped. The beam from the flashlight illuminated a bench. It was rustic, made out of a tree. The ends were still covered in bark. But it was the perfect angel carved onto the smooth and varnished back that held her attention. She sat down as she realized what he'd done, what it was, and outlined the angel with her finger. "It's beautiful."

He sat down beside her and drew her into his arms. "I wanted a place where we could come and remember her. If you want, we can get a plaque. Put the date on it."

"No, this is perfect. Maybe one day we'll have more children. We can make it a family bench. Have us all represented. She'll be at the center, the center of our family."

His arms tightened around her. "We're going to have a beautiful life together, Jill."

As she sat happy and content in the circle of Sawyer's arms, the sound of the water lapping against the rocky shore reminded Jill of the conversation she'd had with Nell that day on the bridge. Sawyer's love filled her with joy and hope, healing the pain of their recent loss, the pain of her past, smoothing over her edges. She smiled up at him and kissed his jaw. "I know we are."

Jack Flaherty has been missing in action and returns as a military hero with no memory of his life in Christmas. But even as he struggles to rekindle the romance with the wife he can't remember, he knows in his heart what he wants: a second chance at love.

Please see the next page for an excerpt from

# Christmas in July

# Chapter One

*T*ill *death do us part.*

Grace Flaherty, owner of the Sugar Plum Bakery, tried to drown out the wedding vows she couldn't get out of her head by humming a song. Her breath hitched when she recognized the melody—"Amazed," her and Jack's song. It was as if he knew what she was going to do and tried to stop her. A warm spring breeze wafted through the screen door, and she closed her eyes, letting its soft caress soothe her aching heart.

Today was her husband's thirty-fifth birthday, and the day Grace said good-bye to him.

"I'm sorry, Jack. I can't do it anymore. I can't keep pretending you're coming home," she whispered as she put the finishing touches on the cake, tying a yellow ribbon to the tiny white picket fence that circled the pink fondant house.

Since the day Jack's Black Hawk went down in Afghanistan and he'd been listed as MIA, she'd clung to

the hope he'd come home to her and their two-year-old
son. But where hope had once sustained her, now, seventeen months later, the gossamer threads held her in limbo.
The not knowing was making her crazy. She had to move
on with her life and somehow heal her broken heart. And
the only way she knew how to do that was to let Jack go.

Kneeling on the stool beside her, her son Jack Junior
dumped a bottle of blue sprinkles onto the stainless
steel prep top instead of the cupcake she'd given him
to decorate.

She sighed, prying the bottle from his small fist.

"Me do." Under a tumble of curly dark hair, a frown
puckered the brow of his sweet face. "Mommy sad."

*So sad that it hurt.* "No, Mommy's happy." She gave
him a hug, touching the tips of her fingers to her cheek
to ensure there were no tears. Grace had been schooled at
an early age to hide her feelings, and it amazed her how
easily her son picked up on her emotions. Then again, she
could never hide her feelings from his father, either.

Forcing a smile, she handed him a miniature American
flag. "Put it on your cupcake," she said as she attached
one to the Victorian's front porch. His hand darted in
front of her. "No…" She swallowed a frustrated groan
when he smashed the flag in the wildflower garden, taking out two poppies and a sunflower.

If she didn't hurry up, he'd destroy the cake. She
quickly retrieved the chocolate sugar plum from the
refrigerator. Typically, the sugar plum contained an engagement ring or a wish. This one held Jack's wedding
band, a good-bye note, and a wish for her future. A man's
man, her husband didn't wear jewelry and had only worn
the ring on their wedding day. Their life had been filled

with such promise then, promises and dreams, like the house on her cake. But while her dreams with Jack might be over, she was determined to create new ones for her and her son. Different dreams, but just as bright.

Instead of hiding the sugar plum in the cake like she always did, she placed it beneath the house. She couldn't risk someone finding it, but she needed the sugar plum to be there. It wouldn't be her signature cake without it. And lately she'd been receiving letters from people whose sugar plum wishes had come true. Something her silent business partner and friend—not that Madison McBride knew what the word *silent* meant—had been happily exploiting. Grace didn't believe there was anything magical about her cakes, but if there was a chance...

The stool wobbled as Jack Junior tried to get down. "Me go party," he said, referring to the gathering Jack's friends had organized to celebrate his birthday at the Penalty Box tonight.

After putting in twelve hours before picking up her son at the sitter—two of her employees had called in sick that morning—the last thing Grace wanted to do was spend an emotional evening with the citizens of the small town of Christmas, Colorado, who believed with all their hearts their hometown hero would one day come home. It wasn't as if she could plead a headache or heartache and drop her cake off and leave. They expected her there, as upbeat and as naïvely positive as they were.

At the thought, Grace wearily scooped her son into her arms. "As soon as mommy's cleaned up the kitchen, we'll go."

"No!" Wriggling in her arms, he tried to break free.

She couldn't handle his Flaherty temper right now, but

nor could she leave the bakery in a mess. She put him down and reached for the broom. "Here." She handed him the dustbin. "Let's play catch the sprinkles."

After an exasperating five minutes, even though the black-and-white tiles were clear of sprinkles, Grace reached for the mop, then stopped herself. She was being ridiculous. Instead, she searched for something to occupy her precocious son while she cleaned the prep top. She latched on to the cupcake liners he'd dumped onto the counter and sat him on the floor at her feet. "Can you put these back in the tube for Mommy?"

He nodded. She ruffled his baby-soft hair before turning to clean up the icing and sprinkles. The crushed flowers called to her. She needed the last cake she made for Jack to be perfect. When an over-the-shoulder glance revealed her son to be engrossed in his task, she reached for the gum paste and cutter.

Less than ten minutes later, she'd replaced the last of the three flowers in the garden and turned to her son. "Jack..." He was gone. Panic overwhelmed her as the memory of another child who'd gone missing on her watch came back to haunt her. She pushed the thought aside as her gaze darted to the narrow space between the industrial ovens and refrigerator.

"Jack, it's time to go to the party," she cajoled, kneeling to look under the prep table. At the sound of a shuddering crash from the front of the bakery, she uttered a panicked "Jack" and shot to her feet, racing through the swinging doors.

Chunks of wet plaster had knocked over a round bistro table, water gushing from a hole in the ceiling above. In one breath she was thanking God her baby hadn't been hiding under the table, while in the next she was crying out his name, her voice ragged with fear.

"I've got him, Grace," a deep male voice called from the kitchen. Sawyer Anderson, Jack's childhood best friend and owner of the Penalty Box, came through the swinging doors with her son in his arms. The former captain of the Colorado Flurries, a professional hockey team, Sawyer had been there for Grace since the day Jack went missing. Incredibly good-looking and laid-back, he was the one person she'd been able to share her fears with. The one person who understood why she couldn't keep pretending Jack was coming home. His support made it easy to be with him. Only lately, it'd been too easy.

She reached for Jack Junior, who wrapped his small arms around Sawyer's neck. She laid a palm on her son's back, the steady rise and fall of his breath and the warm body beneath his navy T-shirt calming the panicked gallop of her heart. "Where did you find him?"

"Back alley. I was coming to check on you..."

She closed her eyes. She'd been so focused on making sure the flowers were exactly right that she hadn't heard the screen door open.

"He's fine, Grace."

"Only because you were there. If you..." She shook her head, trying not to think of what could've happened. Of what had happened that long-ago summer. "Thank you."

From beneath the ball cap pulled low on his dark-blond hair, he scanned her face, then lifted his gaze to the ceiling. "Shit," he muttered.

"Shit," said her son.

Grace shot Sawyer a don't-you-dare-look as he fought back a laugh. "Jackson Flaherty, what did I tell you about using the S-word?" Grace's sweetly innocent child had been spouting expletives with an alarming frequency, and now it seemed she'd discovered the reason why.

"Me no say shit, Mama, me say shh." He grinned at Sawyer, who'd lost his battle with laughter.

She narrowed her eyes at the two of them. Sawyer winced. "Okay, buddy, I'll make you a deal. No more S-words this week, and Mommy'll bring you to the bar for a root beer float on the weekend." He raised a brow at her.

"Bribery?"

He shrugged. "Worked for me."

Obviously it worked for her son, too. He nodded. "Me like beer."

"I'm sure that's just what your mother wanted to hear," Sawyer said, handing her Jack Junior. "We need to do something about the leak."

Distracted by her son's safe return, she'd forgotten about the gaping hole in the ceiling. She wished she could ignore it completely and the dent it was going to put in her meager bank account.

Leaning over the table, she called to their tenant, "Stu, are you up there?"

"Stu, up there?" her son echoed.

"He's not there, Grace. Get me the keys."

"How can you be..." She caught the sympathetic look in Sawyer's eyes. "You think he skipped out on us, don't you?" She groaned. "Jill's going to kill me. She wanted to put him out when he didn't pay last month's rent, but I thought...Jill's right. I am a sucker."

Hefting Jack Junior higher on her hip, Grace rounded the display case and opened the cash register drawer.

"You're not a sucker," Sawyer said as he followed her. He took the key she retrieved from under the tray and held on to her hand until she looked at him. "You were just trying to give the guy a break. Nothing wrong with that."

There wouldn't be if she could afford to, but she couldn't, at least not yet. Stu, a recent divorcé whose wife had had an affair and gotten both their home and their children in the settlement, had easily garnered Grace's sympathy. She hated the thought she'd been played.

"I could be wrong. Maybe he didn't skip out on you. Give me a couple of minutes upstairs and—"

She shut the register drawer and locked it. "I'll go with you."

"You sure? He might have left the place a mess."

"Oh, I didn't think of that." Going into the apartment was hard at the best of times, and this was not the best of times. There were too many memories of Jack there. It was one of the reasons Grace had moved in with her sister-in-law a year ago, the other being the extra income from the rental.

Jack Junior held out his arms to Sawyer. "Me go, Da. Me go you."

A soft distressed cry escaped from Grace, her arms tightening around her son.

Sawyer bowed his head, then raised his eyes. "I wish, buddy," he murmured as he rubbed her son's head and held her gaze.

She averted her eyes, nervously clutching the neckline of her white blouse. "Sawyer, I can't—"

He lifted his hand to caress her cheek. "Yeah, I know. It's too soon. But—"

"What the hell's going on here?" Jill, Grace's

sister-in-law, snapped, keys jangling in her clenched fist as she strode through the front door. Eyes the same vibrant blue as her brother's were dangerously narrowed beneath her dark hair, her blade-sharp cheekbones flushed with Flaherty temper.

Grace went to take a guilty step back. But Sawyer, with a gentle yet firm grip on her shoulder, held her in place. He gestured to the mess on the floor. "There was an accident. I'm going up to see what I can do."

Her sister-in-law looked up at the ceiling. "Son of a—"

"Jill," Grace interrupted her in an exasperated tone.

"Sorry." Hands on the hips of her tan uniform pants, Jill's lips flattened. "So Stu decided to leave us a good-bye present when he skipped out, did he? Wait till I get a hold of the little pri—"

Sawyer cut her off. "I'll take care of it. Help Grace get the cake and Jack Junior to the party." The look in his eyes dared her to argue.

Which she probably would, because when Jill and Sawyer were in the same room together, fireworks were guaranteed. Jack had always thought his sister had a crush on his best friend. She'd been their shadow growing up. If their interactions of late were anything to go by, Jill no longer loved Sawyer; she hated him. Grace released a grateful breath when her son broke their silent standoff. "Me go party."

"Right." As quick as Jill's anger flared, it dissolved with one word from her nephew. "Are you going to show me the cake you and Mommy made for your daddy?"

Jack Junior nodded as Jill took him from Grace's arms and headed for the kitchen. He looked back at Sawyer and opened his mouth.

*Don't say it*, Grace prayed. *Don't call him Da.* Jill would never understand that it was normal for a little boy without a father to be looking for one. She'd blame Grace for spending too much time with Sawyer. Given what he'd just said to her, maybe she'd be right.

"See you at the party, buddy. Save me a piece of cake."

Jack Junior grinned. "Me have beer."

"Nice, Sawyer. Now you're corrupting my nephew."

"Don't listen to her," Grace said as she went to drag the garbage pail over to clean up the mess.

"I'll take care of it." Sawyer stopped her with a hand on her arm. "Don't let her get to you, Grace. You're not doing anything wrong."

"I know. It's just…" She shrugged, then looked up at him with a smile. "Thanks for everything."

"It's not your thanks I want," he said before heading for the door.

\* \* \*

With the cake in her arms, Grace walked the half block along Main Street with her son and Jill. Jack Junior giggled as his aunt swung him up the street by his hands.

"No wonder he'd rather walk with you than me," Grace said.

Jill laughed. "Mommies aren't supposed to be fun."

"Thanks." Grace *wasn't* fun; she was boring and overprotective. She used to wonder what it was about her that her adventure-loving husband had fallen in love with.

Jill cast her a sidelong glance. "I was teasing. You're a great mom." She stopped, lifting a protesting Jack Junior into her arms. "Are you okay?"

*No, I've just said good-bye to the man I loved with all my heart, and if you ever found out, you'd never forgive me.* "Tired. It's been a long day. Not to mention the ceiling caving in and Stu skipping out on the rent." Grace sighed. "I'm sorry. I should've listened to you."

"I'm sorry, too, about earlier, with Sawyer. It's just seeing the two of you..." Jill held the door to the bar open with her shoulder. "Jack's coming home, Grace. You still believe that, don't you?"

*I wish I did.* "Of course I do," she said, smiling in response to the greetings their friends called out. It seemed like half the town had crowded into the rustic-looking bar with its exposed log walls and wood-planked floors. Jack Junior reached for one of the hundred yellow balloons that were tied to the chairs and bar stools.

Gage McBride, Christmas's sheriff, came over. "Hey, Grace, Jill." He kissed both their cheeks and took the cake from Grace, setting it on a nearby table. His wife, Madison, who was not only Grace's partner and friend but also the town's mayor, took Jack Junior from Jill and untied a balloon from the back of a chair. "Here you go, sugar."

Madison smiled at Grace then rolled her eyes when Nell McBride, Gage's great-aunt, sauntered over with her best friends, Ted and Fred, in tow. "Here we go." Madison sighed.

Gage, standing behind his wife, grinned. "You'd better give me Jack Junior."

Madison handed him off to her husband and took a seat, rubbing the barely noticeable baby bump beneath her floral sundress. "I'm sitting, okay?"

Ted pulled out a chair, and Fred plunked Madison's

pink-sandaled feet on it. "Now, you stay put, girlie," Nell ordered.

The three of them shared a couple of their memories of Jack before moving off to join their friends at a large table near the jukebox.

"Gage, you have to talk to them. I can't take five more months of this," Madison complained.

Her husband leaned over and kissed her. "I'll give it my best shot, honey. But the three of them are almost as stubborn as you are when you set your mind on something."

"Hey, I'm not stubborn."

Gage snorted. "Come on, buddy," he said to Jack Junior, "let's go play some air hockey."

Grace felt a sharp twinge of longing. In the beginning, she and Jack had been as head over heels in love as Gage and Madison. She wondered if she'd ever have that again. The thought made her feel horribly disloyal. But who was she trying to kid? The citizens of Christmas, especially Jill, would never forgive her if she moved on with someone else. And it wasn't as if she'd leave town. Her father's military career had taken them all over the world, and Christmas was the only place that had ever felt like home.

"I'll be right back," Jill said.

Madison pulled out a chair. "Come sit with me."

"How are you feeling?" Grace asked as she took a seat.

"Not you, too. I'm fine." Madison looked at her closely. "But you're not. Do you wanna talk about it?"

"We had a minicatastrophe at the bakery. There was a leak in the apartment and part of the ceiling came down. Sawyer's... What's wrong?"

"Nothing."

Grace arched a brow.

Madison grimaced. "It's Gage. He's worried Sawyer—"

She was right. They'd never allow her to move on. "We're friends, that's all."

"Forget I said anything. And don't worry about the leak. Your insurance will cover the damage. Plus, I have an idea that's going to make us rich." Grace's skepticism must've shown, because Madison said, "I'm serious. I've been thinking about all those letters. We're going to create a story about a Sugar Plum Fairy being the one who granted their wishes. We'll sell T-shirts, and books, and wands... Anything we can think of, we can sell."

Grace could almost see the dollar signs flashing in her business partner's blue eyes. She didn't want to be a downer, but she had to ask, "Umm, won't there be an issue with copyright? There's a Sugar Plum Fairy in *The Nutcracker*."

"The Sugar Plum Cake Fairy, then. My friend Vivi can write the stories. Can you do the illustrations?"

Grace nodded. As a little girl, she'd loved to draw, but had stopped the day her sister died. It wasn't until Grace started working on the designs for her cakes that she rediscovered the joy, the deep sense of satisfaction she got from drawing.

"Fantastic. I'm so excited about this, aren't you?"

"Yes, it's a great idea." Anything that had the potential to increase the bottom line was welcome news to Grace. She just didn't know where she'd find the time to do everything, but it was exactly what she needed right now. The perfect way for her to move on with her life.

Madison glanced at the door and reached for her hand. "Okay, just breathe."

"What…" She followed Madison's gaze and swallowed, hard.

Jill followed behind their friends—the twins Holly and Hailey and Sophia and her sister-in-law Autumn—with a life-size cutout of Jack tucked beneath her arm.

A warm hand gently squeezed Grace's shoulder. Brandi, one of Sawyer's waitresses and another of Grace's friends, set a drink in front of her. "This'll help. It's a Hero. Sawyer named it after Jack."

"Thanks, Brandi," Grace murmured, wrapping her fingers around the cold, frosted glass.

"What do you think?" Jill asked, setting up the cardboard likeness beside Grace as the other women took their seats around the table. They placed their orders with Brandi while commenting on the lifelike Jack in his desert camouflage fatigues and Kevlar vest, a helmet tucked under his arm, his sexy grin flashing perfect white teeth in his deeply tanned face.

"There's nothing hotter than a man in uniform. And Jack Flaherty was—" Autumn, the owner of Sugar and Spice, the woman who made Grace's chocolate sugar plums, quickly corrected herself. "—*is* hands down the hottest man I've ever seen."

He was. And looking at him now, Grace felt the same heart-stopping punch of attraction she did on the night he strode into the Washington ballroom to receive his Medal of Honor.

Sophia, owner of the high-end clothing store Naughty and Nice, pointed at Jack and in her heavily accented voice said, "Yes, and he is coming home with me tonight."

"Grace?" Jill said, looking hurt.

She took her sister-in-law's hand "It was a great idea, Jill. It's like he's here with us."

Jill smiled, her eyes bright. Brandi came back with their drinks, and they lifted their glasses. "To Jack."

Everyone in the bar followed suit, and then, one after another, they stood to share their stories about Jack and their prayers for his safe return. By the time they were finished, Grace had downed two Heroes.

Jill clapped her hands. "Okay, time for cake."

They cleared the table and placed the cake in front of Grace. She stood, relieved that her emotional torture would soon be over. Gage, with Jack Junior in his arms, took his place beside Madison.

Sawyer came up behind Grace and whispered, "Hang in there. Not much longer."

Before she could turn to ask how it went at the apartment, Jack Junior yelled, "Da, Da." And put his arms out.

Grace's breath seized in her chest.

Several people said, "Aw," while her friends quietly sniffed. "He'll be home soon, buddy," Jill said, swiping at her eyes.

Grace wheezed out a relieved breath. Thank God, no one seemed to realize he'd meant Sawyer.

But Sawyer did. "How about that root beer float I promised you, buddy?" He went to take Jack Junior from Gage, who gave him a hard look before passing him over. Of course Gage would notice, Grace thought miserably.

"Me want beer."

Everyone laughed as Sawyer carried her son to the bar. After they sang "Happy Birthday" to Jack, Grace cut the cake while Jill handed out the pieces.

She reached across Grace, bumping into her. "Sorry," she said when Grace stumbled.

The knife jerked and hit the house, toppling it over, revealing the chocolate sugar plum underneath.

"Hey, no fair, it's supposed to be hidden in the cake," someone grumbled.

Grace sucked in a panicked breath and dove for the sugar plum. Jill beat her to it.

Her sister-in-law laughed. "Finally, I got a sugar plum."

As Jill opened it, Grace wished the floor would open up and swallow her whole. Jill's laughter ended on a choked sob. "How could you? How could you give up on him?" she said, her voice a strangled whisper.

"Jill, let me explain," Grace called after her sister-in-law, who strode for the door.

From behind the bar came a shrill whistle. "Everyone quiet," Sawyer yelled, directing their attention to the flat screen behind the bar where a newscaster announced breaking news. Sawyer turned up the volume. "We have just received unconfirmed reports that the four crew members of the Black Hawk that went down in the mountains of Afghanistan seventeen months ago have been recovered...alive."

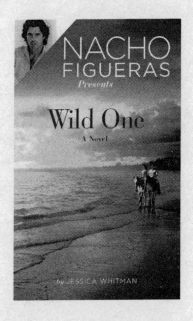

**NACHO FIGUERAS PRESENTS: WILD ONE**

Ralph Lauren model and world-renowned polo player Ignacio "Nacho" Figueras dives into scandal and seduction in the glamorous, treacherous, jet-setting world of high-stakes polo competition. Sebastian Del Campo is a tabloid regular as polo's biggest bad boy, but with an injury sidelining him, he's forced to figure out what really matters...including how to win the heart of the first woman who's ever truly understood him.

"Will get you in the spirit for love all year long."
—Jill Shalvis, *New York Times* bestselling author

Happy Ever After
in
*Christmas*

GREAT
LOW
PRICE!

Debbie Mason

*USA TODAY* BESTSELLING AUTHOR

## HAPPY EVER AFTER IN CHRISTMAS
### By Debbie Mason

*USA Today* bestselling author Debbie Mason brings us back to Christmas, Colorado, where no one in town suspects that playboy Sawyer Anderson has been yearning to settle down and have a family. But when his best friend finds out the bride Sawyer has in mind is his off-limits baby sister, it might be a hot summer in Christmas in more ways than one...

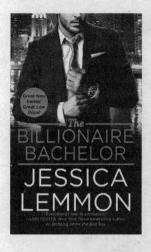

**THE BILLIONAIRE
BACHELOR
By Jessica Lemmon**

Bad boy billionaire Reese
Crane needs a wife to convince
the board of Crane Hotel that
he's settled enough to handle
being CEO. And beautiful
Merina Van Heusen needs
money to save the boutique
hotel she runs. But what will
they do when love intrudes into
their sham marriage? Fans of
Jessica Clare and Samantha
Young will love this new series
from Jessica Lemmon.

**A SUMMER TO
REMEMBER
By Marilyn Pappano**

In the tradition of RaeAnne
Thayne and Emily March
comes the sixth book in
Marilyn Pappano's Tallgrass
series. Can Elliot Ross teach
the widow Fia Thomas to love
again? Or will the secret she's
hiding destroy her second
chance at forever?

*Fall in Love with Forever Romance*

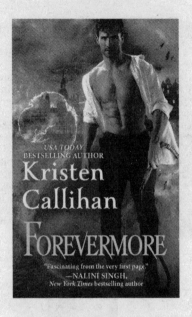

USA TODAY
BESTSELLING AUTHOR
**Kristen Callihan**

FOREVERMORE

"Fascinating from the very first page."
—NALINI SINGH,
*New York Times* bestselling author

**FOREVERMORE**
**By Kristen Callihan**

Sin Evernight is one of the most powerful supernatural creatures in heaven and on earth, and when his long-lost friend Layla Starling needs him, he vows to become her protector. Desperate to avoid losing her a second time, Sin will face a test of all his powers to defeat an unstoppable foe—and to win an eternity with the woman he loves. Don't miss the stunning conclusion to *USA Today* bestselling author Kristen Callihan's Darkest London series!